STRANGE SHAPE OF LOVE

A Novel

HERTA FEELY

CASTLE BRIDGE MEDIA
DENVER, COLORADO, USA

CASTLE BRIDGE MEDIA
Denver, Colorado

Cover photo by Alexander Krivitskiy/Unsplash.
This photo has been modified.

This book is a work of fiction. Names, characters, business, events, and incidents are the products of the author's imaginations. Any resemblance to actual persons, living or dead or actual events is purely coincidental.

STRANGE SHAPE OF LOVE
© 2025 Herta Feely
All rights reserved.

ISBN: 979-8-9917855-6-3

For Andi Rose and Jimmy Fritz,

My inspiration and hope for the future

*You can't go back and change the beginning,
but you can start where you are and change the ending.*

—C.S. Lewis

PROLOGUE

Saturday, December 7, 2019

THE NEWSROOM SEEMED EERILY QUIET, even for a Saturday. Charlotte wove her way to her desk where she stashed her computer and notes, ready for an afternoon of exploring London. She was about to turn away when her eyes landed on a large manila envelope in the wire basket that served as her inbox. She picked it up without intending to open it, but read her name and Thorntree's address, handwritten in a strange loopy script.

She glanced at the world clocks on the wall. Sydney, New York, London, New Delhi, Hong Kong. *Don't be late,* she thought. And yet that writing. She twisted her unruly hair into a knot on top of her head, released it, then ripped open the envelope. She felt the stiff edges of a photograph and yanked it out. Her breath caught as she stared at a nude photo of herself. A grainy black and white shot, an eight by ten.

The image revealed her from the waist up, arms raised overhead, her full lips a finger's breadth apart, her wavy, blonde-streaked hair, tangled and sweaty, reaching for her breasts. She peered inside the envelope, shook it even, but nothing accompanied the photograph to explain who, why, what. Or when.

Could it be a doctored shot? Her face but not her body? A feeling of dread wormed its way into her gut.

With a quick look around to make sure no one was watching, she further examined the image, holding it at arm's length as if it might harm her. When and where had it been taken? Six or seven years ago in New York? Oxford? Ithaca? Three people had taken nude photos of her in her early twenties that she could recall. Why any of them would send her one now was a mystery.

Perhaps Rafe had sent the image as a joke, to recall their frequent struggles as model and sculptor? Of course she could ask him. And yet, if he hadn't, what would he think? What about Russ? A weird form of revenge porn? After all, he'd broken up with her. And that left Zander, the only other person who'd photographed her back then. But they hadn't spoken in over a year.

Charlotte bit her lip. She caught sight of a man absenting the doorway—had he delivered this? More likely, he was just a staffer departing the newsroom.

She gave the image one more uncomprehending look. Not knowing who'd sent it or why irked her. Was it a threat? A warning that you can't have everything at the precise moment she felt on the cusp of success. Cruel after she'd lost so much. She shoved the photograph into her shoulder bag; the envelope she tossed into her desk drawer.

Outside on the street, she found a trash can. Her hands suspended a few inches above a green bin, she began to rip the photo into ever tinier pieces.

The past is the past, she thought, allowing the fragments to flutter into the receptacle like confetti, *let it stay that way.*

Chapter 1

TWO WEEKS EARLIER
New York City
Friday, November 22, 2019

A SHADOW FELL ACROSS CHARLOTTE as she sat hunched over her computer, fighting a rising panic. Her deadline had passed. She was banging away on the keyboard, so engrossed in writing the story that it took a moment before she glanced up. Morgan hovered at the edge of her desk without speaking. If Charlotte ignored her, maybe Morgan would go away. She needed to finish.

"Shelby wants you," Morgan announced, as though she had the inside scoop on all things Shelby.

"Is it about the story? Because if it is, tell her I'm almost done. Just waiting to hear from one more source."

"Really? Which source?"

Normally Charlotte might have engaged in a conversation because she knew what it was like to be *the* bottom rung in a magazine like this, craving for a chance to write. A magazine that—rumor had it—might be heading for bankruptcy.

Charlotte hesitated. Should she confide that she was waiting for the irreverent Italian artist himself, the focus of the piece, which of course meant the story wasn't close to finished. "Oh, just someone at Blenheim Palace, someone in charge of security when the golden toilet was stolen." The lie flew off her tongue. She smiled at Morgan, who squinted at her, as if sensing Charlotte's fabrication.

"I don't know, but she wants you. Pronto."

Pronto? Charlotte suppressed a sigh. What was it now? Surely Shelby wasn't going to blast her for missing a deadline. Her story wasn't that important, was it? Or was it yet one more test in her slow climb up the ladder?

To Charlotte's further annoyance, Morgan lingered until she'd finished typing her sentence. She grabbed her cell phone, just in case the artist, Maurizio Cattelan, called. She absolutely could not miss him. Not a second time. She had a slew of questions, not the least of which included whether he'd stolen the golden toilet himself. As a publicity stunt. Something he'd done with a previous piece of art but ended the fun by returning it a few days later. The golden toilet, on the other hand, had been missing from Churchill's palatial birthplace for nearly two months.

With Morgan close on her heels, Charlotte entered the inner sanctum of Shelby's office, a shrine to immaculate minimalism. Unlike most executive editors at big-name magazines, Shelby eschewed the messy office look. Few books, and even fewer files, and little paper of any sort populated her white lacquered shelves and acrylic desk. One could almost imagine she had nothing to do with the magazine except on occasion to shout orders.

"Hi. Morgan said you want to see me?" Charlotte's eyebrows rose questioningly.

Shelby nodded, then gave Morgan a dismissive wave. "And close the door."

Charlotte felt sorry for Morgan, but knew if she'd remained, nanoseconds later, the exchange would have become fodder for the rumor mill. *Grist?*

Here in Shelby's office on the thirteenth floor of this mid-town Manhattan building, one could only see the skyscrapers across the street. Unfortunately. Because everyone knew she coveted an office with a hundred-and-eighty-degree view, but she'd been thwarted time and again because, well, magazines didn't exactly ooze money, not in this era of online media. And *Savvy Faire* was in competition with *Vanity Fair, Vogue, Esquire, Rolling*

Stone, and every other magazine that concentrated on culture, fashion, style, travel, and art.

"I've got good news for you," Shelby said breezily. "Great news, actually."

Great news? Charlotte remained standing because Shelby's office contained only one chair—Shelby's. The idea being that every minute cost money, hence no time to waste on lengthy conversations. Charlotte slapped on a smile and, adopting her own version of minimalism, said, "Oh?" dreading Shelby's next sentence.

The last time her boss had offered such "good news," Charlotte had gotten violently ill on a trip to Central American museums for a piece on indigenous artifacts. The other time she'd gone to LA for an art opening at The Getty, where an unfortunate night-long encounter with a featured artist still made her cringe because Shelby had blasted her. "You do *not* do that, do you understand, you bleach-blonde idiot?!"

Charlotte wasn't a fan of the white furniture or trademark white outfits Shelby wore—seemed like she was trying to imitate Tom Wolfe. In sharp contrast to all that white, though, Shelby's thick, shoulder-length black hair hovered and floated inside the room like an alien spacecraft.

She waited for Shelby to speak. The woman seemed to enjoy biding her time as she took a sip of coffee from the bone-white porcelain cup. Charlotte hoped this "great news" meant she was being sent on a plum assignment. She could use a vacation. She crossed her fingers. *Please let it be Spain, or Morocco, or even a Caribbean Island.* She could already feel the sun warming her skin. Tanning her pale freckled body. And Thanksgiving only a week away. Without a family of her own, she preferred spending holidays elsewhere.

"We're sending you to London."

"London, why?" The mere words felt like she'd been sucker-punched, not only because England in November and December meant she'd be packing a coat, not a bikini, no, there were other reasons.

"Well, because Thorntree's bought us."

"Really?" This sounded like terrible news. Where was the *great* news?

"Making our magazine online. Only. You haven't heard?"

Charlotte shook her head. She couldn't believe what Shelby was saying. Not on any level. "We were bought by Nigel Thorntree? *The media magnate?*"

"Yes, *him*," Shelby said. "Are you hard of hearing? And he's keeping *me* on." At that her mouth quirked into a tiny smile. "Which means I can keep *you* on." She tilted her head to one side as her fingers drummed the transparent desk. Clearly, she was awaiting Charlotte's reaction.

"Aren't you thrilled?" Shelby asked, examining her red lacquered nails. "Because you should be."

"I am. Yeah, sounds great." Though not thrilled in any way, Charlotte mustered a smile. All her bad luck had begun when that full-length mirror broke during her nine months abroad at Oxford. She'd studiously avoided returning to England for the past six-plus years. "When am I going?"

"Next week."

Charlotte stood mute as Shelby added, "Anyway, don't worry, I'll be joining you soon enough. After I've wrapped things up here."

She had to be kidding. *That's definitely not what I'm worried about,* Charlotte thought, failing to keep a disappointed sigh from escaping her lips.

Shelby took another languorous sip of coffee, her bright red lipstick imprinting the delicate white cup. "You'll need to finish up the golden toilet story; almost done, right?"

"Done? Yeah. Just a few more touches. One last phone interview."

"You're past deadline, you know…" Shelby paused, running her hand along the molded edge of her desk. "Come to think of it," she added, swiveling her chair to face outside, "let's save that story. Soon enough you can visit Blenheim Palace in person. Then you can interview whoever you want about that damned stolen toilet. And get some new photos. Sound good?" She rotated again to face Charlotte.

"How long will I be staying?"

"Where?" Shelby frowned.

"In England," Charlotte said, annoyance seeping into her tone. *Does she think I mean Blenheim?*

"Indefinitely, what did you think?" Shelby said with characteristic disdain.

"Is Morgan going?"

"Morgan?"

"You know, your assistant."

"Her? No. You'll be writer *and* assistant. Cost savings, you know. I spoke with Nigel about it." At the man's name, Shelby's mouth twisted into a smug Cheshire cat grin. At least that's what Charlotte detected. She prided herself in having a sharp eye for facial expressions.

The smile still on her lips, Shelby swiveled once more to face the windows.

Charlotte knew she'd been dismissed and slipped out without another word. She imagined Shelby staring outside, pitying the poor tiny people scurrying along the streets of Manhattan like timid mice. *Am I a timid mouse too,* Charlotte wondered, then reflected on what she'd lost by not returning to England as promised half a dozen years ago.

Chapter 2

Tuesday, November 26, 2019

THE AIRPLANE LIFTED INTO THE sky, rising above Manhattan, its familiar structures glittering against the backdrop of night, almost as if mocking her departure. Charlotte stared wistfully out the tiny window, desperate to stop the tears that tugged at her eyes. How could she leave this city, when it had been homebase on and off for nearly three decades, and when it housed her network of pals? She felt like killing Shelby for upsetting her life, yes, even more than her recent ex-boyfriend. *Thank you very much, Russ.*

Another wave of nausea hit her. She sipped the sparkling water delivered by the flight attendant. And thank you, Daisy and Channing, for taking me out for one last drunken girls' night on the town. "Reject fucking Shelby's offer," they'd said over margaritas at one of several bars, but what options did she have? Not many. Not any, if she was truthful. Besides, she needed the money. More potholes than possibilities loomed ahead. Especially with Shelby slated to be her boss in London.

After she'd woken up with a whopping headache, and finished packing, a thought struck her, one that must have been the work of her mother or father, calling to her from the other side. Her mother had died a dozen years ago and her father nearly three. She gazed into the darkness. Just like them to suggest this move might be a gift in disguise, her chance to switch gears, to dramatically shift her life. So, in a moment of optimism, she'd shouted into her now empty apartment, "Thank you, Shelby, and look out, Thorntree Entertainment. That's right, *Charlotte Cooper takes London by storm!*" Her work options would improve, she decided, even if her boyfriend situation didn't.

Then, her hopefulness waning, she thought: *Of course, I deserve shitty assignments like the golden toilet (pun intended!), and of course I deserve to be sent to London with Shelby harassing me. What I really deserve is worse than that.*

On and off throughout the day, she'd thought of contacting Celia, her very closest friend from Oxford, who now lived in London. What would she say about this move? Most likely, she'd be ecstatic. Celia was a true friend, and despite the distance that separated them, they'd managed to see each other on cheap vacations over the past half dozen years, once in the Caribbean, twice in New York, and once in Malaga. But never in England. No, Charlotte couldn't risk running into Rafe. Wouldn't. She even refused to look him up on social media. Much too painful. And so she hadn't, not in a while.

She'd settle into her tiny rental in Shoreditch, and then one day she'd surprise Celia. That was her plan, as far as plans go. Her decision probably wouldn't last, and that suited her, but she liked the shock element and wanted to get a few days of work under her belt first.

In the early days of living with Russ, Charlotte had taken a stab at travel blogging, but that had turned into a flimsy excuse of a job. She wasn't really cut out for that line of work. *Frugal travel* had been her "niche," but in the end, she'd gotten sick from eating street food in Thailand, survived a brush with petty thieves in Trinidad, and itched from bed bugs at a youth hostel in the Yucatan. No, such work, if one could even call it that, didn't suit her.

Besides, Russ hadn't taken her seriously, and his opinion had been important to her. He was so accomplished, as an archaeologist and then a tenured professor at Columbia at the tender age of thirty, while she flew around trying to get influencers and followers for her blog. Nevertheless, that blog had led to her job at *Savvy Faire*.

And yet, her assignments at the magazine—covering the latest art exhibit and New York fashion (often boring), attending fundraisers and countless other beautiful people events (double boring)—didn't exactly raise her status with Russ or his intellectual friends. He kept telling her she should write "meaningful" pieces for a "serious" publication.

With everything going on in the world, he reminded her—climate change, immigration crap at the US-Mexican border, refugees streaming into western Europe, not to mention an increasingly divided America—surely, she could find work with a reputable news agency. And yet she hadn't. She'd resisted, almost to spite him. So, no wonder Sarah had entered his life.

Now, she wondered what *had* been stopping her. Deep down she knew the answer was linked to events half a dozen years ago—the summer of 2013. The accident that changed everything, and no matter how hard she tried, she couldn't escape its snares.

Charlotte shifted in her seat. The woman beside her appeared immersed in the contents of a lengthy document. Out of the corner of her eye a bold headline—*sex trafficking*—jumped out at Charlotte. She tried to focus on the smaller print, and without realizing it leaned in a little closer.

Abruptly, the gray-haired woman laid the document face-down on the tray in front of her and turned to Charlotte. "Hi." She extended her hand. "Regina. How about you? First time to London?"

Caught in the act of spying, Charlotte felt her freckled skin flush from her neck to the roots of her rippling waves of copper-shaded hair. Shaking Regina's hand, she stuttered her own name, said "no not the first time," and apologized for her visual eavesdropping. "I'm interested in the topic…of sex trafficking," she managed.

"Really?" Regina said.

Was she? "Isn't everyone?" She couldn't believe she'd just said that. "I mean, it's an awful thing. Do you work in that field?" Yes, turn the conversation to focus on the other person. At least she'd learned that much as a journalist. *Lowly reporter*, she reminded herself.

Regina swallowed several sips of her amber drink, scotch maybe, before answering. "I coordinate the human trafficking arm of Human Rights International," she said, adding, "HRI," and gave Charlotte a thumbnail sketch of the work they did. Her tone seemed friendly enough, the accent not quite British. Maybe Scottish?

"In London I could introduce you to the foot soldiers battling human trafficking. That is, if you're truly interested." She opened the small package of airline crackers and popped one in her mouth. "It's an ugly business," Regina continued, peering at her over silver-rimmed spectacles. "Tough to stomach when you see it up close."

Charlotte heard the challenge in her tone and retorted, "I'm a reporter," implying that she was indeed tough enough, though she had her doubts.

The statistics Regina cited raised frightening images in Charlotte's mind. Women and children sold for sex and kept in horrendous, slave-like conditions. By comparison, she'd led a cushy life. Except, well, except she'd survived her parents' deaths, only nine years apart. Without a sibling to lean on. And…well, that summer night in 2013, when her cousin Abbie had ended up dead. The two had been as close as sisters. *All my fault*, and then the aftermath.

Why do I keep thinking about that? It was the return to London, which perhaps, somewhere in her psyche, signaled a return to a time of innocence, one before the accident, to a period of youthful infatuation and love. A time before she was catapulted into adulthood, initiated into the messiness and cruelty of the world. But then why wouldn't her return signal a greater sense of inner peace?

Regina's voice interrupted her thoughts, "Have you ever considered what would happen if—while we're up in the air—well, what if something happened on the ground? Say, an epidemic swept the globe…leaving behind a world in ruins. A lot of devastation can happen in six or seven hours, while we're thirty or forty-thousand feet up—" she waved her arm about, "—in this metal container."

Charlotte grinned at her. "Something you're keeping from me?"

"Indeed," Regina said, and released a chuckle. She took another sip of her drink, then swirled the glass a bit, ice cubes clinking. "But really do you ever harbor such notions?"

"Such morbid ones?" Charlotte stifled a smile, thinking this poor woman's work had left its mark. She imagined getting Shelby and Regina together in a room and locking the door. Who would win? She found herself betting on Regina.

"Not generally," Charlotte concluded, hoping to find something to lighten the mood, then admitted she tended to hoard hotel soaps and containers of shampoo. And she was reluctant to toss out old clothing, in case such stores ceased to exist in some apocalyptic future. "So, yes, I suppose I do think about it."

"I believe it's part of the human condition to worry about and prepare for an impending disaster," Regina said. "Our survival instinct—genetically programmed into us, and certainly history has borne out our fears. Volcanoes, earthquakes, wars, epidemics. Only now it seems ever more likely the impact will be long-lasting. Terminal, if you will."

Charlotte nodded then took a sip of white wine, considering the odd way Regina had said *terminal*. "You know who I'm in total awe of?" Without waiting for Regina to answer, she supplied the answer. "Greta Thunberg. Sixteen and she's *Time* magazine's person of the year. Speaks before the UN. Refuses to fly; crosses the Atlantic in a boat. Twice! All to draw attention to climate change. I wish I…" she hesitated. What did she wish? "I wish I had half her guts. And brains!"

"That's a girl with pluck all right."

Charlotte smiled and gave Regina an earnest look. "If possible, I'd love to stay in touch. Maybe I can help, sometime in the future?"

"We always welcome volunteers. So, you're not just visiting London?"

"No, I've been transferred. Our magazine was bought by Nigel Thorntree."

"Oh?" Regina gazed at her with newfound interest. She took Charlotte's cool hand in her warm one. "With young people like you and Greta, we might be able to save the planet yet. Lovely to meet you." She'd barely spoken those words when she closed her eyes and released a soft snore.

She must be pooped after all that doomsday talk, Charlotte decided, but also noted the grayish pallor of her skin. She looked at her more closely. Not long before her mother died, she'd looked a little like that. Maybe it was just the dimness of the cabin.

Charlotte stopped the flight attendant and asked for another glass of wine, hair of the dog might help after the previous night's partying, then turned her attention to the list of available in-flight movies. She looked forward to something light, a Rom-Com maybe. She found one with Hugh Grant. But now thought about his LA encounter with a sex worker. How he'd been found out. His face in the papers. This brought to mind her conversation with Regina, but also the recent event that had flipped her life upside down.

A few months earlier, she'd discovered Russ sexting his brains out with someone named Sarah, not just sexting but actually fucking her, and it devastated her. The memory ricocheted in her mind. What had she seen in Russ? Stability. Steadiness. Reliability? Yes, exactly those qualities. How could she have been so blind?

Together on and off for three years, she'd even thought they might get permanently hitched. Before that she'd dated around, a steady stream of guys, each one a new opportunity to forget Rafe. Her friend Daisy had insisted that with Russ she'd found the right man. Of course, none of her friends had ever known or met Rafe, because he lived in England, formerly in Oxford where they'd met, and now probably in London.

And none of them knew about the accident. They knew nothing more than she'd gone through a difficult period in her life at age twenty-three accompanied by headaches and a bit of memory loss, and more recently an occasional bad mood because every negative event of the past six years had fused into one unending clusterfuck, beginning with Abbie's death and then her father's, and most recently Russ's betrayal. No one she knew had experienced half the shit she had. And sometimes she wallowed in self-pity. That's when she gained weight and broke out from eating too much chocolate. Or the opposite. She'd lose her appetite and several pounds.

She closed her eyes. They'd all assumed Rafe, "the artist," had been the unreliable one. Temperamental. Egotistical. And prone to screwing around with his models. "Like Picasso," one of her best buds had said. None of this was true. None of these words described Rafe. But she rarely bothered to correct their prejudices, their misconceptions. What would be the point? In the end, it was Russ, the archaeologist, not Rafe, the artist, who'd fit that description.

It seemed ironic that of all the places Shelby could have sent her, it ended up being England, where inevitably Charlotte would encounter Rafe, the talented sculptor she'd met, posed for, then fallen in love with during her junior year abroad at Oxford University. At the end of their school year in 2012, she'd promised to return after graduating from Cornell the following June. Then instead, after Abbie's death, she did everything she could to distance herself from Rafe and England. She couldn't face him after what she'd done. She didn't deserve him.

It made sense to no one but her. Post-accident, she barely spoke to him, refused to explain what happened. How had that made him feel? Lousy, terrible, angry, vengeful? At the time, she figured an abrupt ending was best. Why prolong the agony? Now, she feared running into him. What would he do? Would he allow her to apologize?

Charlotte's eyes stared blankly at the romantic comedy in front of her, but she'd lost interest. She tilted her chair back, an inch or two, feeling the comforting touch of Regina's elbow, for a moment imagining her mother beside her.

If she couldn't fix things with Rafe, maybe she could do something positive in the world? Just before she drifted off, Charlotte imagined breaking a story about the monstrous problem of human trafficking, with Regina's help. She saw her own name in the byline. A faint smile appeared on her lips as she fell asleep.

Chapter 3

AN EXPLOSION OF LIGHT WOKE Charlotte with a gasp. She glanced around and saw that it was nothing but the sun breaking over the horizon outside the airplane window. And her overwrought mind at work.

"A penny for your thoughts," Regina said.

Before turning to face her, Charlotte inhaled a calming breath hoping to erase fragments of a bad dream that clung to her. "A friend of mine used to say that." Rafe's face lit into her mind then disappeared.

In short, clipped sentences, Charlotte described the Tube bombing in her dream.

"*Mea culpa.* All that talk of epidemics," Regina said in apology.

"That's it!" Charlotte exclaimed, laughing. "Definitely your fault."

They were still chuckling as two women and a man in British Airways uniforms moved down the aisle offering breakfast. Charlotte didn't bother to say that sometimes her dreams came true. Like the one about her mother, a year before her death.

Charlotte accepted coffee from the flight attendant and cupping it in her hands, resumed staring at the clouds, now wreathed in gold. Fleetingly, an image of a fully laden Thanksgiving table darted through her mind—tomorrow's holiday that she'd now have to face alone. Unless she called Celia. But she'd promised herself to wait.

As the airplane swooped low, Charlotte told Regina how much she'd enjoyed their conversation, minus end-of-the-world talk, of course, and they again laughed. It seemed like she might have made a new friend.

"I'll call once you've settled into your job," Regina promised. They traded business cards.

Regina Hollyfield, Charlotte noted before handing over her own. "Oh, but I don't have my new phone number."

"Don't worry I'll find you," Regina quipped. "You *and* Nigel Thorntree!"

Below the massive silver-bodied airplane, the spires of London shimmered in the wintry light.

As Charlotte picked her way through the airport to a cab stand, a single thought infused her soul: *This is my chance for a new Life, capital L.* The way she looked at it, the past few hours and several thousand miles now separated her from her old life and opened the doors to a fresh start. She just had to walk through them.

If little else, her parents had left her with a hopeful outlook. They embraced the philosophy that one had to accept life's bumps and bruises, and the sooner one let go of those inevitable hurts and scrapes, wonderful new opportunities presented themselves. This is what she was banking on now. A belief in new beginnings. Endless possibilities. A little magic.

And with that, a bounce arose in her step.

The cabdriver pointed out a few famous landmarks as they drove to her leased apartment. Charlotte couldn't wait to visit all the tourist spots: London Bridge, Big Ben, Buckingham Palace, Kensington Gardens, Westminster Abbey, Shakespeare's Globe theatre, and the many museums. She'd take photos then post them on Instagram for her friends back home. They'd promised to visit. No sooner had she thought this than she realized that if she posted them, Celia would know she'd arrived in London without having called. And she might feel hurt. No, she couldn't do that.

Her gaze fixed outside, she tried to figure out the answer to this dilemma, minor as it was. Buildings blurred by as did pedestrians. At once, though, she caught a glimpse of the back of a familiar figure. Tall, with shoulder-length dreads, his fit physique barely hidden beneath a tight-fitting leather jacket and blue jeans. Could that be Rafe?

She shouted for the cabbie to stop, but before he pulled over, they'd passed the man, and Charlotte saw she'd been mistaken. Nevertheless, the boxy black cab, a London hackney, slowed to a halt and the driver turned, shooting her a questioning look.

"Sorry, keep going," she muttered. "I thought I saw…oh, never mind."

"Almost there," he said.

She couldn't believe the rapid rise and fall of her emotions. The excitement she'd felt a moment ago already gone. "Get a grip," she told herself. "That's over. So over." A monologue ensued. *Breathe. Name three good things that happened today.* She'd bought a book on affirmations before leaving New York and had promised to try them. *Met Regina. Might lead to new options for work…what else? Landed safely. Breathe.* She picked at the brown nail polish on her left hand and watched it flake onto the floor of the taxi.

She'd call Celia. Let her know she was here. Surprise her. Should she call tonight or tomorrow? Her mood shifted again.

Chapter 4

Thursday, November 28, 2019

"YOU'RE UTTERLY AWFUL! HOW COULD you not tell me?" Celia exclaimed.

"You have no idea how many people don't know I left New York!"

"So like you. Slinking about. In and out without a word."

She was right, in a way. Charlotte had a habit of appearing and disappearing. Sometimes for good reason. She didn't like certain people knowing where she was, including back in New York. Of course, that meant social media was a modern-day blessing and curse. She'd have to limit the images she posted.

"And isn't it your Thanksgiving today?" Celia asked, interrupting her thoughts.

"How'd you know? You have time for an old friend?"

"Hmm…let me think." Celia paused. "Are you nuts? Of course. I have a bit of a break around four…you know what? I'll cancel that client. He can wait until tomorrow."

"Anyone famous?" Charlotte asked. Celia's growing reputation as a top-notch interior designer meant she'd done work for some of London's rich and famous. Even for the royals. Lesser ones, but still.

"No one you'd know. I'll come and pick you up. We'll wander a bit. Text me your address."

After they hung up, Charlotte waltzed around her small apartment, placing photos of her parents and a few of her New York friends on a bookshelf. And one of her with Celia. Looked at her parents' images, spoke to them, grew tearful, moved them. She unpacked the Eifel Tower snow globe her mother had purchased on a trip they'd made to the "city of light."

"I bet you don't know how it got that name," her mother had said.

Charlotte, ten at the time, tried to guess. "Because of the light in Paris? It's very bright?"

Her mother shook her head. "Nope."

"I give up."

It was then that her mother told the story of Louis XIV's effort to reduce crime. "He gave one of his men the assignment of making the city brighter at night. That man placed lanterns all through the city. That happened way back in the 1600s. Can you believe it?"

Charlotte had been amazed by the story and hoped someday to match her mother's breadth of knowledge. She picked up the photo of them in Paris and gazed longingly at it. "I still have a long way to go," Charlotte said. As she shook the snow globe, she watched the snow fall on the miniature Eiffel Tower and imagined her mother saying, "You'll get there. Don't worry."

"I will," Charlotte said, then tuned into Adele on her phone's music app and listened to her plaintive voice as she hung up clothes, folded others and tucked them away in the dresser someone had painted a robin's egg blue.

It took her exactly nine pirouettes to cross from the entrance of her bedroom through the family room and into the tiny kitchen, where she opened the small refrigerator and retrieved a can of Pepsi light. Warm from dancing, she allowed the fridge's cool air to waft over her before closing the door.

With a couple of hours to kill and now living in London, Charlotte decided that, like any good reporter, she had to be up on the Royals' latest news. And from the looks of it, Duchess Meghan and Prince Harry seemed far more controversial, and thus newsworthy, than Kate and William. She scrolled through a few articles to discover that only a week earlier Queen Elizabeth and Prince Philip had celebrated seventy-two years of marriage. Scrutinizing the two of them in a 1947 wedding photo, Charlotte decided that then-Princess Elizabeth appeared happy, confident and glowing, while Philip seemed uncomfortable and far less certain about their union. Perhaps already he'd imagined that she'd be Queen, while he remained a mere prince and consort. In fact, he'd earned the title "longest living consort."

Will I even make it to a thirtieth anniversary let alone a sixtieth or seventieth, Charlotte thought. At this rate, even if she married within a year, she'd have to reach one hundred for a *seventieth* anniversary.

As she contemplated the unlikeliness of such an event, a text arrived from Celia saying she got hung up with a client and she'd swing by at six.

With the newfound time, Charlotte checked some more news sites. A link to the "lesser Royals" took her to a scandalous story about Sheik Mohammed of Dubai, seventy, and his attractive forty-five-year-old wife, Princess Haya, the daughter of Jordan's King Hussein. The scandal involved the sheik's abusive behavior toward two daughters, ones by two other wives, and Princess Haya's subsequent escape to Germany, where this past June she requested asylum for herself and their daughter and son, then left for England and filed for divorce. The story compared this divorce to that of Prince Charles and Princess Diana, describing it as a very high-profile royal breakup, at least in part due to the sheik's four-billion-dollar fortune.

Great tabloid fodder, Charlotte thought, and read on. Princess Haya, a renowned horsewoman who'd competed in the 2000 Olympics, had recently been interviewed about the sheik's oppressive behavior toward those two daughters, who'd escaped their compound some years ago. Sheik Mohammed had them tracked down, beaten and imprisoned. No one had heard from them since.

Much of this story intrigued Charlotte. The incredible wealth involved; the oppression of women in the Arab world; and perhaps most of all, why Haya would marry such a man—twenty-five years her senior, and rather unattractive. But the report claimed they'd fallen in love. *Yes, love comes in strange shapes,* she thought. Because now Haya feared for her life and that of her children. It was reported that the unscrupulous sheik would take whatever measures necessary to capture her and the children and lock them up, as he had his two daughters. The story brought Regina to mind. Would Human Rights International consider their welfare a human rights issue? Or was that reserved for people without means?

As the hour of Celia's arrival approached, Charlotte wondered how she could possibly have thought of *not* notifying her friend of her arrival in London? Obviously, her mind for the past few days had been a confused stew of emotions. She didn't know up from down, east from west.

When the buzzer finally blared, instead of pushing the button to open the door, Charlotte flew down the two flights of stairs and let her friend inside. The two embraced for a lengthy hug, loud giggles escaping them. "Oh, God! I can't believe you're here! In jolly old England."

Charlotte led the way to her apartment.

"Not much to see is there?" Celia said after a brief examination.

"It's small but suits me for now."

Celia glanced around again. "It's perfect for a nun," she said smirking. After opening the door to the small fridge and staring inside, Celia said, "Not a damn thing to drink *or* eat. Figures."

"Oops," Charlotte said.

"Can't have you starving on Thanksgiving. Come on, my treat. Let's go to The Crown and Shuttle."

Once settled at a table, they lifted their beer mugs. "Cheers! To best friends!" They clinked glasses and drank.

Wiping foam from her mouth, Celia asked, "How long will you be here?"

"Didn't I tell you? I'm here. For good!"

"Forever?" Celia's dark brown eyes widened. "You swear?"

"Who knows what's forever these days," Charlotte remarked. "I could be sent on an assignment to Mongolia tomorrow."

"You are *not* going to Mongolia. You are staying put." Celia's eyes shifted, moving over Charlotte's left shoulder, down the bar a bit. Charlotte turned to have a look.

It looked like the same guy she'd seen the previous day while in the cab. Well, he must live nearby, she thought. He winked at them. Charlotte blushed.

Celia said something, but Charlotte couldn't hear her over the noisy din of the pub. "What?" she shouted.

Celia leaned in closer to her ear. "Reminds me of Rafe."

"No, he doesn't," Charlotte insisted, with a shake of her head. "Not really. Unless you mean the dreads?"

Celia eyed her.

"Anyway, don't bring him up."

Celia tilted back. "Why ever not?"

"Because. I've recently broken up with my fucked-up boyfriend, and I don't ever want another. Anyway, I'm sure Rafe is taken and doesn't want to hear from me."

Celia gave her an arch look, one that suggested she was harboring a secret. "What if I told you he isn't, and he does."

"Are you in touch?"

"Sort of."

"How sort of?" Charlotte tried to gauge if Celia was up to something. She had a conniving look in her eyes.

"He's come to a few of my parties."

"Oh," Charlotte said with a sigh. "When was the last time you saw him? In person, I mean?"

Celia thought. "A year, maybe. But, of course, I follow him on Instagram and Facebook."

"Yes, don't we all? I mean I don't, but how much can you truly know about someone from social media?"

"A lot." Celia took a final slug of her beer. "I think he's broken up with his most recent girlfriend."

"Oh," Charlotte said, again feigning disinterest. "And who was that?"

"A model. Don't recall her name."

"A model. Figures."

Celia sipped her beer and said, "And what does that mean?"

"Going for looks."

"Well, he went for looks when he fell for you."

"I'd like to think I had brains too."

"Yes, once upon a time," Celia said with a smile.

Charlotte stuck her tongue out.

"So, what the hell happened with Russ?"

"Before I tell you, I want to hear about you! Any fun new clients? Who are you seeing?"

"Mmm…there's a fella named Phil who's kind of cute. We're supposed to get together by the weekend."

"Really? What's he do?"

"Teaches tech stuff at one of the local academies."

"That's different for you…you usually go for the sporty type?"

"I think he likes to bike; you know, out in the countryside."

A smile crept onto Charlotte's face. "This I have to see. Celia on a bicycle tooling around the villages. I love it."

"Don't get all excited. We haven't even met yet. You know how it is; they look good on paper, even on FaceTime, but how do they smell and all that…we'll see." She made a funny face, wrinkling her nose as if she'd detected a foul odor.

"Keep me posted on this *fella!*"

"All right, enough about me. Last we spoke you said Russ cheated on you, but you didn't want to get into it. What happened?"

Charlotte reflected on what to tell her. "Actually, you won't believe how I found out."

"I'm waiting." Celia drummed her fingers on the wooden table.

"I was trying to meditate in our bedroom when I heard this ping." She paused. "Like broken glass. It seemed to come from his iPad. I got curious and took a look. Staring at me was a tantalizing line of text. He was in another room, so I opened the message and saw he was sexting with some girl! The bastard!" The string of texts and nude photos ran through Charlotte's mind. "I confronted him, turned out he'd been seeing her for, like, six months. Was doing it after classes at Columbia. Got to know her in Turkey at one of the digs. Barely apologized. I hate him."

"He did you a favor. I never much cared for him. Too arrogant."

"Really? Why didn't you tell me?"

"I don't know. Thought maybe he'd cure you of your numerous afflictions." She gave Charlotte an affectionate sidelong glance, as if to gauge her reaction.

"Yes, well, instead he added to them!" They both laughed. "Good riddance."

"Truly?" Celia asked.

"I suppose. I mean who wants someone who cares so little about them?"

"A person who cares so little about herself?" Celia offered.

"Is that who I am?"

Celia nodded. "Time to put all that behind you." She picked up the menu and glanced at it. "How's roasted chicken, veggies, and potatoes for your Thanksgiving meal?"

"Sounds fantastic." While waiting for their food, she could feel the jetlag catching up to her. "I'm beat. Four days until I head into the hallowed halls of Thorntree Entertainment. I'm working on a story; have to visit Blenheim Palace."

"Wow, really?" Celia looked at Charlotte with curiosity.

"Need to finish up that 18-karat gold toilet story." Charlotte rolled her eyes. "The one that disappeared from Churchill's water closet in Blenheim Palace."

"Important shite!" Celia said, looking truly impressed.

"You betcha'," Charlotte said, using her best American twang. "I'm a very important journalist, chasing down stories critical to the human race!" Again, they managed a laugh. She briefly thought of Regina.

"Don't underestimate the value of toilet humor," Celia retorted, "it's rescued countless people from depression." She paused to give Charlotte an appraising glance. "But really, now that you're here in London, you ought to call Rafe. I'm sure he'd love to hear from you."

"Stop! I'm leaving if you don't."

"Me thinks thou dost protest too much?"

Charlotte's tone softened. "I am not ready to see him. And when I am, I'll have some serious begging to do."

"I'm sure he'll forgive you."

"And then what?" Charlotte said. "Let's plan a tour of London this weekend? After you and Phil meet up!" On her way out, she could feel eyes following her. When she turned, she caught the man with the dreads watching her. His smile lingered in her mind, as did thoughts of Celia and Rafe on the short trek back to her new apartment. Despite the well-lit path, several times footsteps drew close behind, unnerving her.

Chapter 5

Oxford, Fall 2011

CHARLOTTE AND CELIA OFTEN RECOUNTED how the two of them had met, especially after a couple of drinks on one of their trips. It only took the comment *Remember Marge Whittlesey?* for the two to burst out laughing.

During a moment of drunken banter with several new girlfriends at Oxford, one of them, Grace, mentioned she'd seen a posting at the art department. "They're looking for a nude model. I'll bet it's a fine place to meet some very attractive artists." With a wicked smile, she added, "We can all use a little extra cash. Let's see who can snag the job." She glanced around the circle of four friends. "Whoever gets it, drinks on you."

"You're on," Charlotte said to Grace. "But no, no, drinks are on whoever *doesn't* get the job."

Celia rushed over. "Have it your way; in any case I'm in." They clinked beer bottles and looked at one another mischievously. "May the better woman win," Celia said.

Grace chimed in, "Me too." Which is how Charlotte found herself early the following day face-to-face with the person hiring nude models at Ruskin College—Marge Whittlesey.

"Exactly how experienced are you?" asked the woman with a helmet of curly red hair, completely straight-faced, while Charlotte fought to suppress an upwelling of laughter.

She swallowed twice before opening her mouth. "Why, I've no experience at all." She almost added, *unless you count posing for my boyfriend,* something she'd done a few times. But without experience she'd fail to get the job. Very much hoped so. She'd finally come to her senses in the morning, but her flat mates insisted she fulfill her end of the dare.

"Good," the woman said.

Good? Charlotte thought, examining the metal nameplate on the corner of her desk.

"They want a newbie," Marge said. "Someone without the slightest pretension she knows what she's doing. You're hired." She stared at Charlotte. "Well?"

Charlotte nodded dumbly. That evening she learned Celia had gotten there an hour later, and Grace hadn't applied. Katherine refused to say. Their running joke was that Charlotte fit the bill, because of looking a tad slutty, and Celia didn't because her bum was a bit plush. Charlotte always laughed and said with a toss of her wild mane of hair, "I may look slutty, but you all had to buy the drinks! So there."

A week later, Charlotte found herself without a scrap of clothing, adopting various poses, certain the artists must think she had a permanent sunburn with all the embarrassment she felt. After another week, though, she understood that the students saw her not as a young woman in the buff, but rather as an *object* to be painted or drawn. The turn of her neck held as much challenge and fascination as the curve of her breasts. This realization led to far greater ease posing nude no matter how many eyes latched onto her.

In fact, she became so comfortable that two weeks later, after a long night of studying and "a few drinks down at the pub," she'd fallen asleep on a moss green velvet sofa with only an indigo silk scarf draped across her belly. With her arm thrown over her head, she resembled the model in Matisse's "The Blue Nude." Anyway, that's the image she'd had in mind when striking the pose.

A while later, startled by the noise of someone clearing his throat, she pried her eyes open. Only two feet away a stranger knelt before her, as if about to propose. Who was this dude? The whole thing seemed ludicrous, and for an instant she thought she was still dreaming. But the scene behind this startlingly attractive man with dark probing eyes assured her she was awake. All the aspiring young artists appeared busy, cleaning their brushes and paints, presumably ignoring the tableau before them. She later found out they were all curious to hear the young man's question and her response.

Her instinct on seeing him, with his smooth dark skin and nearly shaved head, was to tighten the gauzy scarf around her midriff. A ridiculous reaction, given the diaphanous fabric.

With one arm resting on his bent knee, the young man again cleared his throat. "I'm Rafe Jackson—sculptor in the graduate program. In…in…uh, search of a model," he sputtered nervously with a hint of a Caribbean accent.

Having traveled the world with her parents on her father's various diplomatic missions, and having an ear for language, Charlotte had a knack for detecting accents. Before she could ask though, he spoke again.

"I wonder if we could talk?" He struggled to keep his eyes trained on her face, dropping only an inch or two below her neck. Either he was nervous, or he'd been well brought up, she thought. Polite. Considerate. Respectful.

She, on the other hand, allowed her eyes to travel over his trim, muscled body only to land on the fingers resting on his knee. Charlotte had a thing for fingers, especially ones like his—long and tapered at the end—artists' fingers she called them. "Let me slip into something a little more comfortable, all right?" She broke into a cocky grin. "I'll just be a minute."

In the dressing room, she took her time and wondered about him. Black men at Oxford were an anomaly. Why had he chosen her? When had he seen her? After she changed into her street clothes, she found him waiting outside the classroom where she'd left him.

"It might be helpful to show you my studio and talk through my work," he said with a questioning look. Though she harbored misgivings about accompanying a stranger to his "studio," a short while later, they walked amiably along the streets of Oxford, autumn leaves crunching beneath their feet. A few times he kicked at pebbles, using the side of his foot like a practiced soccer player, and explained his desire to create a full-size Venus-style sculpture and his need of a model. He'd glimpsed her several times in the classroom and believed that her body "suited" his needs.

Awkward phrasing, she thought, but she liked the idea, if only for selfish reasons. Instead of posing for dozens of students, she'd only stand nude before one artist, someone working toward his master's degree, which elevated her status as a model, she decided. Later, she thrilled at the notion of herself as a life-size sculpture. Forever enshrined in bronze, future generations passing by, perhaps wondering who she was, who she'd been. An artifact. One she'd never had the chance to see and now, seven years after its creation, hoped she might.

Awaiting sleep in her Shoreditch apartment, she basked in that long-ago moment, and admitted to herself that almost instantly, even as he'd knelt before her, she had felt a current running between them. It had been love at first sight, hadn't it? That year, in her English studies, a line from a Christopher Marlowe play captured her young heart, and she committed it to the opening page of her journal: *Where two deliberate, the love is slight. Whoever loved, not having loved at first sight?*

Why else would she have accompanied a complete stranger to his apartment? And why was she so reluctant to see him again now? But she knew the answer to that. She rolled over. Exhausted from her travels, she fell asleep.

Chapter 6

Monday, December 2, 2019

TODAY, HER FIRST DAY AT Thorntree Entertainment, the holding company for Thorntree's media outlets, she'd dressed in her best and most serious work outfit—a dark blue blazer over a white turtleneck with skinny black jeans—to top off her latest gray suede, low-heeled boots. She'd gotten them for a song at a shoe warehouse back in New York. As for her hair, she'd simply drawn back the mass of unmanageable curls with a blue hairband, a nice contrast to her amber eyes. Despite the messy hair, or maybe because of it, whistles and wolf calls often followed her on Manhattan streets.

She entered the elevator, feeling as confident as she ever felt, which wasn't very, but maybe just a smidge better than usual. For the first time in three months, she felt vaguely attractive and a bit happier. That seemed like a step in the right direction.

As soon as the doors closed, though, she caught a glimpse of someone who looked like Rafe. Not again, she thought. Last night's dreams wafted into her mind, curling around morning news reports of Australia's scorching wildfires and the measures their museums were taking to protect their precious art. Now she recalled her dreams had been of Rafe. Frustrating dreams in which she could never quite reach him as he slipped through a doorway, around a corner, always moving away from her. She called out to him, but her words evaporated into the gaping darkness. She released a long exhale and shook her head a little at the memory.

"Long night?" a man's voice asked from behind her.

She cast a glance over her shoulder. "Not really. Just some," she began, about to add "bad dreams," then thought better of it and mustered, "concern about those wildfires in Australia." Only two other occupants on the lift with them and both studiously trained their eyes forward.

He nodded. The silver-haired man had a confident, lean look with a tanned yet still youthful face. "New here?"

"First day," she said.

"Welcome."

Turning further, she extended her hand. "Charlotte Cooper," she said, looking him in the eye. A lesson she'd learned early in life after a teacher admonished her, saying that it showed character to meet an adult's gaze, which for some reason had stuck with her.

"Pleased to meet you, Ms. Cooper." Wearing a tailored suit, he took her hand in his and shook it briefly. "Where will you be posted?"

"Online magazine, I think. I've just left New York. Worked for *Savvy Faire*." The elevator stopped. "The magazine was bought and now will only be online." The man probably knew all that, she thought. A ding brought her eyes forward. *Saved by the bell*. "Ah, my floor!"

"Well, good luck," he called as she escaped, and the doors closed behind her. Nice enough, she thought, and wondered if she'd run into him again, only then aware he hadn't introduced himself.

After a quick glance around, and memories of last night's dreams of Rafe wafting about, she asked the nearest person for the ladies' room.

She stared at herself in the mirror, attempted to fuss with her hair, applied peach lip gloss, then told herself to stop thinking about Rafe. Barely five days in the country and already he consumed her thoughts. Exactly what she'd feared. "Ridiculous! Stop it!" she said aloud. For several years, with a few exceptions, she'd succeeded in putting him out of her mind, and now this.

The loud rush of water of a flushed toilet startled Charlotte. *Talking aloud to myself?* She scampered into the corridor and went in search of the HR department. After filling out some forms, the woman in charge gave

Charlotte instructions for finding her desk one floor up and wished her luck.

The newsroom comprised the entire floor, typical open-plan style. She felt as if she'd arrived in the middle of a beehive, busy worker bees emitting a constant hum of chatter, fingers flying across keyboards, and news arriving on monitors scattered around the room. A woman, roughly her own age, introduced herself as Diane and welcomed Charlotte, who sat down on the neighboring empty chair. Charlotte committed her name to memory by thinking, *Princess Diana.* They exchanged a few pleasantries then Charlotte opened her computer and, using Skype, contacted Shelby as the HR woman had advised.

"I'm in the middle of things, Charlotte. I told you to finish up that piece on the golden toilet. Now get going." Without so much as a good-bye, Shelby hung up.

Nothing new there, Charlotte thought, then worked her way through the morning by reviewing all the latest "hot" news on several sites, including *Esquire* and its Oscar "snubs" list (*how can white males still dominate such a diverse group of talented and creative people*?), and also @*What's Trending*, where she encountered a story about obsessed fans chasing after their favorite YouTube celebrities, hounding them at their homes, demanding photos, etcetera. The price of fame, Charlotte decided, refusing to feel sorry for the "famous" YouTubers, and siding with the fans. *Be grateful; that's how you got famous! Poor you.*

A bit celebrity-obsessed, Celia was a source of infinite knowledge; she'd ask her opinion. Her thoughts turned briefly to the wealthy Dubai sheik and Princess Haya, wondering how she was doing. The woman had millions to protect and insulate her, and yet the story intrigued her. How *did* she feel? Did she truly fear the sheik might kidnap and imprison her and their children? Maybe she'd contact her for an interview. Would Shelby approve? Of course.

Mid-afternoon, after planning a visit to Blenheim Palace a few days hence, the phone on her desk rang. She stared at it; was this actually meant for her? No one knew of her existence here except the HR woman, Shelby, and Celia. Had Celia gotten the vibe she'd been thinking about her? But how would she know this number? When the jangling noise refused to stop, she picked up the receiver.

"Charlotte Cooper speaking."

"Mr. Bradford's office calling," said an officious youthful male voice.

"Mr. Bradford?" she asked.

"Surely you've heard of him?" the voice said in a condescending tone. He sounded like a male version of Shelby. Should she admit she had no idea who Mr. Bradford was? Without a ready comeback, she remained silent.

"Ms. Cooper?" the young man's voice prompted.

"Yes?"

"He'd like to schedule a meeting with you tomorrow at 11:30. Does that suit?"

"Well, sure. Can I ask what it's about?" Charlotte asked.

"May I," the young man corrected. "I don't know. We'll see you then. Top floor. Don't be late. Mr. Bradford's *very* busy. He doesn't like to be kept waiting."

"Of course." Charlotte checked the in-house directory and found that Mr. Nelson Bradford headed up Thorntree Television News.

She glanced at her nails, thinking that perhaps she ought to get a manicure before meeting this man, then wondered what on earth he might want, and how he'd known where to find her? Could he be the man on the elevator? She'd never done broadcast news, so what did he want? *To fire me? Then what? Maybe it's a gag!* Why hadn't she asked the guy's name, the one who'd called? Or maybe Shelby had decided to get rid of her, and asked this man to do her dirty work? None of this sounded the least bit plausible.

"Shite," she muttered, using one of her favorite Brit slang words, and slapped the paper on her desk.

Chapter 7

"LET'S MEET ON LONDON BRIDGE after work," Charlotte told Celia later that day. "I've got something to tell you."

"London Bridge, you're sure? They recently had a stabbing there," Celia replied.

"Oh, Celia, don't you know that's all the more reason to go."

"Good grief, why?"

"Because a repeat event in that exact location is unlikely to happen twice. Plus, they've probably posted police there. Anyway, I want photos."

"Whatever you say. See you at—?"

"Six-ish?"

"As the clock strikes," Celia exclaimed.

"On Big Ben?"

"Yes."

A minute or two before six, they met on the bridge at the midway point above the Thames. The city's lights scattered across the river's dark surface as they listened for the chiming of the iconic timepiece. Charlotte felt her old girlish glee setting in. It was a thrill to see Celia again and she hugged her friend.

But six came and went. Charlotte checked her phone. "That's weird."

"Damn, I forgot," Celia said. "They're working on Big Ben; it won't ring again for a couple of years."

"Wouldn't you know," Charlotte said, her happiness eclipsed by the strange sensation that bad luck had followed her to London.

After a studied look, Celia blurted, "Come. I have a surprise for you."

"Okay, but first—" Charlotte waved her friend over. Leaning against the railing, they made an assortment of goofy faces. Charlotte posted several on Instagram moments later.

She was eager to tell Celia about the call from Bradford, hoping her friend would alleviate her fears that she was about "to get sacked," as Celia would put it. She began to say, "You can't believe who—" but Celia cut her off.

"I assure you that bit of news can wait until we sit down with a drink. Right?" Celia took hold of Charlotte's hand and pulled her along. Together they half-ran, half-walked across the remainder of the bridge, weaving in and out of pedestrian traffic. Five minutes later, they came to a halt before a place with the simple name "George" and stepped inside to the warmth of the pub. "Wait till you taste their Green's Lane gin. With grapefruit. Insane!"

"But I need to tell you my news—" Charlotte said as she glanced around and once more caught sight of a man resembling Rafe, just heading for the men's room. "This is crazy," she said, and for the moment forgot about the call from Bradford's office. Instead, she recounted her near-constant sightings of Rafe the past few days, and the uneasy dreams of the previous night.

"Of course. It's obvious," Celia said.

"What is?"

"You're still in love with him."

"I am not."

"Okay, then you're obsessed?" Celia said, her eyes wide with accusation.

The word *obsessed* caught Charlotte's attention. Was she obsessed? Like those YouTube celebrity fans? She stared across the bar at all the bottles lined up waiting to be poured for every manner of cocktail. "Let's order one of those gin drinks," she said. "The house specialty with the grapefruit. I need it." She sighed.

The two drinks landed before them just as several pings from her phone reached Charlotte. She glanced at her mobile long enough to see that Zander and Daisy had posted responses to her photos. In her excitement, she'd forgotten about wanting her arrival in London to remain semi-private. Oh well, at least Zander wouldn't know how long she planned to stay or where she lived or anything else. Before she could read the reactions, a hand arrived on her shoulder. She glanced at it, momentarily confused. It wasn't Celia's, no, a strange man's hand rested there. A hand with long tapered fingers and a gold ring.

Was this the guy she'd just seen entering the bathroom? When she spun to the left on her barstool, she looked in disbelief at the man standing there.

"Rafe!" she cried. Closeted emotions geysered forth, like a suddenly unclogged fountain. Tears filled her eyes, and she cried, burying her face in her hands, embarrassed but unable to stop.

Through her tears, she heard Rafe say in a waltzing baritone, "I had no idea I had such an effect on women. Shall I leave?" A cock-eyed grin appeared on his face.

Barely able to talk, she squeaked out, "No," and shook her head to underscore her wish for him to stay. "Jetlag," she muttered, the only lie she could think of, and shot a frowning look at Celia, whose broad smile matched Rafe's. She hadn't considered what she'd say *if* or *when* she ran into Rafe, nor was she prepared to see him now. "Gosh, Rafe." She fished in her purse for a tissue and when she looked up, she saw that his expression had grown more curious. She wiped at her eyes.

"Long time, eh, Charlotte?"

She nodded. "Very long. How are you? You look great. I can't believe…I mean whoa. Wow." God, how lame, she thought. *You look great? Whoa. Wow?* Where was the quick retort, something unexpected, or even funny? But, in fact, he did look great. Older, a bit broader, hair in dreads that suited his chiseled features.

His smile returned. He took a step back and appraised her, taking her in from head to toe. "Gorgeous as ever. I knew it." His laughter rolled through the crowded bar, causing a few people to turn and stare. Blushing, she lowered her eyes then lifted them to meet his steady gaze. At last, she slid off the barstool, rose onto her tiptoes, held his arms, and gave him a peck on the cheek. "It's so good to see you."

"Good to see you too." He paused. "Wasn't sure I ever would."

Did she detect resentment? Of course, after all, she'd abandoned him.

Was he mad? No, he probably couldn't care less.

He looked off a moment before angling his body between the two women to order a pint from the busy bartender. Charlotte leaned around Rafe to shoot Celia an "I'm going to kill you" look but discovered her friend had vanished. Her heart sank. With all that history between them, what should she say, alone with a man she'd only dreamt about, a stranger in the flesh right here?

Beer mug in hand, Rafe turned back to Charlotte and sat down on Celia's stool. "What brings you to town?" he asked, sounding strangely casual. Everything he said felt loaded.

"You mean our friend Celia hasn't told you?" She hesitated, wondering exactly what to tell him. He shook his head, though she wasn't sure she believed him. As she began to relay her work circumstance—the magazine folding, her new online reporting job at Thorntree's London office, and her tricky relationship with Shelby—she glanced several times in the direction of the ladies' room hoping Celia would return.

Her discomfort surprised her. This wasn't at all how she'd imagined her reunion with Rafe. It was pointless wishing Celia had waited to do this, but later she *would* kill her. She imagined the headline: *American murders best friend for reconnecting her with old boyfriend!*

"You'll get a kick out of this," she said. "I'm going to Blenheim Palace to follow up on the infamous golden toilet theft."

"Really?" he said, his forehead wrinkling. "Cattelan's getting a lot of ink from that burglary. Maybe I ought to try that?" He smiled at her.

"You know about it then?"

"Of course. Great load of humor for the tabloids, except that it's a damn shame. Security was terribly lax from what I hear."

"Interesting. Maybe I should interview another sculptor for the story."

"Great idea. Know any?" he said.

"Just one."

"Happy to help."

As Celia made her way back to the bar, Charlotte threw her friend an *I'll get you for this* look, but simultaneously wondered what Rafe was thinking and feeling.

She dug around for a witty comment but only managed, "I got a call today to meet with the head of TV news."

"Seriously?" Celia said, an astonished look on her face. "At Thorntree one day and the top guy is meeting with you? Always said you have all the luck."

"Me, all the luck?" Charlotte said. "Well, that's a new twist."

"You got the modeling job," Celia reminded her.

"That?" she said, lifting her brow dismissively. "Probably going to get sacked. On the job today, fired the next." Less anxious now, she hazarded a glance at Rafe. He'd grown quiet.

"I very much doubt that," Rafe said.

"Doubt what?" Charlotte asked.

"That you're getting sacked," he said. "He's probably got his eye on you. Beware of men in broadcast news."

"I've never even met him, but I know what you mean," Charlotte agreed. "All those perverts at Fox and NBC, the whole lot—still shocks the hell out of me." At the thought of this, she grew a little worried. What *did* he want?

With Celia chiming in, the three chatted amiably, but Charlotte couldn't shake feeling tense. At last, she came up with an excuse to leave. "I'm beat. Better catch some sleep. Before tomorrow's meeting." She forced another smile to her lips.

"Get me an appointment and I'll redecorate his office, or better yet, his home," Celia joked.

"I'll sneak some photos," Charlotte promised then faked a yawn. "Better go before I fall asleep standing up." But the encounter with Rafe would guarantee a fitful night.

"Where are you staying?" Rafe asked.

"Small apartment in Shoreditch."

"Seriously?"

"Seriously."

"That's where I live," he said. "Might as well go together."

"All right," she agreed, though his offer sounded less than enthusiastic. Maybe she should take a taxi home. Alone. It had been a long day and being near Rafe conjured such a slurry of emotions she doubted she could relax. Events of that long ago time still riddled her with guilt.

They took leave of Celia, with Charlotte whispering in her ear, "Better lock your door, I'm coming after you."

Celia whispered back, "G'night, luv. I'll sleep like a baby. Don't forget those shots of Bradford's office."

Minutes later, Charlotte and Rafe jumped on a train heading toward Shoreditch. Alone on the ride, their exchanges seemed strained. At best polite.

"Are you missing New York?" he said.

"Yes. Have you been there lately?"

"A gallery there represents me. I go back once a year or so."

She wondered at this. They might have crossed paths, but it had never occurred to her that he might travel to New York. He could have called. But then why would he?

When they emerged from the Tube, he asked, "Which way to your place?"

She pointed down the street to the right.

"How far?"

"A couple of blocks."

"Funny coincidence," he said.

"Why?"

"I live two blocks that way." He pointed in the opposite direction. They took a few steps. "Want me to escort you home?"

"No worries. I'm just over there." She again aimed in the general direction of her apartment. "No need for you to cross that big intersection."

Only then did she realize how remiss she'd been. "Oh, Rafe, I'm so sorry," she said. "Your art, we haven't even touched on that."

"Easy enough to fix. I'll tell you about it next time."

She felt him watching her. "I'd like that," she said.

He leaned toward her. Her heart picked up and she closed her eyes, thinking he was about to kiss her. His low voice sounded in her ear, "Welcome back, Charlotte. Enjoy your time here."

She took a step back. "Thanks, I will," she said, grateful that the darkness of night camouflaged her embarrassment. A tiny nagging voice told her to stop, to apologize right then and there. She hesitated. But even as she did, he backed away, continuing to face her then waved and turned. She waved back, but he didn't see her,

After a few seconds, she allowed herself a backward glance. Was that it? He'd all but disappeared from view, hadn't even asked for her number. Why would he? She turned and kept going, about to cross the intersection.

Quickly, she checked for vehicles coming from the left before stepping into the street. A car from the other direction screeched to a halt, barely missing her as she jumped back onto the curb. The driver leaned on the horn and yelled out the window, "Watch it!"

She lifted her hands in apology. Damn traffic moving the wrong way! Thoughts of Rafe had distracted her. She'd give Celia hell in the morning.

Chapter 8

SOMETIME AFTER MIDNIGHT, CHARLOTTE AWOKE with a start. Maybe a troubling dream, or a noise, she didn't know. But she opened her eyes to the darkness, and in quick succession memories of Rafe crowded into her mind, demanding her attention.

She visualized him—artist, friend, lover—the two of them together almost daily for nine months, she discovering just how deep her commitment and love for someone could be. All the silly love songs rang true: *Deeper than the ocean, wider than the sky!* He was like no man she'd ever loved. And it seemed the same for him. At his urging, she'd stretched her stay in England into July, when she finally returned to New York to finish her last year at Cornell.

She and Rafe stayed in constant touch, planning their reunion, when suddenly the following March he dropped out of sight, and she wondered if he'd ghosted her. But a few weeks later, he reappeared, apologized, and they continued their plan to reunite after she received her BA in English Lit in June. She was days away from returning to London when their bright future together was ripped away. Stolen because of a terrible car accident.

That's when the car that had nearly struck her a few hours earlier came back to her. She needed to make amends, explain to Rafe why *she'd* ghosted *him*, because that's what it was. And maybe he would forgive her. Maybe she'd have another chance. Though she knew it was slim, the possibility existed. Unlike her cousin Abbie who'd died and had no further opportunity at anything.

The gold ring on his finger popped into her head—did that signify a serious commitment to someone else? She hoped not, but did it matter? She needed at least to apologize.

It took her many more minutes to fall asleep.

The next morning, over a cup of coffee and a scone, she checked her Instagram account and found Daisy and Zander's comments on the photos she'd posted of herself and Celia.

Daisy: *Want to meet Celia! Love to visit!*

Zander: *A trip to London?! You need me to take those shots!*

You wish, she thought. And yet he had a point. If Zander had taken the photos, they'd be magazine worthy. She and Celia, if they were famous, would be featured in *Savvy Faire*. The former "what's in" magazine. A step up from *People*. Now in the grave.

Although Zander had been something of a fuck-up at Cornell, a rich boy with little interest in applying himself, he'd risen in the fashion photography world a couple of years after graduation. It surprised her. How had he done it? With help from his father, no doubt, a man worth a fortune who knew everyone in New York. Or rather, everyone wanted to know him. Including Shelby, who'd hired Zander for a few fashion assignments, leaving Charlotte to wonder if she'd done so for his talent or to curry his father's favor.

Though Charlotte had wanted to be rid of Zander after Abbie's death, he continued to pop in and out of her life. He occasionally confided his dreams—he had idols. Diane Arbus. "Love her quirky eye," he said. Richard Avedon. "Someday I'll be as famous as him." The words slid out of his mouth easily. But comments like that annoyed her. Too arrogant, entitled, boastful.

Often, she'd wondered what had attracted Abbie to him. He was handsome enough, just as Abbie was pretty, both of them dark-haired— Abbie petite, Zander athletic. Money? Abbie's parents had plenty. Maybe that's why Abbie felt drawn to Zander. Someone who could perpetuate an opulent lifestyle *and* appear charming and self-confident. So perhaps his eventual success shouldn't have surprised her. But other facets of Zander had worried her, and she wondered whether Abbie had recognized them, or chosen not to. How could a smart young woman like her not recognize that his arrogance depended on his father's wealth and the countless hangers-on? She'd kept from Abbie that he cheated, hung out with other girls, had even flirted with her, believing that eventually Zander would grow up or show his true feathers and bring her cousin out of her romantic idolizing fog. The car crash had ended the need for that.

At work she glanced at headlines and scanned stories—terrorists caught in the Netherlands, elections fair and unfair, natural disasters, a 6.5 earthquake had just shaken Albania. She looked for something humorous to ease her anxiety about meeting with Bradford but instead encountered an interview between Anderson Cooper and writer Afua Hirsch, a woman born to a British father and a mother from Ghana.

She'd written a controversial piece on Prince Harry and Meghan— discussing the media's racist attacks on Meghan, about which she, as a biracial woman, would have some understanding. Afua was one gorgeous, smart woman. Charlotte watched the interview with interest. And imagined herself like that—poised, informed, and confident—as she looked up late-breaking news stories on the golden toilet, hoping she hadn't missed a lead. But no, there was nothing.

Eventually, her phone beeped. Ten minutes until her appointment. She felt nervous but he was only human. Still, her stomach fluttered each time she thought of Bradford's reason for wanting to meet with her.

The elevator rose soundlessly, then released her into a massive lobby with doors that she imagined led to well-appointed executive suites. It was a far cry from the hive atmosphere of the newsroom. Wherever she looked, from ceiling to wall to floor, a gloss, a shine, a sparkle greeted her. If it was meant to impress and intimidate, it succeeded. All that glass and those hard edges sent a chill through her. Not entirely unlike times she'd entered Shelby's office, worrying what she'd done or not done.

The hushed environment made her wish she hadn't worn heels that clip-clopped on the marble floors and echoed throughout the chamber. She'd try to walk more quietly, and since the receptionist's desk was empty, she pulled out her phone and in one slow revolution took a video for Celia.

"May I help you?" a feminine voice called from behind her.

Startled, Charlotte pivoted to see a youthful, conservatively dressed woman behind the desk. She seemed to have materialized out of nowhere and peered at her through attractive lenses. The Thorntree logo, superimposed on a circular map of the world, was prominently displayed on the front of the desk. The message couldn't have been clearer.

Charlotte smiled and said, "I hope it's okay that I took a shot? The lobby's beautiful. My friend is a designer and decorator." The woman nodded and waited. Charlotte rushed to add, "I'm here to see Mr. Bradford."

"I'll let him know you're here. And you are?"

"Oh, of course," Charlotte said, blushing at her own stupidity. Did she expect the woman to know who she was? "Charlotte Cooper," she added with an apologetic shrug.

A few minutes later, alongside Jason, the young man who'd called yesterday, Charlotte found herself nervously entering Nelson Bradford's office, a place that despite its size—at least double or triple her large studio apartment—looked surprisingly comfortable compared to the glitzy, glossy waiting area. In one sweeping glance, she saw couches and tables arranged into various configurations. She wondered where he'd invite her to sit. In fact, where was he?

Surprised by the conservative suit covering Jason's diminutive frame, she followed him into another room, a smaller more intimate one, lined with heavily stocked mahogany bookshelves and a few celebrity photographs, including one with Princess Diana. Mr. Bradford sat behind his desk, facing the window, presumably gazing outside.

Charlotte heard him laugh then realized he was on the phone. Another minute passed before Jason's throat-clearing jarred him, and he swiveled around, tapping the phone off and laying it on his desk. He was a broad-shouldered man with rust-colored hair, tinged silver at the temples, but not the man she'd encountered on the elevator. Like his assistant, Jason, he wore a well-tailored suit, but also a distracted look. The moment his gray-green eyes fell on Charlotte, though, his focus sharpened.

"Mr. Bradford," Jason said, "Charlotte Cooper here to see you." As if on cue, Jason backed out of the room like a servant in colonial England.

Wearing a bemused smile, he stood up and beckoned her. "Come, enjoy the view." He met her halfway and shook her hand.

"Nice to meet you, Mr. Bradford."

"Please, call me Nelson. We're not formal around here." Without letting go of her hand, he guided her to a spot directly in front of the floor-to-ceiling windows.

She eased her hand out of his and stared at the sprawling metropolis of London spread before them. Tall modern buildings knitted between much shorter historic structures; the Thames winding its lazy way through the city. The sight dazzled her. So, this is how some people live, she thought, and imagined how much Shelby would covet this view.

"Pretty amazing," she said. "How lucky to see this each day."

"Little to do with luck, Charlotte. It's all about hard work."

She thought about Zander and the advantages he'd had. Perhaps Nelson had experienced a similar sort of wealth, which inevitably led to high-level introductions that gave them access to professional success. "Is it?" she found herself asking.

As if reading her mind, he admitted, "Well, yes, my family and the Thorntrees go back quite some time." At least he was honest, she thought.

Through her father's diplomatic career and friends from her college days, Charlotte had met some very wealthy and well-connected people. Money often begets money, she'd learned. For some reason this thought gave her confidence. Armored with a poker face, she said, "You asked to see me? I hope it's not to fire me."

He released a loud guffaw. "Heavens no! Fire you. I like that in a woman. Getting right to the point."

Charlotte's mouth had gotten her in trouble before; at times she spoke her mind without thinking ahead. "I'm sorry, that was rude of me. I'm just curious." She gave him a dimpled smile. She needed to be polite; she didn't want to ruin any opportunities and waited for him to speak. At least this much she'd learned. *Don't fill the silences.*

"I was wondering if you'd ever done a screen test, an audition as a TV reporter?" he asked.

Her eyes widened in genuine surprise. "No. I never have."

"Would you like to? We're looking for new on-air talent. Fresh faces."

He paused and gave her an appraising look. "Like yours."

She thought a moment. She'd never considered it, ever. "I suppose it couldn't hurt, but I don't know that I'm cut out for that sort of thing."

This time, she noticed, he waited.

"I'm a bit shy," she added and almost instantly felt patches of red creeping up her neck.

"Really? What I mean is, I'm surprised you've never considered it, and also that you're shy. It's an odd sort of shy."

"You're not the first to say that. I guess everyone's complicated in their own way?"

"Yes, I suppose." They were still standing by the window, though they had turned to face one another while talking. He looked out again. "You're quite attractive, you know. Not in an ordinary sort of way. I mean, that hair of yours…we'll have to do something about it. But then again, I don't want to ruin your…" he stopped, his eyes assessing her looks. "Your uniqueness."

The way he studied her reminded Charlotte of someone, though she couldn't say who. She had been told and believed she was pretty, but her mother had hammered into her head that adage about beauty being skin-deep. True beauty emanated from within. And she agreed. Surface beauty could hide one's inner flaws, but only for a time. And God knew she had plenty of those.

"I'm here to help further your career," he went on, "I was thinking, your assignment…the golden toilet." He chuckled. "Perhaps you could interview a few people…we'll send a video crew with you to Blenheim Palace…and then you'll edit it for the evening news. As a first step, a kind of screen test."

She gazed at him, wondering how he knew about that story. She said, "But I don't know the first thing about editing."

He gave her a shrewd look. "Well, if that's the only thing you have to learn it won't take you any time at all to become a broadcast journalist."

She found herself blushing again. "I meant it's not the only thing I'll learn, it's just that editing is foreign to me. I imagine the reporting won't be so different; it's what I do now, just not with a camera."

"We can teach you the editing."

"All right," she said, adding, "I guess."

"You seem hesitant?"

"No, well, it's—" but she stopped, not knowing exactly what to tell this man. That she wasn't sure she wanted to switch to television news?

"Perhaps the hardest part is to boil into a few words the essence of the story. You can't go on and on as one does in print." He gave her a penetrating stare. "Not everyone gets a chance like this, you know. Too daunting for you?"

"No," she shot back. "It's not daunting at all." She looked at him with disbelief, then gave him her best, bravest expression, forcing her mouth into a smile.

"All right then," he said, "let's see how you do." It was a direct challenge, one she'd accept. But his next move she was unprepared for. With an unwavering smile, he gripped her arm, and with a shrewd look, he added, "Let's grab a drink after your trip to Blenheim and you can tell me how it went."

She didn't know how to respond. Was it an invitation or a command? She stood gawping at him when her cell phone rang. She glanced at the screen. "A source," she said, "someone I've had trouble reaching." It was her escape hatch; she backed away, then turned and hurried toward the door.

Chapter 9

BRADFORD'S VOICE CHASED AFTER HER. "I'll have Jason order a camera crew to accompany you to Blenheim," he called. She turned, smiled, and gave him a thumb's up, all the while pressing the phone to her ear, although the line was dead.

How she left his office without stumbling or stuttering she hadn't a clue. She felt like a massive jellyfish, barely capable of walking to the elevator, pushing the button and getting in. The way he'd touched her made her skin prickle, and the thought of a camera capturing her interviews caused her heart to do a double flip. How could she be herself? Could she ignore the camera's eye trailing her every move and catching every word? She thought she'd done a pretty good job of masking her fear, but then his question about having a drink. What the hell?!

She looked at her phone. The call had been from Celia, not a source. In a few minutes she'd call back. She couldn't wait to tell someone about the meeting with Bradford.

After she returned to her desk and mentioned her apprehension to the guy who sat adjacent to her, he said, "You'll get used to TV in no time. Just wait and see." He introduced himself as Ian, researcher for and assistant to several anchors.

Charlotte reciprocated and they shook hands. "I just realized," she said, looking off into space, "that I should have asked Bradford how he even knew I existed."

Ian gave her a telling look. "Don't be daft, you're attractive. They're always scouting for new talent."

"Yeah, but I got here only yesterday."

"Well then, someone must have spotted you."

"But how would they know my name?"

He shrugged. "True enough. Ask him next time you see him."

She hoped it wouldn't be soon.

A few minutes later, her desk phone rang. She wavered, but after several rings and Ian's curious glance, she picked up the receiver.

"Mr. Bradford wants to know if you'd be willing to go live after your Blenheim interviews air next Monday?" It was Jason. "Maybe get that artist on?"

Her gut tightened; she took a deep breath and asked, "Maurizio Cattelan?"

"You should know, you're the one writing the story."

"Right."

She was flabbergasted. *Go live?* She wanted to shout, *No, no, no. One step at a time.* What should she say? "Uh, well, no, I think I'd better not."

She could hear an exasperated sigh on the other end. "Listen, Charlotte, it's not really a question. You're expected to say yes. Anyway, not everyone," he cleared his throat, "uh, gets such chances. You'd better go after it."

"Really?"

"Yes, really. I don't think I should tell him you're not interested. Right?"

"Okay, right." She hung up and closed her eyes. What the hell kind of test was this? Trial by fire? When she opened them, she noticed Ian's questioning look. "They want me to go on air after my reporting at Blenheim," she explained. "I've never done live TV. I've never even been a broadcast journalist." As those words poured forth, she thought, *am I any kind of journalist?* The work she'd done had seemed second best. Not *real* journalism. Puff pieces. Were they hoping she'd fail?

"I think you've met Diane; she and I will explain the process," he said. He had a kindly look, though not the type of face that lent itself to television—a narrow head with a beak for a nose and tiny eyes, pale skin, stringy hair. So at least he didn't have to worry about becoming an on-air personality.

"That'd be great," she said, feeling some relief. "Maybe after lunch?"

"Yeah, sure. I'll track her down and we can have a cuppa."

She thanked him and left to grab coffee and call Celia. Clear her head. She couldn't believe she'd just agreed to the nerve-wracking prospect of going live. Doing the Blenheim Palace piece on camera was bad enough. Her mind jumped ahead, worrying about keeping her composure, or worse making a fool of herself in front of millions of viewers. Her stomach twisted each time she thought about it. Maybe her on-air debut would be just that. Once and never again. She almost felt relieved at the thought.

She tried Celia, but the call went to voicemail. She thought back on her conversation with Bradford and his suggestion of having a drink. Was it an innocent invitation?

She recalled Rafe's warning the previous night. Which took her thoughts down a different path. Should she contact him? Ask to meet for a coffee?

She needed to review her notes and do some more research on Cattelan's artwork—so much of it aimed to stir controversy—and the toilet theft before heading to Blenheim. That would keep her mind off her fears and thoughts about Rafe. Maybe she'd text Celia.

Charlotte: *Guess what?*

She waited a few seconds then watched the little thinking cloud icon until Celia's response appeared: *What?*

Charlotte: *Bradford—he told me to call him Nelson!—wants me to try TV reporting ... they're videotaping my interviews at Blenheim! And then I'm supposed to go live!!! OMG!*

Celia: *You're going to be a star... Promise you'll still be my friend?*

Charlotte: *Hmm...We'll see. She hesitated before writing: Don't forget I'm still going to kill you!*

Celia: *Whatever for?* 😇

Charlotte: *You know what for!*

Celia: *What I know is you adore Rafe Jackson.*

Charlotte: *I do not.*

Celia: *Yes, you do!*

Charlotte: *Well, seems he may not feel the same about me...*

Celia: *Then why'd he show up last night?*

Charlotte: *Curiosity.*

Celia: *He'll get in touch...just wait.*

Charlotte: *Doubt it. He doesn't have my number.*

Celia: *Shall I give you his?*

Charlotte: *No.* Oh, hell, she thought and tapped in: *Yes.*

Celia texted her his number, added: *Gotta run, luv. Let me know what you're up to later.*

Charlotte sent the photos she'd taken in the lobby outside of Nelson's office and signed it with heart emojis. Then added, *Your thoughts? Garish? Cool? Or...*

Celia: *Chilly. Need to warm that place up...*

Charlotte: *Exactly what I thought. Nelson (!) asked me out for a drink after the shoot.*

Celia: *Yikes.*

So much for hoping Rafe might contact Celia for her number. Now that she knew he hadn't, she tried to settle down to work.

In her research, she'd discovered that Cattelan was described as mischievous and using humor and social commentary in his artwork, like the notorious banana taped to a wall. He sold several versions of it for up to a hundred and fifty thousand dollars to Art Basel Miami earlier in 2019. Cattelan's impetus for installing the now infamous golden toilet in Winston Churchill's water closet was to allow *everyone*, not just the wealthy, to use a fully functioning golden toilet.

Apparently, Blenheim Palace's insurance company had offered a hundred-thousand-pound reward for the 18-karat toilet's return. Of course, they wanted it back. The damn thing was made of something like six million dollars' worth of gold! The stringent rules the insurer attached to receiving the reward was aimed at preventing paying the "villains." But from news reports, she also knew that it was equally likely the thieves had melted the gold into manageable pieces and sold them for far more than the reward monies.

Furthermore, because of his previous prank, initial speculation suggested Cattelan had arranged the heist himself. But several months had passed and the police had nothing more than the suspicion that a group of criminals had committed the theft and images of a Volkswagen Golf they believed had been used to transport the toilet. Unfortunately, the car had "cloned" license plates, and thus another dead end.

She needed to get an interview with Edward Spencer Churchill, a distant relative of Winston's and the founder of the Blenheim Art Foundation, though he'd been elusive when she made the request while still in New York.

She sensed his reluctance could be traced back to August, not long before the theft, when he made light of adding security, saying it wasn't necessary because the toilet was attached to the floor. How he felt about that statement now would top her list of questions.

She was curious about another aspect of his life. He'd married a German photographer, Kimberly Hammerstroem, and she hoped to get an inside track on how that year-old marriage was going. It never hurt to dig around a bit. And celebrity news always sold, even about little-known celebrities.

The story, gaining momentum in her mind, had a delicious quality to it now that she was in England and could actually meet some of the people involved, see Cattelan's entire exhibit firsthand, and experience Winston Churchill's home. She decided that now, just maybe, she'd have better luck getting the artist to commit to an interview.

She picked up her phone to contact Cattelan, yet again. A television appearance might be just the thing to lure him. And using a remote feed meant he wouldn't have to leave Italy. About to tap his assistant's number into her phone, she couldn't help first checking her messages but saw nothing from Rafe.

She didn't like obsessing this way and told herself to get back to work. She'd contact him later and offer to meet. For *one* reason: to apologize.

Maurizio Cattelan's assistant sounded interested in setting up a TV interview for Monday but refused to give her a definitive answer.

End of her workday, Charlotte wrote Rafe a text:

Great to see you last night. Wondering, are you available on Friday? I'm going to Blenheim Palace that day, so after I return? Some things I feel I ought to explain and hope you'll give me the chance. Let me know. Thanks.

Charlotte studied the text, wrote several versions, cut "hope you'll give me the chance," because it sounded too needy, then sent it. And waited to hear back. By the time she fell asleep that night, she'd heard nothing.

Chapter 10

Friday, December 6, 2019

MUCH TO CHARLOTTE'S CHAGRIN, ON Friday morning, a man she didn't recognize stood a few yards from the news truck, emblazoned with the TE! logo, awaiting her arrival. She'd been warned by Jason that someone named Malcolm would meet her with a few tips before heading off on her first assignment. Should she be annoyed or grateful? She wasn't sure.

A man of average height and looks introduced himself. "I'm Malcolm," he said, as if she ought to recognize him. His hair was gelled to resemble meringue that not even a hurricane could disturb. To keep from staring, she eyed the two guys loading the van with equipment.

"Nelson asked me to give you a little advice, because television reporting is different."

Did he think she didn't know that? "I'm all ears," Charlotte replied. "What's your role at the station?"

He looked at her in disbelief. "Mine?" When she stared at him blankly, he added, "Anchor for the evening news."

"Oh, sorry. I'm new. Just arrived a few days ago."

His disapproving look melted into a faint smile. "All right, you listening?"

"Yes."

"One. Just concentrate on your interviewee; you'll completely forget about the camera. Two, focus on what your interviewee is saying so you can compose a follow-up question. Anything that doesn't work you can edit out later.

"Three, take several breaths before you launch into your next question, because that allows a little time for them to say more, which is often where the nuggets are…the sound bites that every broadcast journalist lives and dies for."

She worked hard not to roll her eyes. "Thanks, I'll remember that." Did he actually believe this was novel information? Shelby, in a brief call the previous day, had instructed her similarly. She'd closed with, "Don't fuck it up, Charlotte! This could be your road to fame."

When she'd asked Shelby how they'd identified her as a candidate for TV news, she gave a strange answer. "You'll find out. All in good time."

"What's the big secret?" Charlotte waited for a response, but when silence greeted her, she added, "See you soon?" Of course, Charlotte was hoping for the opposite.

"Next week," Shelby answered.

Back in the present moment, she found Malcolm tilting his head, assessing her looks. "Chloe worked some magic with your hair. Like it?"

She touched the back, which the stylist had twisted into a manageable French braid. Only a few wisps of hair had escaped. "It's fine…better than anything I could do." She was curious though because his comment suggested he'd seen her before. "I don't recall ever meeting you," she said.

In response he gave her an enigmatic smile. First Shelby's cryptic comment and now this. What the hell? Then, eagerly, he added, "I'm tight with Nelson."

She didn't know a response for this so remained silent and faced the camera crew. The two men casually dressed in jeans and t-shirts stood next to the van's side door observing her and Malcolm. One tapped at his phone and aimed it at her, clearly anxious to be off.

"Remember, you're the boss," Malcolm said quietly. "Max and Jack want *you* to give *them* orders."

Great, she thought, I was hoping they'd tell me what to do. "Thanks, I'll remember that."

"Good luck," he said. "Anyway, this is pretty light news, so I wouldn't worry, but if you need anything or run into problems, here's my direct line." He handed her his business card then began taking the wide granite steps that stretched across the front of the building two at a time. She watched his retreat gratefully. In mid-stride, however, he stopped and turned. "You've snagged an interview with Churchill, I hear?" She nodded. "Let me know how it goes. And by the way, Nelson's rooting for you."

She gave him a thumb's up but inwardly groaned, praying that *Nelson* wouldn't turn out to be another lecherous TV exec. There ought to be a prison somewhere, she thought, for the whole lot.

She also hoped he wouldn't be waiting to have a drink with her, because yesterday she'd finally heard from Rafe in response to her invitation, which said: *Of course, some things I'd like to clear up too.* Her heart sank a little at the thought. He'd finally be able to tell her off, she imagined, and had briefly considered canceling, but this was her chance to apologize for all the hurt she'd caused. So, of course, she would go.

Instead of drinks, he suggested they meet for dinner. At least this she found encouraging. At a place called *The Owl and Pussycat*, a name that sounded fairytale intriguing, but the evening, she guessed, would be anything but that.

"What I'd like to know is how we can get our hands on that reward," said Jack, the driver and cameraman, steering the van skillfully onto the four-lane motorway.

"You got that straight," Max answered and broke into a full guffaw. "Imagine gettin' ahold of that hundred thousand pounds! We'd be rich. Retire from this job. No offense, Charlotte."

"None taken. But don't get any ideas. That reward, we split three ways, okay?" she said, grinning. "We just have to track down the thieves."

"Agreed," they both chimed in.

"Thirty-three thousand ain't nothin' to sneeze at," Max added.

"Catch is we need to find the thief *and* he needs to be put behind bars. Prison bars, not gold bars," she explained with a smile.

Again, the two men chortled. The two seemed in their early to mid-thirties, Charlotte guessed, Max taller and fair-haired, Jack with a short-cropped brown mop, but both muscled and fit.

"How'd you get onto this story anyway?" Jack asked.

"You don't want to know how *shitty* my assignments can get. Actually, this is one of the better ones."

"Get the pun, Max?" Jack said with a chuckle.

"I'm not stupid, you know!" he answered with a throaty laugh.

She listened to their lighthearted bickering. As she did, a headline popped into her head: *Posh Toilet Where Winston Churchill Once Shat: Gone for Good?*

The sixty miles to just northwest of Oxford would take about an hour. She rifled through her notes, telling herself she wouldn't be the least bit nervous with the cameras rolling. Before she'd left the office, they took some headshots of her to run over the weekend with promos of the piece: "Watch for a special update on the Blenheim Palace toilet theft with Charlotte Cooper reporting on Monday at six p.m." Nelson Bradford had upped the ante. The option to back out had vanished.

She'd been given a time to edit the day's footage over the weekend. The only thing still missing would be an interview with Maurizio Cattelan. His assistant had passed her call on to his publicist, who said he'd be happy to answer questions via a remote connection if he was available. Emphasis on *if.*

Her mind shifted to her plans with Rafe that evening. If Bradford was waiting for her when she returned to TE! offices, she'd use the opportunity to discuss working on hard news stories, like the Streatham High Road stabbings, another terrorist attack to add to all the others. That might make an encounter worthwhile, but she'd have to make a hasty exit.

She'd been approached by male superiors before and had watched the series about Roger Ailes and the price women had paid to be anchors on Fox News. *No way would I do that,* she thought, and vaguely wondered how those women lived with the choices they'd made. Their dance with the devil. *In exchange for sex, I'll get my own show,* they must have thought. Only the harassment rarely ended with one or two sexual favors. The men in charge kept cashing in.

She'd watched and read the reports about powerful men who'd coerced or demanded sex in one form or another. Harvey Weinstein being among the more opportunistic and disgusting right alongside Bill Cosby. Matt Lauer, another disappointment. Anthony Wiener—ugh! Jeffrey Epstein, whose decades-long abuse of underage girls had ended recently with his arrest and supposed suicide. She was glad he was dead. Good riddance. And Prince Andrew, consorting with Epstein, a convicted sex offender! Poor judgment or was he guilty too?

The mere thought of all this harassment and abuse made her nauseous. It also triggered a memory, a blurry one about a night of sex and sweat not long after Abbie's death. *Everything* from that period was hazy, a blur, and either painfully sad or repugnant. She shook her head, allowing the memory to retreat into the shadowy corners littered with her past, and stared outside as the enormous Blenheim Palace came into view.

"Wow," she said. "That's some kind of place!"

"Imagine livin' 'ere," Jack said. "Get lost trying to find your way to the loo!" That unleashed a good-hearted laugh from all three of them. "Know what ya mean," Max said.

Though impressed, a not so small part of Charlotte rebelled at the sight. One family occupying so much space. What would her parents have said? Of course, there were plenty of mansions on Fifth Avenue, but several of those could fit inside Blenheim.

They parked the vehicle and approached the gate. Inside the massive courtyard carpet of Union Jacks in the shape of a cross greeted them. The playful and subversive Cattelan had titled the exhibition "Victory is Not an Option." He'd dared to turn Churchill's famous quote upside down, installed the toilet, named *America*, and also placed his sculpture of Hitler, *Him*, in Churchill's home. Some people, she'd read, hadn't been amused. But his antics and irreverence made her smile.

The crew began filming a few shots of Charlotte standing by the frayed Union Jacks and gazing off at the magnificent and massive U-shaped Blenheim. She had a brief vision of one of Rafe's sculptures featured in one of the palace's opulent rooms and decided to tell him that. Would he consider it a compliment?

"Ready, Charlotte?" Max said, rousing her from her thoughts.

"Ready as I'll ever be." She watched a primly dressed woman in high heels marching toward them.

"I'm so sorry, but Sir Churchill asked me to send his regrets. He's been called away on business. I'm Ms. Burns, here to accompany you on the tour and answer your questions."

Despite her best efforts, Charlotte frowned with disappointment. She'd prepared several "tough" questions for him and knew his squirming answers would play well on television. *Coward,* she thought.

A few minutes later, they stood staring at the gaping hole in the floor where the toilet had been ripped away. "Do you think it was an inside job?" Charlotte asked Ms. Burns.

Looking somewhat stricken, she answered quickly, "No, no, I don't think so."

Charlotte paused, allowing the camera to capture her expression and giving her time to explain. Knowing the camera was aimed at the other woman gave Charlotte added confidence and time to formulate her next question. "So, who and how?" Charlotte said with a smile. She paused, then added, "If you had to guess."

An hour later, they stopped at the police station for an arranged interview with a spokesman then chatted with a few Woodstock locals at a pub, who had varying versions of events and ideas of who nabbed the toilet. Their colorful accounts would juice up the piece. They wrapped up filming B-roll by four o'clock and were on the road back to London.

"Swear you've never done any television? Like they say in America, you knocked that out of the ballpark," Jack said. "You had Ms. Burns in a corner. And then when you asked her to explain why so little security for something so valuable, I thought she might just fall apart. That stutter! Her look was priceless."

"You got that?" Charlotte asked.

"You bet," Max added. "No surprise Sir Churchill didn't want to speak with you. Maybe he had something to do with stealing it?" He looked at Charlotte in his rearview mirror. She shrugged. "We know the rich ain't innocent," he continued, "and they do need loads o' cash. How much was that toilet worth? Six or seven million?"

"Something like that," Charlotte said.

They arrived back at headquarters shortly after five. Charlotte told Jack and Max how much she appreciated their help. "You made all that camera stuff stress-free…who knew it could be so easy?" And wished them a fun weekend.

With that done, she scurried inside, hoping to avoid an encounter with Nelson. She had no intention of letting him know she'd returned from Blenheim.

Chapter 11

CHARLOTTE LEFT THE OFFICE AS quickly as she could and headed home to freshen up. She stood in her tiny bathroom and applied some lip gloss. Each time she thought of Rafe, anxiety came clattering in. After the way she'd abandoned him, how did he feel about her now? He'd been welcoming at the pub the other night. Was that a fluke? Could they put the past behind them? Would there even be a "them," an us? Like someone examining ancient artifacts, she saw the past—her missteps and failures—more clearly.

Perhaps, for him, this date was a way to tie up loose threads? Resolve emotions that had been gathering dust for the half dozen or so years since… since she promised to return and hadn't. Not only that, but she'd cut him off.

And now, would he understand that had been her way of protecting him from her? She'd done things too embarrassing to share and decided to suffer in silence and alone. But maybe she'd punished herself enough? She wasn't sure. Her gut pitched and roiled as if she were in a tiny raft on a churning sea.

The ping from her phone reminded her it was time to go. Not that she needed reminding. Online, The Owl and Pussycat claimed many considered it the "soul of Shoreditch." *Well, I'll soon find out*, she thought. *Among other things.*

It was dusk as she strolled along Redchurch Street. She glanced at her reflection in the window of a storefront. She'd undone the braid, returning her hair to its usual unruliness. "The color of straw," her father often said in a loving tone, "strawberry blondie," her mother added teasingly. She only wished her parents were alive to see her on TV. They'd cure her butterflies. "Do your best," her father would say, "and no one can complain."

"You'll be wonderful," her mother would assure her.

The thought of the two was uplifting but always brought on a touch of melancholy. She missed them but had also grown adept at diverting such thoughts.

She kept walking and again caught herself casting sidelong glances at her image. How had Rafe seen her the other night? No longer twenty-one or twenty-two, her age while at Oxford, but twenty-nine, nearing thirty. Her running, swimming, and biking kept her in shape. Everything else looked passable, except maybe her hair, and yet Rafe had always loved it. He'd often run his fingers through those curls, massaging her scalp, then, eventually, her head cupped in his hand, he pulled her close for a lengthy kiss, one that often tasted of peppermint.

So lost in that thought as she entered The Owl and Pussycat that she bumped into the person in front of her, a woman who shot her an annoyed look.

"Sorry," Charlotte said and approached the hostess who told her that Rafe had already been seated.

As they drew near the table, Rafe jumped up and pulled out a chair for her. He'd always been old-fashioned, something she loved. Charlotte took in a deep breath as she sat down and glanced around the crowded restaurant. By all appearances, the place, which prided itself for its locally sourced produce, attracted a cross-section of people, perhaps from the neighborhood, as it claimed, to which Rafe belonged, and now she would too. She felt grateful for the comfortable, low-key atmosphere, which hopefully signaled no need for pretension.

Still thoughts flew around in her brain—what would she say in apology and how would he react?—until he touched her hand, and she looked up to see his wide smile. "How was your meeting with Bradford?" he asked.

Her heart slowed, and over her wine and his beer, she proceeded to tell him about the encounter, ending with her visit to Blenheim Palace.

"So, I'm looking at a future TV personality?" He gave her a crooked grin.

"Whoa, not yet. It's only a test. They're looking for 'new faces, fresh talent.' Bradford's words, not mine."

"Taking London by storm," he added.

"That's me, the Charlotte Cooper show, watch it on Thorntree Entertainment!"

"No offense, but that's how men like him operate," Rafe said, giving her an raised brow look and dampening her enthusiasm.

"I know," she said, "but he hasn't done anything yet." No, she thought, but his invitation to have drinks might have been his way of niggling in.

"For the record, be careful."

"I will." She had yet to prove herself, and if this *opportunity* was Nelson Bradford's way of luring her into bed or casual sex, he'd be in for a surprise. Or she'd be out of a job.

They tapped their glasses together. "Now it's your turn. Regale me with Rafe Jackson stories," she said, in no hurry to get to the reason for their meeting. She hadn't gleaned much from his online presence and in a while would sneak in a question or two about his personal life, like who he was dating. Because surely he was.

"I promise to tell you everything, but only if you come to my studio. There I'll show you my latest pieces and bend your ear on my many artistic successes."

The mischievous sparkle in his eyes relaxed her. "Very tricky, Mr. Jackson! I fell for that once," she said, slowly rubbing her finger around the edge of her glass, and added with a half-smile, "And just maybe I'll fall for it again."

Though it was a faint noise, especially amid the restaurant's buzz and clatter, Charlotte's ears perked up at the sound of a broken glass ping. So much like Russ's texting alert that it thrust her into an unwanted *deja vu*. Like the day she'd discovered his betrayal.

"Was that your phone?" she asked.

His mobile lay face down. He picked it up and turned it over. His brows pinched into a frown. "I guess so. Nothing important," he said and returned it to the table, screen again facing down.

"Sure? You look a bit bothered."

He stared at her, a discomfited look on his face. "It's … uh … nothing."

"Doesn't seem like nothing," she persisted.

He shook his head. "Charlotte Brontë Cooper," he said. One side of his mouth curled into a faint grin. "Never could hide a damn thing from you."

"But then…there was no need to," she said lightly, though her stomach did that twisty thing, and she took a swig of her drink, thinking she might need something a little stronger.

"Are you sure you want to know about someone I dated?"

Here it comes, she thought and lifted her chin defiantly. Without smiling she said, "Yes."

"All right, but remember, you asked." He waited, clearly hoping she might change her mind. He gulped his beer and flagged down a waiter. "We'll have two more," he said and ordered a couple of appetizers.

"Actually, I'll switch to a Pinot Grigio, please." It seemed that she wasn't the only one avoiding the reason they'd come here, but a short diversion couldn't hurt, could it?

Rafe looked off, as if trying to decide what to tell her. "Her name's Naomi. We met at one of my openings…at the Saatchi Gallery in Chelsea," he said. "A big deal for me."

She nodded. She recognized the world-famous gallery's name. This alone told her that Rafe's career had leapt into the stratosphere.

"I have to admit," he said ruefully, "she looked stunning. Couldn't take my eyes off her. Her skin tones, the lines of her face, the whole bit. Turned out she was a model, and, well you know how it is with us artist types; I wanted her to pose for me."

Charlotte nodded, tried to keep her face a neutral mask, stop her eyes from growing wide and gaping at him. *Did he really have to* say *he wanted to see her nude?*

"So, I asked her out," he said and took another slug of beer.

Charlotte sipped her wine and listened half-heartedly to the evolution of his relationship with *Naomi.* Her hunger vanished. Why on earth was he going into all this detail? And then she realized he was paying her back for abandoning him, for what she'd done.

To avoid his eyes, she stared over his shoulder at the back wall, painted with a colorful and comical frowny-eyed cat and owl. Half-listening, she watched the movement of waiters and pub-goers, until the sharp edge of his voice drew her back. Did he just say that he and Naomi were getting married? Her heart sank; she wanted to flee, to shove her way through the dining room to stop him from saying one more word.

"Charlotte!" He waved his hand in front of her face. "What's the matter? Are you even listening?"

"I lost you right after you said you wanted to marry her!"

His dark eyes scowled at her. "What? I said no such thing."

"You didn't?"

"No." He shook his head. "I said *she'd* talked about marriage. Not *we*. *We're* done."

"Oh," she said. Her heart slowed. *You're sure?* she wanted to add but didn't.

He shook his head. "Do you really think I'd be here if I was still with her?"

"Then why's she texting you?"

"Don't know," he said with a shrug. "Guess she can't let go. Or she's not ready to. I'm quite a catch, you know."

Wearing another lopsided grin, he reached across the table. When she laid her hand in his larger one, he squeezed her fingers. She knew the gesture should have reassured her, but the thought of Naomi out there wanting him back made her feel a bit wobbly.

She traced his tapered artist's fingers, noticed the gold ring but ignored it. At least she knew he wasn't married or engaged. The time had come to ask what he'd meant in his text and to open the door to her own apology. "You said you wanted to clear up some things? Maybe we should talk about that?"

His eyes probed hers. "I think you know what I meant."

"I suppose." She paused trying to think what she wanted to tell him. "I'm sorry is the long and the short of it. I wish I'd come back as promised. Abbie's death devastated me. I couldn't just come back and live happily ever after with you. There'd be the constant reminder of her being gone. How could I expect you to understand my unhappiness? Especially when we'd been so … so perfect together. No, I knew eventually we'd break up and then I'd be alone in England, and I couldn't handle that."

"Seems like you knew everything. How I'd respond, what would happen to us. The entire thing."She detected the edge in his voice but nodded. She'd deal with those pesky questions another time. For now, she had one goal. "Can you forgive me?"

Without the slightest pause, he said, "Yes."

"Do you? I mean really?"

"Who am I hurting but myself if I don't forgive you?"

"True enough," she said. But it isn't always that easy, she thought. Does he really forgive me?

"Anyway, it happened a long time ago," he said. He stroked his scruffy chin and added, "Time to leave the past behind. Here you are…returned." A radiant smile lit up his face.

She couldn't help the relief and joy filling her up. *Then let's move on,* she thought but said, "All right, Rafe the artist, it's time you tell me all about you."

Tilting his head, he peered at her. "You promised to come to my flat. I'll tell you there."

She hadn't really promised, but she wanted to go. "Then let's get the check. Tell me a little while we wait?"

"What can I say? Life's been good to this poor Jamaican lad come to London to make his way in the world," he said, exaggerating the dialect.

She laughed, for he'd grown up in London, but liked to trade on his Jamaican heritage. Nevertheless, she remembered Rafe's feelings of doubt and insecurity. A Black man in a white man's world. He'd felt the need to work twice as hard, produce the best art. Nor had he wanted to be dismissed or pigeon-holed as a "Black" artist. *Well, I guess he showed them,* she thought. She couldn't wait to experience in person his more experimental sculptures, the ones she'd seen on her computer, the ones she knew had tugged at his soul right from the start.

"I have a new show in the works," he said. "Hope you'll come opening night?"

"Wouldn't miss it." She took a sip of wine. "You've really made it, haven't you?"

"I'm still teaching the occasional class to make ends meet, but it's going in the right direction," he agreed.

"Your father?"

He shrugged. "The same. Still says it's not too late to go into business. That I'm wasting my time. Forcing him to work when I should be supporting him. That'll never change."

"Your mum?"

"She's the same too. 'Raphael,' she says, 'I know someday you'll be famous!' You know how mums can be." He pulled a grin onto his face. With two gulps of beer, he finished the pint, paid the bill, and they left.

Chapter 12

A TINGLING SENSATION COURSED THROUGH Charlotte as she walked beside Rafe, their hands touching now and then. It reminded her of their countless walks and hikes through the Oxford countryside, and on occasion London. For an instant the intervening years shrank, as if only a day or week separated this evening from then. She couldn't believe how comfortable she felt.

At last, he was unlocking his Shepherdess Walk apartment, a second-floor loft overlooking a canal that ran through this part of Shoreditch. He opened the door and waved her into the high-ceilinged room. He flipped a switch, bathing the pale wide-planked floors with a silvery light. She stepped inside the apartment, a Jamaican-spiced meal perfuming the air. "Hope you're planning to feed me a little of whatever I'm smelling."

"Happy to. I'll get it going while you look around."

In a glance she took in the main room's masculine decor, the chocolate brown leather couch, worn and softened with age, the brightly colored contemporary art on the walls, and the sculptures, some clearly his, some maybe not.

Across the room, black metal-casement windows lined the wall. To the left she saw an opening to a space that had to be his studio.

"May I?" she asked as she strode to its entrance.

"Of course," he said. "It used to be the apartment next door."

She peered inside at an area nearly twice the size of the living room, with four white particle-board shelves spanning the length of one of the walls. They were haphazardly strewn with rolls of metal and mesh and assorted plastic tubs and dusty sacks of material. She stood staring at the room's bewildering array of works-in-progress, including a small mound of partially melted-down guns.

She returned to the doorway of the studio and looked across the main living space to the kitchen. An island separated the two rooms. Rafe moved about, stirring something. "Remember your Oxford place off Cowley Street?" she called out.

He looked up at her. "How can I forget?"

She stepped closer as she spoke, "On our way there, I kept worrying you'd turn out to be a serial killer, and how stupid I was for going to a complete stranger's so-called studio." She released a tiny self-deprecating laugh. "All those news reports about that teenaged boy killed in Scotland, remember?"

"News reports? No." He shook his head. "Honestly, you thought that about me?"

"Not really. It's just hammered into us as kids, and even as teenage girls, to never accompany a stranger to his home, and, well, briefly that thought ran through my mind. That I was being stupid. I mean I didn't even know you."

"It had nothing to do with me being a depraved Black man, did it?"

She could feel her face flush. "I hope not. That makes me cringe. *And* feel embarrassed. But who knows? We all have deeply ingrained prejudices." She thought about Prince Harry and Meghan Markle.

"Such a pity, isn't it? I do recall you jumping when I opened the door. Damned hinges needed oil."

"And then you asked me to get undressed; we'd just met, and I think I gave you the stink eye."

"Stink eye?"

"You know, I looked at you, surprised, a little reluctant, like you were inviting me to bed. That wasn't on your mind, was it?"

A devilish grin gave him away. "Course not."

"You scoundrel! Was that it, right from the start? I mean when you watched me model, before you approached me?"

"I plead the fifth, as you Americans would say."

"Well, I'm going to be honest. I fell for you right away. I think I would have liked you, even if you'd been a serial killer. As long as you didn't kill *me*." She laughed. "Mmm…that smell…feed me!"

They sat down at a small narrow table set up near the kitchen window and began to eat. "That first day with you, well, it's imprinted in my mind forever," she said.

"Alright, let's see if our memories match. You know what they say."

"What do *they* say?"

"Very different," he said. "Each person remembers through his own lens."

"And her."

"Her?"

"*Her* lens, Mr. Jackson," she said playfully. "Okay, this part I remember distinctly, and you must too."

He smiled at her between taking bites of the spicy stew. "Go on."

"After you'd asked me to take off my clothes, and I balked, you suggested showing me Venus and Aphrodite statues of the past. Probably to loosen me up."

"Okay, I'm with you."

"That's when we leafed through that great big art book of yours, the one that lay open on a wooden stand."

"Yeah," he said. "I remember it well. 'Did you steal that?' you asked, sounding very accusatory, and of course I could have taken offense—"

"Well, it looked like those stands for oversized dictionaries," she said, even now reacting a little defensively, because back then the words had surprised her; they'd popped out of her mouth. And, of course, they sounded racist. As if all Black people stole, though she hadn't meant it like that. "But then you turned it into a comedy skit," she said appreciatively. "Do you remember what you said?"

"Perfectly."

"What…what did you say?" she challenged, not believing he remembered.

"Why, yes, I did steal it," he said, in a perfect imitation of that long ago time, "how'd you know?"

Looking into his eyes, she responded as she had then, "A wild guess, though I suppose I could have said you seem the type." She bit back her smile, recalling that she'd done that too.

"Do I?" he said.

"Yes."

"I seem like a thief?" he asked.

"Of sorts." The corners of her mouth turned into a quirky smile. "And then it turned out to be true. You stole my heart, remember?" There she'd said it and recalled how her precocious-ness and spontaneity had pleased him. "It was that teasing exchange that put me at ease."

"And now? What will put you at ease now?"

She came around to his side of the table, bent down and kissed him. He pulled her onto his lap, and as they kissed, she savored his familiar smell, the minty taste of his mouth, the roughness of his slightly bearded chin, felt his arms enfold her. How well they fit together, she thought, the ease of their familiarity startling.

When she stood up, she said, "Music's the only thing that'll improve this. You always had the best sound system. Do you still?" But the answer came a moment later with a romantic Al Green tune piped into the room. He reached his hand out, and they danced a few steps before he released her. "Love to see the rest of the apartment," she said.

"Not much to see. I dedicated most of the space to the studio."

"I noticed. Can't wait for you to tell me more about the sculptures you're working on."

"First, my bedroom," he said, waggling his brows up and down cartoon-style.

She laughed, though part of her kept waiting for fissures to appear in his relaxed attitude. Somewhere, underneath it all, he still had to be mad at her, at least a little, didn't he?

Two steps up, through an opaque curtain and they were inside the dimly lit room furnished with a king-sized bed, wicker chair, and two rattan side tables topped with tropical parrot lamps, she assumed came from Jamaica. Colorful pillows made of woven fabric brightened the room as did several fierce-looking African masks against the pale walls.

Charlotte ran her eyes over each item and turned back to him. "Nice," she said. "Suits you." A few photos stood on the dresser. In this light, she thought they looked like his family. She would examine them later.

"Glad you approve." He lingered as if considering his next move, but she left the room, thinking, *Later. Much later.*

They drank more—she wine, he beer—chatted like old friends, and then came the inevitable close to their evening. When he asked, "Stay the night?" she wasn't prepared for it.

Though every cell in her body wanted to, she forced herself to say, "Tomorrow, first thing, it's off to work."

"Tomorrow's Saturday!"

"Didn't I tell you?"

"No."

"I'm sure I did."

"Tell me what?"

"You know Blenheim…my story. *The* story," she added mischievously, "has to be ready for Monday, so they slotted me in tomorrow morning. To give me extra time since I know nothing about editing."

"All right, but I hate to tell you what you'll be missing."

"What?"

"A refresher course on London."

"I promise to be done by noon. Can you pick me up?"

"We'll see."

Despite his insistence, she refused to let him accompany her home. "I'm not a child, Rafe." She watched a series of expressions cross his face before he gave her a reluctant nod. "Text me when you get home."

"Okay…I promise."

"You'd better, or I'm coming over there to check on you," he said. They indulged in one more pleasurable kiss before she tore herself away and began the route home. It thrilled her to think that the ten-minute walk, traversing the few blocks that separated them, might become a well-worn path.

Halfway home, a tingling sensation ran up her spine, as if someone were eyeing her from behind. Without being too obvious, she cast a glance over her shoulder. Nothing but a few pedestrians with no apparent interest in her. Still, she sped up, and once she arrived at her building, she punched in the four-digit combination, but the door refused to budge. She tried again, even more hurriedly. This time she flung the door open, climbed the stairs two at a time to the second floor, jammed her key into the lock, and tore into the room as if someone were chasing her. Not until she'd bolted the door did her heart slow.

After turning on the light, something drew her to the window. Across the street she spotted a figure lurking in the shadows of an entryway, the face turned up as if watching her. Charlotte quickly moved away, but felt certain the person, whoever it was, had stared at her.

Chapter 13

Saturday, December 7, 2019

WRAPPED IN HER THOUGHTS, CHARLOTTE didn't notice anyone or anything as she hurried along toward the entrance of the Tube station. She glanced at her phone—already running a few minutes late. She couldn't wait to meet up with Rafe at noon.

Gregory, the editor she'd be working with, greeted her with a nearly inaudible, "Welcome." He was tall and lanky, with tortoise shell spectacles. Slightly stoop-shouldered, as if years of lowering himself to shorter people's height had created a permanent slouch. "Ready?" he said.

"As I'll ever be." She explained a little about the story she wanted to tell, the footage they'd shot, and the people she'd interviewed. Also, that Sir Spencer Churchill had backed out of his interview. "I'd like to emphasize that," she said, "with subtlety, if possible."

"All right then, let's take a look."

As he scrolled through her footage, he explained that in future there were certain things she'd need to do before meeting with an editor. He described time-code notes, selecting specific soundbites and B-roll she wanted to include, and that it would be helpful to write an outline of the script ahead of time. "But today we'll do it together."

Charlotte appreciated his patience and told him so several times. "No worries," he said each time. It excited her to watch Gregory edit the footage into a coherent, seamless story with only a little prompting from her. A seasoned pro, obviously.

They were close to finished when the door to the editing room opened and Nelson Bradford, his jeans and cashmere sweater a stark contrast to his Savile Row suit, stepped inside. "Thought I'd see how things are going." He smiled at Charlotte and nodded at Gregory. "How about backing up and letting me see the piece?"

"Of course," Gregory said. He seemed unperturbed by the interruption. Perhaps this was the natural course of things, but Bradford's presence curbed Charlotte's earlier enthusiasm. He made her uneasy. Self-conscious. She watched his expression as he surveyed the footage.

"Not bad, Miss Cooper, not bad at all. I'd say you've passed the first test. Good job, Gregory." He turned back to Charlotte. "From now on, though, your future with us rests entirely on *your* performance."

Unsure what he meant, she just nodded and smiled. After an uncomfortable silence, she eked out, "I've learned so much already; full credit goes to Gregory."

"Not full credit, but more than half," Bradford agreed in a circumspect way. He gave Charlotte one more lingering look, his eyes resting ever so briefly on her chest. Then midway out the door, he stopped and asked, "You ever done any modeling?"

A chill went through her as she shook her head. "Not really."

She and Gregory wrapped things up after another fifteen minutes, shortly before noon. She gathered her purse and bag with a change of clothes and thanked him.

"Look," he said, pausing and glancing around as if he might be overheard. He lowered his voice a notch and without meeting her gaze said, "You didn't hear this from me, but be careful of that one."

She frowned, tempted to ask what else he knew, but he'd turned away and occupied himself coiling stray cords. "Good session," he muttered.

"You made it easy. Thanks again."

A little shaken, Charlotte left and arrived at her desk in the newsroom. The place was eerily quiet. Though maybe typical for a Saturday?

After putting her computer and notes away, she planned to sneak out as quickly as she'd come. Scanning her in-box out of habit, she noticed a large manila envelope bearing her name, hand-written in a loopy script. It prompted her to lift it for a closer look.

She flipped the envelope over in search of a return address but found none. No stamps either, so it had been hand-delivered?

She wanted to leave it for Monday—surely it was work-related?—but tore it open planning to give whatever it was a quick look. She withdrew the envelope's contents: a slightly grainy black and white photo. An eight by ten. But not just any eight by ten. A nude image. She stared at herself. The photo showed her from the waist up, in a sexy, sweaty, self-absorbed pose. She laid it down, noticed her fingers tremble, and looked inside the envelope, searching for something, anything to explain why it had been sent, but found nothing.

Could the image be fake? She knew about the dark web and the disgusting things posted there, forever damaging a woman's reputation and scarring her sense of self, just as she'd read about Jennifer Lawrence.

Was this photo meant to be malicious or a joke?

One more glance around the newsroom to make sure no one was watching before she examined the image more closely. The person who'd taken the photo had chosen a moment no one would call flattering. Her eyes looked unfocused, her untamable hair had been the same length throughout her early twenties, the only time an opportunity to snap such a shot existed, she was certain. And she'd rather not think about the circumstances back then, at least not when she was twenty-two. At age twenty-one, it could only have been Rafe who'd seen her nude and photographed her.

Why he would send this now mystified her. What reason would he have? Or could it be from Russ, in a perverse form of revenge porn? No, he wanted nothing to do with her. The only other person who might have taken it, well she couldn't remember the last time she and Zander had spoken. Her thoughts returned to Rafe. Perhaps he wasn't as forgiving as he'd claimed last night. But how could she ask if it was a joke? Because if he hadn't sent it, what would he think?

Charlotte bit her lip and gave the image one more look. It felt like a warning that both irked and frightened her, especially since it had shown up here at work. Could Bradford have anything to do with it? But how would he have gotten ahold of it?

She shoved the photo into her shoulder bag. The envelope she threw into her desk drawer. As she tiptoed out of the newsroom, she felt exposed, like a fraud and a cheat, someone who'd researched celebrities, trying to uncover untidy bits of their past, while hiding her own.

Outside some distance from the Thorntree building, she searched for a trash can. Standing there, with tremendous precision, she ripped the photo, strip by strip, bit by bit until no one could put it together again.

What had Rafe said last night? *Let the past be the past?* Yes, let it stay that way.

She texted Rafe, saying she needed another hour before picking her up. Next, she sent an urgent note to Celia.

Chapter 14

HORNS HONKED, TRAFFIC PULSED, PEDESTRIANS jostled on the sidewalks, but nothing penetrated Charlotte's preoccupation with the image she'd just torn up. It might be in tiny tatters in the waste bin, but she couldn't so easily erase it from her mind.

Who sent that damn photo and why, spiraled in and out of her thoughts, almost in rhythm with her footsteps. Worry creased her brow.

She checked her phone—no response from Rafe, but Celia had confirmed meeting for coffee at a nearby cafe.

Inside, she scouted the tables for Celia, found her, and edged her way through the crowd, aiming for her friend like a drowning person to a lifeboat.

"What's this?" Celia asked, reading Charlotte's concerns as if they were tattooed on her forehead. "Got bad news, have you?"

Charlotte heaved a sigh. "Is that for me?" she asked, seeing two cups of coffee on the table.

"Of course."

Charlotte took a sip, then glanced around before saying, "Why do I constantly feel like I'm a character in a soap opera?"

Celia rubbed her hands together with glee. "Just hope it's something juicy. Something seriously worthy of such a glum look."

Charlotte play-slapped her friend's arm. "It is. I assure you."

"All right then, out with it."

In short order, Charlotte described the photo and explained how puzzled she was by who might have sent it. "I'd hate to think it was Rafe, I mean why would he?"

Celia shook her head in agreement. "No, can't be."

"Very small chance it's Zander, but really that makes no sense either," Charlotte added. Of all her friends, only Celia knew about the period after Abbie died, though not everything. "No, we're barely in touch and he's in New York."

"Doing what?"

Clicking her fingers in front of her face as if using a camera, Charlotte said, "He's a fashion photographer. Pretty successful—probably with his father's help. Shelby knows him, his dad I mean; she hired Zander a few times. As a favor to his dad, I think. I ran into him then. We were working on a spread about Scarlett Johansson. But that was at least a year ago." She stared off, trying to think back.

"No other ideas…who might be angry with you? What about Russ?"

"I suppose it's possible, but why would *he* do that? He's the one who walked out on *me*."

"You never know. Revenge porn? Just a thought."

She didn't reveal she'd had the same thought. "Well, cross him off the list. He's in love with Sarah!" she said with disgust.

"Okay, so let me see it." Celia gave her friend a searching, sidelong glance.

"What *it*?" Charlotte asked.

"You know. I want to see *IT*."

"I ripped *it* up! You think I'd keep that thing?"

"No, truly?"

"Truly."

"Then it *really* must be loathsome! I can't believe you didn't even take a photo of it…or did you?"

Charlotte rolled her eyes. "You should have been a detective."

"Hit the jackpot, have I?" Celia used her index finger in a come-hither motion.

"All right. But it's embarrassing." With reluctance, Charlotte yanked her phone out of her purse and opened it to her photos.

Celia's dark hair swung into a curtain as she looked down. But Charlotte saw her friend's eyes widen. Her cheeks grew warm with embarrassment.

"Naughty girl!! Where were you?"

If only she could remember. If only she hadn't taken so many drugs after Abbie's death. Oh, God. More than anything, she wanted to forget that entire year. Charlotte shook her head. "I don't know. Maybe after the accident, but that's all a blur."

Celia's phone pinged. She smiled.

"Who's that?" Charlotte asked.

"Philip."

"Nice. Second date?"

Celia nodded. "I'm trying not to get too excited, but I think I like him."

"Take it slow. Make him wait."

"What about you?"

"What about me?"

"You and Rafe?"

"Well, after this stupid photo thing, I don't much feel in the mood."

"No, no, you have to ask him about it."

Charlotte looked horrified. "I should show it to him and ask if he sent it? What if he didn't?"

"Hmm…that would be awkward," she said thoughtfully. "But you do need to know, right?"

"I suppose. He's picking me up shortly. Think I'll cancel. I need time to—"

"No jumping to conclusions. I stick with my earlier assessment. You two are meant for each other."

Charlotte stared outside at the pedestrians, shopping bags hanging from their arms. Christmas shopping, she imagined. The potential for a lonely holiday loomed in her mind.

"I've told Philip all about my friend Charlotte," Celia added brightly. "He's dying to meet you."

"Great. Can't wait." She frowned.

Celia glanced at her watch. "Hate to leave you like this, but we're going biking!"

At least this brought a smile to Charlotte's lips. "I'd give anything to see that! Guess I'll sit here and finish my coffee all by my lonesome."

"Oh, poor you."

"Get going. I'll see you later."

Celia rose from her chair. "It'll be all right. Keep me posted."

Charlotte gave her a disconsolate salute.

She stared out the window waiting for Rafe, when she realized she'd never heard back from him about needing some extra time and to pick her up elsewhere. She checked her cell phone. No, nothing. Was he waiting for her at Thorntree? No, he would have texted.

Charlotte: *Did you get my text? I'm not at Thorntree…had to meet Celia briefly.* She added the café's address and sent the text. A few minutes later she heard back.

Rafe: *Something's come up, can we meet up tonight? I'll pick you up at your place?*

Charlotte: *Sure. See you around…?*

Rafe: *6?*

She couldn't help her worrisome mind linking the photo and his delay.

Charlotte walked at a rapid clip along the Thames, trying to empty her mind of the image that hovered and irritated her. Who'd sent the photo? Why? And when was it taken? Those three questions rotated in her mind like the birds circling overhead and releasing their stroppy cries. No matter how much she thought about it, she found no clear answers.

At last, a bench appeared, and she sat, eyes fixed on the river's sluggish movement, sifting through the day's events. The bleep on her phone alerted her to a BBC notification. She glanced down, welcoming the distraction. Prince Harry and Meghan would lose their HRH titles and "will not receive public funds for royal duties, the palace says." Poor Harry and Meghan? No, that's what they wanted, right? Life on their own terms, not everything dictated by protocol, the "palace," or the Queen.

Gazing at yet another image of the handsome couple, she realized she would have loved to have spoken to Harry and Meghan, to find out what obstacles and challenges an interracial couple faced these days. She hadn't given it much thought while at Oxford, though on occasion she'd felt people staring at her and Rafe—on punting expeditions, picnicking along the River Cherwell, at pubs and school dances. But her youth and self-absorption had rejected other people's judgments.

"What do I care?" she'd said to Rafe, who mostly shrugged. Back then she figured his gesture meant he agreed with her, but now she imagined he might have been shrugging at her naïveté, allowing her to be Charlotte at age twenty-one, not insisting she have a more worldly perspective, or forcing her to face people's prejudices, like he did.

And really, it wasn't until sometime in 2017 that she finally understood she'd been living in a bubble because she'd believed the election of Barack Obama signaled the end of racism in the US. She and many others had been rudely awakened with the election of a president who seemed to enjoy racial divisions. It turned out that many in the US still harbored deeply racist thoughts; people hadn't risen above such stupid petty beliefs. Yes, she'd ask Rafe what he thought. And suddenly she wanted very badly to see him.

Chapter 15

IN THE DARK, CHARLOTTE AND Rafe walked along the poorly lit street, clouds of mist exiting their mouths. The chill air crept down her collar. She linked her arm in his and drew closer, hoping to feel his warmth. They'd arrive at his apartment in a moment. All afternoon she'd struggled to erase the nude image from her mind. Now, again, it taunted her, when all she wanted was to be with him and forget the past.

The more she pushed it away, the more it tugged at her. She wasn't sure how to initiate the conversation but knew she ought to. *Where and when was it taken? Who sent it? What did it mean?*

"Do you remember those photos you took of me back in Oxford," she said, gulping in air and keeping her eyes latched to the sidewalk, "you know, when we were trying to come up with a pose for the statue?"

His eyes turned upward as he thought about her question. "I guess."

"Do you still have them?"

"If I do, well, I've no idea where they are. Why?"

"Just wondering."

After a brief pause, he turned to look at her. "Funny thing to be wondering about. Everything alright?"

Grateful for the cover of darkness, she gave a quick nod.

Eager to change the subject, she asked, "What held you up today? I was looking forward to that Rafe Jackson tour you promised."

A shadow of worry flickered across his face. Or was it fear?

"Oh just," he hesitated, frowning, "some business with the gallery. You know the show coming up. My rep wanted to make sure I had all the pieces ready. Which I don't. Not entirely."

"Is that what you told her?"

"Not exactly. No."

"You lied?"

His frown turned into a grin. "Not exactly."

They both laughed. Her mood lifted, and as they arrived at Rafe's apartment, she forgot about the photo.

Moments later, Nina Simone's atmospheric voice streamed through the rooms. She allowed music to travel through her body, relaxing and softening her. As if sensing her thoughts, Marvin Gaye's "Let's Get it On" flowed through the speakers. The sensual music ignited every cell in her body.

Rafe tapped her on the shoulder. "May I?" He wrapped his arms around her waist, and they moved in easy rhythm to the song.

Here I am, she thought, her head on Rafe's chest. Several days ago, she would never have imagined this; now she wanted to drink it in and wondered why she'd waited so long to return. Tried to imagine all the heartache they might have avoided. *Why did I wait?*

As Rafe spun her about the room, she closed her eyes and the answer to that question arrived in the form of Zander's red convertible Porsche spinning out of control.

On that hot July night, she'd woken up behind the wheel, and cousin Abbie, who'd been in the passenger seat of the convertible, was missing. Charlotte's mind, fuzzy from endless rounds of drinks and drugs consumed at the graduation party, took a few minutes to realize that on impact, the Porsche had spat Abbie out of the vehicle. The car's lights shone into the darkness. After a bit of struggle, Charlotte extricated herself from the seat and called out to her cousin but received no answer.

Dazed, she wove unsteadily along the path created by the headlights. In a heap near the tree, she found Abbie, her limbs twisted unnaturally like the roots of a tree. Zander materialized out of thin air, appearing unharmed except for a slight cut on his forehead. In a hushed voice, he told her not to say anything to the police, "Nothing but the truck coming at us; I'll take care of everything."

Truck? What truck, she'd thought.

Much happened in the coming month to alienate her from Zander, but she couldn't deny that she'd done what he asked that night, telling the police she'd seen a truck when she hadn't. Charlotte squeezed her eyes and with some effort drew herself back into the present moment, swaying in Rafe's arms, listening to the soothing sound of his heart.

When the music stopped, he pulled her to his bedroom. Unlike so many of the guys she'd known, Rafe made his bed. A neatnik, everywhere but in his studio. She stole a quick glance around and all seemed the same as the previous night, though she noticed he'd added a photo of her on his bedside table.

One staccato beat and he twisted her a quarter of a turn to face him. "I've waited seven years for this."

In a breathy whisper, she said, "Can it wait a little longer?" She reached for his hand to draw him out of the bedroom. "I want to remember…to savor this moment."

He hesitated. "A kiss?"

She nodded. He took her in his arms and lifted her up as if she weighed nothing. She laced her hands around his neck, touched her lips to his and thought, *I love you.* She believed that saying those words too often rendered them meaningless. Unlike actions.

If you loved me, you would have returned.

I couldn't, but now I'm here to make it up to you. And I will.

These words wound through her mind as they kissed. Eyes closed, she traveled back to his Oxford studio, where their romance began. And for a moment she recalled how dutifully she'd stood in a pose that often erupted into disagreement between them.

Now, as they broke apart, she asked if he remembered those days.

"You must be joking; how could I forget?" He led her back to his sofa, and they sat on opposite ends; he gestured for her feet so he could massage them.

"What a time," she said. The only distraction for her had been to watch him work. His muscles flexing, his body alternately taut and relaxed. His long fingers applying clay to the iron stick figure he'd wrought to resemble her stance.

It fascinated her, his ability to mold lumps of clay into the desired shape. As if he were some kind of God breathing life into his sculpture, his entire being attuned to an image, a final version of her. Her eyes fixed on his every move, aching for his attention, she'd dutifully stayed in a pose that often proved painful after only minutes. Too seldom he acknowledged her, too busy concentrating, staying in touch with his internal vision, trying to see what she couldn't.

She'd heard of this, with sculptors in particular. A piece of wood, a hunk of granite the artist studied to find the sculpture that lay within. They chipped away what didn't belong, until releasing its hidden heart. It seemed to border on the miraculous, and she sometimes envied him that creative urge. If only she had a similar ability. At least an idea for her future self because she saw herself as neither artist nor musician, barely a writer. *What am I,* she'd wondered. *What will I become?* She had no idea back then.

"It was drudgery, too, though," she said aloud, shaking her head as those old images flew through her mind.

"And you complained bitterly," Rafe teased as they sat on the sofa. "Until I gave in."

"Gave in? I had to beg for a break, for you to notice me!" She recalled latching on to his anger as readily as his affection, not caring if he blew up, which he sometimes did. Like many artists, on occasion he displayed an artistic temperament, alternately selfish then slavishly devoted to his muse.

The times that made her love him, Rafe would suddenly look up, his head canted, his face questioning, sensing she'd moved away from him in her thoughts. "Come sit next to me," he'd say, moving a few feet from the evolving Venus-like sculpture to the futon daybed, where he kept a blanket and several pillows. He fluffed them and covered her naked body once she sat down and stretched out her legs. He'd grab her feet and with his capable hands rub the ache from them.

Now, she couldn't help releasing a groan as he tackled one foot, then the other, which reminded her of the sensual creature he was. A paroxysm of pleasure shot up her leg. The very first time he'd lifted her foot to rub her calf, he'd stopped and raised it even higher, brought it to his chest to kiss her toe.

Charlotte had stifled her surprise with a giggle. "Oh, Rafe, I'm terribly ticklish." But he continued, kissing her toes, one by one, despite her desperate laughter.

She leaned back. "Well, all right!" She grinned. "That feels, as you would put it, utterly splendid! So now I command you not to stop! Ever. Please." Again, she'd laughed.

In response, he began tickling her. His hands on her body, moving under her arms, roaming to every ticklish spot. "Stop," she'd roared. "Stop!" Both of them laughing as she tried to fend him off, pretending she hated it, all the while bursting with pleasure.

"Remember how much I hated being tickled?" she asked now, realizing too late that he might torture her again. "No, no. Please," she cried. But this time he stopped.

Back then, it had only taken a few weeks before their childish banter led to something else. But it arrived after a blow-up, when she'd tested his patience and glimpsed her perfect sculptor's fury. A volcanic eruption.

"Charlotte? Are you with me, luv?" Rafe said, lifting her out of her reverie, her feet still draped across his lap. "I promise not to tickle you." Gazing at his profile, admiring his long, curly lashes, remembering, remembering, and now, all at once, life seemed exquisitely lovely. Well, except for the nude photo with that distant look in her eyes.

He massaged the arch of her foot. "Do you remember that time when I ripped the clay off the figure and threw it at you?"

"No! You wouldn't do such a dastardly thing!" she said.

"Do you know how many times I thought about that and worried it was one more reason you didn't come back?"

"Oh, Rafe." It couldn't have been further from the truth and practically made her cry.

"It was unforgivable," he stated flatly. "Hurling that thing at you."

Before embarking with him on the journey to create the piece for his master's degree, it never occurred to her how painful modeling could be. In the classroom, her poses had never been arduous or lengthy; when they were, she was either sitting on a chair or reclining on that moss green sofa. But with Rafe, after a mere ten minutes her muscles screamed for relief because they'd chosen a pose that proved impossible to maintain. First, the blood drained from her arms as she held up her hair; then, the left leg bearing the bulk of her weight felt the stab of pins and needles and threatened to fold beneath her; and, finally, her jutting hip grew weary, achy. And, all too often, she felt the monotony of her task.

That day, the one he'd brought up, she not only grumbled about maintaining this "godawful" position and "what were you thinking," but also about the room being chilly. And he was ignoring her. Again. While at first, his intense frowning absorption had intrigued her, on this day she began sending daggers of resentment his way, hoping her negative energy would elicit a response and he would end, or at least acknowledge, her suffering.

That fateful day, she'd tried asking, "How far along would you say we are?"

He looked annoyed but said, "How should I know?"

She wanted to yell at him, something along the lines of, *Well who else would know,* but asked for a break instead. He gave no verbal response. Deep in concentration, she supposed, though the way his eyes squinted worried her.

A few minutes later the excruciating pain in her hip caused her to wail, "I have to move, Rafe. This is fucking killing me!"

No sooner had those words left her mouth than his expression shifted into a pained grimace. "Please," he said through clenched teeth, "two minutes. I'm almost done here." Instead of looking up at her, his gaze remained fixed on the curve of the clay figure's clavicle as he worked it with his fingers—digging, stroking, smoothing, patting it in place.

The sensation of a knife slicing through her hip caused her to straighten her leg, look down, and rub her hip. She'd just glanced up when suddenly a lump of clay flew at her. The misshapen ball glanced her shoulder then struck the mirror behind her, shattering it into dozens of pieces. The sound clawing the air.

"Rafe, are you mad?!" She stared at the floor, her fractured image reflected in the broken shards of glass. All she could think was, *Seven years of bad luck. Oh, God!* Now, she realized, it had been nearly that long with bad luck sprinkled throughout those years.

Marooned on the small platform, her feet bare and eyes wide with shock, she stared at Rafe. Horror and regret replaced his angry frown. He rushed over, the broken glass crunching beneath his moccasins, and lifted her off the platform and carried her to the futon. "I'm sorry," he said. "Forgive me." He breathed deeply and buried his face in her neck. She felt wetness — was he weeping? — but it was his warmth she sought and hugged him to her.

"Oh, Rafe! All that work and now look what we've done," she said.

He lifted his head, their eyes met, and he kissed her for the first time. His mouth closed in on hers, gently biting her lip. His hands touched her throat, slid along her back, down her front, cupped her head, her breasts, explored her as though he were blind. His fingertips felt smooth and soft — cat's paws. He touched the pale skin on the inside of her legs as she massaged his shoulders through the fabric of his shirt and followed the contour of his muscled back.

She held his gaze and began to unbutton him. He shrugged off the shirt and tossed it away. Discarded his jeans. His skin, it turned out, felt smooth as marble, like one of Rodin's sculptures.

Only then did she realize how much she'd wanted him, and now couldn't get enough, running her hands over the tight curls on his chest, his muscular arms, admiring the contrast of his dark skin against her own freckled pink. *Yin and yang*, she thought. The words swirled together as their bodies sparked with animal heat. The two devoured one another, as if they'd long awaited this moment.

At once a guttural shout forced its way from her throat. He placed his hand gently over her mouth. "Not so loud," he whispered. "Can't have the landlady coming up here, can we?" He laughed and she did too, the happiest she'd felt since the time before her mother's death.

"Yes, but it led to the first time. I'll never forget it," she said, leaning toward him and taking his hand into her own. Stroking it.

"Then you forgave me for that ridiculous burst of anger?"

"You know I did. I can't believe you'd think otherwise."

The concern etched into his brow relaxed. His lips drew into a smile.

"Since we're on the subject, did you have other models after me?" She hesitated. "I mean—" She was about to mention Naomi's name but refrained.

His face contorted into a lascivious grin. "Dozens!" He paused to look at her. "But none like you."

She reached over and pulled him closer so she could kiss him.

A moment later, they were a tangle of black and white limbs, falling onto the bed, kicking off their clothes—pulling, tugging, struggling—sinking into one another. The air filled with yelps and cries of pleasure; each calling out the other's name. *Oh God!* His hand moved between her legs. He touched her lightly, using featherlike strokes, until she gasped. Time collapsed again, and all those years vanished.

The following morning, when Charlotte woke up, she discovered Rafe beside her, his soft snore the only sound in a room hung with the grotesque smiling masks from Africa and a couple of bright squares of woven fabric. Her initial impulse was to touch him, but instead she watched the rise and fall of his chest.

After such a long time apart, it seemed like a small miracle they were together, that against great odds they'd found each other again. She recalled the easy rhythm they'd fallen into the previous night, not much different than at Oxford. This made her so happy and content that to dwell on her good fortune could only bring bad luck, she thought, and they'd had enough of that.

The sun stole into the room, tiptoeing down the wall and onto the bed. A blessing of the gods, she thought and briefly conjured her parents, hoping they might know of her happiness. Her parents had been an unusual couple—"love at first sight," her father often said—strife an almost alien event between the two, until her mother's death cut short their life together. It seemed unfair. And yet, maybe on Earth, we aren't meant to experience too much of heaven? It seemed true enough.

On the nightstand next to Rafe's bed, she noticed the photograph of herself and tried to recall where he'd taken it. During one of their punting afternoons? She imagined he'd placed it there because of her visit. But it triggered the memory of the nude photo. She frowned, then tucked away the thought as a horizontal blade of light slid across Rafe's face and his eyes opened sleepily.

He turned and almost seemed surprised to see her. But he grabbed her and whispered roughly into her ear, "Never letting you go, got that?"

She grinned.

Slowly, hands, legs, lips everywhere, they made love once more, and afterward lay there staring at the ceiling, disbelief coursing through Charlotte. At once, he jumped out of bed, told her to stay put while he showered and then made her breakfast. "I'm an excellent cook," he claimed.

"I *am* ravenous," she said with a sideways grin, watching his naked ass move toward the bathroom door. "But I'll decide how many stars your breakfast deserves!"

As she wallowed comfortably beneath the covers, the unmistakable ping of Rafe's phone caught her attention. Earlier, while they'd been in the throes of sex, she'd heard it too. That awful sound of broken glass. Once. Twice. He hadn't even bothered to look. She, on the other hand, was curious.

Once she heard the shower going, she touched his mobile's screen and saw several texts stacked one above the other.

Can't believe what you told me yesterday.

I bet you're with her.

Please, Rafe, don't do this.

She's the one who left you, not me.

Charlotte stared at the words *told me yesterday* and wondered *what* he'd told her. And exactly when? Those stupid broken heart emojis. What wasn't Rafe telling her?

Chapter 16

"I HAVE A SURPRISE FOR you," Rafe said over a hearty breakfast of eggs, bangers, and toast with orange marmalade.

When she begged for a clue, he said with a mysterious grin, "Then it wouldn't be a surprise, now would it?! I also have plans for the evening, so you'd best stop at your apartment and grab a few things."

She gave him a coy sidelong glance.

"As far as I'm concerned you owe me and I'm cashing in," he said.

"Oh, you," she said, giving him a heartfelt stare. "You're right. I do owe you."

It was mid-morning with little traffic when Charlotte dashed home. Excited to spend another night with Rafe, she didn't notice anyone or anything as she hurried along the street to her apartment. After she'd crossed the main intersection, a funny feeling coursed through her. She spun around and caught sight of a slender woman in a stylish coat and knee-high boots staring at her from across the street. The instant they locked eyes, the woman took off and her thin feminine leg disappeared around the corner of a building.

Tempted to chase after her, Charlotte stopped in mid-track, knowing it was unlikely she'd catch up with her, and besides, what would she say? She continued home. As she packed a small bag with a few clothes, she couldn't help her suspicions pointing to Naomi. Had that been the woman she'd seen?

Rafe's beat-up Aston Martin screeched to a halt in front of Charlotte's building, and she jumped in. Even back in Oxford he'd loved to drive fast with the top down no matter the temperature, like now. She laughed at his daredevil antics, though secretly she wished he'd slow down.

Exiting the car, they embarked on their outing in the cool afternoon, dove gray clouds draped across the city. Charlotte took his hand and declared, "We're twins." She was dressed in a black turtleneck, tight jeans, a snug leather jacket, and a colorful turquoise scarf that emphasized her amber eyes, while Rafe wore black jeans and a brown leather jacket.

With arched brow, he said, "My thought exactly!"

"Not!"

"Can't believe you're here," he said and pulled her close.

"Me neither." *But it is, it is real,* she told herself.

More than once they caught the admiring glances of pedestrians as they traveled by foot across the London Bridge.

They stopped and took photos of each other, then several selfies. Charlotte thought of posting them on Instagram. "London bridges falling down," she thought, though the caption made little sense, and in her mind, she ended the nursery rhyme with "my fair prince" instead of "my fair lady." Several passersby offered to take shots of the couple because, Charlotte imagined, they appeared so clearly smitten.

Every so often, though, she could hear the ping of a text message on Rafe's phone, and that reminded her of Naomi's texts and the earlier encounter with a woman she felt certain had followed her. Both things weighed on her and she tried to think of a delicate way to raise the subject without ruining the day's mood. Timing, she knew, was everything.

Mid-afternoon, as Rafe ushered her through the doors of the Tate Modern, she'd still said nothing about the photo or Naomi. On one of the floors, when they exited the elevators, Rafe suddenly clutched her hand and drew her along. Together they carved a hurried trail through the museum. "Is this the surprise?" she asked, matching his stride and wondering where he was taking her.

"Yes," he said in a loud whisper.

A few seconds later, they came to a halt in a dark, high-ceilinged room with several experimental visual art exhibits, each one making a political statement with an accompanying video. With a flourish of his arm, he pointed to a sculpture on the floor. "That one's mine," he said, pride etched into the smile on his face.

"You've got a piece here? At the Tate? My god, Rafe! Why didn't you tell me?" She rose and kissed his cheek. "Congrats!"

"It's my debut," he said. "An installation. I've titled it 'war, not peace.' Lower case. What do you think?"

She stared at the statue of a ravaged little boy, sitting on the ground, tears streaking his face, arms outstretched. Behind him, in a continuous loop, ran a short film of a screaming child inside a ransacked hut, overlaid with murderous, shouting images of the Hutu chasing after fleeing Tutsis and hacking them to death with machetes. The darkened room and a drumbeat heightened the sense of fear and terror. Film captions stated that as many as eight hundred thousand people had been brutally murdered, including women and children, over the hundred days of the Rwandan genocide.

Charlotte's grip on Rafe's hand tightened. "Oh, how—" she whispered, at a loss for words. A mix of emotions—revulsion, pity, fear, sadness—coiled through her as she watched the film. She forced herself not to look away. She shuddered at the horror of living through such a war—of watching friends and family murdered and the pain of surviving, like the young child at her feet. His arms reaching for his parents, who'd likely perished. The notion brought tears to her eyes.

A few moments later, the film came to an end. The credits included Rafe's name and a brief bio. She released his hand and moved away to view another film depicting war elsewhere in the world. She wondered about the frontline reporters taping and photographing these events and subjecting themselves to frequent danger. All to expose the world's travesties and confront viewers with the brutality of war. Would such knowledge change world events? She hoped so. If not, then what would?

Returning to "war, not peace," she thought of the large and small battles people fought. She thought of Regina and what she'd said about human trafficking; the sheik and his need to control and imprison the women around him, even his daughters.

"When did you come up with your piece?" she asked, feeling Rafe at her side. She vaguely recalled her father discussing State Department reports at the dinner table about Rwandan strife. It must have been in the context of some other event, though, for she'd been only four during the war itself.

With a diabolical grin, he said, "A while ago. I guess I was in a murderous mood."

She straightened, trying to fathom when that murderous time had been. She wanted to leave thoughts of Rwanda behind.

"Probably a rough patch with my father," he added.

She nodded, wondering if her failure to return had contributed more to his "murderous" mood than a "rough patch" with his father.

Holding hands again, they took the elevator to the tenth floor of the Tate. There, Rafe bought her a glass of wine and a beer for himself. They walked from one side of the open space to the other, relishing the glassed-in panoramic view of London and the Thames, silvery and shining, slithering through the city. Directly across the river a domed structure that reminded Charlotte of the capitol building in DC dominated the skyline; it was, in fact, St. Paul's Cathedral, with both low-rise brick and high-rise glass and steel buildings dotting the landscape. In the foreground, boats drifted by, and ant-size pedestrians streamed across the Millenium footbridge. Picturesque clouds festooned a clear blue sky, forming the postcard-perfect backdrop for the city.

The stunning vista and the wine loosened the morose grip the war installations had placed on Charlotte's heart, not unlike a river's current dislodging a pebble. She wrapped her arms around Rafe's waist and kissed his cheek. Mustering the courage, at last, to ask about Naomi and her frequent texts, she opened her mouth to speak. Before she could, Rafe raised his glass. "To love." He kissed her forehead.

"Yes, to love," she said, determined that in another few minutes she'd raise the subject. "Make love, not war," she added with a laugh, referring to the 1960s anti-war slogan.

After visiting a few more exhibits scattered throughout the museum, they returned outside. Streetlamps began to cast their glow across the city, and a warm muted light spilled onto sidewalks from pubs and restaurants as they meandered along the waterfront.

A few phrases tumbled around in her mind until she said, "Rafe, I know it's probably not what you want to talk about, but, you know, after what happened with Russ—those horrible texts—I need to clear something up with you."

He sighed. "Naomi?"

"Yes."

He remained quiet.

"She keeps texting you and you keep ignoring them."

"I know."

"Well?"

"I'm hoping if I don't fuel her imagination with responses, she'll finally stop."

"That doesn't seem to be working, though, does it?" Charlotte said.

"Not yet."

"Rafe!" she exclaimed. How to say what she needed to say next? "I'm sorry but this morning I saw a series of texts while you were in the shower."

His brow dipped. "You read my texts?"

Heat rose to her cheeks. "Well, I wouldn't have but I heard that awful noise and glanced at your phone." She paused and collected herself. "There they were. Several texts. The first one said something about not being able to believe what you'd told her."

"So?"

"Well, what did you tell her?"

He looked off for a moment then stood up. "Let's get going. We'll be late to the restaurant where I've made reservations. I'll tell you on the way, all right?"

At The Prospect of Whitby, a centuries-old pub, Rafe snagged a table by the windows overlooking the Thames. The river shimmered with the reflected light of nearby high-rise buildings. Drinks arrived and after chatting a bit more, an impatient Charlotte insisted, "You promised to tell me on our way here, but you didn't. What on earth did you say to her?"

"*Her?* I told Naomi I was seeing someone else."

"Someone?"

"You, if you must know."

"Oh," Charlotte said, pleased but thinking back on the several lines of text she saw earlier. "She seemed to know about *us*? Our past. Did you tell her I'd 'left' you, because that's not exactly what happened?"

"When we were dating you must have come up."

"Oh." She paused. "But you've told her that it's over, with her I mean?"

"I have."

"Definitively?"

She could see Rafe growing exasperated. "I don't know how much more *definitively* I could say it."

"I keep having the feeling that someone's following me. Do you think it could be her?"

"Definitely not." He laughed.

"You're sure?"

"She's a lot of things, but a stalker? I don't think so, Charlotte Brontë Cooper."

"I wish you wouldn't use that name," she said. "She died an early death, you know."

"She did?" Rafe asked, looking the slightest bit disconcerted. Then he excused himself for a trip to the loo.

No sooner had he left than Charlotte whipped out her cell phone. She might not know Naomi's last name, but she'd thought of another way to find images of her. Rapidly, she scoured Instagram for photos of Rafe, searching for one of him with Naomi. It shouldn't be that hard. She checked all the Instagram names that began with Naomi. And, also, those with the word "model" in them, but struck out. Rafe's Instagram account was hardly worth looking at. It contained a few gallery shots, but none of himself with former girlfriends.

Momentarily stymied, she glanced up, her gaze traveling to the people clustered around the bar, laughing, chatting and drinking. She watched them a bit enviously, so much like the gay nights on the town she'd had with her New York friends.

Charlotte scanned the bar's clientele from one end to the other. This time her gaze halted at a woman, who seemed to be examining her. Had their eyes met accidentally? Whoever this woman was, somewhat younger than herself, she had all the makings of a model: tall, slender, and beautiful, with exotic kohl-lined eyes and caramel skin. Stylishly dressed in high heels and skin-tight pants. The visual encounter ended when the woman steered her glance elsewhere. Had she seen this woman earlier? She wasn't sure.

Two seconds later, Rafe sat down and when Charlotte asked him to check out the gorgeous woman at the bar, his face screwed up into a questioning look. "Which one?" He chuckled.

"Oh, you," Charlotte said, then scrutinizing the knots of chattering people, she found no sign of the exotic beauty. How could she have vanished in a matter of seconds? "She's gone," she said, continuing her search.

They returned to their meal and to chatting about the week ahead—her TV debut, his upcoming show—when Charlotte suddenly asked, "Could I see a photo of Naomi?"

Rafe sighed. "Let me guess, you think the woman you saw was Naomi?"

Charlotte made an embarrassed little nod. "I'd like to rule it out."

"No way that was her."

"Okay, let's confirm it."

"I'm not even sure I have one."

"You don't expect me to believe that?" she said.

He opened the photos on his phone and began scrolling back. "Oh, here's one." He handed his mobile to Charlotte.

Her eyes grew wide. "Rafe, that was her. I swear it."

He frowned. "Impossible."

"Or a very weird coincidence. Or, maybe, she's obsessed with you."

He shook his head, unwilling to believe what seemed obvious to Charlotte.

"So now do you believe me?" she asked.

"About what?"

"That she's stalking you. Us. Me!"

He shook his head but gave her an indulgent look. "Stop worrying about her."

She decided not to push further, but later that night, lying in bed beside Rafe, she had a hunch that Naomi had visited him at his studio, where he'd told Naomi about dating Charlotte, and *that* was the reason he'd delayed meeting up with her. In the next day or so, she'd find an appropriate moment to ask. And, contrary to Rafe's opinion, she was certain Naomi was stalking her. Them.

Chapter 17

Monday, December 9, 2019

"CLOSE YOUR EYES. DON'T SQUINT. Okay, just a wee bit of eyeliner, here. Almost done." The make-up artist, Chloe, was putting the finishing touches on her face, and Charlotte obeyed her commands. Dressed in combat boots, stockings, mini-skirt and sweater—all black—the delicate-featured, light-hearted young woman moved deftly.

"Okay, take a look," Chloe said, stepping back and letting Charlotte examine what she'd done. Freckles minimized, eyes enhanced but not overly so, all good. The only resistance Charlotte had expressed during this makeover was in response to Chloe's attempts at altering her hairstyle. For work, Charlotte kept her hair pulled back, and today Chloe had insisted on undoing her ponytail and straightening her curls.

With a big smile, Charlotte had halted her efforts. "You've given me the royal treatment, and I love everything you've done. But nope, not happening. I like it pulled back, ok?"

"Ach, aren't you a stubborn one? I'm trying to make your television debut sensational. Got word from the top to make you look extra good," Chloe said, her Irish brogue in full lilt. "You don't want to make trouble for me, now do ya?"

"I guarantee I'll feel more confident looking like myself than a fashion model."

Chloe stepped back, admired her handiwork, and admitted her persuasion technique for a new hairstyle had failed. She had, however, talked her into another French braid. "Knock 'em dead, Charlotte."

The moment Charlotte stepped into the studio her knees went wobbly. The lights, the bulky studio cameras, and the fake set where she'd sit beside one of the anchors all served to underscore that she was about to go live on national TV. As she approached, she recognized Malcolm. He patted the chair next to him. She held a few notes in her left hand. How had she let Nelson talk her into going live instead of just airing the story today?

He touched her shoulder. "You doing all right? Commercial's over in a minute," Malcolm said.

She nodded dumbly. *Do I have any choice?* she thought. "I'm all right. Just a little nervous."

"Don't worry; I'm here to make you look good," he said, a smirk on his face.

The arrogance of his comment was the tonic she needed. *I'll make myself look good, thank you very much,* she thought.

"All right, here we go. Three, two, one. A quick smile at the camera then face me."

She did as he asked, drawing herself up to her full sitting height. In doing so, she had a few inches on him.

"Good evening. Here in the studio tonight is Charlotte Cooper, one of our new reporters straight from New York," he said, facing the camera. Then turning to Charlotte, he added, "Tell our viewers, if you would, what you found out on your visit to Blenheim Palace?"

She looked briefly at the camera, smiled, took a breath, then shifted her gaze back at him. "Let me put it this way, Malcolm," she began, "the entire sensational story of the 18-karat-gold toilet has the quality of the surreal. In questioning a spokesman for the Thames Valley police about the theft, which happened during the early hours of September 14th, he admits that since the arrest of six persons, and their subsequent release without charges, the police have become a bit disheartened due to a lack of further leads…and that's despite the £100,000 reward."

After running the piece Gregory had helped her edit, the camera returned full screen to Charlotte who faced Malcolm. "This was my first visit to Blenheim Palace, and I admit," she said with a smile, "as a tourist and as an American, I was quite impressed by the size of Mr. Winston Churchill's childhood home. I wondered what it must have been like to grow up in such a massive and opulent place. And what would he say now, to all this publicity because of the theft of such an unusual piece of art. Would he find it trivial? Or fitting? Or perhaps disrespectful? Would he consider it a humorous commentary on modern society?"

"Indeed," Malcolm said, edging back into the conversation. "Very good question. In fact, I understand we've reached the artist, Maurizio Cattelan, who's joining us live from Italy to provide us with his insights."

Maurizio Cattelan appeared on a screen facing Charlotte as she interviewed him. "How serious were you when you created this toilet? And how do you view it now?"

Maurizio was dressed casually, wearing a dark t-shirt under a flowered white and navy-blue shirt. His short salt and pepper hair topped a strong-featured face with sparkling eyes and a mischievous smile. "I was dead serious," he said. "Everyone must use a toilet, even the rich and powerful. But in this case, I thought it would add a bit of fun to the museum-goer's experience to be able to," he paused briefly, "well, you know, do one's business while sitting on a golden toilet, like we imagine the wealthy might do. People born with a silver spoon in their mouth … a golden toilet under the bum … and all that."

She smiled at his playfulness. "What would you say to the thieves, Mr. Cattelan, if you could?"

"If you're watching, please tell me how much you like the piece and how it feels to pee on gold." He laughed.

"Anything else you'd like to add," Malcolm interjected, appearing slightly ill at ease with the artist's answers. "Any idea who might have committed the crime?"

"We have a tendency to point the finger at poor people, but what about the wealthy, who exploit the poor? I doubt it was the butler or the chef, but perhaps we'd better make sure it wasn't the house owner." He winked at the camera.

"Speaking of which," Charlotte said, grinning at Cattelan, "I tried to interview Sir Edward Spencer Churchill, a descendant of Winston Churchill's and founder of the Blenheim Art Foundation, but he was unavailable. He told the *Sunday Times* that no one would steal the toilet because, and I quote," she glanced down at her notes, "'it's not going to be the easiest thing to nick. Firstly, it's plumbed in and secondly, a potential thief will have no idea who last used the toilet or what they ate. So no, I don't plan to be guarding it.'"

"That is what happens, Mr. Churchill," Cattelan said, again wearing an impish smile, "when the rich look away, someone sneaks off with your stuff."

"I suppose it might be helpful to know what Mr. Churchill thinks now, but we can only speculate since he didn't have time for an interview," Charlotte said.

"I'm afraid we've just run out of time, thank you so much for your time, Mr. Cattelan, and your reporting, Charlotte Cooper," Malcolm said, seeming eager to end the piece, or maybe he was thinking about keeping the station's wealthy advertisers happy. "It's time for a commercial break. Stay where you are; we'll be right back."

Once off camera, Charlotte waved to Cattelan, and he waved back. She mouthed the words, "Thank you." And he winked again.

She rose from her chair, about to walk off the set, when she saw Nelson Bradford in the wings. She hesitated, long enough to hear Malcolm say, "Now that wasn't so bad, was it?"

She had several answers to that question but knew to keep them to herself. "You're a mind reader, Malcolm. Like you said, you made me look good. It was a breeze; thanks," she quipped then kept moving off the set toward Nelson.

He wore a pleased grin. As she drew closer, he lifted his arms and gave her a double thumbs up. He looked like he wanted to embrace her and so she slowed her pace.

When she rounded the corner off the set, though, none other than Shelby greeted her. She put her hands together in a slow subdued clap, presumably not to interrupt the news broadcast. And Charlotte gave her a genuine smile, relieved to see the woman who'd made her life miserable at least once a week over the past two years. At least now Nelson couldn't give her the hug he'd so clearly anticipated.

"Bravo. Well done!" Shelby whispered, giving Charlotte a quick up and down. "I knew I taught you well."

"Thanks," Charlotte said. Taught me well? How quickly some people take credit for someone else's success, she thought, a behavior usually relegated to men. Good to know women do it too!

Nelson stepped toward them. "She's a natural," he said. "Doubt it had much to do with you." He glared at Shelby, who simply smiled at him.

Unsure what to do, Charlotte tried to defuse the situation. "I didn't know you were here, Shelby. When'd you get in? Welcome to London."

"Thanks, great to be here," Shelby said, and ignoring Nelson, added, "Want to go for a drink? We have so much to catch up on."

Charlotte cast a look and a shrug at Nelson, who stalked off without saying another word.

"Sure," Charlotte said, not at all sure she wanted to go. "What's the occasion?"

"I'm here, at last, and you just did your first live TV piece! Do we need anything more?"

In all the time she'd worked for Shelby, she had never invited her out. She wondered what was afoot. Why the sudden change of heart? It seemed to have something to do with Nelson. But what?

Chapter 18

CHARLOTTE COULD FEEL SOMEONE WALKING behind her but pretended not to. She lengthened her stride to speed up her gait. The person kept pace. At once, Charlotte stopped and spun around.

Because of her abrupt halt, the stranger nearly bumped into her and seemed as startled as she felt. Eyes fastened to the sidewalk, the man acknowledged her with a curt nod, then stepped out of her way and kept going.

"Oh, brother," she muttered, and gazed at the stream of pedestrians coursing around her, like water eddying around a boulder. She'd half-expected to see Naomi and now wondered if she was losing her mind. Her phone vibrated with a text from Rafe: *Need to celebrate!*

Definitely want to but having a drink with Shelby at The Marylebone (!!)...pick me up in about an hour? she wrote back. He agreed.

As she dodged crowds, she reviewed her television performance, and felt surprised, even amazed, at how readily she'd adapted to this format. *Maybe I* can *do TV,* she thought and smiled happily as she marched on, forgetting everything but her recent good fortune.

Inside, the maître d' took Charlotte to the bar where Shelby, on seeing her, jumped up and air-bussed both sides of Charlotte's face. This only further confused Charlotte. What on earth was going on?

Her former boss had ordered a bottle of Pouilly-Fuissé and now hailed the bartender and pointed at the empty glass with a haughty stare.

Now that's more like it, Charlotte thought, vaguely happy to see that this woman really and truly was Shelby and not an impostor.

Shelby raised her glass in a toast. "You were splendid, like you'd been doing television for years! You definitely have a future in broadcast."

Charlotte's cheeks grew warm, but she gave her a shy smile. "I did okay?"

"Way better than okay. You gave that Malcolm guy a run for his money. He was hustling to keep up with you!"

"Really?"

"Now, Charlotte, what have I told you about false modesty? Just learn to accept compliments."

Charlotte nodded mutely.

Shelby glanced at her watch, a platinum number studded with diamonds, and said, "We have about twenty minutes for girl talk. Then I've got someone joining me." A dreamy gaze passed through her eyes until she added, "Tell me about Nelson."

"Not much to tell. On my first day his assistant Jason called and told me I had an appointment with…" Charlotte hesitated. She was about to say Nelson but thought better of it. "With Mr. Bradford."

Shelby cut in. "Now Charlotte, you were going to say Nelson, weren't you?"

Shelby was a mind-reader, something Charlotte admired about her, though at times it was a professional liability for those around her. "I suppose so. He insisted on it."

She noticed the wheels in Shelby's mind calculating, running with precision like the mechanical parts of her ultra-expensive watch. "Anyway, the next day we met, and he suggested I turn the golden toilet story into a TV piece."

"And you agreed?"

"Well, yes. I didn't really think I had a choice."

"Why not?" Charlotte felt Shelby's penetrating, narrow-eyed stare. "There was no…you know, quid pro quo?"

On the brink of confiding in Shelby, at the last second Charlotte said, "No, there wasn't. Why?"

"Oh, there've been rumors."

"Really?"

"Yes, really; would I lie?"

"No, of course not. I'm just curious." Charlotte knew that for Shelby truth could be malleable.

"I've been thinking of moving to the TV side," Shelby said, further surprising Charlotte. Maybe this was the reason behind her invitation to have drinks.

"Have you worked in broadcast?" Charlotte took a sip of her wine.

"There's quite a lot about me that you don't know, Charlotte," Shelby said, avoiding the answer as she often did. "And for certain jobs you don't need the kind of experience you're thinking about. I've got management experience; I know how to run a company and that's invaluable."

Charlotte nodded, while thinking that she hadn't done such a great job at *Savvy Faire,* though maybe its demise hadn't been her fault. Current trends in media could be blamed. Was Shelby vying for the top job in broadcast news? If so, she didn't want to get into the middle of a tug-of-war between her former boss and her new one.

"Be sure to tell me if Nelson makes any unwanted moves, you hear?"

Before she could answer, a well-dressed, silver-haired man appeared at Shelby's side and kissed her cheek.

"Meet Nigel Thorntree," Shelby said proudly, and Charlotte tried not to gape. *The* Nigel Thorntree, she thought, *wow*, but also recognized him as the thin, smart-looking man on the elevator that first day. His pale blue eyes met hers. He gave her a small wink, acknowledging, she assumed, that encounter.

"You were spectacularly cool on the set today," he said to Charlotte.

"That feels like quite a compliment coming from you," she said and almost added the word "sir," but it seemed too formal and stopped herself.

"Credit where credit is due."

"I've got someone picking me up, so I'd best get going," Charlotte said, sensing that Shelby was ready for her to leave. "Thanks for the drink." She turned and spotted Rafe near the front door. "Oh, there he is."

About to say good-bye, she saw Shelby staring at him. Nigel too. "Please, invite him over," he said.

Charlotte waved and beckoned him. He crossed the room, kissed her cheek, then, his hand outstretched, he waited for Shelby to claim it. The look on her face was priceless, shock morphing into polite surprise with some effort.

Nigel, on the other hand, offered them drinks, but Charlotte declined. On occasion, Charlotte wasn't immune to enjoying the way people squirmed in the presence of a Black man they didn't know, but not now. Shelby's reaction pained her.

Nigel turned to Rafe. "Her first foray into television, you know."

"So I hear."

Shelby interrupted, "How'd you two meet?" She gave Rafe a sidelong glance.

Charlotte explained their Oxford connection, minus her modeling, and that his sculpture—"war, not peace"—was on display at the Tate Modern. Shelby's face visibly brightened. The smile rose from her lips to her eyes. Charlotte noticed for the first time how attractive she could look when she relaxed. Nigel would be the perfect catch for her. Super successful, wealthy and likely held the keys to London's social scene.

Nigel mused, "Maybe you could do a piece on Rafe's sculpture for *TE!*, Charlotte?"

Shelby wagged her finger at him. "I suppose it would have to be stolen first though?"

Rafe chuckled. "If that's all I need for a bit of publicity, I imagine we can arrange that."

The others laughed.

Nigel lifted his glass. "Here's to firsts, may there be many more! Congratulations to both of you." He seemed to look at them with a touch of envy. Perhaps admiring their youth, the life that lay ahead of them.

After a bit more small-talk, Shelby said, "Now run along, you two. Nigel and I have some catching up to do."

Outside Charlotte thought aloud, "I wonder what that was all about?"

"What?" Rafe asked.

"Shelby's never invited me out, then says it's to celebrate her arrival in London and my debut. Next, she says she's thinking of moving into broadcast, and then Nigel comes along. Maybe it's her way of letting me know they're dating?"

"I'm sure you'll find out."

Charlotte nodded. "At least now I know Nigel's the one who spotted me and told Bradford to give me a shot at broadcast." She felt less beholden to Nelson and this comforted her.

Chapter 19

Tuesday, December 10, 2019

NIGHT ERASES ALL COLOR. CHARLOTTE knew this as she pulled herself out of the car and moved toward the tree, its wide sheltering canopy silhouetted against the moonlit sky. She'd been here before, she knew this too, and felt Zander's presence but couldn't see him. She shouted Abbie's name. She wouldn't answer, Charlotte knew, but still felt compelled to call her.

As if following a proscribed series of movements, she arrived a few feet from the base of the tree, where Abbie lay. She stared at the grotesque contortion of limbs. She dropped to the ground, her heart thumping inside her head, and said softly, "Abbie?" As if her cousin might wake up.

Charlotte knew what came next because it always did. An inner voice told her to touch Abbie's forehead, to see if that dark rivulet was blood or if her skull had cracked in two. She stretched out her finger, hesitating to make contact with that crooked line.

But the moment she did, Abbie's eyes snapped open, and she bolted upright. "What the hell'd *you* do?" she demanded. Abbie's eyes closed and she sank, corpse-like, back to the ground.

Charlotte woke up in the inky darkness of night, bathed in sweat, heart pounding. She took a few breaths, momentarily unsure of where she was. New York? No, she was alone in her Shoreditch apartment. Not until she heard Rafe's steady breathing beside her, did she remember she'd spent the night at his place.

She tried to wipe away the dream, but tossed from side to side, hoping not to wake him. At last, she resorted to reading, using the lowest light possible on her Kindle, and began a mystery novel. Eventually, she drifted off to a fitful sleep.

In the morning, bits and pieces of the nightmare drifted through Charlotte's mind.

"What's wrong?" Rafe asked over a steaming cup of coffee.

"Bad dream," she said with a listless shrug.

"Want to talk about it?"

"Maybe later," she said.

He kissed the top of her head. "Off to the coal mines. See you later?"

"Yes, later," she said, watching him take half a dozen steps and disappear into his studio.

She left with an uncomfortable feeling about the day ahead. Bad things came in threes.

At work, the nightmare continued to distract her. She hadn't had it in a while. Why now when she'd just made her television debut and should be basking in the glow of success? Because Abbie's death lurked in the shadows of her subconscious, and eventually she needed to come clean with Rafe about it. Maybe sooner rather than later?

Around noon, she answered the phone, and to her great surprise, it was Regina with a request to meet for coffee at a nearby Pret café. "I might have a story for you," she said before ending the call.

Well, so far, her day was actually shaping up to be a good one, but she knew from experience not to get smug. Before meeting Regina, she checked the latest human trafficking report released by Human Rights International. Though she felt she didn't have much to offer, as low woman on the broadcast totem pole, she could at least arrive halfway prepared and informed.

She walked at a rapid clip, recalling the statistics. The report's numbers stung. Something like twenty-five million people worldwide were enslaved: twenty million for labor, and the rest for sexual exploitation. Some claimed these numbers were low, and close to twice that many were being trafficked.

Estimates stated that the traffickers earned about a hundred and fifty billion dollars each year, in other words a very lucrative business that authorities would have trouble stopping.

Such numbers seemed more profitable than art theft, Charlotte thought, although experts valued the recent Dresden Museum heist in the hundreds of millions of euros. She wondered if the same criminals who stole art might be involved in human trafficking.

One particularly telling statistic that illustrated her ignorance on the subject was that 71% of the twenty-five million enslaved people were women. And, although only 20% of human trafficking related to sexual exploitation, it represented nearly a hundred billion dollars, or two-thirds of the annual profits.

When she entered the coffee shop, the pleasant aromas of roasted coffee and freshly baked bread greeted her. Both made her hungry and a little guilty when she thought of all those poor exploited people. She glanced around then caught Regina waving to her from a small table in back.

A few minutes later, armed with a raspberry scone and a cup of coffee, Charlotte sat down. The woman looked tired, beaten down. "Are you ok?" Charlotte asked.

Regina mustered a smile. "Honestly no. I've just been going over some wretched trafficking incidents and I find myself daydreaming of flying off to a remote island with a box of escapist literature." She released a small laugh. "Listen to me. Acting like *I'm* the victim when it was me that chose this field, not the other way around."

"You're allowed to grumble," Charlotte said. "By the way did you hear that story coming out of China, some virus? It made me think of you."

She smiled. "I guess that's one way to be remembered, telling horror stories to strangers on airplanes. But no, can't say that I have. Nightly news is nothing but bad news. Who needs it after the kind of days I have? They're all horror stories!" She shook her head. "Actually, speaking of China…no, that can wait. First, tell me how life's treating you?"

"Pretty excellent really," Charlotte said and gave her the short version of meeting up with her Oxford boyfriend, Rafe, and what had ensued on the work front.

"I saw you last night on that news show."

"I thought you didn't watch," Charlotte said, with a guileless smirk.

"It's true, I have a glass of wine and try to ignore most of it. Then I heard what sounded like a familiar voice. You were terrific. That's partly why I called."

Charlotte took several bites of her scone and sips of her coffee. "Yummy," she said. "Okay, well don't keep me waiting. You mentioned China?"

"It's pretty awful…for mature audiences only," she said with a wry smile. "I've just learned that thirty-nine people were found inside a lorry in Essex, dead from asphyxiation and hypothermia. Wretched affair," she said with a frown. "I'm told they were all from China. The youngest a couple of teenagers. Eight women. I can give you my source, but maybe you want to poke around and see what else you can find out? Like, who's behind the trafficking."

"You mean for a news piece?"

"Yes." She eyed Charlotte, perhaps trying to assess her interest.

"Of course, I'd love to, but I'm sure Mr. Bradford has reporters far more experienced than me to cover a story like that."

Regina's eyebrows lifted. "Who might he be?"

"Nelson Bradford. Head of broadcast news."

She gave her a shrewd look. "He's the one, I take it, who's given you the television opportunity?"

Charlotte nodded.

"Then why wouldn't you want to show him exactly what you're made of? Like going after a breaking story?"

Taking a few more sips, Charlotte considered what Regina was proposing. "Look, I'm flattered you thought of me, but I'm so inexperienced I'm afraid I wouldn't do it justice."

Regina frowned at her. "I'm going to give you a bit of advice." She stopped to look into Charlotte's eyes. Her lips turned into a faint, self-deprecating smile, and said, "From an older, experienced woman to a young one. You can't worry about that. You're a bright young lady with a curious mind. Do your research, follow the leads, and you'll do fine. I'll be here to help you."

Charlotte nodded even as she began chewing on a fingernail.

Regina stirred some sugar into her coffee. "Now, back to why I asked you here. On the airplane, you mentioned volunteering for us. That's fine, we'd welcome your help, but I don't mind telling you, *now* you've got something more valuable to me, to HRI. Access to television broadcasts." She paused. "There are lots of stories, Charlotte. We want the world to hear about them. I can give you the inside track on information we get. Tell that to your boss…" she said with an impish smile, "and see what he says." She glanced out the window, then added, "Obviously, we have lots of reporters we feed leads to, but I like you and from what you've told me, you want to do more serious work. Well, here it is. If you want it?"

"I do."

"Enough about that then."

The next thirty minutes they spent in a wide-ranging conversation, including more details of the thirty-nine dead migrants discovered in Essex, Charlotte's concern about the sheik who'd imprisoned his daughter for the past nineteen years, and her surprise at Regina's comment that the US was one of the world's worst violators of human trafficking. "I suppose you won't be going back to the US any time soon," Regina said, "but come February, when you have that Super Bowl event, well, trafficking numbers soar."

Charlotte looked stricken. "You're kidding?"

Regina shook her head. Charlotte noticed again how exhausted Regina seemed. "Are you sure you're all right?" she asked.

"Just getting old," she insisted.

"You're not *that* old," Charlotte said.

"I have a condition—one I routinely ignore. Need to be better about my meds," Regina said with a nonchalance Charlotte found worrisome.

"Please do. I'm looking forward to working with you."

A few minutes later, they were bundling up in their coats and leaving Pret. "Good luck with that sculptor of yours," Regina said, "and let me know how things go with Mr. Bradford."

Chapter 20

THE NEWSROOM BUZZED WITH ACTIVITY. Charlotte glanced around for Ian, hoping to ask him how best to approach Bradford about the human trafficking story, but he wasn't there. She sifted through a few items left in her in-box. On top sat a flyer about joining a few colleagues for drinks on Thursday. Good idea, she thought, because she hoped to make new friends among the staff of reporters. She noted the date on her computer's calendar and replied "yes" by email.

An internal envelope was next in the pile, which contained information she needed to fill out for Human Resources. She tossed it aside. Later. After her job situation was sorted.

Eager and nervous to discuss the trafficking story with Bradford, she dialed Jason's number.

While waiting for him to answer, the next item—a large manila envelope—caught her eye. The script looked familiar. Alarm spread through her insides. With her free hand she fished through a jumble of office supplies inside her desk drawer in search of the envelope that had contained the nude photo. She pulled the drawer open wider, but it wasn't there. She stared at the new envelope, sure its distinct, loopy cursive resembled the previous one.

"Hello?" a man's voice sounded in her ear, startling her.

"Oh, Jason, it's me, Charlotte," she said, barely able to summon the words for a brief meeting with Bradford.

"What's it about? He's busy." His tone was curt, dismissive.

Typical gatekeeper, she thought. "I've been offered the inside track on a story," she said. "And I need his advice."

"Normally," he said, drawing the word out for emphasis, "that's handled by *your* immediate supervisor."

She let his comment go unanswered as she flipped the envelope over in search of a return address. Nothing.

"Last I checked it was Shelby Williams, right?" he asked in a condescending tone. "And she's here, in the building now."

"It'd be great if you could pass my message along to Nelson. If he wants me to discuss it with Shelby, I will, but this is for TV, not a piece for the online magazine."

A great suffering sigh reached her through the phone. "All right," he said. "Later."

Was there a war brewing between Shelby and Nelson? Her stomach did somersaults as she hung up and continued to stare at the envelope.

"You planning to do a magic trick?"

She swung her head in the direction of the voice. Ian had returned. She looked at him quizzically. "Magic trick?"

"The way you're staring at that envelope, I thought maybe you were planning to slice it open with your eyes." He released a self-satisfied chuckle.

"That *would* be a trick," she managed. She laid the envelope down and pretended to turn her attention to the papers on her desk.

"Thought you did well on TV last night," he said.

"Thanks, you were right, it wasn't as nerve-wracking as I thought."

"Will you be doing more pieces like that?"

"Actually, I hope to do more serious ones," she said.

Under normal circumstances she would have gladly engaged in a discussion with him. But the envelope. To look through it, she needed to get away. She was about to excuse herself when the desk phone rang. She leapt at it, grabbing the receiver and putting it to her ear. She gave Ian a shrug, turned her back to him, and said, "Hello," assuming it was Jason. Then, for one, awful second when she heard nothing, she thought it might be someone associated with the two envelopes.

"It's Nelson," she heard instead. "I understand you want to speak with me?"

Why was he calling her directly? She paused before answering. "Mr. Bradford. Thank you. It's about a story a woman at Human Rights International gave me. An exclusive." She swallowed, almost wishing she'd told him it was nothing. Now it was too late. "Thirty-nine people found dead in a lorry just outside London. A human trafficking story."

"I see. Why don't you come up—say five o'clock?"

It was a little past one now. "It won't take long," she said. "Just a couple of minutes of your time. No chance I could see you now?"

"Afraid I'm booked 'til then."

"All right," she said. "Thanks. I'll be there." Scheduling a meeting at five? She shook her head.

As quickly as she could, she gathered her things, shoved the unopened envelope into her leather messenger bag, and practically sprinted out of the newsroom, leaving behind the numerous people talking on their phones, tapping computer keys, and watching news shows on television screens that dominated three walls.

Charlotte again felt the part of furtive thief, stealing out of the newsroom with that envelope—what the hell was inside? She escaped through the corridors of the building, considered taking the stairs, though in the end, she jumped onto an elevator because its doors opened at just the right moment, then fled through the atrium. She kept her gaze forward, as if by seeing someone familiar they might know she had something to hide.

She needed fresh air. She needed to sit down, in private, and look at the envelope's contents, which she dreaded. Until she stepped outside, she hadn't known where she was going, but now she did.

Along the way, Charlotte felt as though she were carrying kryptonite in her bag, a highly unstable chemical that might detonate at any moment. On the Tube, passersby jostled her, and each time they did it sent her heart racing.

Calm down, she chided herself.

Hurrying to her destination, she briefly considered throwing the envelope into a nearby trash can, but that would have been stupid. Rash. Besides her curiosity demanded she see what had been sent. Maybe the person would reveal himself this time. Herself?

Inside her apartment, she opened a drawer and withdrew a sharp knife. Fingers trembling, she sat down at the small oak table beside the narrow window that overlooked the street and again stared at the envelope. It didn't take intuition or brilliance or anything else to know whatever lay inside couldn't be good. *You're being ridiculous,* she scolded. *How bad can it be?*

With a quick inhale, she sliced open one end, reached inside and withdrew the contents—several photos and a typed note clipped to them. Her heart drummed louder as she read each word of the four-sentence threat, then she flipped through the images, each one more revealing than the previous. The fifth one produced a gasp. They were much worse than anything she could have imagined.

She cringed at the memory they unleashed. The sleazy story they painted. The first image with the blurred background had made it impossible to place where she'd been. This time, though, she remembered the location— out on Long Island somewhere near Sands Point, at night, not long after Abbie's death.

But who would send these so many years later? And why?

She glanced at the photos once more, wanting to shred the black and white images of a woman captured in the throes of sex. A bit grainy, but no denying the identity of the young woman in the shots. Each of the first four images showed a little more of her face, arms and naked torso. Until the fifth, which revealed the entire scene, and she recalled the mansion where she'd been with an older man, someone she'd never known, and then had tucked away the memory. Until now.

Her gaze lingered on the fifth image—the perfect one for blackmail. She looked like she was riding a bronco, one hand lifting her long wavy hair from her sweaty neck, while the other reached back, hanging on to the slightly bent knee of the nameless man she was fucking, his face blurred. It was a profile shot of her, perhaps one in which she'd least likely be identified, but still one only had to look. And not too hard. Especially if all five were released at the same time.

She grimaced as that moment returned to her with stunning clarity. There'd been ten or so people in the waterfront mansion, maybe others who might have seen her. She couldn't remember. That night took place half a dozen years ago, but who'd shot the images, she couldn't be sure. It might have been Zander. And yet it could easily have been someone else. Shame flushed through her at the memory of that anonymous fuck. She'd been high on drink and ecstasy to the point of not caring who saw her or what she did.

The total absorption sex demanded had been one of the few things that allowed her to escape her misery, because back then she relived Abbie's death each night and throughout the day. Envisioned her lying on the ground, her pale arms and legs askew, that black trickle of blood oozing from her forehead. Her aunt and uncle's refusal to speak with her, rightfully blaming her for Abbie's death, multiplied Charlotte's pain. A thought she hadn't entertained in a long time now traveled through her mind. *They were right. It should have been me. I should have died.* She'd come close to making that happen.

And after that she'd punished herself by not returning to England. It would have been unfair that Abbie had died while she continued to live and be loved by a man as good and talented and poised for success as Rafe. She'd worried, too, that she would poison that success, suck him into the gutter with her, and she refused to ruin another life.

Then, unexpectedly, she'd gotten this second chance. Or had she?

Sitting on the chair's edge, she read the note again.

Leave London and go back to the hole you came from or these will go viral. Execs at TE will get a copy. You've got two weeks. Unless I change my mind. LOL!

She found the calendar on her computer; today was the tenth. Two weeks fell on Christmas Eve. What a cruel joke. "Fuck!"

She turned the note over, but it was blank. No signature, no contact information. The photos too contained no evidence of their origin. And who would be threatening her? Could someone other than the person who took them have gotten hold of these images? But how and why? Why, why, why?

She got up, kicked off her shoes and lay down on her bed, one she'd spent little time using. She wished she could cry, and her mother would wrap her arms around her and make everything better. Useless wishing.

She didn't expect Rafe to do the same, but would he be so disgusted that he'd tell her to get the hell out? She closed her eyes against such a future. She had to figure out who was behind the threat. Could she possibly manage that in two weeks? What about her job?

And what would she tell Rafe in the meantime? She had to show him the photos, didn't she? Maybe just one. The least damning one. The least revealing. But that only brought to mind her failure to have alerted him to the first one, which from this vantage seemed like a molehill, compared to the mountain she now faced.

Chapter 21

THE BROODING SKY THREATENED RAIN. Charlotte gripped her umbrella tightly as she slipped between throngs of pedestrians. She scrutinized their facial features, trying to decide who among them was capable of locking thirty-nine people into a refrigerated truck and not releasing them until it was too late? And, *who* might have sent her a threatening note?

Some, disheveled and frowning, made her wonder if their lives were messy like hers. Then she caught sight of a tall, stylishly dressed woman, who reminded her of Naomi. Another look and it wasn't her.

The note, the images, and Naomi swam around in her head as she approached the Thorntree high-rise. It was then that an idea arrived—that Naomi had something to do with the photos. The only person who wanted her gone from London, as the note demanded, was the woman from Rafe's recent past. Naomi was still in love with him. She had a motive, with her constant texting and probably even paying Rafe a visit a couple of days ago. Possibly more often.

But how had she acquired those shots? The first image, with the obscured background, could have passed as one Rafe had taken many moons ago. And Naomi might have found it somewhere in his studio. But the other images were not Rafe's doing. And with that her theory fell apart.

As usual at this time of day, Thorntree Entertainment's atrium filled up with people filing out of the building. For this sizable crowd Charlotte felt grateful. She kept her head down, eyes locked to the marble floor, as she moved against the tide of departing reporters, editors, producers, assistants, executives, and assorted other daytime workers.

The elevator doors slid open on Bradford's floor. His secretary had gone for the day and no one else seemed around. Early for everyone to have left, with the many shows the network produced and aired at night.

The door to Nelson's office stood ajar. She peered inside, then jumped at the sound of someone clearing their throat behind her. She turned to find Jason approaching. "No one was around," Charlotte said. "Just taking a look."

"No problem, he's expecting you."

From the smile on his face, she assumed that Jason was in a better mood than earlier in the day. He joked and complimented her on-air debut. "Nelson's the king of spotting new talent, you know," he said with a grin. She now knew Nigel not Nelson had been the one to "spot" her but kept the comment to herself.

He ran his fingers through his thick shock of auburn hair then rested his hand on his slender hip. He cut quite a figure. She could imagine him on TV. "What about you?" she asked.

"Me? Gosh no. I'm awful in front of a camera. Completely fall apart. I'm best behind the scenes." He grinned as he ushered her into Bradford's office.

"'Ere she is," he said, using a funny Cockney accent. "Our new talent, fresh off the streets o' London. Or should I say out of the gutters of New York City?"

Nelson Bradford looked at him as if he was half mad, then allowed his lips to form a smile. "Thank you, Jason."

"If there's nothing else, I'll be off." He bowed as he left.

Concern washed over Charlotte as she watched Jason close the door behind him. Her eyes shifted to Bradford, seated on a leather sofa, as she settled into an upholstered chair across from him and dove nervously into her conversation with Regina, telling him how they'd met on the flight from New York, the woman's high-level position at HRI, the news about the horrible Essex deaths, and the human trafficking angle. "This is the kind of story I'd like to do. I know I'm still a newbie here, but maybe I could be paired with a more experienced reporter, and then when, um, if you think I'm ready—"

"Whoa, whoa. Slow down."

She looked at him, embarrassed. Waited.

"I think a broader conversation about your work for Thorntree News is probably in order. Don't you agree?"

She nodded, unsure whether or not he'd just admonished her. Her gaze traveled over his shoulder at the inky sky outside his window. "Yes, and—"

He cut her off. "You'd rather do hard news, than say covering arts and culture?"

"That's right." She turned back to him, willing herself to look him in the eye. "I want to do news that matters. That makes a difference."

He sat, appearing relaxed, one arm draped over the back of the sofa. His sea-green eyes studied her, almost as if she were a piece of art. She shifted positions, crossing her legs.

"You're an interesting young woman," he said. "I heard that a Black fellow picked you up after you had drinks. Your boyfriend?"

She nodded, surprised he and Shelby had spoken after the hostility between them the other night. "Yes, he's a sculptor," she felt driven to say, as if somehow this improved his standing. Not just any *Black fellow*, but an artist. "He's got a piece in the Tate Modern."

He grinned. "And if he didn't, would you still be in love with him?"

"Of course, I would," she said, hearing how defensive she sounded. Modulating her tone, she added, "We met at Oxford, when we were students."

"I see," he said. He appeared slightly agitated. "Well, we're here to discuss your work not your personal life."

She wanted to tell him that she knew Nigel had "discovered" her and that he should have some say, shouldn't he?

As if reading her mind, he said, "Nigel mentioned that he thought you had possibilities as a TV reporter, but we didn't discuss hard news. The work's a lot tougher than your golden toilet story. You've got to work fast. Nights, weekends. Is that what you *really* want?"

"I do," she said eagerly. "Does that mean I can work on the story Regina offered?"

He canted his head to the side, watching her.

"Yes?" she asked.

He nodded.

"That'd be great. Really excellent. Thank you."

"All right then," he said in a more agreeable tone, as if something else had occurred to him. He jumped up and glanced at his watch as he strode across the room. "We didn't get to have our drink last night," he said over his shoulder.

He opened a cabinet door, behind which stood a small refrigerator. He pulled it open and withdrew a bottle of champagne. With his other hand he grabbed two champagne flutes and set them on a small coffee table. He wiggled the cork up and allowed it to explode into the air, the champagne bubbling out of the bottle and into the glasses.

Charlotte hadn't moved but rather twisted in her seat to watch him.

"Come, come," he said. He extended one of the filled glasses toward her.

Reluctantly, she rose and reached for the glass. "Thank you," she said. They stood an arm's length apart.

"Here's to our cub reporter, our new talent—Charlotte Cooper!"

They lifted their glasses and drank.

"You've gotten what you wanted. Aren't you thrilled?"

"I am. Thank you. I'll work hard. I promise. You won't regret your decision."

"We'll see. Now come sit with me; I promise not to bite." His gaze rested on the leather couch.

"I'd love to stay, really, but I've got an engagement…at six…it'll take at least half an hour to get there."

His eyes narrowed. With a disgruntled nod, he said, "Off to meet your boyfriend, eh? All right then, but you owe me, not to mention you're missing out." He took a long sip of champagne. "Expensive stuff. A little more?"

"No. I mean not today. Another time?"

He paused to watch her gulp her drink. "Don't forget, we're expecting great things from you."

"No, no, I won't! I'm so grateful. Really." She heard herself blubbering more nonsense and grabbed her purse from the floor. She backed out of the room, nodding and smiling like a frightened servant. "Thank you so much!"

Out in the lobby, she pushed the elevator button and waited, drumming her fingers on her thigh. When, a minute later, the elevator hadn't arrived, she took the stairs, two at a time until she landed on one of the lower floors, and there she returned to the bank of elevators and waited, more patiently this time.

Chapter 22

I SHOULD BE HAPPY, CHARLOTTE thought, *for getting the go-ahead on the trafficking story*. She swung open the door to The Princess of Shoreditch, recalling Bradford's come-on. And almost instantly those hideous nude photos appeared in her mind, eliminating every ounce of joy. Her new albatross.

She glanced around and found Celia at a window table. Outside, lights were strung for the coming holiday, one that created a tangle of emotions in Charlotte. Happy memories intermingled with sad ones. She missed her parents most at this time of year. Time that should be spent with family. And now? She might end up in New York celebrating alone.

She leaned over to kiss Celia's cheek and plopped into the seat across from her. "You'll never guess what happened today," she said, then noticed Celia's frown. "What's wrong? Everything ok?"

"Yes, no," Celia said. "I don't know if Philip's coming. He's so damn focused on work I can hardly stand it. Not a good beginning, is it? Me complaining already," she said. "So, what's your news?"

"Back up a sec'. You were head over heels for Philip last week. He seems very nice. Maybe you're imagining things?"

"You're right. I'm too demanding. But really, at the beginning aren't you supposed to be constantly texting, wanting to see each other, touch each other, kiss, hop in the sack, and all that?"

Charlotte took a sip of Celia's wine. "May I?"

Celia smiled. "I've ordered you one. Should be here any second."

"I bet he'll show up. Philip, I mean. You watch."

Celia nodded without conviction. "You were saying?" she said, still distracted. "About today?"

Charlotte reached into her messenger bag and pulled out the manila envelope. "Here's the source of my troubles for the day," she said and handed it to Celia. "Look at the photos quickly then put them back. I can't risk Rafe seeing them, not yet, and I'm afraid he'll be here any minute."

"Ooh, I like the sound of this," she said, her mood lifting, her brow arched, one corner of her mouth curving into a smile. She opened the envelope just as the waiter swung by with a glass of pale wine for Charlotte. He set it down and asked if he could get them anything else.

"We're just about to look at the menu, okay?" Charlotte said, watching the expression on Celia's face.

"I'll be back shortly." He hesitated, and Charlotte saw him watching Celia's expression. With each photo, her eyes grew wider.

"Yes, thank you," Charlotte said, hoping he couldn't see the images. She cleared her throat, and he moved off to another table.

"Oh, dear. You are in trouble, you bad girl. Where'd these—"

"The worst part is this," Charlotte said and handed her friend the threatening note, exchanging it for the envelope and photos.

Celia's eyes perused the note. "What the fuck?" she said. "Who sent this? Who took those?"

"God, I'm so embarrassed. I don't know. I've got ideas, but none of them make sense. You remember Zander, the photographer friend I mentioned, he might have taken them, but why he'd send them now ... I just don't know." She paused, thinking. "And then, of course, there's Naomi; makes more sense she's involved. Somehow. I mean she's the only one who wants me gone. And that cursive on the front. Well, that looks like feminine handwriting, doesn't it?"

Celia nodded.

"But how would she get those photographs?"

"Good question," Celia said. "I do like mysteries, but this one's a bit scary." Her grin turned into a tight-lipped frown. "You're not going back, are you?"

"Where?"

"New York?"

"God, I hope not. But I can't let those images get posted on the Internet, can I?"

Celia shook her head.

"What should I do?"

Celia's brows rose. "Oh, look," she said.

Charlotte's gaze followed Celia's to see Philip heading their way. "And you thought you were being stood up; guess not. But this whole thing…" Charlotte pointed at her purse. "Oh, I can't even…" Her voice trailed off.

"Definitely weird. I'll think on it, and we'll figure it out. Try not to worry." Celia slid out of her chair to greet Philip as Charlotte pushed her purse further under the table.

Once they were seated, Charlotte fixed a smile on her face and glanced at her mobile, hoping for an update from Rafe about meeting here. The three chatted a while, with Charlotte explaining the migrant trafficking story she was about to pursue. "I can't believe I got Bradford's approval," she said, but refrained from mentioning his obvious come-on.

"Oh, God that incident sounds wretchedly awful. You sure you want to do hard news?" Celia asked.

"I do," Charlotte insisted, glancing at the front door, but still no sign of Rafe.

"We don't want to leave you, but we're meeting some friends of Philip's," Celia said.

"Go. Have fun. I'm sure Rafe'll be here soon."

"How about dinner on the weekend? The four of us?" Celia said.

"I'll cook," Philip said.

Celia looked at him in disbelief. "You cook? What else don't I know about you?"

"Long list. Shall I begin?"

She swatted him. "Talk later?" she said, giving Charlotte a don't worry wink. But how could she not?

After their departure, she nursed her glass of wine and stared outside at those twinkling Christmas lights. If Rafe didn't show in the next five minutes, she'd go home and wallow in self-pity. Just as she was about to leave, he arrived, dropping heavily into his seat. She looked at him, annoyed.

"What's that for?" he asked, a bit gruffly.

"Where have you been?" Charlotte asked, glancing at the time on her Apple watch. He was half an hour late. "Why didn't you text me?"

For a moment, Rafe seemed unsure how to respond. Then he shrugged, got up, and over his shoulder said he was getting a pint without asking if she wanted anything.

When he returned, he still seemed preoccupied.

"Is one of your pieces giving you trouble?" she asked.

He looked at her in confusion. "What?"

"Your work, you've been getting ready for that show, and you were late."

"Was I?" he asked, glancing at his phone.

"Yes," she said a little more emphatically. "Was it because of something you're working on?"

He shook his head.

"Then what? Why are you being so vague? What's going on?"

He looked off a minute, swallowed, then stared at her. "Naomi showed up."

Charlotte took in a deep breath but said nothing. A fork or a spoon clattered to the floor at a neighboring table. They both turned and watched a waiter retrieve it then shifted their eyes back to one another. "Well, what happened?" she asked.

"She wants to get back together." He frowned.

"Well, that's been obvious. What did you say?"

"Let me finish."

"Please." She waited, staring at him impatiently.

"She asked if I really knew you."

"What does that mean?"

"Well, according to her, you've been keeping secrets from me."

"Like what?" Charlotte managed, her eyes veering away from his.

"She said you were involved in Abbie's death."

Charlotte felt her stomach disappear into her spine. "What…how?" She reached for her water. Trying to keep her hand steady, she took a sip. "How would she know something like that?" she eked out, forcing herself to meet his gaze.

"Well, were you?" His eyes penetrated her.

Charlotte's thoughts swirled in confusion. What should she say? Should she tell him everything? Now?

He waited a moment, then, his voice raised, he said, "You've been secretive about that entire period, Charlotte. What the hell happened?"

"Stop shouting. It's embarrassing."

"I'll tell you what's embarrassing: having my former girlfriend know things I don't have a clue about." He stared at her with knitted brows.

She couldn't tell him everything, not when he was like this. And what exactly did Naomi know and how had she found out?

"Looks like you're not about to come clean, even now." He drained his glass of beer and banged it on the table. "Let's call it a night."

"No reason to break the glass," she said.

"If I'd wanted to break it, I would have," he retorted.

They both jumped up and he paid the bill, but she didn't wait. She marched outside, thinking how she'd been about to broach the subject of the photos, and now there was no need. She hurried along the pavement, tears welling up. Damn him, damn her!

Rafe caught up and grabbed her by the elbow. "Where are you going?"

"Home, where I belong!" She turned and left. He didn't come after her as she hoped. And then she was alone in her apartment with the photos, her memories, and a thousand regrets.

Chapter 23

Wednesday, December 11, 2019

THROUGHOUT A MISERABLE NIGHT OF sleep, Charlotte agonized. What secrets could Naomi have possibly unearthed? And how? Whatever she'd found, she imagined they'd spell the ruin of her and Rafe's already tenuous relationship.

In the morning, despite her sleeplessness, she jumped out of bed and raced to work. Between the moments of fear and doubt that punctuated the night, she'd committed herself to providing some justice to the thirty-nine people who'd lost their lives. At least that story would keep her focus on something more meaningful than Naomi, and she could add it to the positive side of her own life's ledger.

Regina's source at the Essex police sounded stern as he passed along new information: the thirty-nine victims were Vietnamese, *not* Chinese, *and* a young Irishman, age twenty-five, had been driving the "lorry" in which they'd died. She understood the subtext: This young man was about to be arrested.

The human trafficking story was developing quickly, and she decided on a trip to the town of Grays. A police official would meet with her and show her the refrigerated trailer in which the people had suffocated. Perhaps he'd even reveal the name of the lorry driver.

"How soon can I meet you?" she asked.

"In a couple of hours," he said.

The story was filled with anguish on many fronts, and intermittently Charlotte felt on the verge of tears. She questioned if she had the stomach for hard news. It wasn't like the fluff she'd covered for Shelby. But then her father, who'd faced many challenges in his diplomatic career, came to mind, and she imagined how proud he'd be to hear of her work. She told herself that yes, she could handle it. Of course, she could. If only time weren't ticking on that other front.

And that reminded her of Rafe, who hadn't called or bothered to text. In light of the threatening note and the photographs, maybe that was best.

Before heading to Grays, Charlotte stepped out to get a cup of coffee at Pret. Along the way, she felt a vague churning in her stomach as her thoughts flipped between her nude photos and the poor people who'd died from lack of oxygen. Or maybe they'd frozen to death.

Walking helped her think. The nude images revolved, one after the other, and as they did that long ago night materialized and Zander with it. His hooded eyes, his trademark smirk, his dark hair flopping onto his forehead. They'd lost touch for a few years, until a gala event Shelby asked her to cover, one she and Russ attended early in their relationship. A week later, she received several photographs in an email from Zander. One of herself smiling gaily as she spoke to a celebrity, another with her champagne glass raised in a toast, and the last, a pensive moment alone at a table cleared of plates but filled with empty glasses. He'd attached a note to the latter image: *You don't look happy. Is he really* the *one? Z.* Russ had been in none of the pictures.

Oddly, she hadn't seen Zander there. And she'd wondered when he'd taken those shots. In the end, she simply deleted the email.

A year or so later, she'd forgotten all about the photos until she ran into Zander at a Metropolitan Art fundraiser she was covering. "You on assignment photographing the beautiful people?" she joked, because fundraisers weren't his usual fare.

"Nah," he said, smiling, "trying to make the world a better place. I donated a bit of money; you know the drill."

Actually, she didn't since her funds were meager but wondered if he was trying to get on her good side. He wrapped his arm around her shoulder and asked someone to take a quick shot of them with his phone.

When she mentioned the email and photos he'd sent, he brushed it off with, "We're friends, right? I don't know, you just looked sad. So, thought I'd tell you in case you needed someone to confide in." Later, the shot of her and Zander appeared on Instagram and Facebook.

On her way back to TE!, her thoughts returned to Naomi. Had she hired a private investigator to dig into her past? Charlotte's police records in New York were sealed as far as she knew, but she imagined for a price anything was possible. And maybe the photos too, but how would Naomi have tracked them down?

Back at her desk, she checked the clock, another forty-five minutes or so before she needed to leave for Grays. She stared at Zander's number in her mobile for a solid minute. Should she call or not? With only twelve days until Christmas, did she have a choice? She tapped the number and listened to it ring. Would he answer? What should she say?

Contemplating Zander raised the very worst memories of her life. Without a doubt, those vile, incriminating, and humiliating photos were taken shortly after Abbie's fatal accident. Now, those memories stirred to life, she'd never be able to erase that single night. And she would never know whether Zander had something to do with them until she asked, and looked into his eyes, watched the muscles of his face, the flush of his skin. Searched for a telltale sign that proved he was blackmailing her. Or at least had been the one taking the photos, in which case, if he hadn't sent them, he might know whose hands they'd fallen into.

The phone rang at least ten times. She waited for his voicemail to kick in. And yet, what sort of message should she leave?

"Rusikov here," a brusque voice said.

"I didn't think you were going to answer," she said on hearing his last name.

"Life's full of surprises," he said, his tone suddenly jovial, "and on occasion they're even pleasant."

After only those few words she recalled Zander's playful attitude combined with a certain air of authority. As a fashion photographer, she imagined he could charm the most reluctant of models into poses they otherwise might not consider. She could see his lanky body contorting to catch just the right angle.

"Zander, it's Charlotte, Charlotte Cooper," she said despite feeling certain he'd recognized her voice.

There was a pause on the other end. "Charlotte? *My* Charlotte?"

"I realize it's been a while."

"Yeah, far too long," he said, dropping all pretense of formality.

"Listen, I need to talk with you about something."

"Of course. Love to. Charlotte…I can't believe we're speaking. Damn, it's good to hear from you. You were, well, not so happy the last time I bumped into you."

She liked his honesty. It helped her to remain calm, despite her suspicion he was involved with the shots. "By the way, congratulations," she said. "I've seen you written up, now and again, as the up-and-coming fashion photographer."

"Don't know about that, but yeah, I'm making a living. A pretty good one." He chuckled. Ever self-confident and a bit arrogant, she thought. "What's on your mind?" he asked.

"Well, actually, I'd like to see you…in person," she said. "You're in New York, right?"

"I'm still based there, but I'm on a shoot in Paris right now. You know, models wearing the latest outlandish fashions…on the steps of Sacre Coeur, outside the Louvre, on the grounds of Versailles. We'll be wrapping up in a week or two." He paused, as if wanting the picture he'd painted to sink in. "I'll be back in New York after that. You still in the city?"

"No," she said, "not really."

"Not really?" he said. "Still the same Charlotte. Ever elusive."

She noted the dig but didn't react.

"So, where the hell are you?" he asked.

"You know where I am—in London. You commented on some pics I posted on Instagram, remember?"

"Didn't know you'd moved there. Thought you were just visiting."

Of course, why would he think otherwise? she thought, but said, "New job at Thorntree News. Arrived right around the time of that stabbing on London Bridge in late November. You must have heard?" she said.

"I did. Fucking shitshow these European cities."

"Honestly." Returning to the purpose of her call, she said, "Would it be possible to pay you a visit, maybe later this week?"

"Pay me a visit? You? Of course. I might have to squeeze you in between shoots, but hang on, let me check my schedule."

He sounded eager to see her, not even bothering to know why she wanted to meet him. Or had he expected her call?

Zander came back on the line. "How about Friday?"

"Thursday wouldn't work?"

"'Fraid not."

The trip to New York would have been complicated. Now, with him in Paris, it was so much easier. The "chunnel" train from London to Paris took no time at all. She could manage the entire trip in a day, which meant she wouldn't have to tell Rafe. She knew that was a lie, one of omission, but a lie nonetheless. Like the photo she'd intended to show him and still hadn't. Did he even still care?

There was a bit of back and forth regarding timing—Zander wanted to meet at night, she during the day—and the question of where. Because they'd agreed on Friday, he suggested she spend the weekend, take in the sights.

"I'm sorry, but I've got the weekend shift. You know, cub reporter." Another partial lie, but one that didn't bother her.

She heard him heave a sigh. Then he rallied and said with great enthusiasm, "Can't wait to see you, Charlotte. Been way too long."

Just write, she told herself after returning from Grays. The horror of it rained through her. She had to write the story for both online news and broadcast. Once she began typing, though, the words unfurled with uncanny ease.

According to police sources, she wrote, *the thirty-nine men and women found dead in a refrigerated trailer on Monday in Essex were not Chinese, but Vietnamese nationals. Eleven of the victims have been transported to a nearby hospital for examination.*

Officials have notified the Vietnamese Embassy.

The driver of the lorry was stopped at an Essex industrial estate; he has been arrested on suspicion of murder and is being questioned. Maurice "Mo" Robinson is twenty-five years old and apparently from County Armagh in Northern Ireland. His father claims to have heard about events and his son's arrest solely through social media and a news report.

Detectives have traced the route of the trailer, which arrived in the UK at Purfleet via Zeebrugge in Belgium just after midnight on Monday, and the front of the lorry, or the tractor, which came from Dublin, entered the country on Sunday.

She checked the video for the interviews she'd done, one with a police spokesperson and another with Regina. She typed in what they said:

An Essex police spokesperson explained, "The lorry then picked up the trailer (with the thirty-nine occupants) at the port of Purfleet and left about half an hour later."

We also spoke with Regina Hollyfield, head of human trafficking for Human Rights International in London. "It is impossible to imagine what these thirty-nine people endured," Ms. Hollyfield said, "when it is known there was insufficient oxygen in this container to keep them alive. Although it was a refrigerated unit, the refrigeration had been turned off." Ms. Hollyfield believes it is highly possible that criminal gangs are behind the deaths, "a pretty clear example of human trafficking."

Another lorry was stopped yesterday containing nine people, according to police in Kent. Fortunately, they were still alive.

Then she made some adjustments for the broadcast piece, including the videotaped interviews, and concluded the story with:

We will be following this story closely. Charlotte Cooper, reporting from Grays for Thorntree News.

She checked her script, went to edit the piece with Gregory, and knew countless television viewers would be watching her and this sordid story a little after five o'clock.

Would those same viewers be seeing her nude image on the Internet in less than two weeks' time? She shuddered at the thought.

Chapter 24

WHEN SHE FINALLY LEFT THORNTREE, a dreary London drizzle fell from the night sky. It matched her mood. Her umbrella popped open.

At the same instant, a horn honked, and she looked up. The sound came from a slightly dented, gray Aston Martin parked less than fifteen feet away. She pretended not to notice either the car or its occupant and continued walking along the pavement past the vehicle. Her heart picked up a little though. How long had he been waiting for her?

A few steps later, an arm wove its way around her waist, causing her to twist away and continue on.

"Let me give you a ride, luv," Rafe called after her. "It's raining."

She stopped and turned to face him. "And why should I go anywhere with you?" she said, having every intention of doing so.

"Because I … because I'm sorry and I want to make it up to you." Glistening droplets of rain gathered on his dreads, his face, and his scruffy beard. "Anyway, I'm getting soaking wet. Please?"

"All right," she said and made an about face. Together they returned to the car which he'd left running.

He opened the passenger door and waited until Charlotte closed her umbrella and tucked herself into the front seat before running to the other side and getting in. He grabbed a cloth and wiped his face. "The things we do for love," he sang, giving her a cock-eyed smile.

"I know you'd rather not, but we need to talk about last night," she said.

"You're right." He put the car in gear, stepped on the gas and launched into traffic.

The roar of the vehicle prevented Charlotte from talking. She was dying to discuss their argument, though clearly Rafe seemed happy doing what guys do best—avoid difficult topics.

"Where are we going?" she shouted over the noise of the engine.

"It's a surprise."

As always, Rafe sped through the city streets, took corners too fast, and chuckled the entire way while Charlotte clutched the door handle, pressed her foot on an imaginary brake and begged him to slow down. "Come on," he said, wearing a huge grin, "you must be used to my driving by now. Always deliver you safely, right?"

"I guess," she said, although his driving reminded her of Zander's irrational self-confidence behind the wheel. But, of course, it was her own driving that had led to the accident from which there'd been no recovery.

Could she really tell Rafe the awful truth? Yesterday she'd decided that she would show him one of the photos and explain the details of the crash and share some things he was unaware of. She hoped he'd confide the details of Naomi's visit, but where in the world was he going now?

The car pulled up to the curb in front of a glass and steel building on Hopton Street, near the Thames, a block or two from the Tate Modern. "What's this?" she asked, wondering who lived here.

"*This* is a building," he said, with a slight smirk. "Converted into flats. Nice, isn't it?"

She looked the unusual cylindrical structure up and down, maybe twelve stories tall, with a funny jagged top. At least that's how it appeared from the ground. "Lovely. Who are we visiting?" At work she'd slipped out of her business attire into jeans, a turtleneck, a pale blue peacoat and a plaid scarf. "Am I dressed all right?"

"You're perfect!"

"Yes, I know, but first let's clear up last night. We've got to have honesty between us, right?"

"I was thinking we'd go to a nice restaurant afterwards, or my flat, your choice, and there we can have a long talk and sort it all out. What do you say?"

"You're a rascal, you know that?" she said with an eyeroll then leaned over to peck him on the cheek. Though relieved, she wasn't sure he'd feel the same after she revealed her unsavory past.

At the front of the building, she watched Rafe push the buzzer beside the initials "PH" and vaguely wondered if Celia's Philip might live here. She didn't know his last name.

A female voice answered, "Hullo?"

"Rafe Jackson here."

A click sounded and Rafe pushed the massive glass door open, motioning for Charlotte to step inside.

"So … where are we going?" she asked as they stepped inside the elevator.

"A surprise," he said again.

When Charlotte frowned, Rafe added, "You don't like surprises?"

The photos she'd pulled out of that nefarious envelope appeared in her mind's eye. "Well," she said, "not always."

"Do I know who lives here?" she asked.

"Are we doing one hundred questions?"

"Only if it'll provide clues to the answer."

"It's unlikely but go ahead."

It suddenly occurred to her that he was taking her to see Naomi. No, that was absurd. "Are we going to see someone *I* know?"

"No."

"Then why are we going here?"

"I only answer questions with a yes or a no."

"Okay, is it someone you know?"

"Yes, but only slightly."

"That was more than a 'yes' or a 'no.' Is it someone interested in your art?"

He hesitated before answering, "I don't think so."

This brought a smile to her face. "Oh, I see," she said, though he still hadn't told her who lived here. "You mean there's actually someone who doesn't love your art!?"

He grabbed her by the waist, hugged her tight and planted a kiss on her lips before releasing her.

They took the elevator to the floor marked PH, which Charlotte now realized stood for Penthouse. So, they were visiting a rich acquaintance of Rafe's, perhaps he was hoping to turn the person into a collector of his sculptures.

The elevator doors opened into a dazzling living space. A smart navy-blue suit bedecked the slender woman whose back faced them. Her hair reminded her of a style she'd seen on Naomi. When she turned, Charlotte knew right away it wasn't Naomi and felt greatly relieved. This time Charlotte's smile was genuine. The woman took her outstretched hand and shook it. "Hello, you must be Charlotte?"

"I am. And you?"

"Pamela Ashcroft," she said. "Mr. Jackson's estate agent."

A brief look of confusion creased Charlotte's brow. Was this woman showing them the penthouse apartment because Rafe wanted to rent it?

"What do you think, Charlotte?" Rafe asked, motioning his hand at the entire L-shaped room, which featured an arched wall of glass overlooking the Thames and the jeweled city beyond.

"It's splendid," she managed, wanting to ask about his plans and the need for an estate agent, which she knew was the equivalent of a real estate agent in the US.

"Come, let's take a look." He took her hand and guided her toward the narrow spiral staircase that rose to the next level. Charlotte eyed the thin metal railings from which the wooden steps were suspended.

"It's safe. Don't worry," said Pamela. "I'll be right here to answer any questions."

Upstairs, he led her into what appeared to be the main bedroom, fully furnished, with its own sweeping views of the river and the city. "That's the Tate Modern," he said, grinning and pointing to a structure a short leap away.

"Yes, where one of your sculptures resides."

"Thought I should live close enough to visit more often," he joked.

"Do you mean you want to rent this place?"

"Well, not exactly. A bit of luck has come my way," he said. "A few days ago, I learned I'm the recipient of a rather sizable artist's grant, and I got two new commissions. The owner of some of my work is willing to sell this unit quite reasonably in exchange for two more sculptures. Done over time, of course."

"Really? That's epic! I'm so glad for you."

"Not for me. For *us*," he said. He tilted his head. "Eventually anyway."

Us? she wondered.

They stood side by side before the bedroom's floor-to-ceiling window, his arm pressing her to him. "It came to me last night. Don't you think it would be nice to have our own place, not one tainted by the past."

A part of her wanted to scream yes, yes, but she only nodded. How she wished they could live together—if only disaster would stop courting her.

"What do you think?" he asked.

"I hope you know I'd live in a tent with you?"

"An elaborate, elegant tent, no doubt?" he said.

She gave him a quirky look. "No doubt." Her gaze traveled outside, back to the world, where so much torment and evil existed. She felt his kiss on her neck and closed her eyes.

"Good?" he said.

She nodded, keeping her thoughts to herself. At a moment like this, she ought to feel exuberant, joyous, but all she could do was give him her best and most hopeful smile. What would he think later in the evening when she showed him the photo and explained a bit more about her past.

Would he scoff or be horrified? Men could become unbelievably territorial when it came to their women, fending off potential challengers as if they were predators, which perhaps they were. But then men were not entirely unlike women, she decided. Trying to protect what's theirs. Like Naomi.

"What about your studio?" she asked. "It's so nice to have just a few blocks between your apartment and mine."

"That's true, but I'll have my place at least another month or two before making the transition."

Of course, Charlotte thought, during which time her whole life could implode. She might be forced to leave London. Her palms grew sweaty. She smiled hard to keep the tension from her face. They'd returned downstairs and Charlotte decided to take another look around while Rafe discussed some details with Pamela. She'd daydream about a life together. Before it all went to hell. Though maybe, if she was lucky, it wouldn't. "Mind if I look around a bit more?"

She went from room to room snapping photos, imagining how she might arrange Rafe's furniture. No, she'd let him—the man with the artistic vision—make the important decisions on decor unless he deferred to her.

Upstairs, off the master bedroom, she found the door to a rooftop garden. She stepped outside to take in the vast city below, and all the secrets it held. Secrets like hers. Somewhere in the distance, thirty-nine people had died, hidden inside a truck by men who cared little about them, lured only by money. She imagined the pitiable cries of the people in that container.

The buzz of traffic seeped into her consciousness. *It's not too loud*, she thought, conjuring an image of sitting out here on a warm night with Rafe. And yet, loud enough to mask Rafe's arrival at her side. "Beautiful, right?"

She jumped a little at the sound of his voice then leaned against him as they gazed at the Thames, a ribbon of shiny obsidian passing so near that Charlotte could imagine Rafe hurling a rock into it. The slow-moving current flowed beneath bridges and past buildings, some skyscrapers that clearly belonged to the new millennium and others that heralded antediluvian times. From their perch, the past and present mingled into an unseeable future.

They took their leave, with Rafe telling the estate agent he'd be in touch.

Charlotte noticed the slightly flirtatious look Pamela cast at Rafe, a look that reminded her of other women she'd witnessed eyeing him. Perhaps, like them, Pamela found him all the more alluring because of the color of his skin. It wasn't only men who laid claim to sexual thoughts. She savored that Pamela couldn't know how quiet and interior Rafe could be. Or how delicious in bed.

"Let's go have some dinner and drinks," Rafe said with a grin. "Okay?"

"Dinner and drinks seem to be all I do," Charlotte said, swallowing a smile. If only he knew, she thought, what I'm about to tell him.

Rafe pulled up in front of Swan, a restaurant housed inside Shakespeare's

Globe, jumped out of the vehicle and handed the valet his keys. With a jokingly gallant bow, he opened the door for Charlotte. "Come, my luv…" he said, then brushed her cheek with his lips and whispered in her ear, "my lovely, gorgeous girlfriend."

Everything he did this evening seemed destined to hinder her confession, but she vowed to tell him, at least some of the story she'd hidden thus far.

The candlelit restaurant hummed with quiet conversation. The waiters floated among the tables. Delicious smells wafted about and renewed her hunger.

Looking over the menu, she ran a finger along the rim of her wineglass. "You're pretty sure about this place, this new apartment, I mean?"

"I am," he said, frowning a little. "I don't want a place haunted by the past."

"By that," she said softly, "you mean Naomi?"

His gaze shifted past her shoulder and off into the distance. "Yes."

"Has she been stalking you?" She sipped her wine.

"Well, she's made several unannounced visits."

"Like the other day when you were late to meet me?"

"Yes, like that. And then, there she was last night invading our relationship with her malicious gossip." He paused, thought, then added, "I've never had this problem. Maybe no one's ever said 'no' to her." He screwed up his mouth and shook his head.

"Are you willing to share what she told you about me?"

He inhaled deeply. "Of course, although she was rather cryptic. Just said that I didn't know everything about your past, especially what happened with your cousin. That if you loved me, you wouldn't keep secrets."

"I suppose she's right. In a way." Charlotte's gaze softened and her voice fell to a whisper. "But she's also wrong, because I do love you."

He reached for her hand. His fingers brushed hers, a tiny shock running up her arm. "After thinking about it last night, I've decided I don't care about the past. It's the present that counts."

She marveled at the way his touch and his words brought her to life. Like Adam touched by God, the famous image of "God's Creation of Adam" appearing in her thoughts.

"You know I've never seen Michelangelo's Sistine Chapel. With my favorite artist as tour guide, of course."

"I think we can arrange that," he said, adding, "When shall we go? Next weekend? Cheap flight to Rome from here!"

Oh, yes, she wanted to say, but instead, with the need for honesty pressing on her, she said, "Very soon! Surprise me!" Her countenance must have betrayed her, because as soon as she said the word "surprise," she couldn't help thinking of the sleazy truth that lay in store for him.

"What's wrong?" he asked.

She so wanted to confide in him, and this was the opening she'd been waiting for. At the last second, she also knew she didn't want to ruin the evening. It can wait a little longer, she thought. "Nothing. Absolutely nothing."

"Let's drink to this new place then," he said.

They clinked glasses, each taking a drink, eyes locked, free hands clasped.

Their food arrived. Over a plate of Scottish salmon and roasted fall vegetables, he spoke exuberantly about decorating ideas. It seemed he was moving in the direction of living together, and she so hoped that could happen. Furnishings meant nothing to her, as long as their relationship remained intact. Now and again, she nodded or added a word of encouragement.

During a lull in the conversation, Charlotte took a long sip of wine, and gathering her courage, said, "I never told you what happened after the accident. And I need to. In case you want to change your mind about … about me. And us."

She gazed into his dark eyes, which glittered in the candlelight. He blinked. She watched his Adam's apple bob up and down as he swallowed then said, "Nothing you say will change my mind."

"I think you'd better wait until you hear what I'm about to tell you." She sipped her wine. Liquid courage. "Okay, here goes. You know that Abbie died, but you don't know it was *me* behind the wheel." She paused. He said nothing. "And that *I* was arrested for her death. For 'involuntary manslaughter,' because I was drinking and driving. Some places they call it negligent homicide."

A glimmer of fear flashed through his eyes. "I can't imagine how awful that must have been," he muttered. "And that's why you couldn't come back?"

"Not exactly. But it *was* awful, and I hate talking about it, much less telling you. Anyway, Zander's father hired a very good lawyer for me. My dad could never have afforded someone like that. She got me an excellent plea deal, which meant I spent no time behind bars, other than the few hours right after the crash. And that scared the hell out of me. So, Abbie died, and I got no prison time. Zero. I guess you could say I got off scot-free."

"Charlotte, you've been blaming yourself ever since. Isn't that enough punishment?"

"You know, in some ways, it might have been better if I *had* served time. I might have felt like I'd paid my dues, that some justice had been done. And maybe so would Abbie's parents. My aunt and uncle.

"The worst of it was, they disowned me. Until then I'd been like another daughter to them. Afterwards, I was nothing. No amount of apology made any difference. And poor Dad, he was a wreck. They even sued us, but they're rich, and they ended up dropping the lawsuit."

"Care for any dessert?" a voice said. Charlotte gave the waiter a startled look.

"I'll have another glass of red," Rafe said. "How about you?"

Earlier, a drop of red wine had stained the white tablecloth, and now Charlotte stared at it, recalling that long ago drunken night. All that blood. And Zander, despite his own drunkenness, saying, "I'll take care of it," over and over.

Though she didn't answer, Rafe ordered her another glass as well.

Charlotte pulled out her phone to show him the one nude image she'd planned to share, but then thought, *enough damage for one night.* She'd be brave again tomorrow.

"Charlotte, look at me," Rafe said. "You've suffered plenty for your mistake. Why do you need to keep flogging yourself?"

"Because I took her life, Rafe. I killed her. Do you have any idea how that feels?" Tears welled up in Charlotte's eyes. "She'll never come back. Never. I'll never hear her voice, her goofy laughter. And neither will her parents. I have to live with that." She covered her face with the napkin, using it as a handkerchief. "I'm sorry, Abbie. I'm so sorry," she whispered.

Chapter 25

Friday, December 13, 2019

AT HER DESK EARLY THE next day before heading to Paris, an item in *The Independent* caught Charlotte's attention. It contained the photo of one of the thirty-nine victims, a beautiful twenty-six-year-old woman, Pham Thi Tra My, who'd sent her mother a text saying, "I can't breathe," at the exact moment that the container was making its way from Belgium to the UK. Her next message said, "I'm dying."

This story touched Charlotte deeply. The poor thing looked so pretty and innocent. Charlotte grew outraged by the people who'd committed this crime. Staring at the image and thinking of the loss the young woman's mother felt brought Abbie's parents to mind; they had lost their daughter too. Grief rose up in Charlotte, and before she knew it, she was weeping.

"Oh, my, are you alright?" Ian asked.

She looked at him. "I just read this." She aimed a finger at her computer screen, where the image of the young woman stared at them.

He read the text. "Tragic all right," he said.

Diana arrived a moment later. "What's going on?"

"A sad story. You know that awful bit about all those Vietnamese dying in a lorry," Ian informed her.

"Such a piece makes me question how objective I can be—the way a serious journalist needs to be," Charlotte lamented.

Diana shook her head at her. "We're still human. Not robots. Even serious journalists have a heart. Well, most of them." She released a small chuckle. "The best part is you get to expose such horrid stuff. Then maybe someone will do something about it." She pushed a pile of bushy hair off her face and into a clip atop her head.

"Thank you, I needed that." Charlotte looked at Diana gratefully. She hoped she was up to the task of exposing this terrible injustice and that it would trigger a response as Diana suggested. One thing she knew for sure. She couldn't let Regina down, but that thought was chased by another: no wonder she looked so haggard.

On the elevator going up, she tried to think of something to tell Shelby about being gone all day, as a courtesy and to stay in her good graces. Certainly nothing about the trip to Paris. Her thoughts drifted elsewhere, and it occurred to her to approach Diana about Bradford. *Note to self*, she wrote on her phone, *ask Diana re NB—any gossip?*

She knocked on Shelby's door, which stood open. With perfectly coiffed hair, Shelby turned. On seeing Charlotte, her frown turned into a smile. "Where have you been hiding?"

Simultaneously taken aback and emboldened by her friendliness, she got to the point. "I've been working on something I thought might be adjusted for the online arts and culture magazine."

When Charlotte told her the basics of the story, Shelby's perpetual frown returned. "Are you mad? How shall we plug it? Here's a young woman from Vietnam who might, in other circumstances, have become a model or an actress, a productive member of British society, but now she's dead. Is that it?" she said mockingly.

Charlotte stared at her. "I thought we could tell it from the heart. Contact her mother and speak to her. Do a little exposé on the issue."

Shelby released a long breath of air through pursed lips. "No. If you want a piece on *my* magazine, think of something else." Shelby seemed upset or angry. Or both. Hard to tell.

"All right. I'll try. Do you have any ideas?"

"I'll think about it." She turned her back on Charlotte, who took that as her cue to leave.

That went well, Charlotte thought. *Not.*

Shortly after "take-off" the train crossed the English Channel through the long tunnel, then sped across the plains of France. Though Charlotte had bought a croissant, she only picked at it as she gazed out the window wondering if Rafe had seen through her charade the night before. She'd told him she needed to sleep at her own apartment because of a very early morning and a long day ahead investigating the Vietnamese trafficking story.

"Why can't you leave early from my place?"

"I just haven't been sleeping well," she claimed. "Trust me I'd rather be with you and not work on this story."

"It's gotten to you, has it?"

She nodded somberly. "So sad. It's making me wonder if I'm cut out for this sort of thing." At least that was the truth.

"Would you rather go back to writing fluff?"

She shot him a fiery glance. "No, but there has to be something in-between, right?"

He came over and put his hands on her shoulders. "You are fully capable of all manner of journalism. Consider this your opportunity to explore. It's what I do with my art. Try this. Try that. You can do that as a writer too."

"I suppose you're right." His comment made her feel lighter, but then she remembered her lie about staying at her apartment. She sighed.

Instead of saying anything more, he kissed her. "It will all get sorted. You'll see. Especially once we start living together." He smiled at her. "Trust me."

"I do," she said. If only it were that easy.

She'd barely finished her cup of coffee, and most of her croissant remained on the white plastic plate, when the Eurostar train pulled into the Gare du Nord station in Paris.

As she exited, some of her travel excitement caught hold and she wished she had another reason for being here. That she and Rafe had traveled together for their first time to Paris to stay on the Île Saint-Louis in a quaint inn.

In the taxi, heading to her rendezvous with Zander, Charlotte reviewed what she planned to say. They were meeting at Honor, a café on the fashionable rue du Faubourg Saint-Honoré around noon. She weighed several approaches, silently rehearsed the lines, then decided to play it by ear, because who knew what he'd say? She believed in her gut instincts, but knew she'd have to stay alert. More than anything she needed a big dose of confidence.

The cab entered the central streets of Paris, and her gaze shifted outside, many of the neo-classical buildings all at once familiar. The Eiffel Tower stood guard in the distance. She wished most fervently that Rafe was sitting beside her in the cab, holding her hand, the two of them about to visit the Louvre or the Musée d'Orsay. *With any luck,* she thought, *by this afternoon I'll have solved the problem, and be free of this wretched business shadowing me.*

Chapter 26

EVEN FROM A DISTANCE, SHE recognized him. Zander with his dark-haired, olive-skinned good looks sat at a table facing the street, watching passersby, perhaps imagining how he would photograph them. She'd wanted to arrive ahead of him, was in fact twenty minutes early, but instead she now saw him waving at her. Take a breath, she told herself, and smile.

She exaggerated the exuberance of her last few strides. Catch him off guard. He'd never suspect she'd figured out he was the culprit. And yet why wouldn't he? Because who else could it be? Who else would have taken those photos and sent them? Someone who'd found them? But who and how? None of it made sense.

Nattily dressed, a scarf flung around his neck, he rose from his seat and took several steps toward her. Grasped her arms, leaned back and looked her over, brought her close and kissed her, first on one cheek and then the other.

"*Ma cherie*!" he said in mock French. "You are a wonder to behold." He seemed in high spirits. "Will you join me in a celebratory drink?" he asked. "A Lillet? Remember those?"

"Sure, why not?" She studied him. His face had filled out, more masculine to be sure, but he remained the slender man she remembered.

So far, this encounter wasn't going exactly as she'd imagined. He seemed far too relaxed and happy to suggest he'd written that awful note or sent those photos.

Zander flagged down a waiter and ordered two Lillets.

"I'm afraid we only have beer," the waiter said in French-accented English.

"If I'd known *that* I wouldn't have come here," Zander groused.

Still spoiled, Charlotte thought. "I'm okay with a beer," she said, hoping to avoid any unpleasantness.

"Well, all right. Make that two," he told the waiter with a scowl. "And a bottle of Perrier with two wedges of lime. Two glasses. And ice, *s'il vous plaît*."

The waiter gave a curt nod and strode off.

"Did you know that Russ and I split up?" she asked, hoping this question might lead to the real reason for meeting up with him.

He shook his head no. "He broke up with you?"

"I suppose," she said, feeling slightly embarrassed.

"Fell for someone else?"

She nodded, wondering if he knew the details.

"Well, guess I was right?" he said.

"Right?" she asked.

"Remember, I told you he wasn't *the* one?"

She recalled the note and photos he'd sent after the event she'd attended with Russ.

"So, the break-up's good news or bad?" He canted his head to the side, watching her.

She considered her response before saying, "I'm not permanently scarred, if that's what you mean."

"He wasn't right for you. Your basic loser."

She frowned at him. "He may be a louse, but he's not a loser. He's quite an accomplished archaeologist," she said, coming to Russ's defense, though perhaps Zander's intent was to soften the blow of the break-up.

"Digging around for old bones—I guess we all have to pass the time somehow. I much prefer live, healthy, beautiful bones," he said, giving her another appreciative look.

The waiter returned, carrying a silver tray laden with beer, several extra glasses, a bottle of Perrier, lime wedges and a glass of ice. He quickly unloaded their drinks and disappeared.

Zander gave her a coy smile. "You've finally come to your senses then?"

She squinted at him. "How so?"

"Well, here we are. Both single. *And* available?"

"Oh, Zander!" She managed to produce a chuckle, wondering how to sidestep his question. "Tell me about *you*. I want to hear about your work! I'll never forget how opposed you were to a job after we graduated."

"Well, yes, I hate the idea of *work*, but following your passion, now that's a fucking joy ride," he said, his eyes flashing, a satisfied look on his face. "And I'm still on it."

"I'm in awe of your success! Really. Wonderful."

"What about you? Still working for Shelby…at that new job at Thorntree?" He stirred ice into his glass of Perrier.

So, he remembered, she thought, and instantly wondered if he hadn't called Shelby. It would have been so like him. Nosy and gossipy.

"Actually, I'm not really working for Shelby anymore. They're trying me out as a broadcast journalist."

"Journalist! Listen to you," he said with a smile. "Sounds like I'm not the only successful one."

"About time for me." She told him a little about the golden toilet piece and then the human trafficking story.

A shadow crossed his face. "That sounds downright depressing."

Charlotte picked up the menu, and as she stared at the short list of lunch items, she tried to figure out how to raise the real reason for coming here.

Zander's hand shot up to catch the waiter's attention. "Ready, Charlotte?"

She nodded as the man arrived. "I'll have the smashed avocado on sourdough crumpets," she said with an encouraging look.

"Make that two," Zander said, and thrust his menu at the waiter.

Charlotte watched him retreat and hoped he wouldn't spit in their food.

"You didn't answer my other question," he said.

"What? Which question?" She looked at him, confused. What had they been talking about?

"The one about being available." He smiled.

That question. At least ten minutes had passed since he'd asked her that. "I'm not," she said, wondering what she should say next. *Taking a break? I'm done with men for a while.*

His forehead wrinkled; a slight dip at the corners of his mouth replaced the smile. "So then, uh, what brings you here?"

She looked at him, trying to read his thoughts. Could he have hoped she wanted to date him? She cleared her throat.

Before she could speak, he said, "Look, don't get me wrong, I've got plenty of girls…these models, they're like—" he thought a moment, "like locusts, you know, dime a dozen. But I haven't found *the* one." He gave her an odd, knowing smile.

Tempted to respond, she stuck to her plan and said, "I received a ticking time bomb the other day." She scrutinized his expression.

"What's that supposed to mean?" His brow furrowed with incomprehension.

He has to know, doesn't he, she thought, *otherwise this trip was a mistake.*

She decided to risk it and reached into her purse. Once she withdrew the photos from the envelope, she saw the startled look on his face. "Oh, God, Charlotte. Where'd you get these?"

"That's what I was going to ask *you*." She watched his eyes widen with surprise then narrow to a puzzled squint. She pressed ahead. "You recognize them? You took them?"

"No, but I remember that night," he said, "how could I forget?" His cheeks flushed as he nodded his head. Then he seemed to catch on to why she'd bothered to make the trip to Paris. He examined the envelope, stared at her name, Thorntree's address. "But these aren't from me. I swear. That's not my writing, you can see that."

"Easy enough to get someone else to write my name and address."

He continued to stare at her, an incredulous look on his face, but said nothing.

Either he was a very good actor or—or what? "So, you're saying someone else sent them?" she asked.

Just then the waiter arrived with a tray of food. He placed their dishes before them and asked if they wanted anything else.

"I'll take another beer," Charlotte said, continuing to scrutinize Zander.

"Me too," Zander chimed in, watching the waiter depart. He turned back to Charlotte, shaking his head. "It definitely wasn't me."

"Then who?"

"Look, other people were there. You remember?"

"Yeah, but others taking photographs? Of me? Fucking some stranger?"

Pain contorted his face. He rubbed his arm, as if she'd just taken a knife and stabbed him. "Yes," he said.

"Who?"

His eyes rolled up as if trying to recall. "I've tried to forget. Haven't you?" His mouth curled in disgust.

Charlotte stared at him. Yes, she *had* tried to forget and now everything depended on her remembering, on finding out who'd been at that stupid party and who'd taken the photos and who wanted her to leave London.

She took in a deep breath then said, "A lot depends on *you* remembering, Zander. They're threatening to put these up on the Internet if I don't leave London…by Christmas. I've got less than twelve days."

"Really? Wow," he said, his brow arching with disbelief. "That sucks. What are you gonna do if you can't find whoever sent them?"

"What choice do I have?" She studied his face. He was frowning. What the hell was he thinking? Had he taken the photos or not? "Damn it, Zander, you have to remember. My whole life depends on it."

"Your life?" He appeared startled. "No one's threatening to kill you, are they?"

She glared at him. "No, no one's threatening to kill me, but it'll mean my job, my relationships, *and* I'll be forced to move back to New York."

"At least moving to New York isn't so bad," he said.

His complacency was maddening. "Zander, for heaven's sake, whose house were we at?"

"A guy named Evan." He thought for a moment. "I don't think I ever knew his last name. But I could probably find his house. Or somebody might remember him. One of the people I used to hang with."

Well, that was a start, she thought.

"I hate thinking about that night," he said.

"What do you mean? It was your idea."

He nodded and looked over her shoulder, as if trying to remember something. "You were so unhappy…so filled with self-loathing. You blamed yourself for Abbie's death. But it was an accident. I thought somehow that night might help. Might jolt you out of, well, whatever it was you were hung up on."

"Hung up on?" She gaped at him in disbelief. "Abbie was dead, Zander. You thought a night like that might help?" She shook her head then took another sip of her beer.

"Yeah, I did. So stupid of me. It was disgusting…painful."

"Painful?"

He sighed. "Watching you with that man and then those two guys."

Shame washed over her. She remembered the man but not two guys. If only she could erase all that. "Don't think about it," she said. "I hate to even ask about it, it's so damn embarrassing, but I don't know what else to do."

"Of course, you should ask. We're friends, Charlotte. That's why you called, right?"

She nodded, though it wasn't the truth. She hadn't forgiven him.

"I'll help you," he added. "Any way I can. Because you're right this *is* partly my fault. I took you there, and I'm sorry. Really, I am."

Charlotte gazed off. She hadn't touched her meal. She'd put so much energy into thinking that Zander was the culprit, that she hadn't thought about what would happen if he wasn't. After all, why would he be? That never made any sense.

They chatted a while longer. Zander promised to get in touch with anyone he could think of from that night or at least contact Evan through a friend he thought still hung out with him. "They still do a bunch of drugs," he said, "and I don't, not anymore."

"That's good to hear," she said. "I don't either." She checked the time and saw that she needed to leave if she was going to catch the return train to London.

They stood up and she gave him a half-hearted hug. "You know," she said, "I still dream about Abbie. I still miss her. Do you?"

His eyes clouded but he nodded. "Of course. We'll never forget her." Then he added, "If you decide to go back to New York, let me know. I should have things wrapped up here in a week or so."

"I'll stay in touch. Let me know when you get those names."

"Will do."

Chapter 27

ON THE TRAIN BACK TO London, Charlotte stared outside, her thoughts turned inward. She and Rafe were supposed to spend the weekend together. What—if anything—should she tell him? She'd made precisely zero progress.

Well, Zander had offered to find out Evan's contact info. At least that was something. Was it? If he did, she'd ask Evan who else had been at his home that night. What were the chances of him remembering? She didn't even know who she'd been fucking! Should she have asked Zander? The memory of it had pained him, so, no, she shouldn't. And in a way she was glad she hadn't. And yet, she'd have to face this awful truth sometime.

It was then that it occurred to her: that man, specifically, or maybe two men, might be behind this whole thing. She'd fucked him…them? Perhaps she'd made promises and hadn't kept them? Revenge porn of a sort? But no one had ever contacted her afterward. Right? The entire episode was so deeply buried and her questions about that night so exasperating because they led to nothing but more questions.

The train's smooth rocking caused her eyes to close, but sleep refused to come.

She pulled out her mobile and texted Celia: *Can you meet at St Pancras Station around five? Booking Office…the bar in the hotel.*

Celia: *What's there?*

Charlotte: *Me. Returning from a quick trip to Paris.*

Celia: *You didn't tell me…naughty woman! What took you there?*

Golden toilet artist?

Charlotte: *I wish! Can you make it?*

Celia: *For you, of course, but hot date with Phil tonight.*

Charlotte: *Who's the naughty one? We'll stick to one drink.*

Shortly after five o'clock, the Eurostar train rolled into St Pancras station. Charlotte gathered her things and rushed to exit not wanting to be late. At the entrance of the restaurant, which featured an old-fashioned "booking office," she searched for Celia and caught sight of her long dark hair trailing down her back, her slightly oversized bum pressing against the bar stool.

Anxious, she hurried between tables, failing to appreciate her surroundings. Under other circumstances she might have noted how the soft glow of lights and the orange leather booths and upholstered chairs gave the place both a sophisticated and comfortable "home away from home" feel.

On reaching her friend, Charlotte embraced her as though they hadn't seen each other in days. Celia laughed. "Me thinks my friend needs a drink. What'll you have, darling?"

"Thought you'd never ask. Hmm, let's see. Maybe something radically strong!"

The bartender came over and took their order for dirty martinis, two olives each.

"All right, where on earth have you been and what the hell is going on?" Celia said.

Charlotte sped through the last two days, ending with meeting Zander in Paris, interrupting herself with rhetorical questions, and ruminating about what it all meant without giving Celia time to answer. At last, she took a breath and a long sip of her martini.

"So, basically, you don't think this Zander fellow's behind the threat?" Celia asked.

"No. It makes a lot more sense that Naomi sent the note. She wants me gone from London."

"But how did she get the photos?"

"That's the million-dollar question."

They were both quiet for a moment. At once Celia burst into laughter.

"You're amazing, you know that?"

Charlotte looked at her, brows pinched together. "What do you mean?"

"Never a dull moment with my dear Charlotte."

"Well…I could use a dull moment right about now." Charlotte took another sip of her martini and munched one of the olives. "I need your help, Celia. I'm completely exhausted. Trying to write stories, figure out who's behind the threat, not to mention what to tell Rafe. I've been meaning to show him the photos, but I'm afraid he'll be so disgusted that'll spell the end."

"Better sooner than later."

"That's why I went to Paris. Hoping that Zander was behind this whole stupid thing, that I'd get him to confess, and then stop this madness." A tiny "V" formed between her eyes.

"I've got another half hour or so before I need to run. By the way, you haven't forgotten that Philip's making us dinner tomorrow?"

"Thanks for the reminder." Charlotte glanced at her phone. "Let me send Rafe a quick text. I think he's expecting me right about now." She fired off a note, already feeling a little lighter after unloading her concerns on Celia. When she turned back to her friend, Celia wore a thoughtful look.

"I'm sure we can figure it out, but maybe you ought to tell me more about what happened between you and Zander," she paused, "after Abbie died."

Charlotte half-closed her eyes, as if gazing into the past, searching for the right place to begin. Once she launched into the story, though, it unspooled effortlessly—the entire awful saga that detoured her life.

Two words described the weather on the day of Abbie's funeral—*hot* and *clammy*—typical for Manhattan in July.

Zander showed up afterward, waited for Charlotte out on the street, leaning against his new black Porsche, convertible top down. The old red one had been mangled beyond repair. At the sight of the shiny car, she almost didn't get in. But he put his arms around her and said, "Come on, whatever you're feeling, I'll make it better."

He had any number of drugs at his disposal, some of which would help her sleep and forget the thoughts that strained her sanity: Abbie sprawled beneath the tree, the police and their endless questions, the horrified looks on her aunt and uncle's faces. Not to mention her own father.

After nearly an hour of driving, they reached Zander's father's Sands Point estate on the north shore of Long Island. He took Charlotte by the hand and guided her to the back of the mansion. Though the images registered in her brain, she hardly noticed the Olympic-size pool they passed or the Italianate statues and fountains, and then the gardens lush with flowers, shrubs, and exotic trees. At last, they arrived at Zander's cottage with its own view of the Long Island Sound. Tacked beside the front door, a narrow driftwood sign bore the painted word "Nautilus."

No sooner had she stepped inside than she felt like running to the bathroom. What was she doing, hanging out with Abbie's boyfriend only days after her cousin's death? She swallowed, pushed away the feeling and followed him into the tiny family room. His bedroom and a second room, that alternated as study and sleeping quarters for friends, and a galley-sized kitchen made up the rest of what used to be a guesthouse. Its nautical theme featured seashell lamps and blown-up, framed images Zander had taken of sailboats and marinas, a turbulent ocean, and shorebirds in flight; navy blue cushions adorned the wicker furniture; and a fishing net weighted with green glass globes hung from the ceiling.

She asked for water, plopped down in one of the chairs and stared outside.

"Okay, let's fire her up," she heard Zander say from the kitchen. She wondered what he meant. "Come here a minute, then we can sit on the couch and watch the ocean. Okay?"

She rose, zombie-like, and joined him. He stood beside the narrow white enamel stove, one of the gas burners lit. In his right hand he held a butter knife, its tip discolored. On a small plate next to the stove lay a dark wad of what looked like volcanic putty.

"What's that?" she said.

"Come here and you'll find out."

She moved closer, watched him place a pea-sized piece on the flat blade of the knife, then hold it above the flame. The substance released a vapor that Zander sucked into his lungs. "Now you; just inhale."

"What is it?"

"A miracle," he said, arching his brow mysteriously.

"Come on," she said.

"Opium."

Why not, she reasoned. She tilted her body toward Zander and breathed in the acrid smoke. They each inhaled a few more times before he poured two glasses of Corona, squeezed in some lime, and walked her to the sofa.

At first, she didn't feel much, but after a few sips of beer, her mind wandered. Her thoughts floated over the ocean chop and into the blue heavens, a feeling of quiet well-being spreading through her limbs. One minute she'd been despondent, and the next she felt inexplicably released and buoyed up like a balloon rising into the air. Like everything was okay with the world.

"Feel good?" Zander said. She could only nod.

She drifted in and out of consciousness for some time. When night fell, it seemed as if a dark curtain had dropped over Zander's cottage. She thought she'd eaten something and drank more beer. "Shouldn't I be waking up?" she asked. And he said, "Why bother?"

She only had a vague awareness of him leading her to his bedroom and helping her peel off her clothes. She kept on her bikini underwear and grabbed the white tee-shirt he offered. She felt his eyes scouring her chest, her nipples, as she arched to pull the tee-shirt over her head, but it didn't matter. Nothing seemed to matter.

She lay down on the bed, her legs draped over the edge.

"Will you do something for me?" she heard him whisper.

"What?"

"Lift up your t-shirt."

"No."

"Just enough to expose one of your beautiful tits."

She sighed.

"Please?" he said, "for picking you up. And making you feel better."

She couldn't deny he'd done both. With eyes closed, she did as he asked. An instant later, she heard several clicks accompanied by bright flashes. Then he lay down beside her and kissed each breast. "Don't," she groaned.

"Open your mouth," he said. "This'll help."

It was all she wanted. The sweet oblivion of sleep. She opened her mouth and felt a tablet hit her tongue. "Swallow," he said, and again she obeyed.

The next morning, she woke with a start. Light shot through the blinds, slicing into her brain like a blade; she squinted, her head throbbed, her mouth felt parched like the Gobi Desert. She got up, a little unsteady on her feet, then finally realized where she was. In the bathroom, she went to tug her panties down only to realize she wore nothing but a t-shirt.

Like pieces of a puzzle, her thoughts fell into place. "Zander! What'd you do? What the hell'd you do?"

He opened the door to the bathroom and leaned against the doorjamb, a cocky grin stretched across his face. "What?"

"You know what!" She pulled her t-shirt down to cover herself.

"I made you feel good, babe," he said, leering at her. "Should have heard you moan."

"Fuck you! Get out!"

He gave her a quick salute, swiveled on one heel, and left her gawping after him. The whole thing made her sick. She wanted to throw up and turned to face the toilet. When nothing came, she turned on the shower and got in.

The steam rose in billowing clouds as she scrubbed between her legs. Tears finally came, but she couldn't rid herself of what he'd done. What she'd done. How could she face Rafe after this? What would she tell him? "Oh, God," she muttered.

She returned her gaze to Celia and took a last sip of her drink. "I had the most awful feeling that Abbie had seen the whole thing. I felt sick. Wanted to end it. Everything was ruined."

Celia waved at the bartender. "I think we'll each have a sparkling water." To Charlotte she said, "And you're still beating yourself up over that?"

"Oh, no, that's not the worst of it," Charlotte said, returning to the story. "Zander offered me a mug of coffee that morning. I took it and calmly told him I hoped he knew the only person I loved was Rafe."

"That *wannabe artist* in England? Fuck him!" Zander said. His mouth twisted in disgust, he turned back to the stove, cracked an egg into a pan. It popped and sizzled. Then he dropped in another.

Charlotte swallowed, trying to think straight, wanting to come to Rafe's defense, though she didn't know how. She met Zander's silence with her own. Her errors in judgment were mounting. She needed to get out of there. But how could she go home and face her father?

About to walk out the door, she decided to hurl one last taunt at Zander, whose back faced her. "You know I'm leaving in a few weeks," she said. "To go back to that *artist* in England. And I promise I'll never see you again. Ever."

"I wouldn't count on that," he said without turning around. "You've got a court date in a week. Doubt it'll be the last."

How could she have forgotten? A few days later, she returned to Sands Point. "That night he took me to a party," Charlotte explained. "A 'special' party, where everybody drank, took E, fucked whoever was around. I don't recall names, but that one shot of me says it all." She lowered her voice. "Any idiot can see I'm riding some guy's cock. I may not be a celebrity but if those go on social media, my career's done. And what do I tell Rafe?" Her face had misery written all over it.

"You all right, miss?" the bartender asked.

She nodded.

"You must tell Rafe the truth? Somehow, we'll figure this out."

"We will?" Charlotte cast a desperate look at Celia. "I don't see how I'll get out of going back to New York, do you?"

"Maybe not, but what'll happen there?"

"I don't know."

There was a lull in the conversation when suddenly Celia's eyes lit up. "I know. I think I know the solution."

"You do?"

"Yes."

"What?"

"I can't believe we didn't think of this already." Celia took one last sip of her drink and looked off. "Go to the police."

"The police?"

"That's right. Tell them someone's trying to blackmail you. And they need to stop them from going through with the threat."

Charlotte looked at her skeptically. "I don't know. That means I'll have to show them the photographs."

"Yeah, so?"

"I'd rather not."

"It's worth a try," Celia said. "Don't you think?"

Chapter 28

THAT EVENING, CHARLOTTE APPROACHED RAFE'S building with faltering steps. She lingered at the small bridge overlooking the canal that flowed beneath his apartment windows and glanced up. She couldn't decide how to broach the subject of the photos. What should she say? Where should she start? How would he react? Would he wonder why she hadn't told him sooner?

Earlier, she'd glanced at a headline and realized it was Friday the thirteenth. Just my luck, she thought, recalling the broken mirror and the seven years that followed.

She turned her gaze back to the canal. The dark water reflected a few streetlights. She stooped over to pick up a pebble, found several and tossed them into the water. The tiny stars of light shattered as the pebbles struck the surface. Seconds later, the black surface grew still, and the streetlights returned to perfect circles of light.

She continued to stand there, feeling the chill air and summoning her courage. *Waiting won't make this go away,* she told herself. Celia's faith in her gave her a boost. "You've got this, Char. He loves you." But did he love her enough? She wouldn't blame him if he didn't.

"There you are," Rafe called out from the kitchen. "How's Celia?"

"I think she's in love," she said, dropping her messenger bag near the front door. "She asked if we were coming to their place tomorrow? Philip's cooking. I totally forgot."

"Do you want to?"

"I guess," she said, then paused before adding, "but I have to tell you something. And after that, I'm not sure you'll want to go, at least not with me."

He came over, took her by the shoulders and gave her a long hard look before kissing her. With the swirl of emotions that stirred inside of her, his look compounded her worries; she tried to interpret what he was thinking.

"What are you talking about?" he asked as he released her. "Something about Celia and Philip?"

She shook her head. "No, not them. Me."

"Now what have you been up to, Ms. Cooper?"

Did he know she'd gone to Paris?

"Nothing you say will change how I feel about you," he added. "I've missed you all day. Hope you missed me too?"

She tried to smile. "Of course, I did." *Could this be our last night,* she thought as she looked into his dark searching eyes.

"What's going on? World coming to an end?" he asked.

Yes, mine just might be.

"Let's go for a walk? Maybe head over to The Eagle?" What she needed to show and tell him might be easier to reveal in the dark, while walking. More than anything she couldn't bear to see the disappointment in his eyes.

They walked together, their long strides matching. "Before I start, let me just say that the last two weeks have been my happiest in a long time. Thank you." She allowed those words to sink in before adding, "My past kept me away from you, and then it seems fate tossed us together. Now the past's back to haunt me, and you may decide I'm damaged goods."

"What the hell are you talking about? We all make mistakes. No matter what, I'll be here for you."

"Hear me out."

"Shouldn't we have something to drink?"

"No, I need to be sober. And I want you to be sober too. Maybe later," she said, *if there is a later.*

She began with Abbie's funeral, and when she finished with all she'd told Celia, a palpable silence followed, interrupted by a distant siren that somehow seemed appropriate to the moment. At last, he released a sigh. "Charlotte, I can't say I like hearing this, but this orgy, or whatever it was, happened years ago. We've both been punished by the past; it's time to forget about it. Why should we care what happened then?"

"Well, I was getting to that."

"Oh?" he said. "Maybe I need a drink after all."

"Please, before we go in let's just sit on that bench over there." Her desire to avoid alcohol wavered.

She could see inside The Eagle, filled with people, chatter and music. Though everything there appeared the same, for Charlotte nothing was, least of all in her private turbulent world. Once seated, she dove in and told him about the nude photos. "I know they were taken at that wretched orgy, but how they appeared in my in-box, well, that's a mystery." She pulled the envelope out of her purse and handed it to him. "Please don't gasp…they're awful," she said in a whisper.

"I won't," he said, "but that's odd."

"What is?"

"Delivered to your work."

"Why's that odd?"

"Because who even knows you're working there?"

"Good point. I have no idea. Except it happened after my on-air debut, so a few people might have known."

He withdrew the photos from the envelope and examined them one by one. They were organized from least offensive to the one that qualified as X-rated. Charlotte watched the expression on his face. As he stared at the last one, she saw his eyes narrow despite his best effort to maintain a neutral mask.

"Bloody hell. When did you get these?"

She hesitated before telling him the truth. "The first one came last week. I wasn't even sure it was me, so I ripped it up and tried to forget about it. But then the others showed up a few days ago…with a threat."

The lines on his face deepened. "A threat? What kind of threat?"

"That if I don't go home—to New York—by Christmas they'll go viral *and* be sent to Thorntree."

"And you failed to tell me?"

Charlotte couldn't tell whether it was concern or anger etched into his brow. "I tried, no, I wanted to tell you, but each time something came up and I felt like I was just going to ruin things. Then I got this idea that I might know who'd sent them and if I could just get him to admit it, the whole thing would go away!"

"Charlotte, that's what you did six years ago."

"What do you mean?"

"You kept me in the dark. You refused to let me in, and then you did all that shit so that you couldn't come back. You wouldn't let me help you. Christ, haven't you learned anything?"

Charlotte felt her face grow hot. "You're right, of course…please don't be mad," she begged. "But I haven't even told you all of it."

"There's more?" He took in a gulp of air.

"Like I said, I wracked my brain trying to figure out who could have sent them, and why. I mean after all that time it made no sense. But …"

"Based on what you've told me, the only logical person is this photographer fellow in New York," Rafe said.

"I know but I saw Zander, and he convinced me it wasn't him." She pushed the words out of her mouth before she grew too cowardly to say them. "He's in Paris; I took the train there today."

"*Today*?" Rafe's face twisted into a dark scowl. "Which means you lied to me last night?"

"I told you I had an early day."

He stood up and said, "Let's go; I need a beer." She gladly accompanied him across the street and hoped he'd forgive her.

Ten minutes later, inside The Eagle, they nursed their beers in silence.

Rafe placed an order of fish and chips and glowered at her. "The implication last night was that you had to work, not that you were taking the train to Paris to meet an old boyfriend."

"Rafe, that's not fair. He's not an old boyfriend, not by any stretch. I could hardly stand him by the time …well, after my court appearances and all that horrid stuff. I could hardly stand myself. But I owed his father a huge debt of gratitude. And Zander convinced him to help me."

His back against a wall, he flipped through the photos once more. To Charlotte it seemed he was torturing himself. *Why's he looking again,* she wondered, *so he can hate me?* When he finished, he returned them to the envelope and extended it to Charlotte. Before she could retrieve it, though, his hand retracted the envelope. He stared at the elaborate curlicues that spelled out Charlotte's name and Thorntree's address.

"What?" Charlotte said.

"The photos came inside this?" The pinched brow returned.

"Yes. Why?"

"That handwriting, it's familiar."

Back at Rafe's loft, he plowed through papers on his messy desk to see if any notes from Naomi had survived.

For Charlotte, the theory had obvious appeal. "It certainly makes sense that she's behind the threat since she's the only person I can think of who wants me gone from London."

"But how the hell did she get ahold of the photos?" He continued searching but eventually lifted his hands in defeat.

"I don't know, but maybe you can find out," she said hopefully, "and while you're at it, get a sample of her handwriting."

"And how will I do that?"

"You're clever. You'll think of something."

They made love that night with passionate abandon, perhaps secretly worried their time together might soon come to an end. Charlotte lay in his arms afterward, praying they'd be spared this latest ordeal—her second departure from London followed by an uncertain future.

Chapter 29

Saturday, December 14, 2019 (10 days)

CHARLOTTE WOKE UP HUNGRY. SHE hadn't eaten much the previous day. After lying there a few seconds the aroma of coffee reached her. She slipped into Rafe's white terrycloth robe, cinched the belt around her waist, and walked barefoot to the kitchen where she spotted a pot of freshly brewed coffee but no sign of him.

Then the grating sound of a buzzsaw, or something, ground into her ears. She found him in his studio, covered in dust, smoothing a large piece of light-colored stone with a sander. Once he saw her, he put it down. He ran the back of his hand across his sweaty forehead and reached for a towel to wipe the pale grit off his face but only managed to transfer dust from one place to the other.

"Couldn't sleep?" she asked.

"No, you?"

"I did all right, considering."

She clasped her arms around his neck and kissed him on the cheek, then used her sleeve to wipe the particles of sand off her mouth. In a subdued voice, she said, "I just want to tell you how sorry I am. About all of it. Not sure how this will end, but having you here…well, thanks…it means… everything."

He nodded, but she could see something bothered him. "What?"

"I heard from her."

"Naomi?"

"Who else?"

"Already?"

"Said she needs to talk with me."

"You mean you hadn't already contacted her?"

He shook his head. "I've no idea what she wants."

Charlotte retrieved her computer from her messenger bag and sat down at the kitchen table with a mug of coffee. "Mmm," she said after taking a sip.

She hadn't bothered to check her emails after she'd returned to Rafe's the previous evening and now found several emails needing her attention. She groaned. "I don't feel like working today."

"It's Saturday," he said from the other room. "No one works today!"

"You do! *And* reporters do. News doesn't just screech to a halt on weekends!"

"Maybe you should switch jobs."

"Fat chance," she said as she opened an email from Nelson Bradford. *How's the Vietnamese story coming along? What's new? Imagine you're coming in to work? Stop by my office. I should be in by 11.* Her mouth turned into a frown.

She puzzled over how to answer Bradford's query when another email arrived. She didn't recognize the sender's address, a series of letters and numbers, but opened it.

You've got 9 days. If you don't leave soon you'll regret it. Be the fuck gone! (What are you waiting for?)

Charlotte gaped at the email then opened her computer's calendar and counted to December twenty-fourth. *Ten days, maybe even eleven, but not nine,* she thought then read the email several more times. *If you don't leave soon you'll regret it.* Her jaw tightened.

"Rafe," she called, "take a look at this."

He entered the kitchen, poured her more coffee then read the email over her shoulder. "What a cock-up!" He sat down opposite Charlotte and glanced out the window at the canal below. Slowly, he sipped his coffee then buttered a piece of toast. She could see the wheels of his mind turning.

Without thinking she began to type: *Who are you? I'd like to meet you. And discuss whatever it is that's* …that's what, she wondered. Pissed you off? *Upsetting you,* she wrote. *That's made you so crazy you want me out of the country,* she thought. Unsure what else to say she pressed "send" and turned her attention to other emails, mostly marketing junk and a couple from friends in New York, wondering how things were going.

She wrote a group email to her New York gang, was about to send it, when she heard the ping of a text arrive on Rafe's phone. The sound put her on alert, and she cast a questioning look at Rafe.

"Speak of the devil," he said.

"Were we?"

He nodded. "She asked if I'm available this afternoon."

"Seems like a weird coincidence."

"Why's that?"

"A threatening email and Naomi wanting to see you."

Rafe shrugged, picked up his phone and tapped in a text.

Charlotte heard another ping and watched as Rafe looked at his phone and sipped coffee. "We're meeting around three, but before this damn encounter," he said, "how about an adventure? A tour of some of my favorite sculptures in London?"

"Lovely. Anything to distract me." She glanced back at her computer. "Oh, brother, I just got a response."

"What's it say?"

"*Nice try! Signed, Anonymous,*" she read. "Almost positive it's Naomi. Getting rid of her competition, aka *me*, is the only way she sees of getting you back."

He released a resigned sigh. "I guess we'll find out."

An hour later Charlotte popped out of the tube and felt the brisk air hit her skin. Over the past few days, temperatures had steadily dropped. She shivered as she stretched her fingers into a pair of gloves. She hurried along several streets strung with Christmas lights and past stores decorated for the holidays. Once upon a time, she'd loved this time of year, but now her stride slowed. The festive windows roused her anger. She refused to let Naomi win, and yet was she to blame?

She turned away and continued toward the Thorntree building. Where recently she'd wanted meaningful work and gotten it; now she just prayed she'd be with Rafe for Christmas.

She opened the door to Bradford's office and stood in the entryway. She was hoping to make this quick. He looked up from his desk and smiled at her. "Come in," he said.

She had the feeling he'd been waiting for her. He was casually dressed in jeans, loafers, and a pullover gray sweater with a black t-shirt underneath. Though in his fifties, he looked sufficiently handsome, and she imagined he'd had numerous affairs with aspiring young women at Thorntree. However, she wouldn't be among them.

She left the door wide open and walked toward his desk. "I've only got a minute. It's Saturday and I'm meeting my boyfriend at one o'clock."

He glanced at his watch, a Gucci, she guessed. "That gives us at least forty-five minutes…plenty of time," he said. "Come let's sit over here," he gestured to the upholstered chairs, "it's a lot more comfortable."

"I have some things to sort at my desk, so I just wanted to let you know that I'd like to dig into the general topic of human trafficking in the UK, and perhaps even do a story in the US. Apparently, we lead the world in sex trafficking."

He eyed her. "Last time I checked *I* was assigning stories."

"Of course, but I was hoping you'd like the idea of a more in-depth piece on the problem, using the recent Vietnamese incident as the basis for it." She stood her ground, not moving toward the chair, where he now stood.

"I'll give it some thought," he said, though his tone suggested the opposite. "Send me a memo about it." He paused, as if making his mind up about something. "You're still in the trial phase of broadcast reporting. I hope you realize that?" His brows now bore an angry slant.

She nodded, her heart leaping. "I appreciate the opportunity. I'm sorry if I overstepped. But I'll send you a memo with details about the issue and how I might go about it."

"In the meantime, I'd suggest you provide us with an update on the victims, as I requested in my earlier email," he said and walked toward a door that led to another room in his office without turning to say good-bye.

Chapter 30

SHE ARRIVED AT ENZO PLAZZOTTA'S *Jeté* on Millbank with an uneasy feeling. She glanced around but saw no sign of Rafe. The bronze dancer, both legs fully extended, seemed to fly through the air. After the dressing down she'd received from Bradford she failed to appreciate the statue's exuberance. She stared at it, recalling that Rafe had mentioned *Jeté* several times—how full of energy and life it was.

"It's what I was trying to achieve with *Running Doesn't Pay*," he'd told her, "even though the two couldn't be more different. *Jeté's* a dancer in full artistic expression, while my sculpture's a kid from the harder neighborhoods trying to survive. I hoped to achieve the explosive energy Plazzotta captured."

"Seems to me," she said in response, "a black kid running for his life, with a bullet aimed at his back, is pretty 'explosive' and far more relevant to today's world than *Jeté*." Shrugging, Rafe had shown her a photo of his sculpture, which was owned by the famous musician and rapper, Tinie Tempah. "I'm not disparaging the other artist's work, but if I could own one, it would be yours, Rafe."

"You're biased," he said.

"In the best possible way." She'd given him an adoring smile.

Rafe's sculpture was inspired by the abundant US police murders of young Black men, and also the police brutality that disproportionately targeted Black men in the UK. He began to focus on this issue, he told her, his voice gaining uncharacteristic vehemence and indignation, after the 2014 shooting of eighteen-year-old Michael Brown in Missouri. He'd been in touch with one of the three women who founded the #BlackLivesMatter movement in the US and planned to meet with her on his next trip to New York.

Perhaps he could come with me to New York, she now thought, and meet with this woman. She jumped a little when a voice behind her said, "Boo."

"Oh, you," she said and leaned her head against his chest.

They stood before the sculpture, chatted about it, stared off, until finally they left, recognizing their minds were elsewhere.

Ambling along, Charlotte argued with Rafe to let her accompany him to get a peek at Naomi. "We'll split up long before you arrive at Pret."

"And what? You're going to peer in through the window? Or worse yet, you're going to come inside thinking she won't notice or recognize you?"

"I promise not to go inside."

"No."

"I just want to see her," she said in a pleading tone. "Please."

He shook his head. "Short of tying you to a chair in my apartment, I know you're going to follow me. In which case we are not getting on a train together. I'll take an Uber. You do what you like."

"Thank you." She smiled. "Maybe later I'll take you up on some kinky sex!"

"Careful." He gave her a cock-eyed grin.

Shortly after he left, she wondered if he might throw her off the trail by switching the meeting with Naomi to another Pret café. She hurried to the nearest Tube station.

Careful not to be too obvious as she passed the designated café, Charlotte glanced inside and surveyed the room. It took a few seconds to see that Naomi and Rafe weren't there.

"Damn him," she muttered to herself. She couldn't believe he'd tricked her. *Now where?* she thought. She'd finagled Naomi's address from him before they'd parted ways. She checked the GPS on her phone and discovered her apartment building was only a couple of blocks away.

She began moving in that direction. To her surprise, a second later, she saw Rafe's head towering above other pedestrians some twenty or thirty meters away. She took a step back, caught sight of Naomi beside him, and ducked into the entryway of a store neighboring Pret. She peered out and watched as the couple came toward her.

Scowling, Rafe stared ahead while Naomi tried to keep up, taking two mincing, high-heeled steps for each of his.

As they drew closer, Charlotte entered the store, pretending to examine delicate dishes and crystal glassware displayed on tables and shelves. She said hello to the woman behind the counter then positioned herself so she could watch Rafe and Naomi pass by. Neither said a word, but Naomi cast a longing glance at Rafe. In that moment, Charlotte felt something other than resentment and anger toward her. *Poor creature*, she thought, *there've been times I felt exactly as you do.*

She allowed the feeling to settle then departed the store, waited a few minutes before walking past Pret. Once again, she looked inside. This time, she spotted Naomi at a small table and Rafe in line to place an order.

Naomi sat primly, one leg crossed over the other, her back ramrod straight, as if posing for a shot. She wore black leggings and a loose white, V-necked sweater, her hair bound tightly in a knot atop her head. She was staring at her phone, which lay on the table. She picked it up, put it to her ear, frowned and spoke; her hand lifted to cover her mouth.

Charlotte wondered who might be on the other end. Then she saw Rafe approach the table, carrying two paper cups. Naomi quickly turned the phone upside down and placed it back on the table.

Had she actually hung up? A little alarm went off inside Charlotte's head until she told herself she'd seen too many detective shows. Now there was nothing to do but take a walk and wait. She tore herself away from the cafe's large picture window and explored the neighborhood, a vision of Naomi in her mind.

She looked young and fragile, unhappy. Again, in spite of herself, Charlotte pitied her. And no denying she was a beauty. Now, she had seen Naomi a second time. Large eyes, crescent-shaped brows, voluptuous lips—her epic features assembled to rival the world's most attractive models. All of this atop a slender stalk of a neck.

Charlotte recalled Rafe saying that it was her skin he loved. The color so lovely. Not pale, not dark. Caramel, and it had appealed to his artistic sensibility; he'd tried to capture it on paper, once using charcoal and then watercolors. "Sure, she loved the idea of sitting for me, but our sessions never lasted. She grew bored," he told Charlotte. "Just like you," he teased.

She wondered how long they'd talk and imagined the young beauty's mouth, its beguiling yet innocent curve. Charlotte pulled up her jacket collar and after noting Naomi's building, nothing special, she strolled aimlessly along the street, trying to avoid returning to Pret and spying on Rafe.

Forty-five minutes passed before her phone vibrated. *Meet me at Pret?* Something told Charlotte to go elsewhere, and she suggested an outdoor café several blocks away. She arrived first and snagged a table, her legs crossed, one of them bouncing nervously.

The moment she saw Rafe's tight uneasy gait and his furrowed brow, she worried. Once he sat down, they ordered tea and an almond croissant. Charlotte eyed him. "So, what are you waiting for? Talk. I'm dying."

"That's just it, she made me promise not to tell you."

"And you promised?"

"I did."

"That's idiotic, Rafe." Charlotte couldn't help the words bursting forth.

"I know. But she wouldn't have told me one word if I hadn't agreed."

"Oh," Charlotte said. "But you *will* tell me?"

"Yes, and then I'll have to kill you," he said, forcing a smile. "Where to start?"

"The beginning?" she suggested, her patience thin.

Sipping Earl Grey tea, Charlotte noticed how discomfited he appeared. Unable to wait any longer, she prompted, "Please?!"

He frowned. "She thinks she's pregnant."

Charlotte's eyes grew wide. "You're kidding?"

He shook his head, staring at the vehicles passing by, looking shell-shocked.

What was he saying? My God, this was even worse than she'd expected. She hesitated, but finally brought herself to say, "And you're the father?"

"So she claims."

Her mouth felt dry. In a timid voice, she asked, "You're not going back with her, are you?"

He seemed unable to meet her gaze.

"Rafe, *please,* tell me."

"Of course not, but I need time to think. A baby! Me, a dad?" He looked forlorn. He sipped his tea and took a bite of the croissant she'd ordered. "You don't mind, I'm starving?"

"No, Rafe, I don't mind." Her leg swung back and forth. "But I don't see how you can be hungry right now."

After several more bites and a lot of chewing, he said, "She asked if I remembered her mentioning a guy who'd helped her break into fashion when she lived in America. I vaguely recalled someone. 'Yes, a photographer,' she said. 'A guy named Alex Rusikov.' Apparently—" he stopped. "What? Why are you looking at me like that?"

"That's Zander she's talking about!" she shouted. She stared past Rafe, struggling with this revelation, then lowering her voice, added, "He's Alex Rusikov."

"Oh," Rafe said, as if all the objects inside a kaleidoscope had just clicked into place. "It all makes sense now."

"What?"

"She said Alex would be furious to hear I got her pregnant, which is why she insisted I not tell you. Because *you'd* surely tell him, and then there'd be hell to pay." He paused. "I couldn't make heads or tails of it— thought she was spouting nonsense—anyway, all I could think about was the fact she was pregnant, and I might be the dad."

Now it was Charlotte's turn. "Oh, but Rafe, you've just given me the missing piece."

"I have?"

"Yes. If she knows Zander, then she might have had access to the photos…if Zander took them, and *if* he'd kept them. Or *if* he'd somehow gotten them from whoever took them. Don't you see?"

He looked dubious. "Seems like an awful lot of *ifs.*"

Chapter 31

Monday, December 16, 2019 (8 days)

CHARLOTTE'S PHONE RANG. WITHOUT A hello, she heard Shelby's voice in her ear. "The Prince Andrew scandal is sensational, but you need a new angle. An interview with him or someone close to Epstein, otherwise it doesn't have legs. 'No news is good news' and all that, but not when you're in the news business." She chuckled, sounding pleased with herself.

"Okay, if I can't get an interview with him or find a new angle in the next five minutes, what's the runner-up?" She'd sent Shelby a few story ideas on Sunday in case Bradford fired her.

There was a long silence before Shelby said, "Well, if you'd read your emails once in a while you'd know that I said human trafficking might actually be interesting, but only if there's a juicy story. I mean a little more research into the Jeffrey Epstein suicide or murder or whatever it was might work. Then again, I could live with the fashion piece. The competitive nature of it appeals to me. Especially if you can get interviews with the designers. Say something like, 'I hear Givenchy has fallen behind Gucci,' to Matthew Williams. And see what his reaction is." She chortled with laughter. A rare sound coming from Shelby.

Charlotte stopped listening. Instead, she searched the Internet for stories on revenge porn. Shelby was still talking, obviously enjoying the sound of her voice, when Charlotte saw a piece on revenge porn victims. She read quickly and learned that in the UK the police were largely untrained, unsympathetic, and often incompetent in dealing with such cybercrimes. Her heart sank. Since Celia mentioned it on Friday, she'd hoped going to the police might be an answer to her quandary. Or at least a beginning. Since Naomi lived in London and the handwriting on the envelope very likely belonged to her. But as she read on, the hopelessness of her case sank in because she couldn't with certainty identify her blackmailer. She could imagine the police, shocked by the photos, shaking their heads at her.

Shelby's voice moved back into her consciousness. "So…?"

Damn, she hadn't heard a word since several sentences ago. "Wh… what did…" she paused to collect herself. "What would you think about a piece on revenge porn?" she said as she stared at the article on her computer. She read fast. "Apparently, we've had something like 1,400 cases in the UK this year alone, most of them women, and contemplating suicide is common. It's the latest hot cybercrime!"

"Hmm," Shelby said, "I like it. Run with it."

Just as she hung up, an email landed in her in-box from Bradford. *If you can get Robinson to talk, you're a better reporter than I thought!*

She'd sent him an email earlier suggesting an interview with "Mo" Robinson, the man police had charged with the deaths of the thirty-nine trafficking victims. She knew he wasn't innocent, but also that he hadn't acted alone, and she hoped to dig deeper in a one-on-one.

Reading Bradford's email prompted anger, resentment, and annoyance to race through Charlotte. She knew the implication of his comment—that she was just another pretty face—well, she'd show him.

After saving Bradford's email and making a copy of it, she did a revenge porn search and found a heartbreaking story about thirteen-year-old Ann, who began a secret online relationship with John, a guy considerably older and to whom she sent numerous nude selfies. He'd ask for them then compliment her looks. Young Ann couldn't wait for their online chats, which continued for several years. At some point, John convinced Ann to meet him.

At first, as she read this, Charlotte feared he might want to lure Ann into sex or even rape her, but in the end, with little in common, it merely turned into an incredibly uncomfortable encounter at a restaurant. Charlotte felt grateful for this and kept reading, while also fearing the story's eventual outcome.

After the awkward meeting, their contact lessened. In time, though, they communicated again, and became what Ann, now a young woman, thought of as online friends, nothing more. She did continue to send nude photos. Eventually, Ann moved to another town for work, stopped sending selfies, and believed all was going well until a work friend told her she'd seen dozens of nude selfies of her online. When Ann looked up the link, five years of nude images of her changing figure appeared.

John had posted them on Twitter. Her colleagues and thousands of other people saw them. As one might expect, Ann felt exposed and embarrassed and could tell that her work friends no longer viewed her in the same positive way as before; worse yet, the images drew stalkers who harassed her almost daily. But when her images appeared on amateur porn sites, Ann went to the police because now a cybersex crime had been committed.

The person who interviewed her seemed unfamiliar with the law and said that's what she got for taking such photos and sending them. Not only that, but also that she was lucky nothing worse had happened. As a result, Ann grew so depressed and desperate that she considered suicide. She got as far as taking a boxcutter into the bathtub with her.

The computer screen grew blurry, and through tearful eyes, Charlotte realized how much the story had touched her, but even more so she identified with her. Ann had been at the mercy of a man who became vindictive, a man she'd foolishly trusted and considered a friend.

The parallels to her own life were obvious. How would Rafe feel once her images went online? Would he be so embarrassed that his affection would falter then disappear? Would she lose her job? Undoubtedly. How about Celia and Philip? What would they think?

Another thought crept into her mind. Something that hadn't occurred to her until now, though it should have. Once those images went up, they'd never come down. Even if Twitter or Facebook or Instagram removed them, people could take screenshots, download them onto their computers, keep them circulating and reappearing online forever.

The thought horrified her and reminded her of something she'd read about Jennifer Lawrence, whose nude photos had gotten hacked and posted on the Internet. "There's not one person in the world that's not capable of seeing those intimate photos of me," the actress had complained.

Charlotte left her desk; she needed to find the person behind the threat and beg them not to post the images. *Demand?*

The distance between someone having the images and posting them amounted to a nanosecond. And yet it would take an eternity to remove them. No wonder so many women considered suicide.

After she'd walked around the block, she stopped at a coffee shop and purchased a cup to go, then returned to her desk. Ian asked if she was okay. He must have noticed her earlier tears.

"Just needed some fresh air," she said, and with an apologetic shrug turned to her computer and logged in. "I can't believe two weeks ago I had nothing to do and now I'm swamped," she muttered.

"Welcome to the club," he said.

After reading Ann's story, instinct pushed Charlotte to check her own Twitter account, which Thorntree's IT department had created after her broadcast debut. She scrolled through the morning's tweets. There were bits responding to the Vietnamese trafficking story, updates on human trafficking stats, reasons for outrage, and calls to action, all lifting her out of the doldrums until she ran into one that stopped her: *7 days and counting!* The Twitter handle belonged to *@NotKidding*. There were quite a few retweets and responses along the lines of: *7 days to what? Good luck, Bad luck?, Who's Not Kidding?*, and *@NotKidding about what?*

Who the hell was this and why did he, or she—?—keep confusing the deadline? She had eight days, not seven. A chill climbed up her spine, knowing this crazy person held all the cards.

When she checked the profile connected to the Twitter handle, she found nothing but an unidentifiable silhouette of a man. One more thing to report about her blackmailer. But to whom? Based on "Ann's" story, Charlotte knew as long as the image hadn't been posted on the Internet no cybercrime had been committed and doubted the police could or would help.

She felt the world closing in on her; first the images and threatening note, then an email, and now social media taunting and harassing her. She checked the time. Philip had mentioned a detective friend on Saturday over dinner and suggested she give him a call. She felt almost certain Naomi was behind the twitter handle *@NotKidding* messages. But doubted her ability to create her own Twitter account. Could it be someone else entirely? Evan? Zander? Who?

Chapter 32

CHARLOTTE WROTE: *REVENGE PORN, AS defined by UK law, is "the non-consensual sharing of private sexual materials with the intent to cause harm or distress."* Charlotte's blackmailer certainly intended to cause her harm unless she obeyed the demands of the note. And it definitely caused her distress. But they had not shared the images. Not yet.

She wondered if the police had become any more sophisticated since the "Ann" story. She continued to write: *According to the Revenge Porn hotline, statistics show that one in ten people in Great Britain have been victims of this cybercrime. Of this number, 70% are women.* No surprise there, Charlotte thought.

Such crime leads to cyberstalking and harassment. Not surprisingly, there is a psychological toll. All too many revenge porn victims consider suicide. According to the End Revenge Porn campaign, that number is at about 51% for US victims.

Further searches produced an even more disturbing piece on BBC News, written by Monika Plaha: "Inside the secret world of trading nudes."

Charlotte was shocked by what she read. The social media platform Reddit apparently allowed the sharing of women's intimate photos and videos, including personal details, without their consent. As a result, they got blackmailed by strangers who remained anonymous. When she reviewed the site, which Charlotte was reluctant to do, Plaha said it contained hundreds and thousands of photographs and wrote, "A seemingly endless stream of naked or partially dressed women. Underneath, men were posting vicious commentary about the women, including rape threats."

How to make this stop, Charlotte wondered. Now she worried that her own photos would enter this maelstrom of traded images along with threats to her safety. She couldn't understand why Reddit was doing so little to stop this vicious treatment of women. Seemed like another facet of human trafficking, about which she wanted to consult with Regina. Lower in the article the author stated, "It seemed like a new evolution of so-called revenge porn, where private sexual material is published online without consent, often by embittered ex-partners."

There was no surfeit of articles. Next a piece in the *New York Times* drew her attention. It had happened in October, when a Democratic congresswoman from California resigned from office because nude photos of her had been posted on "Red State," a conservative website, and traced back to staffers of the Republican congressman she'd beaten.

In her resignation speech, as reported in the *New York Times*, Representative Katie Hill said she would continue fighting "this type of exploitation that so many women are victims to" and added that she was leaving because of "a misogynistic culture that gleefully consumed my naked pictures, capitalized on my sexuality and enabled my abusive ex to continue that abuse, this time with the entire country watching."

So unfair, Charlotte thought. The double standard applied to men and women in the same position seemed to be the article's focus. Numerous men, including President Trump, had had affairs or accusations of affairs, and yet remained in office, the *Times* article said. But Katie Hill was harassed out of office.

Charlotte knew that when Shelby read her piece, she'd undoubtedly want her to interview Katie Hill and get the "details," which meant as much dirt as possible. Shelby always referred to *dirt* as "details."

Charlotte summarized the *BBC* and *New York Times* pieces, added them to the Ann/John story, and with a few final flourishes sent it to Shelby, identifying it as a draft.

Charlotte's telephone alarm clanged, jolting her. She glanced around the newsroom as she tapped Philip's number on her phone and listened. The raised television monitors were set to BBC News, CNN, a local TV news channel, and, of course, whatever was airing on TE!. She got up and left her desk just as Philip answered.

"Charlotte," he said, "how are you?" He seemed a good complement to Celia, she thought with a smile.

"I'll get right to the point," he said. "My mate, John Smith—don't laugh, that's his real name—works independently these days, and he agrees that it probably won't get you anywhere to contact the police, but he'd be happy to track the IP address of that email."

"Thank you, I'd love that. And, of course, I'm happy to pay for his time. Maybe I should meet with him to discuss the situation in more detail?" She paused, wondering if Celia had told Philip about the nude photos, then added, "There might be some other things he can do for me. What do you think?"

"Great, I'll pass that along. Can I give him your number?"

"Of course."

"He wants you to have his contact info so you can forward that threatening email…and he can try to crack the code, so to speak."

"I can't tell you how much I appreciate this. Thank you."

"You're most welcome. I'll cross my fingers that it all gets sorted; I mean it would be awful if you had to return to New York."

"Agreed."

She ended the call, and almost instantly received a text with John's information. She opened her Gmail account and entered his email. Another few seconds and she sent John the offending email, a photo image of the original threatening note, and a reference to the tweet and Twitter handle *@NotKidding* with a brief note about getting together and charging for his time.

Times like this she appreciated technology, the very same technology that routinely destroyed people's lives.

Chapter 33

IN HER EFFORT TO KEEP her job, Charlotte placed calls to Regina and her police contacts for an update on the Vietnamese trafficking case.

As a result, she discovered several good options for the story.

First, according to Regina, she might want to look more closely at migrant smuggling gangs. Next, sadly, ten minors had been discovered among the thirty-nine dead, two of them fifteen-year-old boys, and one a teenager who'd escaped from an migrant asylum center in the Netherlands.

And, lastly, from one of her police sources, four more people, including a twenty-three-year-old man from Northern Ireland had been arrested.

She typed quickly and sent the latest news and story possibilities to Bradford.

Moments later her desk phone rang. She felt sure it would be Bradford. When she picked up, she heard Jason's voice. "Mr. Bradford wants you to see if you can get any of the men who've been arrested to talk to you, and to get an interview with home secretary, Priti Patel."

"All right, I'll see what I can rustle up," she said.

"As in the cowboy films?"

"Exactly," she said.

"Stay in touch. He'll want to see you tomorrow."

"Uh…okay," she said and hung up, wondering what excuse she could find to avoid him.

Instead of sending an email, Charlotte got up from her desk, took the elevator to the eleventh floor and knocked on Shelby's door.

Shelby stared at her with dark-eyed surprise. For an instant, her look seemed to carry a welcoming spark. As if she'd just relieved her from a more loathsome task than speaking with none other than Charlotte Cooper.

"What are you smiling about?" Shelby said, crossing her leg and bouncing her foot hidden inside a skinny Jimmy Choo boot. "You look like the Cheshire cat. You didn't come here to gloat, did you?"

"No. Actually I came to ask your advice."

"Well, that's a new one," Shelby said. "What is it?"

"It's about Mr. Bradford."

"Nelson?" Shelby said. Charlotte nodded. "Sit down," Shelby barked, "you make me nervous standing there like that."

Charlotte had never, not once, been asked to sit down in Shelby's office. This office, in contrast to her other one, featured two chairs facing her desk. Charlotte sat down.

"All right, what's up? You want some coffee? I can have *that girl* out there get you one."

Charlotte tried not to wince at Shelby's remark. "No, I'm all right. I'll make it quick. I know you're busy."

"Not busy enough. By the way, I love that piece you wrote. Can't believe you hammered it out so fast."

"Thanks. Glad you liked it."

"See, I knew you were a print reporter at heart."

"You might be right."

"Oh?"

"I like television reporting, partly because I think more people rely on broadcast than print these days, which gives me better reach." She tried to assess her former boss's reaction, but Shelby stared at her, poker-faced. "But I also like print. That's true. The problem is I'm uncomfortable around Bradford."

Shelby frowned. "Uncomfortable how?"

Charlotte tried to describe his overly friendly behavior, his repeated invitations to take her out for a drink and sit close to him in his office, and, finally, his rude email, which she'd brought and handed to Shelby.

Shelby glanced at it and then back at Charlotte. "Look, I told you I've heard rumors about him, but this, well, it's nothing. You might as well toss it in a wastepaper basket." Which Shelby did. "Men coming on to women in the news business is as old as the hills and you need to learn how to handle them."

"But you said…haven't you been reading the stories about men like Roger Ailes, the NBC execs, Matt Lauer? They're all being fired. You have heard of the 'me too' movement?" Charlotte said, incredulous.

Shelby ignored her question. "Until Nelson forces you to have oral sex, or attempts to rape you, well, I'm not sure you have a case, my young friend."

Charlotte gaped at her. "All right, but can you at least tell me how to handle him? He knows he has the upper hand because if I don't please him there's ten more women lined up to take my place."

Shelby's eyes bore into Charlotte's. "Okay, here's the secret." She paused to get Charlotte's full attention. "You string him along. Have a drink with him. Make a name for yourself, and then when you can, jump ship to another news outlet. Or come back to print. I promise not to flirt with you!" she said wearing a silly smile.

"Okay, got it," Charlotte said, thinking how truly unhelpful her advice was. "By the way, have you heard from Alex Rusikov lately?"

"No." She seemed to be thinking, then added, "I think he might be in Paris. Why?"

"Oh, I just wondered. You were friends with his father, right?"

"I guess you could call us friends. Mostly, I didn't want to get on his wrong side."

Charlotte tilted her head. "Meaning?"

"It means he has a lot of connections and they're not all the kind you want to cross. He's of Russian heritage, you know." As if that should explain everything.

"You're not referring to the Russian mafia, are you?"

"Who knows?" she said, "but why not? Some shadiness in his past. Don't ask. I have no details."

Charlotte got up. Paused, trying to think how to end this encounter.

"Well, thanks for the advice."

"Thanks for nothin'," Shelby said with a thick New York accent Charlotte had never heard. She gave Charlotte a lengthy stare before adding, "Listen, if Nelson really misbehaves, I mean if he's a real bastard, let me know. I have connections upstairs," she said, by which Charlotte figured she meant Nigel.

In an Asian-style thank you, Charlotte put her hands together and bowed. "By the way, I might have to go to New York for a week to deal with some family business."

"What family business?" Shelby asked, just as Charlotte had imagined.

She had a ready response. "My aunt and uncle. Their only daughter, my cousin, died a while ago, so they rely on me for help. My aunt's not doing well," Charlotte lied, hoping that wasn't true.

Shelby gave her a disbelieving look. "You know you can't go running off to tend to your aunt and uncle every time they have a problem. Don't they know you're working in London?"

Charlotte felt as if Shelby was reading her mind. *No,* she wanted to say, *they don't know I'm in London, and sadly, if they did, they wouldn't care.* "Sure, but I really need to go. So, can I take a week? After all, it's almost Christmas."

Shelby took in a deep breath. "Well, all right, but you just got here. You'd better make other arrangements in the future."

Charlotte studied Shelby for a moment. "You know that both of my parents died, right? My aunt and uncle are my only family. I probably shouldn't have moved to London."

Shelby looked stricken. "Oh, Charlotte, I'm sorry. How heartless of me. But why haven't you ever told me?"

"I don't like to talk about it."

"You could have told *me*," Shelby insisted.

Doubtful, Charlotte thought.

"Anyway, you have that wonderful artist boyfriend. You can't leave him, can you?"

She shook her head. "No, I'll be back." She managed a smile. "Any chance you'd contact Bradford for me and explain all this?" she said, almost whispering.

"Sure. When are you going?"

"Before Christmas, I think, but I'll keep you posted."

Shelby was leafing through her daily calendar, one of the few people Charlotte knew who still kept one.

"Christmas is a good time," Shelby said. "Can you finish that story for me first?"

"Definitely. Thanks, Shelby. I owe you."

"You do and I won't forget."

"I didn't think you would," Charlotte said with a grateful smile. She was on her way out when she stopped. "I could do a little research on how America's the number one consumer of sex…in the world. Did you know that tons of kids are being sold as sex slaves? American kids. Kids in foster care, homeless kids, and, of course, undocumented kids. It's shameful."

"Pretty awful. I'm glad you feel so passionate about it. I'll make a good writer out of you yet. Sure, sniff around. Get some leads." She looked out her window, appearing lost in thought. "That's what I'll tell Bradford. You're working on a story for me. An exposé. Sex sells. So does scandal. Keep up the good work, Cooper!"

"Really? Thank you! When you next see Mr. Thorntree, would you please tell him how much I love working here?"

"I'm seeing him tonight." Her lips drew into a lopsided smile.

As Charlotte rode the elevator down to her floor, she couldn't help thinking the bit about Bradford, protecting her from him was probably the kindest thing Shelby had ever done for her.

Charlotte stepped off at St Pancras station, where Rafe had asked to meet her. She'd barely exited the Tube train when Rafe put his arm around her shoulder. "There's something I want you to see," he said. "But first, let's go outside before it's completely dark."

Her previous time here, for her trip to Paris, she'd paid little attention to her surroundings and afterward she'd met Celia, her focus entirely on what had transpired with Zander. Now she saw the station with different eyes, through Rafe's expansive artistic lens.

"Look at the color of the sky," he said, once they'd stepped outside.

A pale rim lined the horizon, while overhead the heavens had turned a deep shade of blue, like a Maxfield Parrish painting. Then he directed her gaze to the elaborate elegance and antiquity of the massive structure that made up St Pancras. "It dates back to 1865," he explained, "which is when they first built the hotel, and the station became a railroad hub."

"If sculpture doesn't work out for you, I think you'd make boatloads of money as a tour guide," she said, giving him a mocking look. "You'll have women swarming back for second and third visits." Despite her teasing, the building's magnificence captivated her. She used her phone to take photos. "It looks slightly Moorish, doesn't it, with all the arches and columns and mixed colors of brick?"

"Very observant, Ms. Cooper. You get an A+!" he said, following her gaze. She batted his arm. He reached for her, pulling her to his side. "The real reason I brought you here, though, is something else. Come."

He grasped her hand and led her back inside, through the high-ceilinged lobby of the Renaissance London Hotel and several dining areas, exposed brick throughout that echoed the exterior. At once he slowed his pace. "Okay, now close your eyes and I'll guide you."

She walked slowly but trusted him to keep her from stumbling or falling. Once they came to a halt, he said, "Now, tilt your head up and then open your eyes." She did as he asked and when she opened her eyes, she gasped at the sight. A bronze statue of a man and a woman rose several stories high, arms wrapped around one another in an eternal embrace.

"Magnificent," Charlotte said.

"It's Paul Day's," Rafe explained, his eyes raking the colossal figures from head to toe. "Everyone refers to it as 'The Lovers,' for obvious reasons, but officially it's 'The Meeting Place.'" He squeezed her hand. "Listen. If anything ever happens and we get separated, this is where we'll meet, okay?" he said in a solemn tone.

His words felt ominous. Tears clouded her eyes as she nodded yes. He took her in his arms and kissed her, the two of them a life-size replica of the giant statue.

Chapter 34

Wednesday, December 18, 2019 (6 days)

ALTHOUGH SHE SAT AT HER desk inside the newsroom, she left Jason a voicemail saying she couldn't meet with Bradford because she was out pursuing a lead. "I'll call when I return." Her stall tactic would end soon enough; in the meantime, she perused the rest of her emails until she saw John Smith's. *I checked carefully but the emails are coming from a dead-end server. There's no IP address like the one they're using.*

Someone appears to be very clever, Charlotte thought. Smith added, *I have some other ways of tracing these. But maybe I should find out what this woman (Naomi?) is up to…I can spend a day following her if you'd like. Reduced friend rate.*

Charlotte considered his offer. Would it come at a price she could afford and still have money to travel to New York, a trip that seemed inevitable? And, what if she lost her job? She didn't have much of a cushion. Could she rely on Rafe? Surely Celia would put her up if all else failed. Should she or shouldn't she hire John?

Out of the corner of her eye, Charlotte watched a pair of hands place a vase filled with yellow roses on her desk. Several heads turned to look. About to say thank you, she only saw the backside of one of the mail delivery people weaving between desks.

She called out anyway, "Thanks."

Grinning, Ian said, "Well, well, well. Who's the lucky fellow?"

With a coy look, Charlotte replied, "How do you know it's not a woman!?"

Ian's pale skin turned crimson.

"Just kidding," she said.

"It's true though," he said.

"Actually, I don't know who it's from." She reached for the card and opened it, imagining Rafe had sent them, though he didn't really seem the type to send roses. Too boring. *Call me*, the note said. She frowned.

"What's wrong?" Ian asked.

She handed him the card. He stared at it with puzzlement. "You really don't know?"

"Would you?"

"Now that's not fair. I'm sure you have many suitors. Unlike me."

She smiled at his choice of words. "How nice to think I have many. No, I just have one and we're practically living together. An artist," she said.

"Anyone famous?"

"*I* think so; he's got a piece at Tate Modern," she said. "Rafe Jackson."

"I'm impressed," Ian remarked.

Her desk phone rang. She thought twice about answering then picked up. If it was Jason, she could always say she just got back.

"You need to come to my office," a woman's voice shouted into her ear. "Pronto!"

Pronto? Charlotte thought. She hadn't heard that in a while. "Okay, coming."

The entire ride up the elevator, Charlotte worried that something awful had happened. But what? She knocked on Shelby's office door.

"Door's open, for God's sakes," Shelby called. She had an odd look on her face when Charlotte walked in.

"This," Shelby said, waving a piece of paper in the air, "what the hell is this?"

Even from her distance, Charlotte could see one of the damaging images dangling in Shelby's hand. She reached for it. It wasn't the worst one, but not the most innocent either. Not that she looked innocent in any of them.

Resigned, Charlotte said, "It's why I need to go to New York."

"So that family business stuff was a lie?"

"Not exactly. But it wasn't the whole truth either. I'm sorry," Charlotte said. "Was there a note?"

"Of course. How else would I have known why I'd gotten a nude shot of you?" She lifted the sheet of paper from her desk and thrust it at Charlotte.

She read the typed note: *More where this came from. Fire Charlotte B. Cooper or these will go online with TE! footage of her. Hot social media story, huh?*

Charlotte slumped into one of the chairs opposite Shelby. "Oh, god, I'm so sorry."

"Care to tell me what this is about?"

Charlotte remained silent, thinking what to tell her. Her stomach churning, she gave her an outline of the story, as much of the truth as possible, and began with Abbie's death, then her arrest, and Zander's father paying for a lawyer. She trod carefully around the awful night of the images and focused instead on trying to resurrect her life with the help of her father, eventually, after her failed blog, landing the job with Shelby. She concluded with the arrival of the images and the threatening note.

"I thought maybe you were one of those sex slaves you told me about the other day," Shelby said, her mouth curved into the faintest hint of a smile.

"No, at least that would be an excuse." She couldn't believe Shelby wasn't yelling. "You're not mad? Or disgusted?" Charlotte added.

"Why should I be mad? It's your life you screwed up, not mine."

"No, but I am endangering the reputation of Thorntree Entertainment," Charlotte said.

"Not if we fire you today. Or tomorrow. If the minute we found out about this," she picked up the image and looked at it again, "and we sent you packing. Right?"

The lump in Charlotte's throat made it hard to speak. "I guess that's what you have to do. So, basically, I've lost my job?"

Shelby stared off into the mid-space of her office, slightly less meticulous than the one in New York. "I don't like people telling me what to do, but I don't have much choice. So, let's say as of tomorrow you stop coming in. Finish what you're doing. Okay?"

Charlotte nodded. She felt a vast empty space in her mind. No more thinking about the Vietnamese, about Ann and revenge porn, or anything else that got her through the day, just the tricky puzzle of how to extricate herself from this mess.

"What's your plan?"

"I need to go to New York to find out who's behind this." She didn't say it, but she still hoped to avoid the trip. If only Rafe could get Naomi to talk. Her gut told her the woman had everything, or a great deal, to do with the photos and the threat. "What if I can fix all this in the next couple of weeks?"

"Let's see what happens."

"What about Bradford?"

"What about him?"

"We have to tell him…something…about all this?"

"We?" Shelby gave Charlotte an annoyed look. "No, it's your problem, so you ought to."

"Oh, Shelby, what will I say? It's so embarrassing."

"I don't know, but you have to stop going on-air, so you'll need to tell him something."

"I think he's expecting another story from me. Can I just tell him I'm doing some work for you and need a week or so off?"

"I suppose. When are you leaving?"

"By the weekend. I need a couple of days to clear out my apartment."

"Really? That sounds pretty permanent."

"Maybe it is, but I hope not," she said, her voice dropping to a whisper. She was on the verge of tears, closed her eyes and got up. "I'd better go." As she ran from the room she nearly slammed into Nelson Bradford, but managed to avoid him and mutter, "Sorry."

He turned and stared at her. "You okay?"

Her gaze lowered, she nodded but kept going. She prayed Shelby wouldn't show him the photo.

Chapter 35

SHAKEN, SHE ENTERED THE NEWSROOM, possibly for the last time, when her mobile released the Night Owl ringtone. She'd recently set that sound for one person. She fumbled for the phone in her purse, found it and hesitated a moment before answering, her stomach twisting into knots about what to say and wishing he hadn't called.

She juggled her coffee into the other hand then tapped "accept."

"Hello?" she said, pretending not to know the caller's identity.

"Charlotte," Zander said, "I haven't heard from you. Everything okay?"

"What do you mean? Was I supposed to call?" Instead of continuing to her desk, she turned around and retraced her steps out of the newsroom.

"Don't tell me you didn't know the roses were from me?"

She tried to laugh lightly. "Oh, they were? I had no idea. Sorry!"

"Who else sends you yellow roses?"

"Have you sent me yellow roses before?" she said, her brow furrowed, attempting to recall such an occasion.

"Of course, I have. You don't remember?"

Afraid of saying the wrong thing, she went ahead and thanked him. "They're beautiful. But since you wanted me to call, I'm assuming there's a reason?"

"Don't you want to know what yellow stands for?" he asked.

"Sunshine? Happiness?"

"Well, I suppose. But something else. Yellow roses signify friendship and loyalty."

"In that case, a double thanks. Very kind of you."

"And yes, I do have news. And it *is* good."

"Oh, tell me."

"I told you Evan might recall who came to his house that night. Well, I've reached him, and he recently saw one of the guys who thinks he knows who shot photos that night."

She wasn't sure she'd just heard him correctly. A friend of a friend *might* remember?! "That seems pretty vague, Zander."

"Have you thought about coming back?"

"Not really," she lied.

"Might be best if you did."

"And why's that?" she asked, refusing to tell him her plans.

"Because then you can confront the guy in person—I think that's the only way—and I'll help you."

"Help me?"

"You know, get him to turn over those awful images. And promise not to post copies or anything."

"But we don't even know who it is, Zander. Come on, this sounds like a wild goose chase." She wanted to bring up Naomi, but knew she couldn't, not when she'd promised Rafe.

"By the time you arrive back in New York, we will have tracked down the culprit. Positive."

"Who's we?"

"Well," he said, pausing, "I took the liberty of hiring a private eye. He's very good."

Oh, sure, she thought. Knowing Zander, he probably did have a detective on his payroll. Who else had this guy followed, she wondered. Tempted to ask, she said instead, "Thanks for doing that. What about you? Are you still in Paris?"

"I'll be home this weekend, latest on Sunday. So, you're coming? I mean you can't wait until the last second, right?"

"I'll think about it," she said.

Silence on the other end. She pulled the phone from her ear to see if the call was still active. "Zander?"

"I'm here. Someone just came in. All right, well, keep me posted," he said breezily.

"Will do," she said and stared at the phone trying to decide her next step.

Instead of texting Rafe, Charlotte called him. "Don't ask how my day is, but here's a quick summary: I got flowers from Zander—he claims to have info about who took the photos, but it sounds flimsy—then Shelby called me upstairs, sounding furious. She waved a nude photo at me and showed me a threatening note demanding she fire me. Or they'd post stuff all over social media with TE! footage. I guess it doesn't get any clearer that I need to go to New York."

"What would happen if you didn't?"

She thought before answering. "Are you prepared for that? Those images of me all over social media. For anyone to see. Probably drag you into it too." Her face contorted with dismay as she described Jennifer Lawrence's nude photo experience and the BBC's trading nudes article to Rafe.

"You were younger, who'll recognize you?"

"Rafe, you're not listening. They're ready to use TE! footage of me on social media platforms. And, of course, this devil person will add my name to the postings."

He was silent.

"What are you thinking, Rafe?"

"Murderous thoughts."

"I have one last idea," she said.

"I'm afraid to ask."

"Please call Naomi and ask her *if* or *what* she's got to do with this whole thing. I'm sure she's involved. It's my only hope."

Chapter 36

CHARLOTTE ENTERED THE EAGLE AND spotted Rafe at the bar nursing a pint. She sat down beside him. When he turned, his face appeared deeply troubled in a way she'd never seen before.

"What's going on?"

"I called her. She insisted I see her in person, but not at her apartment. We met at a café. She looked a little nervous, kept glancing about. 'What is it?' I said. She claimed someone'd been following her and she needed to make sure they weren't around."

Charlotte wondered if John Smith had followed Naomi, though she hadn't yet given him the go-ahead. Reluctant to tell Rafe about it, she said nothing.

"Then she admitted there was more to her relationship with Zander than she'd told me."

"She dated him. I knew it!" Charlotte shouted.

"Sort of. More importantly, he not only helped her modeling career in the US, but he got her the job in London a couple of years ago. When the time came, she didn't want to go back to New York. We'd already begun dating, though she didn't tell him. Even so, he got really pissed. Threatened her, saying he'd end her career as fast as it began."

Charlotte asked the bartender for an IPA then turned her attention back to Rafe. For the first time all day she felt hopeful though she didn't know why.

"She'd never truly considered herself his girlfriend," Rafe said, "but it was clear to me they'd had a sexual relationship, and his threat was as much about not losing that as anything. While she wasn't explicit, I think he backed off his threat when she agreed to continue seeing him. With *privileges*."

"In Paris, I got the impression that Zander sees himself as quite the international playboy," Charlotte said, "so I suppose he didn't take kindly to one of his models ending things. But honestly, Rafe, can you just tell me what this has to do with blackmail?"

"Patience, luv." He took a long swig of beer.

Her foot tapped the rung of the stool. "I'm all ears."

Rafe seemed hesitant, but eventually said, "Apparently, he grew furious when he learned she and I were dating. She begged him to explain, and he began ranting about me. Called me nothing but a *goddamned nigger*! 'Well, I'm a nigger too,' she told him. His response: 'How can I lose two girlfriends to that bastard! Tell me that.' And then apparently, he said, 'It's not happening.'"

"He's the bastard if Naomi's telling the truth." The "n" word repulsed her. She felt herself coiling up, ready to protect Rafe by striking out at anyone so insensitive, so brutish. She'd never experienced Zander this way and hoped that maybe Naomi had exaggerated. "I can see how he might have thought Naomi was his girlfriend, but not me," she added. "No idea what fantasyland he's living in. Just hope this story has a happy ending."

Rafe shook his head. "In another universe, maybe. Anyway, Naomi knew she owed Zander for her spot in the fashion world. Very unlikely she would have made it without him."

"Yeah, okay, so?"

"So, he asked her to help him. But before she told me more, I noticed she was again glancing out the window. That's when I got impatient. 'For heaven's sake, what does he want help with?'

"'You'll see,' she said and pulled a large envelope out of her purse."

"The photos? I knew it!" Charlotte interrupted.

"That's what I thought, but not exactly. They were shots of Naomi, in awful, degrading poses…with a white guy, a Black dude, an Asian. Touching her breasts, coming at her from behind, smiling crookedly at the camera.

Disgusting stuff." He stared off, then drank more beer. "Underneath the shots of her were yours. I wanted to rip them up. All of them." Rafe rubbed his temples. "What a twisted bastard. I was stunned that he would do such a thing to two people, ones he supposedly cares about."

"Sounds like a sick fuck alright," she said, hardly able to connect Zander with the man Rafe described.

"According to Naomi, he truly hates *me,*" Rafe went on. "'Why me?' I asked. 'He's lost two women to you,' she said, 'and the best revenge is to get even.' Aims to split you and me up. I guess he figured you haven't shown me the photos and you'll do what the note says to keep them from going live. He enlisted Naomi's help, and yes, the writing's hers. If you don't go to New York, Naomi's photos will go up too. And he'll make sure no one hires her. She told me she hated him and began crying."

"So, presumably *he* took the photos of me," Charlotte said, sipping her beer. "Or someone else did and he got hold of them. I can understand him hating you, but why ruin my reputation? Strangest revenge porn I've ever heard of."

"Naomi said that 'fucking Zander' is obsessed with you," Rafe said. "Her words not mine. Between that and hating *me,* well, he's killing two birds with one stone. He'll get even with me and maybe have a chance of winning you back."

"That's insane. Winning me back by threatening me? I don't know if I believe it. Like I said, we never even dated." *But,* she thought with distaste, *there was the date rape at his cottage.*

"You really didn't detect he was lying when you met in Paris?"

"He seemed genuine." She thought for a moment. "You don't think it makes more sense Naomi's the driver behind this?"

He scratched his cheek. "She might have more motivation, but I doubt she could pull it off on her own."

Charlotte agreed. "In that case, I *have* to go to New York. Play him and get him to fucking back off." She said *fucking* with enough vehemence that someone's head turned. Charlotte's cheeks flushed. She cast her eyes at the bottles lining the wall behind the bartender.

"Maybe, but Naomi said he'd do whatever it takes, which sounded dangerous." Rafe looked worried. "I think we should call the police. People can't get away with such shite."

"Even if he's the predator, I doubt they'd be able to do anything; he doesn't even live here," she said with a puzzled frown. "Did she say how all this started?"

"Apparently, he paid her a visit on his way to Paris. That's when he shared your pictures with her. She didn't know I'd already seen them, so I think she was hoping I'd be shocked."

"It's all shocking, quite frankly," Charlotte said, trying to imagine when he'd passed through London.

"She said Zander gave her your shots, dictated a note, then told her to put it in the mail."

"Did she tell you what the note said?"

"Yeah. She grew quite agitated when I asked what would happen if you didn't leave London. She said you *have* to go and that I have to make you go. Otherwise, your photos go up. And he'll do the same with hers."

"What a bastard," Charlotte said again. Despite all Rafe had described, a shred of doubt lingered in Charlotte's mind that Zander had masterminded this.

"Funny thing, she asked if I'd go with you, to New York, because then what would Zander have accomplished?"

"What did you tell her?" She watched his expression shift into a frustrated frown.

"I told her I wasn't sure, but that I very well might. What I really want is to meet up with this prick and—" he hesitated, "and give him a piece of my mind."

"A piece of your mind?"

"He's pushing me buttons. Inciting primitive impulses. *Kill the asshole* is more like it!" Jaw clenched, he wore a pugilistic squint. "Here's the thing, she begged me *not* to tell you Alex—Zander, whatever—is behind all this. She seemed frightened."

Charlotte twisted on the barstool to face him. "How convenient! And then you comforted her? Maybe even kissed her?"

"You know I only kiss one woman." He gave her a sidelong look. "And that's me mum!"

"Ha ha," Charlotte said and pinched his arm. "Only good news I can figure is that *maybe* Zander's the father of her child. *If* she's pregnant. Which could be a pretty big if."

"I had the same thought," Rafe said.

"So now what?"

"First, I need to order some food. I'm starving. Okay?"

They placed an order of burgers and chips, which arrived in a flash. He continued. "It's important, please don't tell Celia. And, of course, you can't let Zander know anything, so play along when you communicate with him. Can you do that?"

"I can. I think. Crap. Just not sure what the next step is, short of going back." She watched his expression shift to a crestfallen look. She took his tapered fingers in her own. "I love you," she said. "Nothing can change that. Are you having doubts?"

He gazed back at her, his eyes weary and despondent. "Not doubts. Just wishing that things could go smoothly for a change. I'm having flashbacks of the day you promised you'd come back and didn't."

"Oh, Rafe, please don't say that. You do understand what happened?"

"Yes, but that doesn't make it any better. You left and didn't come back, and now you're leaving again."

"Come with me."

"My show's in a little over a week. I've still got work to do."

"Then come as soon as you can. You've got a gallery in Manhattan. I'm sure they'd love to see you?"

He watched her push food around her plate. "Lost your appetite? Me too. So…when are you thinking of going?"

"Sometime this weekend. Maybe Sunday."

He speared one of the chips, studied the morsel before shoving it into his mouth.

Chapter 37

SHE AND RAFE WALKED ARM in arm. She waited until they were less than a block from his apartment to say, "I got one more charming email from Naomi, or Zander – however, you want to think about it. It asked what I was waiting for. *A miracle?* I guess they're right. I am."

Rafe kicked a stone in their path and sent it skittering across the pavement. "Damn them."

"My sentiments exactly. I guess I need to make a plane reservation."

"I suppose so," he said with an audible exhalation of air.

Up the flight of stairs to Rafe's apartment, they were silent, Charlotte dreading the trip back to the US and desperate to think of some way to avoid it.

Rafe unlocked the door and let Charlotte enter first.

She looked forward to their evening alone, probably one of their last. Thinking this, she dropped her bag on a nearby chair, and only then noticed a woman sitting on the leather sofa.

She gasped at the intruder, who a moment later she recognized as Naomi. Close up, she was an intimidatingly gorgeous creature. Her large eyes, outlined with kohl, appeared forlorn, though not red-rimmed from crying. Charlotte detected Naomi's curly halo of dark hair as a strategic change, a look that softened her appearance from the day she'd seen her at Pret.

Naomi stared back at Charlotte as if daring her to say something. But

Rafe beat her to it. "What are you doing here? How'd you get in? I thought you returned my key?"

"I made another," she said, obviously feeling no need to lie. Her shoulders lifted into a small shrug. Again, looking at Charlotte, she said, "I'm pregnant, you know. With Rafe's child."

Charlotte stood there, arms slack at her sides, thoughts crowding her mind, part of her considered challenging the claim. She'd wanted to meet Naomi, and yet now she only wished her to disappear. She stared and remained silent.

Rafe took a couple of steps toward the couch. "Naomi, why are you doing this?"

"I want her to know. She needs to know." Turning back to Charlotte, she added, "Our child's future is in your hands."

"And apparently my future is in yours," Charlotte retorted.

Naomi glared at Charlotte then twisted her head to throw Rafe an angry confused look. "I told you not to tell her; you promised," she shouted. "He'll kill me!"

Charlotte jumped in. "Oh, come on, Naomi, you don't mean that. Zander won't kill you. Not literally," she said, but the look of panic on Naomi's face made her wonder.

"I do mean it," Naomi said. "None of this would have happened if you'd just stayed where you belong."

"And where's that?" Charlotte asked.

"New York," she said sullenly.

She was right, of course. And, also, entirely wrong. This woman, while gorgeous, was childlike. She now understood what Rafe had once said. On the one hand, Naomi could no more be his partner for life than a girl of fourteen, but, and it was a big but, on the other hand, the alluring and sexy girl-woman exuded the need to be taken care of. Protected. How does one respond to each of those impulses?

"I'll be back in a minute," Charlotte said. "I'm going to *our* bedroom to change." Her words were innocent enough, but they were designed for maximum impact. And, just as she'd expected, Naomi's veneer of self-assurance crumbled beneath a flood of tears. Or was she truly distressed by the fact that Charlotte knew what she'd told Rafe in confidence?

Charlotte walked away, slowly enough to hear a distraught, "You love 'er, don't you?" The young woman's accent caught her attention. It sounded American—New York, maybe?—not like someone who'd come from Namibia, as Rafe had recently mentioned. Though what did a Namibian accent sound like? Confident in what he would say, she didn't bother to listen to Rafe's answer.

Charlotte changed into a comfortable top coupled with black leggings. She washed her face and hands and stared at herself in the mirror. She shook her mass of ginger hair, twisted it several times, then with a scrunchy pulled it into a bushy ponytail. She sought a simple look without pretense or ornament and hoped she could get Naomi to see her not as competition, but as a potential ally, a kind of older sister. If I can pull this off, she thought, I'll deserve an Oscar.

When she emerged from their bedroom, she found Rafe sitting beside Naomi, his arm draped over her shoulder, speaking softly. A series of emotions whipped through Charlotte's gut—surprise, jealousy, fear. At her entry, Naomi looked up, a wary expression crossing her face before her gaze shifted away. Or had it been a sly look?

Rafe dropped his arm and stood up. "I'm taking Naomi back to her apartment," he announced. "She's afraid to go home alone."

Charlotte took in a breath to steady herself. "Perhaps I should go with you?" she said. Turning to Naomi, she asked, "Is everything all right?"

"Nothin's all right," Naomi said wearily. "Because you messed everything up." She looked at Charlotte through hooded eyes.

Charlotte waited for Rafe to speak up, but he remained mute and appeared conflicted, or confused, she didn't know which. Was Russ's not-so-distant betrayal coloring her thoughts? She didn't like the off-kilter way this made her feel. If only she could talk to Celia. She'd find some way to delight in the drama. What would Celia suggest in this situation?

"Rafe, could I have a private moment with you?" she said, already moving toward their bedroom. Without turning, she felt Rafe following her.

When he entered, he fidgeted with his car key. She extended her hand to him. After stuffing the key in his pocket, he took her hand and looked at her expectantly. "If you want to take her back alone, it's fine. I was trying to be helpful. There might be less drama if we both go?"

"I see what you mean. But, of course, Naomi doesn't want that."

"Yes, of course."

"She really meant that; she's afraid of Zander," he said.

"She said that before. But how can he hurt her if he's not even in London?" Charlotte asked.

"He's threatened her, saying if she didn't do what he said he'd have someone disfigure her face. You know, so she can never work as a model again."

The idea conjured various images in Charlotte's mind. "Oh, God, I don't know if he's capable of something so dreadful. But if she's telling the truth, he's a monster."

She waited for Rafe to agree.

Instead, he grabbed hold of her and kissed her. Hard. And held her close. "I love you, Charlotte. No matter what happens."

No matter what happens? she thought. She kissed the stubble of his beard, ran her hand over the rough contour of his dreads, then stepped back. "Would you mind terribly if I spoke with her? Alone? For a minute?"

He shrugged. "Okay." He seemed on the verge of adding something but checked himself.

She returned to the main room and saw Naomi gathering her purse and a coat. Her long legs were wrapped in skin-tight leather pants and black suede, high-heeled boots. She stood nearly six feet tall, at least half a head taller than Charlotte, who drew as close to Naomi as possible. A space of two feet between them seemed necessary. "I wonder, if for just a moment, we could speak to each other, like friends? I don't mean you harm, you know that, right?"

Naomi looked at her, working hard to appear bored, not saying anything.

"There are two men who've had an influence on both of our lives, and in some way I think that binds us. Do you agree?"

Naomi gave her an almost imperceptible shrug.

Charlotte continued. "One good man and one not so good. Yes?"

A nod, with a quizzical expression on her face, probably wondering where this was going.

"One's Rafe and the other's Zander, right?" Charlotte said.

"Yeah, so what?" Naomi said.

"Well, I think as two women, we ought to support each other, not fight like cats. And I want to know how I can help you?"

Naomi's eyes took on a fiery glint. "Why do you even ask? You know how. Leave! I want you to leave London! Leave Rafe!" she shouted. "Because I love him. Because I'm going to have his child, and I won't be able to work. Not for a few months. Because I'll be pregnant, with a belly." In her high heels, she towered over Charlotte, but her eyes bounced around the room. "I'll need money…" she said, and with a whimper added, "I need him, you don't."

"But what if," Charlotte paused and said softly, "what if Rafe loves *me*?"

"He doesn't!" she cried. "You stupid bitch! He just thinks so. If you hadn't come along, do you think we would have broken up? Of course not!"

"He broke up with you before I came along," Charlotte insisted.

Naomi swayed slightly. "Shut up, okay? We're not friends. Never will be!"

Charlotte felt the energy in the room shift. Naomi's eyes roamed past her shoulder. Rafe had entered. "Let's get you back to your apartment," he said. Two seconds later, they left.

Charlotte itched to call Celia, but she'd promised Rafe not to tell her the latest details. Instead, she picked up a Jo Nesbo thriller as she waited for Rafe's return. Although her eyes took in the words, her mind traveled elsewhere. How long would it take to drive to Naomi's and back— half an hour? With traffic, maybe an hour. The minutes ticked by with insane slowness.

Half an hour later, she got up and paced the apartment, then stopped at the large window where a few plants she'd bought awaited her care; she gazed into the black night. How long before she'd arrived in London had he broken up with Naomi? She recalled those constant texts. Had Rafe told the truth?

Taking three long steps back through the living room, she reached the kitchen, suddenly aware of the constraints of his flat. Another reason to move to a larger place. She picked up the paper, but that was no good. Gossipy headlines. Endless stories on Brexit. Trump. Royal family squabbles. Nothing but bad news, some of it exaggerated to attract readers. She hadn't yet gotten used to British tabloids.

She picked up the remote to turn on the TV. Briefly watched a banal talk show, then turned it off at the commercial. She thought of Celia, again considered calling, but didn't want to interrupt her evening. It was Philip's last night before a trip to Istanbul. Which made her think of Russ, ever so briefly, and plagued her with thoughts of how he'd cheated on her.

At length, she wandered into Rafe's studio. Admired his work. As she passed, she grazed the sculptures with her fingertips, thinking of all that had gone into their creation. She lingered by a fallen woman cloaked head-to-toe in a burqa, rocks strewn around her. Could she be a Syrian woman lying in the rubble of Aleppo? Or one who'd been stoned to death, the victim of an honor killing? Or struggling to survive a war? In Yemen, perhaps. Charlotte's heart pined for struggling widows and mourning mothers.

With everything she'd been reading about revenge porn and sexual exploitation, she felt compassion for women the world over. How long until we're safe from predators, she thought, her mind shifting to Zander. Was he really threatening Naomi? Why would she make that up?

She wandered over to a shelf stacked with roughly hewn missiles. She touched them. The cold penetrated her fingers. The words he'd used earlier—*no matter what happens*—seeped into her thoughts. Had they been prophetic? Something he feared? Why hadn't she asked what he meant? The phrase had caught her off-guard. She glanced at the time on her phone— at least forty minutes had passed. Tempted to call him, but not wanting to interrupt his dealings with Naomi, she decided to wait a little longer.

Please come home safely, she prayed.

Another very long half hour passed before Rafe walked through the door, appearing disheveled and exhausted. Eyes bloodshot. A deep frown was etched into his forehead, and his mouth was screwed up like he'd tasted something bitter. His gaze swept the room but stopped a short distance before landing on her face. Instead, he glanced over her shoulder at the window.

"What the hell happened?" Charlotte cried.

His mouth opened, but nothing came out. His breath seemed labored, and his eyes still refused to meet hers. They dropped to the floor where they remained as if studying the scrap of carpet near her feet. "What is it, Rafe? For God's sakes, tell me."

At last he spoke, though the effort seemed to cost him. "It's … it's time to face facts, Charlotte," he said, each word emerging with ponderous slowness, like a worm trying to wriggle out of the hardened earth. "This… it's not working." His eyes searched the room; his voice tapered off, nearly inaudible. "It's a mess," he whispered.

A mess? This can't work? What the hell? "Do you mean us? Are you talking about *us*?" She took a step forward, wanting to run to him, shake him, but he stood there, a distant look on his face like one of his statues.

"That's it?" she said, not knowing what else to say, willing herself not to cry. She could take anything, anything but him leaving her, and that's what she thought he was trying to say.

"Charlotte, I shouldn't be telling you this," he said, hesitating as if trying to make up his mind. He shook his head. "I can't. I shouldn't."

"Rafe, please!"

His eyes scanned the room as if the walls had ears. One of his hands clenched into a fist. He opened and closed it. "I'll tell you what I can, but then you've got to go. There were two of them…at her apartment; they threatened us, Charlotte. They said they'd do things so Naomi and I could never work again." He shook his head. "They weren't kidding. One of the guys held a knife to her cheek and drew blood. The other one told me he'd smash my hands to a bloody pulp." Rafe raised his left hand so she could see his bloody pinky. "Used a hammer. The guy did. Taste of what's to come if I don't get you to leave."

"Oh, God, Rafe. You need a bandage. We have to call the police."

"No!" he shouted. "They'll harm Naomi. I think one of them's outside, waiting for you to leave. Hurry up. Grab your stuff; make it look like you're devastated."

"That won't be hard," she said, feeling herself choke up.

He ran his hands over his face. "Act like I just kicked you out."

"Oh, Rafe, that's exactly what you're doing, isn't it? Do I have to go?"

"Yes!" he shouted at her. "You need to go!"

She wondered if he was raising his voice for the benefit of whoever lurked outside. "Okay, but how can I reach you?"

"I don't know. I can't think. They're monitoring my phone. Can they do that? This is fucking bloody hell awful! God, Charlotte." He clutched his head. "How can I let you go?!"

The last thing she wanted was to leave him, but moments later she was shoving her clothes into a suitcase. She wiped tears away. "I'm afraid to go to my apartment. Where should I go?" *Oh, fuck,* she thought, *I did this, it's my fault, why am I asking him?*

"I don't know. A hotel? Call an Uber but be careful; make sure you're safe. I'll reach you tomorrow. At work, maybe. Best not to call me."

She fought for control. "Work?" She didn't have a job anymore as far as she knew. "I love you, Rafe."

He nodded. As she stumbled out the door she glanced over her shoulder and saw his helpless forlorn look.

Before she exited Rafe's building, she contacted an Uber. She remained inside until the car arrived. Closing the short distance between herself and the Uber, she kept her eyes trained on the backdoor of the car, afraid to look around for fear of alerting anyone who might be watching, just as Rafe had revealed.

Halfway to her apartment she asked the Uber driver to take her to a hotel. She looked up hotels near Celia's apartment and found one. She'd feel safer there. And going to a hotel wouldn't appear suspicious if someone was watching her. She shifted slightly to glance out the rear window but saw no evidence of a vehicle following them.

Once safely inside the hotel room, Charlotte broke into tears, then fell onto the bed and sobbed, all the while feeling that she deserved exactly this. How could I have thought not going to jail was a victory? It's a simple matter of chickens coming home to roost, she thought. A phrase she'd heard both her mother and father use. *Consequences, Charlotte.*

"But how do I fix it?" she asked aloud. "I can't turn back the clock. I can't bring Abbie back! I just wish I'd never met Zander. I wish Abbie hadn't liked him. If we hadn't gone to that party…oh, fuck!"

And now the one person she wanted to spend her life with seemed beyond reach. She needed to protect him at all cost. And Naomi too. "If this is your doing, Zander, I'm going to get you," she said.

In the next moment, pacing the perimeter of the room, she cried, "I wish you were dead!!"

Chapter 38

Friday, December 20, 2019 (4 days)

IN HER HOTEL ROOM, SHE used make-up to cover her splotchy tear-stained face, ironed and dressed in the best outfit she could find in her suitcase, then, armed with faux courage, she entered Thorntree Entertainment!'s soaring atrium lobby. She took in her surroundings, knowing this would be her last time here.

At her desk, she pretended to concentrate on work, hoping to avoid Ian and Diana for fear of breaking into tears. She wrote a quick email to Zander, letting him know she'd decided to head back to New York on the weekend and would keep him posted on her exact flight.

"Great news," he shot back, almost as if he'd been waiting to hear from her.

She responded, "Have you heard anything more about who was at Evan's that night?"

"Still working on it, but don't worry. We've got this!"

Really? Charlotte thought.

As she composed an email to Bradford, she couldn't help wondering if Shelby had shown him the nude photograph. She told him that she would pass all her information and contacts for the Vietnam trafficking story to Ian and Diana, but an emergency in New York required her presence there. "I'll be digging into the Ghislaine Maxwell story (her role in procuring minors for

Epstein) for Shelby." She ended the note with: "Hoping to be back in a week or so. And hope you can give me the time off?"

She copied Shelby.

It wasn't long before she received a terse note from Bradford, saying that as far as he was concerned her on-air reporting had just ended. What she did for anyone else was their business.

Charlotte's fingers shook as she forwarded the note to Shelby and wrote: *Thanks for everything. I'll be in touch.*

Shelby wrote back and copied Bradford: *Do let me know what you find out. About Ghislaine! Juicy story.*

Classic Shelby, Charlotte thought. About to leave, her desk phone rang.

"I wish there was something I could do, Charlotte. I've grown used to having you around." It was Shelby.

"Even after everything I've told you?"

"Let's say I've grown fond of you. You're not so different from other people. We all make mistakes; that doesn't make us bad, unless we don't care that we've hurt others."

Charlotte had never heard Shelby speak this way and wondered about this new version. She also heard her father's words in Shelby's statement, and even Rafe's. Though they didn't erase her current predicament, they helped buoy her.

She barely heard Shelby's good-bye as she lowered the phone into the receiver.

Charlotte was dying to call Celia but knew she shouldn't for fear of telling her everything. She needed a plan that wouldn't endanger her friend.

She tapped in John Smith's number and waited for him to answer, but when he didn't, she left a voicemail. She gathered a few personal belongings and waved good-bye to Ian and Diana. No way she could speak to them just now. Later she'd send them emails.

With leaden steps and a final tear-filled gaze, she managed to walk through the several doors that led out into the street, doubting she would ever enter or exit those doors again.

Walking to her apartment, Charlotte had the uneasy feeling she was being followed, but whenever she glanced around, she detected no one suspicious. Paranoid thoughts swarmed through her mind, not unexpectedly after what Rafe had described the previous night.

Not for the first time she wondered again if she should have gone straight to the police. Based on all she'd read, though, she imagined they'd bungle it and cause more harm than good. Especially if Zander was as ruthless as it seemed. Trying to deal with him herself still seemed like the best plan. She convinced herself he wouldn't hurt her; why would he if he so desperately wanted her? Nevertheless, unease stuck with her like an unwanted friend.

Inside her apartment, Charlotte picked up a plate from beside the sink, and with great force threw it on the floor, shattering it, then spent several minutes cleaning up the mess through teary eyes.

She made a plane reservation for Saturday, not Sunday, then sent her aunt and uncle an email saying that she'd been in London for the past few weeks working as an on-air reporter but was coming home briefly and would like to see them. She hoped they might get together.

She wanted to say, *I hope you can forgive me*, or *I hope we can reconcile*, but left the email as she'd written it.

She then sent an email to the blackmailer, saying she'd given up and was returning to New York on the weekend. *Please confirm that the images will NOT go up since I'm complying with your demand,* Charlotte wrote.

Two texts from Celia she ignored, though finally she sent a response saying she was on a deadline and would call later.

That she'd heard nothing from Rafe worried her and made her alternately nauseous and weepy. He said he'd get in touch. *He will,* she told herself. Though she also imagined it might be too fraught with danger. Or he'd given up on her.

She took great care packing her suitcase, taking only what she needed. The rest she'd put in storage. Would she be back for it? She hoped so, but one could never know the future. In her short life, she'd learned that much.

The estate agent who handled her apartment responded with British politeness. "You'll still be responsible for the remainder of the month's rent," he said.

"Of course," she replied.

She pulled the Eiffel Tower snow globe from its perch on a bookshelf and shook it. Nostalgic family memories stole over her. *Be strong, Charlotte,* she told herself. She prayed that her parents would watch over her, then in the next breath told herself such thoughts were fairy tales, childish wishes. She took in a deep breath and changed her mind about not contacting Celia. She had to say good-bye to her friend. She wrote:

Sorry I've been out of touch. Crazy events. Can you meet me at the café near Primrose Hill Books? Meantime: Rafe and Naomi in danger. Please say nothing to Phil. Please.

Charlotte stared at what she'd written and knew not to send it. She turned back to her boxes and continued packing.

When the urge to connect with Celia came over her again, she distracted herself by checking the news. The increasing unrest in Venezuela, the food lines, the growing poverty in that nation could only mean its children and women would be at increased risk for being trafficked. The warring factions in Yemen, the growing hunger, meant innocent children would be caught in the crossfire. She read on: Gang warfare in Honduras, gender-based violence in El Salvador, and in Nicaragua President Daniel Ortega and his cronies had turned out to be much like Somoza, the dictator the Sandinistas had deposed nearly forty years earlier. How often did history repeat itself? So much corruption, so little concern for human rights, the endless disparity between rich and poor. Far too many female and child victims.

Working up a little anger helped Charlotte manage the tightness in her gut. *And what can I do about all of this when I'm running off to stop someone from posting nude images of me?*

She thought about the answer, closed her eyes, and concentrated. *If I succeed in stopping Zander, then I promise to pursue stories that illuminate the injustices around the world,* she thought. Which reminded her to update Regina about her plans.

Chapter 39

GLANCING OUT HER APARTMENT WINDOW at the traffic below, Charlotte lifted her cell phone, about to call Zander. First, she decided to check if the blackmailer had responded to the email in which she'd informed him, or her, of her impending departure from London. Nothing yet. She assumed beating the blackmail deadline by several days would stop the images from being posted. But without a response, how could she be sure the person would keep his or her end of the bargain? His *and* her?

For that reason alone, she dialed Zander's number. After two rings, she heard his familiar voice. "Charlotte!" He paused briefly then asked, "Everything all right?"

He sounded so damn nice. So near to fucking normal. "Quite honestly, no. Everything's not all right." She wanted desperately to yell at him about threatening to maim Rafe and Naomi but knew she couldn't. Zander couldn't be aware that she knew, and she'd promised Rafe. She waited a moment to see what he'd say.

"Sorry to hear that. What happened?"

He was fishing for what Rafe had told her about events at Naomi's, she felt certain. But she'd prepared for his question. "I really don't want to lose my job, but whoever's behind this damn blackmail sent a photo to Shelby. You don't know anything about that do you?"

"Char, why the hell would I? What did she say?"

"Basically, she fired me. And Nelson Bradford seconded that. I suggested doing a story for her from New York, and she said, 'Maybe'—a small maybe—if I could figure things out."

"Well, that's not so bad, right?"

"Guess not. It's a trafficking story. You've heard of Ghislaine Maxwell?"

There was silence on the other end.

"Z?"

"Yeah?"

"Oh, thought I lost you. Anyway, I'm flying back tomorrow," she said.

"Well, that's good news too, right?" He sounded almost jubilant.

"Is it?" she asked. "Have you heard from Evan?"

"No, but I'll check in with him."

"I sent an email to my blackmailer, but I haven't heard back," she said.

"Going back should do it, right?" he asked.

"Damn well better." She paused. What else should she say? "I suppose we'll see each other at some point." She was toying with him. "Rehash the good old days."

"Definitely," he said, apparently not catching the sarcasm in her voice. "Let me pick you up at the airport."

"You don't need to."

"No trouble. I'd love to."

He pressed her until, reluctantly, she gave him her flight info and time of arrival.

"Where are you staying?" he asked. "If you need a place, you know you can bunk with me. For you, I'll kick out my other girlfriends." He broke into chortling laughter.

"Thanks, but I'm staying with my aunt and uncle." The words had popped out. A Freudian slip. An unfulfilled wish.

"Oh? You finally made up with them?"

"Yeah." A lie. On that note, she ended the call.

This might be her last chance to make everything right with them. Although they hadn't responded to her email yet, she was determined to pay them a visit, and this time she didn't intend to screw it up.

Again, she checked her emails. Still nothing from the blackmailer or Rafe.

On her way to purchasing a disposable phone, Charlotte finally sent the note to Celia she'd written earlier and asked to meet at four o'clock at Sam's Cafe.

Charlotte arrived early, browsing the shelves of neighboring Primrose Hill Books, purchasing a couple of novels then left for Sam's, where original art and more shelves of books greeted her. There she glanced around for any suspicious persons, but as usual identified no one who might be watching or following her. Then again, what would such a person look like? She imagined an eyeglass-wearing man hiding behind a newspaper. Her thought elicited the chilling thought that it could be anyone sitting at any of the tables doing what people did in cafés: drinking coffee, reading, and checking their phones!

She planned to do the same, grabbed a coffee and waited, glancing out the window at passersby. As she people-watched, she caught sight of someone who resembled Zander. She craned her neck to look more closely, but he melted into the crowd and disappeared.

At last Celia waltzed through the door and joined her friend. "For me?" she asked, pointing to a second cup of coffee.

"Yup."

No sooner did Celia sit down than in hushed tones Charlotte described the previous day's encounter with Shelby. Celia shook her head in disbelief. "I can't believe they sent that image to Thorntree. I'm so sorry."

"When Shelby held up the photo, it was a blow. The final straw, as they say. Now there's no doubt that I have to find this person. Get them to stop once and for all."

Celia studied her coffee for a minute, stirred more sugar into it. "By person you mean Zander and I guess you think Naomi sent Shelby the photo?"

More than anything Charlotte wanted to share more details about the thugs at Naomi's apartment and the physical threats they'd delivered but knew she shouldn't. "I guess. But what difference does it make?"

"None, I suppose."

"I'm going to miss you," Charlotte said with a sad little frown.

"Don't say it like that. You'll be back. Of course you will, right?"

Charlotte gave an unconvincing nod then conveyed her flight information to Celia and told her about the charade of a conversation she'd had with Zander, and that he'd offered to pick her up at the airport.

Celia stared at her. "Usually, I love you because you liven up my dull life, but right now I'd vote for less drama. Maybe I should go with you?"

The corners of Charlotte's mouth lifted into a grateful smile. She reached across the table for Celia's hand. They clutched one another and squeezed.

"Be safe, ok?" Celia said.

"I'll be fine." Charlotte then explained her theory that Zander wouldn't hurt her, because, according to Naomi, "It's me he wants. So don't worry about me. But, please, look after Rafe?"

"Of course, I will," Celia said. "But I don't trust Zander. Please be careful and if he—"

"Stop. He's obsessed with me. He won't do a thing. Anyway, I can take care of myself."

Celia looked at her askance. "Call me if he tries anything."

"Right, and you'll speed across the ocean and rescue me? You bet. Stop worrying."

Celia drained her coffee and rose to her feet. "I hate to run but I'm sending Philip off on his trip and have a client meeting after that. Give me a hug."

"Hang on." Charlotte reached into her oversize bag and retrieved a wrapped item. "I want you to keep this for me, and someday, when all this is over, let's go there."

Celia ripped the tissue paper off. "Oh, Char, this is precious. Are you sure?" She shook the snow globe and watched the Eiffel Tower disappear in a flurry of pretend snowflakes.

"I am." In that moment it seemed to Charlotte that half of life felt unreal, and the other half, well, she wasn't sure.

After a lengthy embrace, she watched her friend's retreat—Celia was wrapped in a fashionable beige cashmere coat—and couldn't help the nagging feeling that she wouldn't see her again; that this marked the demise of her relationship with Rafe; and her time in London had truly come to an end.

Chapter 40

Saturday, December 21, 2019 (3 days)

AFTER HER SEVEN-HOUR FLIGHT, she moved through JFK airport, keeping an eye out for one of Zander's thugs, for suspicious and unfriendly faces. Anyone wearing dark sunglasses could easily fit the bill of spy, private detective, assassin.

She inhaled deeply and relaxed a little. *Ridiculous*, she thought again, although she wasn't entirely naïve and knew that such people existed, it's just that they'd never inhabited her world. She continued her watch.

Once she stepped through the doors that separated international travelers from people picking up friends and family, she wondered if she could act happy to see Zander?

Minutes later, she saw a short, balding, dark-mustached man with a sign bearing her name. *Charlotte B. Cooper,* it said. He wore a shapeless dark suit, white shirt, and black tie, like many limo drivers and chauffeurs.

She approached him with a pasted-on smile. "Hello?" she said. "I'm Charlotte."

"Hullo," he replied without smiling. "Mr. Rusikov ask me to meet you."

"Oh?" She noted his accent. Middle Eastern? Russian?

"Yes. Come. He wait," he barked and grabbed her suitcases. She'd brought two filled with her most essential things. She picked up her pace to keep up with him.

With so many unsavory memories of the past fresh in her mind, the idea that Zander was waiting for her caused her insides to clench. They wove their way through travel-weary crowds and finally stepped outside the airport to the waiting cars. She felt as if she'd walked halfway to Manhattan before he escorted her to a black Town Car and opened the door.

She peered inside. Zander. He broke into a big grin. "Come in, come in," he said, patting the seat next to him. "You must be parched after that long flight? I have your favorite drink." He pointed to a bottle of Perrier. "Airplane rides can be so exhausting. Dry me to the bone."

She resented him already. How dare he suggest he knew her favorite drink. *Stop it,* she told herself as she slid onto the black leather seat. He pulled her toward him and gave her a hug. She tried not to stiffen and hoped he didn't notice when she did.

"Thanks, that sounds great," she said half-heartedly and managed a smile.

As he poured Perrier into a glass with ice, she searched her purse for a pair of sunglasses and put them on. She waited for him to talk, fearing her own voice might quaver now that she was face-to-face with a man who was malicious, probably obsessive and capable of who knew what. And yet, listening to him, he sounded completely normal and sane. She wondered if *she* might be insane. Or if most everything Naomi had told Rafe was fantasy? And that an entirely different person had ordered the injuring of Naomi and Rafe?

"I have a surprise for you," he said.

"Oh? What's that?" Her stomach cartwheeled.

"If I told you, it wouldn't be a surprise."

As the Town Car wound its way to a remote part of the airport, she initiated banal chatter, feigning interest in his work, asking how the shoot in Paris had gone, what he was up to next, and offered inane details of her flight.

The vehicle stopped at a squat building. "Okay, here we are," he said.

"We are? Where's this?"

"Heliport."

"Oh?" she heard herself saying for the third or fourth time, but what else could one say when feeling unbalanced like a bird with one wing?

"Have you ever taken a chopper?"

She shook her head.

"Then you're in for a real treat."

"Where are we going?"

"Another surprise," he said, grinning. "Trust me?"

Glad to be wearing sunglasses, she only nodded yes. "I'm pretty tired though."

"I imagine you are. No worries, you can take a nap once we get there."

She wanted to tell him she needed to get into the city, that her aunt and uncle were expecting her, but also feared lying. She'd appease him by letting him have his way for the next couple of hours. Then she'd tell him she needed to go.

Barely inside the tiny terminal, he said, "Okay, ready?"

Through the large plate glass windows, she could see several helicopters parked outside.

"Can you give me a sec? I need to use the ladies' room."

He aimed his head across the room. "Over there."

She wondered how many other women he'd brought here.

Inside one of the stalls, she pulled out her cell phone and texted Celia. *Zander's taking me somewhere in a helicopter. Says it's a surprise. Stay tuned.*

No! Don't go, was Celia's immediate reply.

I have to! Can't let those pics go live. Need him to trust me… What other way was there, she thought. Besides, around her he was harmless. If not harmless, then manageable. Right?

Celia: *Text me as soon as you get there. Wherever that is!*

Will do, Charlotte wrote, then deleted her entire exchange with Celia, to make sure Zander wouldn't somehow find it. Next, she located the chain of texts with Rafe, and hurriedly scrolled through his many love notes, jokes, and affectionate teasing, stopping on the most recent one of several days ago. Before that horrid night. *I love you,* it said. Feeling the pressure build behind her eyes, she collapsed the text messages, then swiped left on his name, tapped the red "delete" button, and his name and all the messages disappeared.

She exited the stall. At the mirror she blinked several times, wiped away the tears, washed her face and hands with cold water, dried them, applied lip gloss and with a deep inhale left the bathroom and rejoined Zander.

"Ready?" he said, appearing boyishly exuberant, as if little separated them from their early days of knowing each other at Cornell to now.

She pasted on a smile and nodded. He might be devious, he might be attracted to her, but was he also dangerous?

She'd tread carefully and stay alert. "As ready as I'll ever be," she said.

Chapter 41

AFTER AN INITIAL UPWARD JERK, the helicopter lifted into the air like a bird gliding on a current of wind. It reminded her of childhood roller coaster rides, both frightening and thrilling. If only Rafe sat beside her. That thought was swept away when the helicopter, in a sudden stomach-churning maneuver, twisted sideways and took off in a new direction.

Through its glass-bottomed belly she could see the buildings below shrink into toy-sized structures. Based on the direction of the afternoon sun, she believed they were traveling northeast. Away from Manhattan.

"Where are we going?"

He arched his brow in a way that indicated she obviously failed to understand the meaning of surprise.

She figured they were heading to his home but then realized she'd never bothered to ask where he lived. She'd assumed Manhattan.

The helicopter flew over highways, residential areas, and water until they slowed at a wooded area, where many of the houses hid beneath a thicket of branches, trees now bare. A little further and the estates grew more sizable, acres of land surrounding mid-size mansions with water views. They crept along the coast, which, playing the role of tour guide, Zander explained was the north shore of Long Island. If memory served her, his father's estate had been nearby.

"What's the name of the town?" she said, shouting to be heard above the roaring noise of the engine. She wanted to confirm their location and later text Celia.

"Sands Point," he shouted back, a proud look transforming his face. It *was* where his father had lived—one of Long Island's enclaves for the wealthy. He couldn't still be living with him, could he?

"I'm on the board of the preservation efforts here," he added. They were flying over manicured gardens and a late nineteenth-century mansion, which could only be described as a castle with turrets and a fairy tale appearance. Not two minutes later, the helicopter flew inland a hundred feet or so, hovered, then touched down on the expansive lawn of an ultra-modern home, all glass and sharp angles. The antithesis of the castle. They'd landed ten feet from an enormous oval swimming pool.

"Okay, let's go," Zander shouted to Charlotte, who stared out, first at the intricate mosaic floor beneath the rippling water, then the well-tended gardens, and finally the mansion's wall of cloud-reflecting glass which faced the Sound. At least now she had a vague idea of where she was.

Stooping slightly, they ran out from under the rotating blades of the helicopter and onto the nearby gray slate path. The pilot unloaded her suitcases, placing them along the edge of the pavement, and with a brief salute to Zander flew away.

"Is this yours?" she asked in an incredulous tone, gawping at the grounds and the house. It wasn't his father's place, the one he'd taken her to all those years ago. But like his father's estate, this must have cost a fortune.

He cocked his head, appearing chagrined, proud, and slightly amused. "Yeah, it's mine. What'd you think?"

She didn't answer. From the patio, they stepped inside a spacious room both diminished and enhanced by the three-story high windows and view of the pool and the Sound beyond. In a swift glance, she took in the luster of glass, metal, and Roche Bobois furnishings—an extreme case of form over function.

"Maria," she heard Zander call. The woman appeared, and after a quick exchange in Spanish, she disappeared and so did he.

"Make yourself comfortable," he called to her.

She surveyed the room a bit more, then wandered over to a built-in bookshelf, where she found several oversize books of well-known photographers—Diane Arbus, Annie Leibovitz, Richard Avedon, Henri Cartier-Bresson, Edward S. Curtis, and several others — but also a dozen or more photographs, all of them framed in silver. To her surprise there were two of her. One of Zander, Abbie, and her from their days at Cornell, and one just of her at a daytime party at his parents' house in Sands Point after graduation.

She recalled that shot, because Charlotte had hidden her disgust with Zander behind sunglasses. He'd enticed Abbie with his coke habit, she'd succumbed, and Charlotte could do nothing to convince Abbie to stop.

A few minutes later, a short Latino man brought Charlotte's luggage inside. At the same time, Zander and Maria returned, he empty-handed, she bearing a tray laden with glasses of ice, a large bottle of Perrier, an attractive platter of fruit, crackers and cheese. Maria's sweet demeanor shifted when she barked orders at Gustavo, who stood beside the suitcases, apparently wondering what to do with them. He gave a curt nod, lifted them up and disappeared from the room.

"We can have wine, or champagne if you prefer," Zander said, dropping onto a modern sofa stitched together in squares of scarlet and mustard felt.

Charlotte sat down opposite him in a chair of similar style, but in hues of blue and gray. "If I have alcohol, I'll fall dead asleep. I still have to get into the city tonight."

"To your aunt and uncle's?" he asked, pouring Perrier into a glass.

"That's right."

"They know you're coming?"

Her heart fluttered at those words. "What do you mean?"

"Craziest thing, I spoke with them." Smiling, he gave her a penetrating look.

Her mouth suddenly dry, she grabbed one of the glasses of Perrier and took several swallows. "Spoke with them?" she said, trying to sound casual. "When?"

"Pretty weird coincidence, but I ran into them at the airport when I arrived."

"Oh," she said, knowing the unlikeliness of accidentally bumping into them. Should she challenge him? *No, keep cool, think fast.* "I was planning to show up and hope they'd finally forgiven me."

"Sounds like a flimsy plan if you ask me. What if they aren't there? Or don't invite you to stay? Why don't you spend the night here and approach them tomorrow? After you've gotten a good night's rest."

How clever, she thought, of course he wanted to keep her here overnight. Coming from any other friend, this seemed like a reasonable plan, but not from him. She recalled how he'd drugged and raped her. "What did they say?" she asked.

"Who?"

"My aunt and uncle."

"They weren't all that friendly. It was your uncle I spoke with. I don't think they ever liked me, especially not after what happened."

Charlotte recalled her aunt's anguish and grief and almost rolled her eyes. "No, I suppose not. Exactly what did you say to them?"

"I said I heard you were coming back to New York, from London, that is. He said they hadn't been in touch with you in a long time."

She felt her face flush with the knowledge that he'd caught her in a lie, but then he'd done much worse things. And so had she.

"They must not have checked their emails," she said.

Chapter 42

SHE THOUGHT HE WOULD ACCUSE her of having lied, but he didn't. Stalling for time, she leaned toward the tray of food, picked up several grapes and ate them. "When are we going to meet up with Evan?"

He hesitated, his mind appearing to search for an answer. "There's no reason to meet him. It's the guy who took the photos that we'll meet up with. I'll kill the bastard myself."

She knew to tread lightly. He'd caught her in a lie and now it seemed she'd caught him in one. "Look, I hate to be a pain, but I came back to find the guy who's threatening to post nude photos of me. I want to meet with Evan and anybody else he remembers from that night."

He was listening, though he seemed distracted. "Okay. But I told you I have a guy working on this."

"Yeah, and I'm running out of time. Please, Zander. Are you going to help me or not?"

He gave her a circumspect look that prompted Charlotte to wonder if he might confess or laugh it off with his usual, "Everything's under control."

Instead, he said, "I'll call Evan, set something up for tomorrow. How's that?"

"And the private eye? What about him?"

"I'll get an update."

In college and right after, she'd often witnessed Zander's wily, selfish behavior. He'd make dates and break them, then come up with excuses. He seemed adept at knowing what people wanted to hear and came through about fifty percent of the time. Mostly, people didn't catch on, so his strategy worked. But she'd watched how he treated Abbie and didn't like it.

"Don't you see how unreliable he is?" she asked her cousin after he'd blown her off again.

"No. It was just a library date," Abbie said. "Anyway, he had an excuse."

"Right," Charlotte said. She wanted to add, *but that's the third time in a row and I saw him hanging out with Victoria.*

A short while later, Charlotte said, "Well, if I'm going to stay here then you'd better show me my room?" Spending the night might give her a chance to look around and search for the photos, and any other evidence of his scheme with Naomi.

Zander jumped to his feet, a look of happiness brightening his face. "Of course, what a terrible host I am. Let's go; I'll show you the place."

As they made their way through his mansion, he acted the part of proud tour guide. All the rooms, designed and decorated in a minimalist style, contained honeyed wooden floors and modern furniture—composed of steel, glass, and leather, some Le Corbusier-inspired pieces.

But nearly every room featured at least one, or more, black and white image taken by the great portrait photographers of the recent past. He seemed especially fond of Arbus, Avedon, and Leibovitz. Later, she'd ask about them.

One room exhibited nothing but three sculptures. He moved more slowly through it. Her gaze fell on a racing horse, hooves in mid-air, constructed of wire and colored glass; it appealed to her, perhaps because it was the perfect metaphor for how she felt—trying to run free but trapped in place by the past.

She wondered, of course, what Rafe would say. If he would find the horse too kitschy, or superficial, or simply an overly commercial piece, something someone with little real appreciation for sculpture would buy. Someone like Zander, whose ego clearly needed a display of wealth and everything that came with it. But the modernity of it all, though having a certain appeal, lacked warmth. Like walking through a museum, and all these pieces carefully curated, probably by an interior designer.

For a moment, she imagined Zander wandering this house, lonely and wanting. Never having found the true love he desired. Or did he regularly fill it with guests and parties, like that last one they'd gone to in Easthampton, where he'd dispensed all those drugs to girls swarming around him like greedy guppies.

When at last they arrived in the room he indicated would be hers for her stay, she first felt overwhelmed by yet one more floor-to-ceiling wall of glass and its stunning view of the Sound. Light poured in, splashing nearly every surface but one — the wall opposite the windows, which featured three larger than life-sized black and white photographs of women, each one barely clad, animal skins covering vital areas, like gorgeous, brazen Amazons.

She knew Zander treasured these images, which he'd taken. But the one in the middle took her breath away; the effect could only be called electric. The girl's eyes dug deep into the camera, almost defiant, her nearly nude figure, if a bit too lean, was perfectly muscled, her slightly open mouth gave her face a sensual, half-starved, wolfish look. Her brown skin tones against the pale desert backdrop provided just the right contrast to rivet one's eyes.

Naomi several years younger. In Namibia?

She felt Zander watching her as she scrutinized the image and tried to laugh at the irony of it. "You want me to sleep *here*?"

At once everything about this situation swerved toward the surreal. From being in the home of the man most likely to have engineered the blackmail, to resting in the bedroom where Naomi, his partner in crime, would watch over her as she slept. The woman who hated her, but perhaps now was content that she'd left. And maybe, if Naomi truly was pregnant, she would entice Rafe to return.

A smile bloomed on Zander's lips. "No, I'd rather you slept with me," he said, his response so slick that she knew he'd prepared it in advance. But she also felt it to be true, spoken with a mix of desire and wishful thinking. "Let me show you that room," he said, grinning, "in case you change your mind."

For a moment, she hesitated.

"Oh, come on, I don't bite," he said.

Like hell you don't, she thought, wishing she could be as honest as he seemed to be. For now, she would keep up the charade and followed him.

His bedroom, done in shades of gray, white and black, with clean lines and little ornament, was as attractive, if not as cold, as all the others. She peered inside for a quick look, long enough to know his geographic relation to her room. After a perfunctory peek, she told him she needed a nap and returned to the space she now thought of as Naomi's. She'd confront him about her later.

He showed her the remote to lower the linen blinds, opened his arms as if to embrace her, then, perhaps noting her reluctance, thought better of it. "Sleep well," he said and left.

She waited by the door to hear the retreat of his footsteps. After assuring herself he'd gone, she turned the latch to lock the door and tested it to make sure it worked; indeed, it did.

She wrote a brief text to Celia, telling her she was going to spend the night at Zander's and not to worry. *I'll call you tomorrow,* she added.

Turning her back on Naomi and the two other women, one Asian and one tall Caucasian with curly, long hair and a body eerily similar to her own, she dropped into a dreamless sleep.

Chapter 43

SEVERAL RAPS ON THE DOOR startled Charlotte awake, her heart stampeding through her chest like wild horses. She glanced at the unfamiliar surroundings until her eyes landed on the image of Naomi. As recognition took root, the pace of her heart slowed.

"You'll never sleep tonight if you don't get up," Zander called through the door.

It had grown dark outside.

"I'll be down in a minute," she called, trying to roust her sluggish self. "Think I'll shower first." She checked the time and saw that her short nap had lasted over an hour.

The steam in the shower coiled around her body as water gently pummeled her face, shoulders, and back, helping to loosen her muscles and thoughts. Rafe's face surfaced and so did a fierce longing for him. Her salty tears mingled with the water. Not now. She took in a deep breath. *Oh, Rafe. If I ever catch up with you again, and if you'll open the door for me, I'll never let you go.*

With resolve she got dressed. She needed to stay focused on what she'd come to do. Fix her problem. Could she get Zander to admit he was behind the threat and promise never to post the photos? Better yet, get him to destroy the images and ensure no copies remained. Was that even possible in this digital era? She recalled young Ann's devastating experience and those women whose images were traded on the dark web. She shuddered.

Before leaving her room, she decided to check Twitter for a note from *@NotKidding*. She'd fulfilled the blackmail demand ahead of schedule, and Zander knew she had. There shouldn't be any more threats, but a chance still existed that Naomi would post a snarky comment out of spite. Or even an image.

Charlotte's phone connectivity was zilch, and the Twitter feed refused to load.

When she checked her texts, she saw that her earlier message to Celia, about spending the night at Zander's, hadn't been "delivered." She frowned, turned her phone off and on, hoping the reboot would pave the way to better reception, but it didn't. The little wheel at the top of her phone spun. Annoyed, she decided she must be out of range. She'd ask Zander for his Wi-Fi and password.

She found him in the kitchen putting together a salad. The rest of the meal, in the oven, wafted delicious aromas into the air. She sniffed the air and said amiably, "Smells great." Then added, "I can't seem to connect to the Internet."

"Believe it or not reception here is crap. I'll get you the Wi-Fi and password. Let me finish up the meal."

"Can I help?"

"Sure. Take the wine and the glasses to the table. Thought we'd eat in the dining room. Special occasion, right?"

She nodded absently and noticed the bottle had been opened but did as he asked.

In the dining room a long glass table had been set for two people. She sniffed the wine but couldn't detect anything off and set it down on a silver wine trivet. She couldn't help recalling the night he'd drugged her. Unwanted thoughts of him crowded her mind along with an urgent desire to flee.

Zander sat at the head of the table with Charlotte to his right.

"I thought maybe you'd put me at the other end, like in those movies where two people sit twenty feet apart," she said, trying to sound relaxed.

"I'd never do that," he said, without responding to the joke. He helped himself to the salad then passed her the wooden bowl. Maria had prepared roasted zucchini and red peppers, a white fish covered in a pale sauce, and mushroom risotto. It all looked delicious, but her appetite was nonexistent.

Reflected in the wall of glass at the foot of the table were a half dozen wavering candles, sending flickering light across the otherwise unlit room. She wondered if this was intended as a romantic touch or Zander's way of limiting her ability to see his expressions.

He lifted his glass of red wine and said, "To you, Charlotte. So fabulous to see you. Who would have thought this day would come?" He extended his glass toward her. The cut crystal glasses chimed as they clinked. His face glowed, as a lover's might.

She painted on a wide smile, then drew the glass to her lips, unafraid to take a sip, because she'd watched him swallow after the toast. This time, she wasn't taking any chances. If she fell asleep, so would he. Besides, she planned to limit how much she drank.

"Tell me about Naomi," Charlotte said, surprising even herself.

He leaned back in his chair with a studied look. "Do we have to?"

"Yes, I'd like to understand your relationship."

He laughed lightly. "And here I thought we were just going to have drinks and dinner and spend time catching up." She refused his eyes' search for warmth or tenderness.

"Indulge me," she said.

After a loud exhale he said, "It's both a long story and a short one."

"I'll take the long version," she said.

He took another sip of wine and twisted the glass in his hand. "I met Naomi about five years ago, when I took that photo of her in Namibia, where she'd won some beauty contest. She was desperate to get out of there and away from her family—you know, poverty, few opportunities, no future—so I helped her get a visa to the US. She's gorgeous, right?" Charlotte nodded. "The next thing I knew she'd fallen for me."

Charlotte sighed and cast him a dubious look.

"Okay, I fell for her too. I'll give you that."

"Thank you," she said.

"We had good times for a couple of years. I introduced her to people in New York, modeling agencies and so on, took her to LA, San Francisco, all kinds of hot spots, no expenses spared, luxury she'd never known. It gave me a kick to see how excited she got. Eventually, since we were together all the time anyway, she came to live with me. That was her private dressing room, the one you slept in."

"I figured," Charlotte said. *And you wanted me to sleep there, when you have other bedrooms.* "Sounds like you did a lot of traveling. When'd you have time to work?"

He shrugged. "She had raw talent when we met, no real modeling skills, no connections in the industry, which makes things tough. Cut-throat even, especially for a Black girl," he paused, as if to watch Charlotte's reaction to those words, "so I introduced her, made things happen. Got her gigs. I know lots of people. I helped her circumvent some of the prejudice in the modeling world."

"And you have a father who knows a lot of people."

"Had," he said, watching her.

"What?"

"He died last year. You didn't know?"

She felt embarrassed and shook her head. "I'm sorry." Why hadn't Shelby told her?

"Don't be. He was a bastard." She watched his mouth curve downward. "Didn't treat my mother very well."

"Maybe so, but he helped me and for that I'll always be grateful," Charlotte said.

He appeared annoyed by the reference.

Charlotte stared at her food. Where to go from here?

But Zander went on, ignoring the detour. "Anyway, after three years in Manhattan, I got her the job in London. That's where she met," he hesitated, "that Black artist."

She could see it pained him to mention Rafe's name. "Rafe?"

He nodded. "Next thing I know she decides to stay in London, and we broke up. The rest you probably know."

"*We* broke up? Don't you mean she left you?"

He shot her a look. "You know how to rub it in, don't you?"

"Fair enough. Sorry."

"Anyway, call it what you want," he said.

She eyed him. "The rest, well, I know when I came to London, she and Rafe had broken up—"

"Correction," he said. "*He* broke up with *her.*"

"That's right," she said. "And it seems to me, *Zander,* that's why she's the most logical person behind the photos and the blackmail. Naomi wants me out of the picture to get Rafe back, don't you agree?" she said, pressing him. "And, somehow, she magically got ahold of photos from my past. Guess what? You're the only connection between us. So…"

Zander frowned. "What are you saying?"

"Damn it, Zander, you gave her those images, didn't you?"

He looked up in alarm.

But she wasn't buying it. "How about being truthful…for once. Please!"

Zander held up his hands to stop her from saying more. "Charlotte."

"Yes?"

"You've got it wrong. I didn't do it." Pause. "How about more wine?" He filled both glasses.

"Then how'd she get those images?"

"Beats me." He shrugged and added, "she's resourceful."

Such a liar, she thought, based on everything Naomi had told Rafe. Unless, of course, Naomi had lied. Frustration was about to get the better of her when she stumbled on another tack. She raised her glass. "Here's to Abbie, who we both loved."

Chapter 44

"YOU REMEMBER THAT PARTY? THE one in East Hampton?" Charlotte asked. Ordinarily she chose not to recall that graduation event. But now, something prompted her to mention it.

"How can I not?" Zander asked with a regretful smile.

They both fell silent.

The view from the terrace of the East Hampton mansion that day had been nothing short of spectacular. The sun sat on the ocean, fat and smug, casting a golden glow on everyone but Abbie; she seemed frustrated and unhappy. Zander and Abbie hadn't spoken much on the ride over. Charlotte had assumed the noisy rush of wind had made it impossible to hear one another in the convertible.

Once they arrived, her cousin lagged behind as the three wound their way down the sloping gardens toward a cluster of partyers. Charlotte glanced over her shoulder, signaling a "what's wrong" question at Abbie, but her cousin refused to meet her eye. As if timed perfectly to further agitate her, Zander called out, "Char, come on," and reached for her hand.

She refused, instead turning to her cousin. "Abbie, come on," she said, but Abbie fled in the opposite direction.

She wanted to follow her, but Zander clutched her elbow and dragged her across the lawn toward a group of his friends she'd never met. If he were to be believed, everyone at every party qualified as his friend.

"You know I never asked," Charlotte said, now turning to Zander, "do you know why Abbie was so upset at the party?"

"You didn't know?" he asked, appearing surprised.

She shook her head.

"We'd broken up."

She stared at him with incomprehension. "What? She was crazy about you."

His face widened with a complacent smile. "So were ten other girls. But that was about the drugs, not me."

Stunned, Charlotte stared at him as this news sank in. *They'd broken up?*

Zander broke the silence, saying, "You really didn't know?"

"No, she didn't say a thing."

"Maybe she was hoping we'd get back together." He looked off. "I'd fallen for someone else."

How could Abbie have kept this from her and why? "Who?" she finally asked.

He gave her a dubious look. "As if you didn't know."

Frowning, she shook her head. "No."

He touched her left hand which rested on the table. "You, silly."

"What?" She looked up, shaking her head. "No, that's crazy. Don't—" *touch me,* she wanted to say.

"Not so crazy," he said, his smile fading. "I always liked you. As we got to know each other better I liked you even more. You weren't like the other girls. Way too much fawning back then." He stared off. "You were distant, I guess because of your plans to return to London, and your dedication to Abbie. So, it was a twofer…hang with Abbie and I'd get to be with you. The two of you were inseparable, as you may recall."

How could she have been so wrapped up in herself not to notice or even get a hint of his thoughts and desires? "Did Abbie know? I mean that you, uh, liked me?"

"I think so."

"So that's why she avoided me all afternoon."

"Maybe."

"But we told each other everything." Her voice sounded plaintive.

"Maybe not."

To think Abbie had died angry with her or hurt. Probably both. All this time and she'd never known. She stared at Zander. "Not only did I kill her, but she died, and we never had a chance to talk, to resolve this." Tears accumulated in her eyes. "No," she said, shaking her head. "No." The candlelight blurred, and her cheeks grew moist. Her head fell into both hands.

At once she felt Zander behind her, his hands on her shoulders. "Don't cry, Charlotte. It wasn't your fault," he said in a soothing voice.

"Of course, it was."

"No, it wasn't," he said more forcefully, then sat down and poured more wine into their glasses. "Look at me," he said. He took a deep breath as she turned to face him. "*I* was the one who'd broken up with her, not you." Pause.

"And *I* was driving," he said, lifting his chin and straightening in his chair. "I thought you knew, and that's why you lied for me."

"Hold on. What?!" Charlotte stared at him, confused. *Lied for him? Knew* he *did it?* Was *he* lying now? To make her feel better? "No, no, *I* was driving," she insisted, her fingers rested on her forehead and cheek, propping her up. "I remember getting out of the car after the accident. Driver's side."

He looked at her as if weighing what to say next. He cleared his throat. "I hate to tell you this, but do you really think my dad would have paid for your lawyer if *you'd* been driving? I convinced him you'd tell the truth if he didn't pay. *You* were innocent."

"So...*you* were driving?" she asked, her brow knitted in confusion. "Why are you telling me now?"

"Because I want us to start over. I love you, Charlotte," he said, his voice tender and earnest. "Always have. There should be no secrets between us, not now, after all this time."

She stared at him, her eyes wide, her mouth open, trying to take in the enormity of what he'd just said. *Not my fault? He* was driving? She shook her head a little. After all the years of guilt plaguing her, keeping her from moving on. She could only think he was mad.

He didn't seem to notice her shock and went on. "I promise, I thought you knew. Otherwise, I would have told you. Jesus, forgive me?"

His lighthearted tone made her want to scream. Forgive him? She wanted to punch him. Beat him to a bloody pulp. She squeezed the edge of her chair and searched for calm.

He gave her a sheepish look. "Forgive me?" he asked a second time.

She couldn't say yes, and so said nothing. As if sensing her reluctance, he filled the silence with, "Just for the record, I was nuts about you."

Being "nuts about her" meant she should forgive him? She was still struggling to understand which of the words pouring from his mouth were true. "What about the nude photos?"

He looked startled, raised his hands. "No, I've told you. I have nothing to do with that. Honest."

"You're sure?" She sat there, dazed.

"I promise. I told you, no more secrets between us."

Her mind swirled with all he'd revealed. Should she ask about the men who'd hurt Rafe and Naomi? An inner voice cautioned against it.

Maria appeared with two small bowls of creme brûlée. Charlotte gazed at hers, said it looked delicious and thanked her, knowing she couldn't swallow a bite. She was grateful though not to be alone in the house. How else could she sleep with this maniac nearby? He'd clearly lost touch with reality.

"Anything else, Mr. Zander?" Maria asked.

"Yes, bring us the wine, please. The one in the kitchen." Turning to Charlotte, he excused himself. "Too much drinking. Gotta visit the little boy's room."

Charlotte shot daggers at his retreating back. She'd never hated anyone, not like this. Unable to come to grips with all he'd said, especially that she hadn't killed Abbie, she stared into the black night, anxious for morning to come. *Then I'll leave. He can't keep me here.* She imagined he'd come up with all manner of reasons for her to stay. She thought of the door in her room. It locked. She'd be safe until morning. And then she'd get the hell out.

In Zander's absence, she realized that the strain of the day and the revelations this evening, not to mention jetlag and too much wine, had left her foggy, disoriented, and exhausted. She had to stop drinking and get some sleep. She was desperate to call Celia and pulled out her phone. A dark screen greeted her. She cursed herself for letting the device lose its charge.

It was getting late and with each passing minute, she grew more tired, and her situation seemed more unreal. And hopeless. She'd confront him once more about the blackmail in the morning before she left. Despite his protestations, now more than ever, she felt certain he'd taken the shots. How would she get him to surrender the images? And how could she believe that no duplicates existed?

For an instant she felt like dashing outside and running away. And yet, she had no idea how to get back to the city. Certainly not without a phone to call an Uber. And without GPS, how would she find her way to safety?

Zander reappeared carrying an open bottle of wine. Had he spiked it? Hadn't he asked Maria to bring it in? Before sitting down, he poured them each a glassful.

Until Zander took a sip, she wouldn't either.

"I thought maybe you'd help me decorate this place for Christmas," he said, the corners of his mouth lifting into a hopeful smile. "Here we are, two orphans." He couldn't be serious, could he? She watched him raise his glass in another toast. "Have a sip; it's the good stuff," he urged.

She touched her glass against his and pretended to drink. She watched him swallow. *No way, I'm not drinking any.*

She picked at her dessert, glanced outside, heard the rush of wind, something tapping, maybe a tree branch against the glass. The thin separation between her and the outdoors made her uneasy. As if someone might be observing them.

Naomi popped into her mind. "How'd you feel when Naomi broke up with you?" she said meanly, keeping her eyes fastened on the creme brûlée, hoping to avoid his stare.

Without the slightest edge he said, "I never did think of Naomi as a permanent fixture."

Permanent fixture? she thought.

"I mean I never thought of marrying her," he said, as if he read her mind. "She's beautiful and all that, but not that interesting when you get right down to it."

What he said echoed something Rafe had once told her. Brow arched, she asked, "You weren't upset?"

"Look, I'll admit, at first, I was pissed; you know, two girls stolen by the same guy. What are the chances? But then, well, I thought what the hell. Like I said…" Suddenly his eyes narrowed as if he'd just thought of something. "Why? Did Naomi say I was upset? She's an incredible liar." His face flushed a little and he reached for his wine and took another drink.

At least this matched Naomi's version about Zander being enraged by Rafe, perhaps wanting revenge. She had to be careful how she responded, though he looked a little drunk. "I just wondered. Because, if you're dating and she dumps you for someone else—"

"She didn't dump me!" The vein along his temple pulsed; his body radiated fury. He took another swallow of wine.

Charlotte cleared her throat. "What I meant is, even if you're not deeply in love, it can feel like rejection when someone ends a relationship. At least that's what I've found."

"Take another sip of your drink," he said, staring at her wine, a morose look on his face.

"Long travel day. Need to hydrate." She pointed at her glass of Perrier then took a long gulp of water.

He slumped back in his chair and expelled a breath of air through puckered lips. He suddenly looked like a sack of bones lacking all energy.

"Did I say something to upset you?" she asked.

His mouth opened and closed, a little like a fish, as if he wanted to speak. Instead, he swallowed then gripped the table's edge and pulled himself up. His eyes looked unfocused as he mumbled something about a long day and needing some "shut-eye." He stumbled a little. "Sorry," he said, "for being a lousy host. I'll make it up to you tomorrow."

"Get some rest," she said, watching his unsteady gait.

After he left, she sat there staring at the windows. All he'd said turned and twisted in her mind. If only she could get in touch with one of her friends in the city. Why hadn't she thought to contact Daisy or Channing?

The uneasy feeling she'd had earlier, of eyes watching her, returned. Her gaze traveled the room, coming to a brief halt near the ceiling at the intersection of two walls. A small rectangular-shaped device with a tiny red light stared at her. It was either part of an alarm system or a camera. Trying not to be obvious, she shifted her gaze away slowly, as if she'd just been glancing around the room.

She'd never been prone to paranoia, but now, in Zander's home, her suspicions and fears bubbled up. She should leave. She picked up her creme brûlée and wine glass and took both to the kitchen.

There she bumped into Maria, who told her not to bother cleaning up. "I do it. Don't worry, okay?"

Charlotte smiled and thanked her. "I'll take the wine upstairs?"

"Sure, sure," she said. "You want fresh glass?"

Grateful for the woman's kindness, she said, "No, not necessary. But thanks." If only she could question her about Zander, but that was not a good idea. Just having her around felt reassuring.

Before heading upstairs, Charlotte moved quietly through the first floor of the house. After a few wrong turns through various rooms, she found, just as she'd suspected, a security system closeted inside a panel near the front door. The red light indicated someone had armed the system, which likely meant if she opened the door a screeching sound would shoot through the house.

She stood there, thinking. All the doors that led outside had to be similarly armed against intruders. Who would have thought such a system could equally lock someone inside?

Now she could search Zander's study, but where was it?

"You need help?"

Charlotte gave a start on hearing Maria's voice. "No, no," she said, abandoning her search and heading upstairs.

She hesitated at Zander's door and listened. His snore calmed her, and she moved on. Once inside Naomi's room she turned the lock as quietly as possible. She felt almost certain he'd put something in the wine but had forgotten when he grew angry and took a couple of swallows without thinking. She sniffed her glass and discerned nothing unusual, certainly not whether he'd roofied the wine. She located her water bottle and poured the liquid inside. She'd have it tested once she escaped this damn house.

Everything he'd said during dinner meant he needed to be locked up, in a prison or an insane asylum. And she didn't care which.

Chapter 45

Sunday, December 22, 2019 (2 days)

AFTER WASHING UP, SHE LAY on her bed fully clothed, her imagination a jumble of thoughts and theories. Despite her worries and desire to escape, after only ten minutes, her eyes closed, and she drifted off.

Early the next morning her eyes popped open. Her first thought: *Get out!* Her second: *Why am I fully dressed?* The third involved checking her phone for messages. But she couldn't find it, not on the desk, where she thought she'd plugged it in, and not elsewhere.

She searched her purse, the bathroom, everywhere she could think of, but failed to locate the damn thing. When she checked the room's door handle, it was unlocked. Last night her brain had been dull with fatigue, maybe she'd forgotten to lock it? Was Zander playing games? She retrieved her computer, then realized he'd never given her the Wi-Fi password. She released a frustrated sigh. Today she would leave. He couldn't stop her.

As if hearing her thoughts, Zander entered her room. "Sleep good?"

"Yeah, but have you seen my cell phone?"

"You left it in the kitchen, to charge it, I guess."

She'd absolutely done no such thing. Zander was a pathological liar. "Okay, great. Could you bring it up?" she said, trying to maintain an even voice. "I'll be down in a few minutes. Just need to wash my face, brush my teeth."

"Sure thing."

When she'd finished in the bathroom, she found the phone on the bed. She entered her security code and checked it for messages but found none. She moved to another part of the room, closer to the window and hit "deliver" to the text she'd sent Celia earlier. *This time,* she added, *I need to get out of here. I'll get the address and send it.*

She longed to speak to Rafe and called him, but it went straight to voicemail. She wanted to tell him how much she loved him and left a message.

"I don't blame you for not wanting to have anything to do with me," she said. "As for me, I'm stuck here in New York, my heart broken. Perhaps someday you can forgive me for all the craziness I've caused you."

She hung up and began to sob. It took her several minutes to collect herself. In the mirror, swollen red eyes stared back at her.

The smell of bacon wafted up from the kitchen. She hadn't eaten much the previous night, and now her stomach growled with hunger. Using a cool, wet washcloth to wipe the tears away and soothe her eyes, she took a deep breath and applied a little make-up, regaining her courage as she did. In the bright light of day, she didn't feel nearly so afraid. Anyway, what could he do to her? Maria was here. Even so, she would leave his house as soon as possible.

Downstairs, she found Zander in the kitchen turning the bacon. "You're cooking? Where's Maria?" she asked casually.

"Her day off; she left earlier," he said.

Her stomach twisted.

"Beautiful out there," he added.

She followed his gaze. It was a picture-perfect day, with only a few clouds dotting the sky. "Chilly."

"So, what do you want to do?" he asked.

What do I want to do!? "After breakfast, I should get going."

He frowned. "It's Sunday. What's the hurry?"

"I made plans with my friend Daisy. She's expecting me. She'll be worried if I don't show up." She said this in a matter-of-fact tone, but kept her eyes trained on the kitchen window, pretending to look outside.

He canted his head to the side. "This isn't an imaginary friend, is it?"

"No, Zee, it isn't." She knew he liked being called by his nickname.

He smiled. "Not like spending the night with your aunt and uncle?"

She ignored his comment. "That reminds me," she said coolly, "I need to stop by their place. I promised myself I'd make every effort to patch things up."

He wore a cagey look on his face. "You mean you're going to tell them that I was driving?"

"I hadn't thought of that," she said. "But maybe I should." She couldn't show him any weakness. She knew he despised that in people.

He ladled scrambled eggs and bacon onto two plates and handed her one. "Coffee?"

"Of course. Thanks," she said.

"So, call her. Daisy, I mean. Tell her we're going for a sail out on the Sound."

"It's freezing out there." She almost said, *are you crazy?*

"No, it's going up into the fifties. With a little gear it'll be great."

"You know, Zander, my life is kind of messed up right now. I'm not really in the mood to go sailing."

His jaw tightened. "Oh, so what *are* you in the mood for?" The air suddenly filled with static.

She looked at him without speaking. Waiting for whatever else he might throw at her.

"A flight back to *fucking* England…" he sneered, "so you can be with *him*?"

She bit back fear and anger, refusing to let him bully her. "Maybe so," she said, her chin jutting out defiantly. "But because of whoever's blackmailing me—my guess is that's you and Naomi—he's had enough of me. So that's not really an option." She put her plate of food down, turned her back to him, and began to leave the room.

In an instant, he stood behind her, his hands latched onto her arms. She could feel his breath on her neck. "Goddamn it, Charlotte, you're wrong!" he hissed. "It's not me. Can't you just give me one fucking day? I care about you. You know I do."

Shrugging his hands off, she turned and with narrowed eyes, looked at him like he was crazy. She shook her head. "No, you don't. Not really. What's the address here?"

His face flushed, his eyes darkened with anger, his body grew rigid. He looked explosive. She shrank back. Then, as quickly as it had arrived, his rage drained away. In a quiet and resigned voice, he said, "I'm sorry, but I can't give you the address."

"What do you mean?"

Lips pressed together he said nothing, merely studied her.

"I'm leaving," she said.

His answer came quickly. "If you walk out, that image of you, the one where you're fucking that guy…it'll be everywhere. Naomi'll make sure of it. It'll be the happiest she's been in a while." His mouth smiled, but his eyes glinted with malice.

She stopped. Tried to imagine her life after such exposure. It all flashed before her—the humiliation, shame, endless embarrassment and harassment. If it had seemed real before, now she could taste the aftermath of the image burned into a million minds. How long before people lost interest in such postings? Even if she survived the public shaming, she doubted Rafe would want her back. And then, what would be the point of returning to London? For her reporting job? The likelihood of reclaiming that was just as slim.

"So, it *was* you?" she said and sat down at the kitchen table.

"I know you don't believe me, but it wasn't me who put her up to this."

Ignoring what he'd just said, she took a few bites of breakfast then said, "Okay, we'll go sailing. But promise me that Naomi won't post that image."

"Good news is she does what I tell her. Done!" Wearing a confident smile, he gave her a few minutes to change into more appropriate clothes.

She marveled at his ability to think she believed him. His incessant, convoluted lying had no limits. Most likely he believed at least half of his own lies.

As she got up, he said, "Leave the phone with me." Though he said it quietly, she knew it wasn't a request. She imagined he'd hold on to it as insurance and left it on the table.

Trudging upstairs, Charlotte kicked herself for not having called the police earlier. But what would she have said? I think the guy who lives here is dangerous and you ought to arrest him? Now she could tell them he was holding her against her will and threatening to post nude images of her on social media. And even on sleazy Reddit subculture sites.

She rummaged through her suitcase in search of suitable clothing: her heaviest sweater, a turtleneck, and the warmest leggings she'd brought. As she dressed, she felt the life-sized photo of Naomi taunting her. Charlotte wanted to take a Sharpie and scrawl a mustache on her face or better yet to blow-torch it. If she could, she'd rip it off the wall and smash it to pieces.

Taking the steps back down, haltingly, and trying to calm herself with deep breaths, she couldn't seem to stop the thoughts that flew through her head. She wished she'd been able to send Celia the general location of Zander's home. But what good would that have done? Though she didn't live here, Celia, if nothing else, was resourceful, and if she didn't hear from Charlotte, she'd do something. But what?

She turned her thoughts back to Zander. She had to get him back to trusting her. Perhaps she should have been more afraid, but he insisted he loved her, which gave her the slightest bit of confidence she needed.

Chapter 46

AT THE BASE OF THE winding staircase, Zander awaited her, wearing white jeans and a navy blue and white striped sweater, a dark blue woolen scarf looped around his neck.

She reached her hand toward him, and he took it as if no cross words had passed between them. He handed her yellow rain gear. "Just in case it gets too windy, or the weather turns ugly."

She accepted it without a response. What was the point?

As they walked past the pool and then along a winding pathway that led to a small pier on the Sound, she took note of her surroundings, especially the back of the neighbor's home they passed. Did he think his seemingly endless money and toys would win her over? Slightly hidden behind a copse of trees, a sailboat and a motorboat bobbed in the water. The sun shone brightly on the boat's dark-blue hull, its name painted in white letters: *Jane Eyre*.

"Do you like it?" he said in all innocence.

The paint looked fresh. "Did you do that for me?"

"Who else? I thought of calling it 'Rochester'," he said, making air quotes with his fingers, "you know after the guy, Edward, in the book. Sometimes I feel just like him."

"Really?" she said, "Which I guess means you haven't forgotten that used to be one of my favorite novels?"

"No, Charlotte Brontë Cooper, I haven't forgotten anything about you." He hauled a white YETI cooler onto the teak deck and helped her aboard.

He wore a sailing cap and seemed to enjoy playing the part of captain of his twenty-seven-foot Catalina. As if he needed to explain the reason for the small craft, he said, "You can race it or have fun just sailing, besides maintenance doesn't cost an arm and a leg."

Would that really be an issue, she thought. "Do you race?" she asked.

He shook his head. "No time for it." After motoring out a little way, he raised the sails, and they set off.

Seeing few other craft on the Sound, she leaned against the seatback of the boat's narrow bench, closed her eyes, and basked in the sunshine, trying to imagine how this day would end. The waves gently rocked the boat.

A few minutes later, a cloud swallowed the sun, and she opened her eyes, expecting to see the sun hiding behind a puff of white or gray, but instead Zander was leaning over, blocking her light. He reached for her face, clearly intending to kiss her.

She inched sideways and shook her head. Then realized too late it might have been better to play along. But she couldn't bring herself to let his mouth touch her lips. What would he expect next? "Please, Zander, don't."

He backed away without complaint and returned to steering the boat. He kept his eyes on the horizon, and his mouth curved into a smile, as if to signal that he had infinite patience and that he knew, eventually, she'd come around.

More time passed, and Charlotte dared to ask for her phone. "Can I have it back? To memorialize this day with some photos." She hoped there might be a moment when she could send such an image to Celia.

He smiled at her without answering.

She asked a second time. "Not yet," he said.

The wind fingered her hair, which she'd tied back, but loose tendrils escaped and tickled her face. She again tried to relax as the boat plowed through the water.

His voice broke into her reverie. "Charlotte, is there any way," he hesitated before adding, "that we can be together? Forever?" His question and the tone of his voice sounded genuine, laced with hope. Almost the way a normal person, albeit a young one, might sound asking such a question.

She thought a moment. "How can we, Zander? After all that's happened between us.”

“Exactly. After all that, it seems inevitable. Everything we've shared… who else has such close ties?”

She tried to hide her incredulity. He again seemed like someone from an alien world. “Zander, for God's sakes, your reckless driving killed my cousin—something you revealed to me yesterday…after years of blaming myself—and then you raped me,” she said and paused. Yes, that's exactly what he'd done. Fed her drugs and raped her. “And now you're holding me hostage. Is that the kind of shared past you think would charm me?” As she heard herself speak, the memories of those events surfaced, along with the years of pain and anger she'd suffered.

Disbelief etched itself into the curve of his mouth. After a long stare, a deep sigh escaped his lips. “I did *not* rape you.”

Once again, she hid her astonishment. “You did. That is, *after* you drugged me.” She paused, waiting for recognition to arrive in his expression. “I hope you don't consider that consensual sex. How can you expect me to love you when you do things like that?” He looked startled. “You didn't think I'd remember?” she added. “I yelled at you the next morning. You roofied my drink and then fucked me.” She stared at him. Something was truly off with him. “You think you can get away with shit like that, but you can't.”

He laughed, a wild look in his eyes. “You'd be shocked what people get away with.” His look grew bitter, then a moment later, he turned thoughtful, emotions rolling across his face like waves across the nearly empty Sound, and she wondered what he might be referring to. “But you offered to take the blame,” he said. “That's what someone does who truly loves you.”

“I told you last night that I woke up in the driver's seat. Which reminds me, I meant to ask, how did I get there if I wasn't driving?”

He frowned. “I think you climbed there from the back. You seemed pretty out of it. Banged up, and then you just sat there.”

She tried to return to that night. She pressed her eyes closed and pictured the scene. Memories shift and change over time, she'd read. Maybe he didn't remember correctly.

“When we got to the car after the party, you said, 'let me drive,'” Zander said, “and I said, 'no way.' Remember that? And then you asked Abbie to put on her seatbelt, but she refused. She was mad at you. Mad at both of us, I guess. You climbed in back, just like on the ride to the party."

At once, something clicked in her mind. She saw Abbie fiddling with the glove compartment of the Porsche and reach inside. That's where Zander kept his stash of coke. Charlotte knew they'd all had enough and suggested the two of them slow down with the dope. Abbie yelled at her. "Shut up, Charlotte, just shut up."

She repeated it in a sing-song voice, "Shut up, Charlotte. Alliteration, right, Miss English major? It's got a real ring to it!" Then she invited Zander to say it and howled with laughter.

Charlotte shrugged off her cousin's drunken behavior—Abbie always apologized the next day—and kept an eye on the speedometer. He was going at least eighty.

When Abbie handed him the tiny glass container of coke, he used his knees to steer, one hand holding the vial and the other dipping a silver straw into the coke. He took a long snort, the car veering into the oncoming lane, but at the last second, he righted its course.

She was annoyed, but also fearful, and again shouted at him to be careful.

"Chill, Charlotte, chill," he yelled and roared like a maniac. Abbie joined in.

It was the next snort that caused the crash. He'd again removed his hands from the wheel and relied on his knees to guide the car. It happened on the heels of their laughter; one second they were careening along the road, and the next the car flew sideways, screeching, skidding, resisting the forces of gravity.

Charlotte, her eyes squeezed shut, felt a heavy object strike the car. With a spine-jerking thump the vehicle vaulted into the air. Her memory insisted that the car flipped twice. She could still hear the creak and groan of twisting metal. Then, finally, the car came to rest. And that was it. The roll bar had saved her, that and the crazy way she'd buckled herself in.

"Do you remember how scary that accident was, Zander?" She decided to let him believe whatever he wanted. He had his version of events, and she doubted she could change that.

"Yeah." He tipped the boat into the wind and watched it accelerate. "Fun, huh?" he said as they flew across the water.

Spray dappled her face with moisture. She was about to say, *Slow down*, but instead released a fake chuckle. "You're a good sailor."

"Thanks," he said, smiling, pleased with himself.

She wasn't sure this was the right moment, but thought she'd try. "Could I have my phone now? I need to contact Daisy."

He pulled it out of his pocket, weighing it in his hand. Stared at it. "Damn things."

She put her hand out to catch it.

"Will you leave after we get back?" he asked.

She needed to be careful. "I think so," she said, slowly nodding her head. "Why?"

"Wrong answer," he said. In one smooth arc, she watched the phone rocket into the sky then splash into the water and sink beneath the waves.

Gulls wheeled overhead, shrieking and complaining. As she stared at them, a line from *Jane Eyre* arrived, one she'd memorized at Oxford: *I am no bird, and no net ensnares me: I am a free human being with independent will.* She repeated the words in silence when a can of beer appeared before her eyes. Zander grinned at her. She needed to keep her wits and shook her head. "No thanks."

The sun dipped behind a bank of clouds. Chill air seeped through her clothes. She grabbed the yellow rain jacket, and wished they were heading back. Maybe they were, but she'd lost all sense of direction on the water. She hadn't spoken more than a few words since he tossed her phone into the water. And she wouldn't. She felt his eyes on her.

At last, he broke the silence. "I was willing to take you back."

His words jarred her. What the hell was he talking about now? She looked at him but didn't speak.

"That night when you fucked the guy in the photo." He stared at her as if trying to shake loose a memory.

Though she was trying to resist, he had an uncanny ability to draw her in. "Why are you looking at me like that?"

"You know who that guy was?"

"No. Who?"

"A real bastard," he hissed.

Her eyes narrowed. "Who?"

"I think you know."

She shook her head no, although the awful truth was dawning on her.

He nodded. "Yeah, you do."

"Your father?" she whispered.

He gazed off. "Had to do it. Sorry."

Had to? Revulsion whipped through her. "Why?"

"That was his price…to pay for your lawyer. I had to supply his other asshole buddies too."

He'd *trafficked* her! She looked at him in horror.

He didn't seem to notice. "Anyway, I was willing to take you back," he repeated.

"Are you saying what I think you're saying? That *you* were willing to take *me* back after having to fuck your dad so he'd pay for my lawyer for something *you* did?" She tried unsuccessfully to keep the sharp edge out of her voice.

"Yeah. Even though it killed me to watch. You looked like you were enjoying fucking him." His brow pinched together, and he shook his head.

"Correct me if I'm mistaken, but that whole thing—it was your idea?"

He studied her a moment. "Going there, yeah, but fucking that other guy wasn't."

Her memory of that night was hazy—the fault of the drugs he'd offered, and she'd willingly taken. "I thought it was an orgy, everyone fucking everyone. Like you said. What was your plan then?"

"It wasn't really *my* plan. After you fucked my dad, I thought *we'd* make love."

"There? In the middle of all those people?"

"Why not? If you could do it with strangers, why couldn't you do it with me?"

"I fucked people I didn't know precisely because I didn't know them. I'd never see them again. I just gave myself up to whoever. A few moments of not thinking, of not caring…about anything or anyone." The notion of what she'd done now made her nauseous.

"And I could have been one of them?" He seemed like a boy struggling to understand.

"Maybe. I don't know. Like I said, that night's a blur. I wish it had never happened, and I still have trouble not hating myself for it. And by extension, you. Despising you for taking me there." She didn't say *and despising myself for ruining part of my life and giving you the chance to take those photos*. But now with this latest revelation she had someone else to despise. His father. How could he ask his only son to bring her there to fuck her or he wouldn't pay for her lawyer? What if Zander had stood up to him? A question she now asked.

He stared at her blankly. "I couldn't do that."

"You really think he wouldn't have paid, or he was bluffing?"

"He didn't bluff." He appeared to be staring at the leaden water.

When she looked in the direction of his gaze, in the distance, she saw a dark blotch against the horizon. By squinting she saw a larger boat headed their way. A ferry of some sort. After several minutes, over the rush of wind, she called, "Don't you have to give the larger boat the right of way?"

He ignored her and stayed the course.

In a few minutes they'd collide if he didn't alter his boat's trajectory. "Zander!" she shouted. The ferry was growing more and more distinct.

Still no response. She got up and shook him. He seemed in a trance, staring past her. "For heaven's sake, what's going on with you?"

As the ferry drew closer, its horn blared. An unmistakable warning. In a couple of minutes, they'd crash. Giving way to larger vessels was one of the few sailing rules she knew.

"Zander," she shouted again, "we have to stop…or something." She also knew that sailboats couldn't just turn on a dime, but if she could lower the mainsail, it would slow the boat. She ran over to the lines and tried to release them, but the mainsail didn't respond. Several times she called Zander to help her. "Which line? Which one?" she cried. The large boat blasted its alarm again.

"The halyard," he whispered.

She tugged on several ropes, not knowing which was which, but finally must have released the halyard because the mainsail began flapping in the wind; the sheets and metal hardware pinged and clanged against the hollow mast.

The collapse of the sail brought the boat to a near standstill. The ferry passed by so closely that she could see the concerned and relieved faces of people on deck, some of them waving.

Her heart was still pounding as she said softly, "Zander, let's go home. Ok?"

He finally looked at her. "You'll stay with me?"

"Of course," she said.

Chapter 47

STORM CLOUDS BREWED OVERHEAD. IT looked like a Nor'easter heading their way. They docked the boat, grabbed all their gear, and walked swiftly along the path back to the house. Large drops of rain splattered on their jackets and slammed into the pool, the water spitting and dancing. By the time they reached the back door their rain slickers were drenched, and Charlotte shivered.

Zander ushered her inside. "Come on, I'll make you some hot tea," he said. She looked at him. Was he serious, acting as if nothing weird had just happened? A mystery how quickly he regained his equilibrium; Charlotte only knew she hadn't. She also knew she couldn't spend another night in his house. He was unhinged, capable of almost anything. Even self-destruction, something she hadn't counted on.

"No thanks, maybe later. I'm taking a warm bath, and then maybe a nap," she said. "I'll be down in about an hour." She headed straight for the stairs, glancing at the front door as she passed.

The large tub in her bathroom took a while to fill. She lit a lavender-scented soy candle that sat on the ledge and found the novel she'd just begun—*An American Marriage*.

The bathroom door had no lock, but she cast aside her concern, already aware he had ways of opening locked doors, since he'd stolen her phone. After placing her suitcase in front of the bedroom door, she gave up worrying about whether he'd come in or not. She just prayed he wouldn't.

At last, she entered the steaming bath and sank down until the water reached her chin. The warmth sent a shiver down the length of her body. For a time, she just lay there, waiting for the heat to seep into her bones. Before she could make any sort of meaningful plan, she had to warm up. She couldn't believe how frozen she felt.

The revelations of the past twenty-four hours tugged at her mind, and though she wanted to think about Abbie and all that Zander had said, she had to stay focused. She recalled one of her professors saying that every puzzle, every problem had an answer, but the solution to how she would escape evaded her, she just knew she had to.

She cared little about leaving behind her clothing. Essentials, like her computer, she'd stuff into her backpack and somehow smuggle it downstairs and hide it in a closet near the front door. Without a phone, she was handicapped. If she got outside, and that seemed like a big if, she'd find the nearest house and beg the neighbor for help. Flag down a passing car and ask to use their phone. That was the extent of her plan.

For a few minutes she tried to relax by reading, but it was useless. At last feeling warm, she sat up to unplug the tub. As she did, she noticed the same electronic eye in one corner of the bathroom that she'd noticed in the dining room. Whether reasonable or not, she covered her breasts. In one rapid motion she stood up and pulled a towel around her body.

The rhythmic clatter of the rain against the windows in her room continued. Naomi's room. She wished she'd thought of closing the blind to ease the sensation of eyes watching her as she dressed in layers, as many as possible, several favorite items included. But she had to be careful not to rouse his suspicion.

Plus, night was approaching. She imagined being outside in the dark, in the rain, without an umbrella, not knowing which way to turn. Without her cell phone. No matter, she had to go; braving the elements was the least of her worries.

Downstairs, she found no sign of Zander. Not in the kitchen, not in the great room with its three-story tall windows, and not in several other rooms she peered into. Instantly, she knew she needed to take advantage of the moment.

Retracing her footsteps, she entered her room, where she slipped her own rain jacket over her head and slung the backpack over her shoulder. She threw a quick glance down the hallway toward Zander's room. No sound. She tiptoed down the stairs then raced to the front foyer, which was well lit.

Here she stopped. Unable to see how the door unlocked, she tested the knob and felt it turn. Could it be as easy as this? After several deep breaths, the backpack firmly over both shoulders, she was ready to pull the door open and dash outside. The instant she did, a screaming noise erupted and traveled through the house. He'd set the alarm! Why hadn't she noticed the red light? Because she was too intent on getting away?

Nevertheless, in that heart-jolting instant, she sprang into the black night, took a few steps and entered his driveway that curved downhill and out of sight. The loud sound of the alarm continued as rain struck her from every angle.

She pulled her hood up and took one quick glance over her shoulder, suddenly remembering something she'd read: when escaping never look back. Too late. In the open doorway, she saw Zander's silhouette. Again, she leapt forward, this time nearly tripping on the slick gravel driveway. But her luck held, and she regained her balance. She jogged as fast as she could.

If Zander was close behind, the sound of his footsteps was lost in the relentless downpour, the pounding of her heart, and her gasping for air. At once she stumbled, then slipped, and her legs gave way, her hands reaching back to break her fall. Rocks tore into her skin, but she scrambled back to her feet, ready to take off again.

A hand clutched her arm and stopped her. "You can't get out this way, Charlotte," Zander said calmly. "The front gate's locked and there's a tall fence around the property."

"Let go of me!" she cried, trying to shake his hand loose, but his grip grew firmer. She caught the dark glint of something in his other hand. "What's that?" she said.

"Oh, this," he said, waving a gun.

"Were you going to shoot me?"

"I heard the alarm and thought it was an intruder."

"People get killed that way, you know," she said.

"I wouldn't shoot you. Not intentionally," he said. "Let's get you inside. Out of the rain."

Back in the kitchen, her hair drying, her hand bandaged, Charlotte sat on a bar stool, watching Zander prepare a salad and heat up some leftovers.

"I'm disappointed is all," he said in a strange voice. "You running away like that. Without even saying good-bye." So quietly she almost didn't hear it, he added with a shake of his head, "Just like Mother."

She recalled the story Zander told her not long after they met in college. That his mother had died without saying good-bye to him. That it had been like that all his life. She'd been forever leaving him in the care of others and hadn't the common decency to at least kiss him and give him some mother-to-son advice before dying. He'd dwelled on it. Unable to forgive her.

"Zander, I need to leave, and you won't let me. Do you think you can keep me here forever?"

At this he frowned. "I want you to stay because you want to be with me. Just like her."

Her? she wondered. His mother? Naomi? Abbie! She needed to tread carefully. "I think you know the answer to that."

He took a long gulp of his beer from a dark brown glass bottle featuring a fanciful label of a beastly dog. The gun lay on the counter within his reach. She eyed it.

"What happened to you?" she asked, truly questioning what had gone wrong in his life. "I can only imagine lots of women chase after you."

"But none like you." His eyes latched onto hers, as if wanting her to understand him. A moment later, his look shifted, and a sly smile appeared on his lips, replacing the softer, gentler Zander. "You're still beautiful." His eyes slid over her breasts slowly, as if remembering something.

She tilted her head to the side wanting to understand what he was trying to tell her. "What do you mean?"

His smile widened. "I saw you."

She gave him a questioning look.

"In the bathtub." He waited a moment, letting the words sink in, letting her know he'd tricked her. "All of a sudden you looked shy as if you felt me watching. Did you? I have been watching you, Charlotte." His eyes and smile grew as the words spilled out, clearly hoping she recognized his cleverness. "I watched you pack."

She closed her eyes. *Oh, God. If only Celia weren't so far away.* Charlotte couldn't help taking a long swig of beer, a bottle she'd opened herself.

After a long pregnant pause, she forced herself to bring the conversation back to her original question. "Why haven't you married?"

"It's never been right." He looked past her, as if recalling a string of lovers. "After the initial flush of excitement, they always seem disappointed. After the first few times we have sex, I can tell they just want me for my money; sometimes they want me to photograph them, make them famous, but they don't really care, not about me." He sounded childishly petulant, unhappy. "Not like you. You didn't care about all that shit." He was remembering another time. "You liked me."

"Zander, we were friends in college," she said, trying to keep the frustration out of her voice. She recalled what he'd told her the previous night about breaking up with Abbie. Had he imagined that she felt about him as he claimed he did about her? "If we had gotten together, how do you know I wouldn't have become just like—"

The doorbell interrupted her. A slow mellifluous chime that seemed to suggest his home welcomed angels not people. But the peaceful sound had no effect on Zander. He grabbed the gun and scurried off. "Stay here," he demanded.

Chapter 48

CHARLOTTE DISREGARDED ZANDER'S ORDER, FOLLOWING him but staying back and stopping once he did.

"Who's there?" Zander shouted through the door. She tried to imagine who'd come to visit, but whoever it was, her heart leapt with joy.

"It's me. Evan! Open up," a male voice shouted.

Zander holstered the gun into the back of his jeans and opened the door a few inches. "Not a great time," he said.

Ahh, there actually is an Evan, Charlotte thought and moved closer to the door so Evan could see her. How had he gotten past the front gate? A key code?

A burly guy, he shoved his way inside and said, "Hey, man, what're you tawkin' about? You ask't me to come, remember?" He checked his phone. "Right on time, too. Fuckin' miracle with the rain and holiday traffic." He turned sideways. "Ahh, this must be the infamous Charlotte?" He gave her a quick up and down glance. She smiled. Anything to get him to stay.

Zander seemed flustered. Then finally, "Yeah. Charlotte meet Evan," he said.

She stepped toward him, a bushy-haired guy wearing a flannel shirt over his sizable gut, not sure if she should shake his hand or hug him. "Nice to meet you," she said.

"Yeah, likewise." He gave her a lopsided grin, and a quirk of his eyebrow. "I could use a brewski, man. Got any Six Harbors?"

Charlotte heard *hawbors* and recognized his Long Island twang. A local, she thought. A wealthy local who'd hosted that long ago party?

"Love their Kolsch and the pilsner."

Zander looked at him with annoyance. "I don't have any fuckin' *Kolsh*."

Unperturbed, Evan moved further inside and led the way toward the kitchen, obviously knowing the layout of Zander's place. "Yeah, they named Buddy's Golden Kolsch after their dog. Pretty fuckin' cute, eh?"

Zander plodded along behind him. This was the Evan he'd talked about. The one who might know who'd taken photographs of her. She seriously doubted it, but no matter. He was her savior just now.

They settled in the kitchen, and Charlotte kept the conversation going by tossing questions at Evan. She wondered if Zander would raise the topic of the party and the photos, as he'd promised. It seemed unlikely, she thought, as Evan prattled on, and Zander looked increasingly irritated.

"How about some tunes? This place is like a fuckin' tomb." Evan's laughter filled the room. Zander complied, shouting at Alexa to turn on "classic rock."

With no sign that Evan intended to leave, Charlotte announced, "Stay for dinner, Evan?" He nodded agreeably, while Zander shot her a look. She gave them both an innocent smile and added, "I'll be right back. Little girls' room." With that she waltzed out of the room. In the hallway, she pulled off her shoes, rose up the stairs in her stocking feet, and entered her room.

As quickly as possible she put on a new sweater and her parka, slipped into sneakers and tied them securely. Just before she left, she raised her middle finger at Naomi's image. "Screw you!" she whispered.

She trod lightly. Once she reached the bottom of the stairs, she looked both ways, then headed for the mud room and side door they'd used for the boat trip. She could hear Evan still talking, though not exactly what he said. At once she thought she heard Zander hiss at his friend. *Hurry up,* she thought and braced herself as she opened the door.

There was a low-level beep, but she prayed Zander couldn't hear it for Evan's loud chatter and the music he'd turned on. Jagger was singing "Wild Horses." And for some reason, as she looked outside, Charlotte saw herself racing away on a black stallion.

Chapter 49

IT HAD STOPPED RAINING. THE wind whipped through the trees and even the bushes rustled as Charlotte made her way past the pool to the path that ran along the water's edge. She looked for house lights to guide her, but once she exited Zander's backyard, darkness greeted her. She knew to be careful. The paving stones had grown wet and slick. And then they came to an end. She tested the soggy earth and kept going, searching for lights at the neighboring home.

At last, she saw the English-style country house she'd seen earlier in the day, but its numerous narrow windows appeared menacingly dark. Still, she wove her way through the garden, slipping once on pebbles, slowing down, then speeding up again when she heard Zander shouting for her.

She hesitated, glanced around. Saw plenty of places to hide, even wide tree trunks where she could briefly find cover. She edged along the neighbor's house finally reaching the front. There she found the buzzer and rang the bell. Held her breath to hear any movement inside. *One, two, three, please, please, please.* Should she ring again? *No!*

If this house was like Zander's there'd be a gate, one she might not be able to open or scale. Nevertheless, she had to try.

"Charlotte!" The voice drew closer.

Should she run or try to hide? She kept going.

This driveway, unlike Zander's, was asphalt. *Slippery, be careful,* she thought. As she soon saw, this drive led to the street. No walls, no gates. For an instant she wondered why Zander's property was like a fortress. Had he held other women captive? She ran, carefully placing each foot, and once she hit the street, released a sigh and took a deep breath. Looked left and right. Which direction? To the left, the road curved. *That way,* she decided.

A hundred yards further and the road ended. She had to turn back. And pass Zander's house. She prayed. "Please, please, please," she muttered. Just as she got close to his property, the gate swung open and car lights swept the driveway inches from her. She lurched back and ducked behind a bush, making herself small, a turtle retreating into its shell. She dared not breathe. The car, an unmistakable black Porsche, turned to the right, its motor purring. On the prowl for her.

She wondered if he'd left Evan behind or taken him along. She glanced up the driveway and saw a white pick-up truck—Evan's. The type of vehicle surprised her. Should she see if he was still inside?

No. Nothing could drag her back into that house. And if he'd left Evan with instructions to call if she showed up, well, then she'd be worse off than before.

She kept going. Searching for a house with someone home. A few minutes later, she saw lights behind a tall hedge, two houses down and across the road from Zander's. She ran to the driveway and crept toward the front door.

Light from the windows splashed white rectangles onto the lawn. The hedge lining the property hid her from the street. Zander would have to pull into the driveway, and why would he unless he knew she'd come here.

She approached the front door, trying to think what to say. *I'm lost? Someone's after me? Do you know your crazy neighbor, Alex Rusikov?* None of these options seemed suitable. She rang the doorbell.

And then she rang it again.

She heard footsteps. The door creaked open a few inches. A chain stopped it from opening further. An elderly woman in a robe peered out at her. "Yes? What do you want?" she said in a quavering voice.

"Help. I need help," Charlotte said, trying to keep the desperation out of her voice. "I'm without a phone. I need to call the police." The words leapt from her mouth.

She sensed the woman's hesitation. "I can show you my ID," she added, trying to think what might reassure her. "My name is Charlotte Cooper. I've been kept in one of your neighbor's homes against my will. If I could just make a call?" She heard a car and flinched, instinctively moving closer to the woman.

In the next instant, the door shut in her face.

Chapter 50

CHARLOTTE HEARD A NOISE—THE rustle of a chain? A moment later, the door swung open. The woman leaned outside to glance in both directions before waving Charlotte in. "Come now, it's all right."

In the foyer, Charlotte studied the patchwork of black and white marble at her feet and tears sprang from her eyes. "Thank you so much," she said between sobs of relief. "I'm so grateful."

The entrance featured spindle-legged antiques, a small black granite statue of Mercury, and a full-length heavily ornamented mirror in which Charlotte caught her reflection. She tried to fix her damp messy hair. Useless.

The woman—she introduced herself as Mrs. Whitehurst—put her arm around Charlotte's waist, walked her into a tastefully done family room and invited her to sit in a comfortable chair near the fireplace. "I'll get Gerald to make you some tea," she said, "and you can make your calls. To the police?"

Charlotte nodded and sat down. A fire burned, flames leapt excitedly, warming her feet. A sigh escaped her. An old-fashioned portable phone sat on the mahogany table beside her. She picked it up and dialed.

A few minutes later the doorbell rang, and she could hear Mrs. Whitehurst's footsteps. Charlotte sipped her tea and felt her insides warm up. She listened and heard talking at the front door. She was glad the police had arrived so quickly.

Suddenly the voices grew louder and a moment later a man barged into the room and blocked the fire.

Charlotte shrank back. "How'd you find me?"

Zander looked at her like she was an idiot. "You go to one of my neighbors and think I won't?" he whispered.

Mrs. Whitehurst shuffled in. "Young man, what on earth are you doing?"

"Just taking my friend back home," he said, trying to smile. "She's with me, Mrs. Whitehurst. I'm sorry she interrupted your evening." His jaw was locked tight, obviously furious that she'd embarrassed him. Lips pressed together he nodded his head toward the door.

Charlotte stared through him as if he were a ghost. "No," she said, making no move to get up.

He reached behind his back and moved closer to Charlotte. "You'd better come, or I'll hurt her," he hissed through gritted teeth. "Don't think I won't."

She knew the gun was hidden beneath his jacket, but would he shoot Mrs. Whitehurst? She couldn't take the risk. She smiled sweetly at the old woman. "I'll just be over at Alex's across the street. Thank you so much for the tea." She uncurled herself from the chair.

Her brow knitted in confusion, Mrs. Whitehurst said, "Well, if you're sure?"

"I am."

They crossed the street, Zander dragging her along. The gate stood open. As they reached the end of his curving driveway Charlotte saw no sign of Evan's truck. Panic rose inside of her. She couldn't return to that house. Her footsteps slowed. At the door, Zander handed her the key. "Open it," he said.

"No."

He pulled out his gun and shot it into the air. "Open it," he repeated, his tone flat.

Her hand shook as she inserted the key. Once she'd gotten it to unlock, he shoved her inside. "When you're ready to apologize, let me know," he said.

"*Me* apologize? For what?" Charlotte shouted.

"For being so ungrateful!" He paused, used his fingers to tick off all he'd done for her. "I took you out on my boat, fed you last night, gave you a helicopter ride…need I go on?" He studied her. "What exactly do you want me to do, Charlotte, to show how much I love you?" He shook his head as if she were an unruly, spoiled child. "Most women would be scrambling to get me upstairs right about now. But not you."

"Maybe that's what you find so appealing," she muttered.

"What?" he said.

"Nothing."

They remained silent for a few minutes. He left the room then returned carrying a bottle of wine. She stared at it as he opened it. A part of her wanted to drink and fall into a drugged stupor, while another part knew she could do no such thing. She accepted the glass when he offered it.

"I'll tell you what will endear you to me," she said at last.

"What?" His eyes brightened. "Anything."

"The truth. About Naomi and the photos. Everything."

His shoulders slumped a little. "Everything?"

"Yes."

"And then we'll start over?" he said hopefully.

"Yes, exactly." *Well, not exactly,* she thought.

He began by telling her about the night at the sex party and how painful it had been to watch her, especially with his father, all of which she already knew, but she had to act patient, and so played along, urged him on. "I can't tell you how sorry I am for making you feel like that." She gave him her most apologetic sad-faced frown.

"Really?" he said.

"Really."

"When I got Naomi the gig in London and she told me she was dating some artist named *Rafe*," he said, spitting his name disgustedly, "well, I couldn't believe it. What were the chances of that? Two of *my* women…and then she told me you'd moved to London—without telling your old buddy Zander, by the way—and that you'd started going out with him again, and how fucking mad it made her that Rafe dumped her for you. Well, she wanted revenge. That's how it started." He stopped to see if she believed him.

She nodded and he continued. "She saw the photos at my place." He gave her a sly glance then admitted, "Sometimes I get them out to look at them," he said and leaned toward her confidentially. "So, yes, it was me who took those shots. But *she* suggested we threaten you. See, it wasn't me. I swear it."

Charlotte watched how easily he unburdened himself of lies and added new ones. She was taking another tiny sip of wine just as the door chime rang out. The one that heralded angels. Her heart picked up a little, wondering who'd arrived this time. Evan? The police? Please.

Once more, she saw him reach behind his back for the gun. "Zander, no."

"Shut up," he said. "I'll handle this."

Chapter 51

IN THE FOYER, HE HESITATED long enough to disarm the security system then threw the door open.

Charlotte gawked disbelievingly at the visitors who stood there. Instead of the police, it was Rafe and Celia. The sight of her friends sent such a shock through her that she froze before shouting, "Watch out, he's got a gun!"

In that same instant, though, Celia came bounding through the door and a loud crack barreled through the room. Charlotte shrieked. Celia slumped to the ground, her body lying across the threshold.

Hop-stepping over her, Rafe pounced on Zander and wrestled him to the ground. They tussled on the pale wooden floor, blocking Charlotte's path to her friend. She held her breath, eyes wide, as Zander brought the gun toward Rafe's head.

"No," she screamed.

With a grunt, Rafe slammed Zander's arm to the floor. The gun slipped from his grip and shot across the polished wood.

"I'll kill you," Zander hissed through clenched teeth.

"Sure you will," Rafe shouted with a snort.

She watched, helpless, then rushed around the two wrestling men to her friend. Celia lay where she'd fallen, moaning and touching her shoulder lightly. Charlotte knelt beside her. "Oh, Celia. My dear Celia."

They both turned their heads at the sound of running footsteps. Coming up the driveway, several men materialized. "Hold it! Sands Point police," one shouted. "Everyone freeze!"

Charlotte jumped up and yelled, "We need an ambulance. The maniac who lives here shot her. He's got a gun."

Three policemen rushed in and two aimed their guns at Rafe. "Hold it, right there, buddy," one of the white cops said.

"No, officer, not *him*," Charlotte said, looking angrily at the uniformed man. "The other one. The white guy. Alex Rusikov. He lives here." She pointed at Zander.

The policeman turned and stared at her, his eyes narrowed in disbelief. Rafe's hands were outstretched in surrender.

Zander smiled. "What a relief, sir. He just barged in and beat the shit out of me. Fuckin' crazy Black dude."

"Sir," Celia croaked. "I know who shot me and it was him." She aimed at Zander.

"It's not true," Zander yelled, shaking his head.

The three officers—one white, one Latino and one Black—exchanged looks. "You two," the white one said to Rafe and Zander, "stand over there." He aimed at the wall opposite the front door.

Charlotte repeated the request for an ambulance as she crouched down beside Celia and stroked her forehead. "Oh, dude, are you okay?"

"I think the bullet…" she groaned "…just grazed me."

"Let me take a look?" Charlotte carefully peeled Celia's jacket from her injured shoulder. Blood had seeped through her white turtleneck. "Ooh."

"Hurts like hell," Celia said. "My favorite jacket, too!"

"We'll get you fixed up," Charlotte said. Under her breath she added, "We'll get the bastard to pay for a new one." One side of Celia's mouth slid into a smile.

Charlotte rose to her feet and in an urgent tone addressed the police. "When's the ambulance coming?"

"It's on its way. A few minutes," Officer Garcia said, glancing at Zander and Rafe.

"Officers, I know what happened here," Charlotte said. "And you need to know this guy," she pointed at Zander, "held me hostage for the past day and a half. There's a lot more to the story—"

"You know who I am," Zander shouted, interrupting her. "I'm Mr. Rusikov's son!"

"Yeah, and he's dead," Garcia said.

"All you have to do is check our records," Zander said loudly. "See who was arrested…for drunk driving…she's the one who killed her best friend! And then check mine. You'll know who the liar is."

Charlotte stared at him. He seemed like two people. Everything he'd told her and now again lying to save his own skin. "I pity you," she said to him.

"Stuff it," he said and muttered, "bitch. Why did I even bother?"

"Good question," Charlotte said.

At last Officer Holmes turned to Rafe. "And who are you?"

Rafe identified himself using his most proper British accent. "Rafe Jackson. I'm a sculptor, arrived today from England to meet with my New York agent, and—" he looked at Charlotte, "and to bring her home."

Charlotte returned his gaze with a relieved grin.

A siren drowned out Zander's sneered comment.

"We'll have to question the three of you," Garcia said, waving a hand at Rafe, Charlotte, and Celia, "and you're under arrest, Rusikov. Three people say you shot the gun." He read Zander his Miranda rights as the emergency medical technicians loaded Celia into the ambulance and gave Charlotte the name of the hospital.

"We'll be right there, okay? Hang in there."

Celia gave her a thumbs up.

"Welcome to New York," Charlotte shouted. Once the ambulance rumbled out of sight, she turned to search for Rafe.

At last, when she found him, they gathered each other in a lengthy embrace. "My sweet crazy Charlotte," he said. "Celia's right, you know."

"How so?"

"Never a dull moment with you."

She smiled and asked how he and Celia had found her. "And when did you even have time to fly here?"

"I'll tell you everything later, when we're having dinner. I'm starving."

"You're always starving at the strangest times!"

"Man's got to keep up his strength. Right, luv?"

They accompanied the police to the station, answered their questions, then ordered a cab to a hotel near Sands Point.

Over a quick meal, Rafe told her, "The minute you sent Celia the text about going in a helicopter with that idiot, she enlisted the help of Philip's friend. In no time, John Smith located Rusikov's address…property records, or something like that. She called me, and we decided to fly here. There's more, and it involves Nigel Thorntree, but I'll tell you after *dessert*." He gave her a lascivious grin.

"Don't give me that look, after you finish, we're going to visit Celia."

"Don't worry it'll be quick," he said with a chuckle.

Ignoring him, Charlotte mused, "In case you wondered, after I escaped, I called the police from a neighbor's house; she must have sent them to his house. I'll have to thank her." She sat beside him and leaned her head against his chest. *It's over,* she thought. But it wasn't. Not entirely.

Chapter 52

Tuesday, December 24, 2019

THE PROSECUTING ATTORNEY, A WOMAN named Kameisha Gordon, told Charlotte she couldn't return to England without promising a court appearance once Zander's trial began, which might not happen for several months, even a year.

"You don't have to ask twice. I promise," she said. "I wish you could put him behind bars for good. He's evil."

"Oh, we might be able to swing that," she said with a grin. "We've got a lot more on him than what he did to you."

"Really?"

"Yes. Trafficking."

"You mean people?"

She nodded. "Sex workers. Drugs. The usual."

Charlotte wondered if he'd taken over the illegal part of his father's business. Aloud she asked if he'd get out on bail.

"Undoubtedly his lawyers will aim for that, but the judge could set it so high that Zander can't pay it. If he does, he'll be required to wear electronic monitoring that won't allow him to leave New York."

But it worried Charlotte that no matter how high the sum, he could afford it.

"If we get lucky, they'll deny bail altogether because of the flight risk," the prosecutor said, echoing Charlotte's concern.

"What about Naomi, she was assisting him in London? He'd threatened to mutilate her face if she didn't do what he asked, including posting those nude photos of me and awful ones of her."

Kameisha gave her a concerned look. "There's little we can do except let authorities in London know what he was up to. They'll have to deal with her."

Later, when she told Rafe, he revealed that he'd spoken to Naomi and conveyed all that had happened. In the course of the conversation, she promised to destroy the photos. "I, uh, encouraged her."

"Meaning?"

"I recall saying something along the lines of, 'We'll have to report you to the authorities if you don't.' And then I asked her in a very kind way if she was pregnant."

Charlotte inched forward. "And?"

"And she said, 'I think so.'"

"Yours, Rafe?"

"She doesn't think so."

"That's good. Really good." Then an awful thought struck her. "Oh, God, what if it's Zander's?!"

Rafe nodded. "I know."

The following day, Charlotte placed a call to Shelby. "I hear thanks are in order?"

"Least I could do. Anyway, it was Nigel's plane, not mine. Thank him."

"I will," Charlotte said.

"Well?" Shelby said.

"Well, what?" Charlotte said innocently.

"Oh, for God's sake," Shelby snorted, "what the hell happened?"

Charlotte recounted everything, from the helicopter ride to Zander's spacious home to being held captive, to the frightening sailing excursion, and finally to Rafe and Celia arriving at just the right moment, then Zander shooting Celia and his arrest.

"He shot Celia? Are you kidding? No, don't answer that. Of course you're not. No one could make up such a story. Well, I didn't tell you this before, but Zander and his father are clearly cut from the same cloth. I alluded to it before…you want to hear more?"

"Please," Charlotte said. "Without a job, all I have is time."

"Oh, for heaven's sake, Charlotte, of course you have a job." Shelby then proceeded to tell her how Alex Rusikov, Sr. was killed in his home on Long Island the previous year. A couple of mafioso Russians, posing as carpenters, came in and simply shot him. They rummaged through his stuff and took everything of value—jewelry, paintings, anything that could be pawned. As soon as the police were on to them, they fled to Russia and authorities there refused to extradite them.

"How did I miss that news item?"

"As I recall, it happened while you were on that trip to Mexico, the one where you got deathly ill. Soon after, it stopped making major headlines, except maybe in the Long Island papers."

The idea catapulted into Charlotte's brain that Zander might have played a role in his father's death, which she mentioned to Shelby.

"What a thought!"

"Can I look into it?" Charlotte asked.

"Of course. In fact, I expect a damn good story when you get back. God knows you've got plenty of material."

"I guess I'm back to print?"

"I wouldn't be so sure about that."

"Really?"

"Yes, really," Shelby said, and if Charlotte were to guess, she imagined Shelby wearing a smile—a very smug smile as she gazed out the window from her elevated perch.

"Thank you, Shelby. Really and truly."

"Don't thank me."

"Then who? Bradford?" she asked with a quizzical frown.

"Hell no. Not him. Nigel!"

"Really?"

"Yes, really. And stop saying that, okay?"

"Okay." She'd get details when she returned but imagined Bradford had gotten the boot. Most likely other women had reported his sexual harassment and misbehavior to TE!'s HR department.

"I do have another bit of news," Shelby said, interrupting Charlotte's thoughts.

"What?"

"Ding dong," she said merrily.

"What?"

"Wedding bells!"

"Rea…" but Charlotte caught herself. "Who's the lucky man?" she asked, pretty sure she knew the answer.

"Oh, come on."

"Nigel?" she said tentatively. There'd be hell to pay if she was wrong.

"That's right," Shelby gloated.

"Oh, that's wonderful news, congratulations. Can't wait to see the ring."

"Quite a rock!" Shelby said. "Can't wait to show it to you! All right, that's enough. I'm exhausted. Need to get my beauty sleep." And with that the call ended.

That evening, Charlotte entered Elio's restaurant on the Upper East Side and smiled when she saw Rafe and Celia already sitting at a table in front, her friend's arm in a sling.

"How'd it go?" they both asked.

"My aunt was stand-offish at first but after explaining all that had happened, including Zander's arrest, they both believed me, and we had a big cry fest," she said. "They even asked to visit me after we get back to London."

"Us," Rafe corrected.

"What?"

"Visit *us*!" he added. "We'll finally get moved into that apartment."

"The one with a view of the Tate?" she said.

He smiled and nodded.

Celia announced, "This is my last night, you two lovebirds, so drinks on me."

"You're feeling well enough to travel?" Charlotte asked.

"Horses couldn't keep me here. Still can't believe Shelby and Nigel are tying the knot. Next'll be me, you wait. Philip's just returned from his trip to Istanbul, hopefully with a gorgeous piece of jewelry. I'd best be heading back." She grinned as she flagged down a waiter and ordered a bottle of champagne.

Chapter 53

A few days later, December 27, 2019

RAFE AND CHARLOTTE SAT ON beach chairs beneath a low-curving palm staring at the turquoise waters. Their feet covered in sand, the two clinked plastic glasses, foamy with citrus and pineapple, heavily doused with rum. Jamaican rum.

"Here's to us," Rafe said. They both sipped the tropical drinks.

"To us," Charlotte agreed. "You know I could get used to this. What a lovely, lazy life."

"So, let's stay, and you can make me breakfast and dinner, like a proper woman," he said.

"What about lunch?"

"We'll have something else I crave for lunch!" He gave her a sidelong glance.

"Oh, you!" With her toe she tossed sand onto his leg.

Yesterday she'd met his grandmother and some remote branches of his family not far from the Robinson Crusoe-style beach hut he rented in Negril.

The family encounter had been a surprise, but not the first one. After they arrived in this little corner of paradise on Christmas day, he'd shown her to their room-on-stilts with its exquisite view of the perfectly aqua Caribbean.

On stepping inside the place, which featured several glassless windows open to the lush jungle on the hills behind them, he asked her to take off her clothes. "Rafe Jackson, what have you got in mind?"

"It's not what you think," he said mysteriously.

"Damn," she said.

"Then lie down on the wicker sofa and put this on." He handed her a diaphanous moss green scarf.

It seemed like an elaborate way to get her into bed when he only had to ask.

"I'll be right outside," he said. "Shout when you're ready."

She smiled mischievously. A few minutes later, she called out, "All set!"

Before he came in, he asked her to close her eyes. She did. She thought she heard some shuffling about, and then he said, "Okay, open up."

He knelt before her, resembling his pose the day they'd met. She smiled at his antics—would he ask her to model for him again. And then what? Throw a lump of clay at her? One arm was hidden behind his back. He pulled it out, and in his hand he held a bronze statue about ten inches tall. At first glance, it appeared to be a miniature of Paul Day's *The Meeting Place*, the sculpture at St Pancras station. On closer inspection, though, she saw that it was the two of them—she and Rafe—in a full-fledged kiss.

"Do you like it?" he said.

"I thought you said Day's statue was romantic kitsch." She kept her inner smile in check.

"Well, it is, but, oh, such wonderful stuff when one of the figures is you. Remember, we said we'd meet at St Pancras if ever we got separated? Well, here we are."

She ogled it. "Is it for me?"

He nodded. "Forever."

She rose onto her tiptoes to kiss him.

"Live with me?" he said, now holding an emerald ring between his thumb and index finger.

"In a tent," she said, her eyes glittering.

Epilogue

FOREVER IS A VERY LONG time, but that was exactly the amount of time Charlotte had hoped Zander would get for his many crimes. In fact, he received a twenty-year sentence, which meant with good behavior he could be released much sooner. And return to being a scourge on society.

But that was not the only scourge released on the world. No, in March 2020, an epidemic called the coronavirus, or Covid-19, circled the world, killing thousands. In those early months, Charlotte often thought of Regina, who succumbed to the virus in June because her body had been compromised by lung cancer. No funeral, only a Zoom memorial celebration could be held for her mentor and friend. Tears flowed freely during the many eulogies, including Charlotte's.

Similarly, via long distance Zoom, Zander granted Charlotte an exclusive interview less than a week after he'd been sentenced and a few days before entering prison. He admitted he'd paid the men who killed his father. She jotted in her notes that *the thirty-one-year-old seemed not the slightest bit repentant.* "He deserved worse," Zander grumbled. "At least you have to give me credit for ridding the world of that bastard."

"You know this is on the record, right?" Charlotte said.

"Is it?" he asked, appearing confused. "Thought you were here because you cared."

He's not well, she thought. *Should have gotten help long ago.* Shortly thereafter, she concluded the interview to write up her story.

After he'd begun his prison sentence, Charlotte received a call from Kameisha Gordon. "Guess who was found dead in his cell in an apparent suicide?"

In the story that followed, Charlotte wrote, *Sources speculate, however, that he had numerous enemies and someone inside the prison had been instructed to kill him and make it look like suicide.*

THE END

Author's Note

THE INSPIRATION FOR THIS STORY came from several places. First, back in 2017, as I thought about my next novel, the idea arrived of a woman receiving nude images of herself with a threat they'd go viral, most likely because such stories, including revenge porn, were circulating on the internet and in the news media. It was frightening to think that a person's life could so easily be derailed. The next thought was who would do such a thing? And to what lengths would a person have to go to keep the images private? If exposed, a person could lose their job, their family or significant other, and where they lived, causing many victims to commit or consider suicide.

Second, I read Ronan Farrow's provocative *Catch and Kill*, which, simply put, exposes that elite and powerful group of men in Hollywood, in the news media and in corporations who exploit and oppress women, then protect one another by hiding the truth of what they've done. I'm sure you recall the names of a few people at the center of such news reports.

Third, the #MeToo movement caught on, using social media to expose the world of sexual harassment, predation and abuse. By using the hashtag #MeToo, women began to openly share their experiences and unmask the men who'd committed acts of harassment, oppression and exploitation.

Fourth, many years ago I worked at Amnesty International in San Francisco. I became knowledgeable about human rights violations worldwide. In doing research for this novel, I was shocked by some of the recent statistics, though perhaps I shouldn't have been. Human trafficking is an international scourge perpetrated in large part (about 75%) on women and children, though men are not exempt. According to a variety of sources, some 50 million people are subjected to slavery, which includes forced labor and sexual exploitation. In the UK, where much of this story takes place, some 90% of those trafficked for sex are women and children.

Fifth, only while writing this novel did the phrase "revenge porn" entered my awareness, and I realized that it was "a thing." In England, in 2015, it first appears as a crime in that country's legislation (in an amendment to the Criminal Justice and Courts Act).

While these facts contributed to the inspiration and writing of this novel, the characters of the story bring these problems to life. I have posted some additional information on my website (hertafeely.com) that contains links to some of the above facts.

Finally, throughout *Strange Shape of Love,* I referenced actual events and stories about human trafficking, sexual harassment, female oppression, revenge porn and art theft that appeared in news reports and online. I've taken some liberty regarding their timing. When these events occurred in the story and when they happened in real life may differ slightly.

Acknowledgements

FEW BOOKS ARE WRITTEN WITHOUT outside assistance, comments, edits. *Strange Shape of Love* is no exception. A number of people chimed in over the years, but no one was more helpful in bringing this novel to its current state than Anne Brewer, my editor. I'd written three other versions before coming to Anne, each one significantly different from the previous. Though each contained a biracial love story, the nude photographs, and the theme of female sexual harassment, other elements of fiction differed—the settings, the characters (all but Charlotte), and aspects of the plot. After a thorough evaluation, Anne encouraged me to begin again. It took six months to mull this over and figure out where to start. I did, though with some trepidation. Now, I firmly believe these characters and this plot was the right way to go. So, a huge thank you, Anne.

It is my agent, Emily Williamson, that I credit for finding my publisher, Castle Bridge Media, led by the intrepid and incredibly brilliant Jason Henderson and his partner in crime, In Churl Yo. I am grateful to Jason and In Churl for taking this book on with its "cinematic quality," as they put it, and for final edits, layout, book cover and so much more. And, of course, a big thank you to Emily, for representing me, reading and offering ideas, listening to me whine (on occasion), and being a critical and essential pillar of my fiction writing.

In the creation of this novel, I'm grateful to so many people, not least the friends who kept demanding to see my next book. I certainly couldn't let them down. The list is too long to include everyone (so forgive me for this short list) but thank you to all those who read and commented along the way. A special thanks to Kathleen Pasley, Jackie Mears, Darlynn Slosar, Rangeley Wallace, Marian Wernicke, and Gail Wilkins.

And always a heartfelt thank you to another pillar essential to my writing: my family—a constant source of encouragement and love: Jim, Max, Jack, and Megan Feely; and my brother, Gary Burbach, and sister-in-law, Joan Feely.

CASTLE BRIDGE MEDIA RECOMMENDS...

If you liked this book, you might also enjoy reading the following titles from Castle Bridge Media available on Amazon or by order at your favorite book store:

The 23rd Hero
By Rebecca Anne Nguyen

ANIMAL CHARMER
By Rain Nox
Animal Charmer
Magic & Melody

Austinites
By In Churl Yo

Bloodsucker City
By Jim Towns

SOUL CATCHER
By Don Sawyer
The Burning Gem
The Tunnels of Buda

THE CASTLE OF HORROR
ANTHOLOGY SERIES
Volume 1
Volume 2: *Holiday Horrors*
Volume 3: *Scary Summer*
  Stories
Volume 4: *Women Running*
  From Houses
Volume 5: *Thinly Veiled:*
  The 70s
Volume 6: *Femme Fatales**
Volume 7: *Love Gone Wrong*
Volume 8: *Thinly Veiled:*
  The 80s
Volume 9: *Young Adult*
Volume 10: *Thinly Veiled:*
  Saturday Mournings
Volume 11: *Revenge*
Volume 12: *Ripped From*
  The Headlines
Edited By Jason Henderson
and In Churl Yo
*Edited By P.J. Hoover

Child of Dark Water
By E.G. Rand

Castle of Horror Podcast
Book of Great Horror:
Our Favorites, Top Tens
and Bizarre Pleasures
Edited By Jason Henderson

Cherry Dark
By R.L. Wilburn

Dream State
By Martin Ott

Dominic
By Lee Guzman

FRENCH DECEPTION
By Janice Nagourney
A Forgery in Paris
A Forgery in Lyon
A Forgery in Marseille

FuturePast Sci-Fi Anthology
Edited by In Churl Yo

GLAZIER'S GAP
Ghosts of the Forbidden
By Leanna Renee Hieber

Hellfall
By Jay Gould

Isonation
By In Churl Yo

JAYU CITY CHRONICLES
By Chris M. Arnone
The Hermes Protocol
Necropolis Alpha

Junk Film: Why Bad
Movies Matter
By Katharine Coldiron

Nightwalkers:
Gothic Horror Movies
By Bruce Lanier Wright

MID-LIFE CRISIS THRILLERS
18 Miles From Town
By Jason Henderson
Lost Angel
By Sam Knight

Ties That Kill
By Deven Greene

THE PATH
By David Bowles
The Blue-Spangled Blue
The Deepest Green

Strange Shape of Love
By Herta Feely

SURF MYSTIC
By Peyton Douglas
Night of the Book Man
Dark of the Curl

The Thing That Happened
When We Were Little
By Caroline Kelly Franklin

Tick Town
By Christopher A. Micklos

Yesterday's Tomorrows:
The Golden Age of
Science Fiction Movies
By Bruce Lanier Wright

Please remember to leave us your reviews on Amazon and Goodreads!

THANK YOU FOR
SUPPORTING INDEPENDENT
PUBLISHERS AND AUTHORS!
castlebridgemedia.com